GIVE ME SHELTER

DAVID B. SEABURN

Black Rose Writing | Texas

The author grants the final approval for this literary material.

First printing

This is a work of fiction. Names, characters, businesses, places, events, and incidents are
either the products of the author's imagination or used in a fictitious manner. Any
resemblance to actual persons, living or dead, or actual events is purely coincidental.

ISBN: 978-1-68513-084-8
PUBLISHED BY BLACK ROSE WRITING
www.blackrosewriting.com

Printed in the United States of America
Suggested Retail Price (SRP) $22.95

Give Me Shelter is printed in Garamond Premier Pro

*As a planet-friendly publisher, Black Rose Writing does its best to eliminate unnecessary waste to
reduce paper usage and energy costs, while never compromising the reading experience. As a result,
the final word count vs. page count may not meet common expectations.

To my brother, Rick.

ACKNOWLEDGEMENTS

Many thanks to Reagan Rothe and the team at Black Rose Writing.
Special thanks to Alan Lorenz.
My deepest thanks to my wife, Bonnie, for all her support.

GIVE ME SHELTER

CHAPTER 1

Willie lies on the floor behind the couch, his back against the wall, because that's the safest place to be. He turns on his belly and rests his chin on his fist. He hears the wall clock ticking over the fireplace, but he can't see what time it is. "Smoochy, come-ere." Smoochy is sprawled on the throw rug, her tail thumping the floor. "Come on girl. You don't want to die, do you?" Smoochy gets up, shakes her head, her long ears flapping, and then crawls in, her nose pressing against Willie's forehead. "'Atta, girl. Now you're safe." Smoochy licks Willie's face.

Willie and Smoochy cock their heads when a siren, screaming like a coyote, goes off again in the distance. He squeezes his dog and closes his eyes. "You'll be okay, girl. I've got you." Smoochy squirms to get loose, but Willie holds on tight. "Just another minute, Smooch." Willie presses one ear against Smoochy's side and cups his other ear with his hand. It feels like the siren is inside his head, right between his ears, whirring, whirring, whirring. "C'mon, enough."

When the siren stops, Willie sighs and pats his dog. Smooch tries to wiggle her way out just as the siren blasts again---RRRRrrrrrrrRRRRrrrr. She slips away. "Smoochy! Smoochy!" Willie digs his nails into the carpet. He can't see his dog. He holds his breath. A spider slinks slowly down the wall beside him. He reaches out and smashes it. He closes his eyes and buries his head in his arms. He inhales carpet dust. This has gone on every day for, like, ever. Test after test. The siren stops and then starts blaring a third time.

"Pop! Where are you?"

This must be it, he thinks. The end of the world.

Sounding like air screaming through the pinched end of a balloon, the siren subsides again. Willie shuts his eyes tight, and muffles his ears with the palms of his hands. He curls his toes and tries to pull up his knees. He gulps air and waits for the next blast.

It's quiet for a few minutes. He takes one hand from one ear and turns on his side to see if he can hear anything. The clock on the wall is still ticking. There are voices outside. Happy voices. Kid voices. He takes another deep breath and blows through his puckered lips in relief.

There is a knock at the door. He pushes as hard as he can against the couch, feeling like a turtle struggling to get off its back. The knock is louder the second time. He slides out backwards inch by inch. Smoochy watches, bemused. Willie goes bug-eyed when he sees it's 12:45pm. Nuts! Lunch time is long gone. He hasn't eaten a thing. Another knock at the door.

He goes into the hall and peeks through the curtains. Lucy's face is pressed against the glass. Preston is walking on the porch railing, his arms out for balance. Lucy smiles and waves. He holds up one finger, he'll be out in a minute. He races up the stairs to his bedroom where he yanks a Clark Bar from his pillow case, shoves it into his jeans pocket and flies back down. He feels his heart beating against his striped jersey. He looks in the hall mirror. His hair is plastered to his head from all the sweat. Can he soak it at the kitchen sink and quickly dry his hair with a hand towel? There is another knock. He looks in the mirror again, shrugs and runs to the front door.

When he opens it, Lucy is sitting on the porch, rocking in Pop's favorite chair. Preston is still balancing on the porch rail.

"Hey," says Lucy.

"Hey." Willie takes a deep breath.

"How's it going?" Preston slides off the rail.

Willie breathes hard, his face is white.

"What's the matter?" says Lucy.

"What do you mean 'what's the matter?'?"

"You look, well, you look like death warmed over," says Pres. Preston shoves Willie and laughs.

"Like what?"

"That's what my grandma says if someone doesn't look right. She says, 'What's wrong? You look like death warmed over'."

"I've seen your grandma. She looks like death warmed over," says Willie.

Lucy sneers and punches him in the arm.

"So..."

"So, what?"

"You still haven't answered me," says Lucy.

A group of kindergarteners pass by holding hands, one of their mothers leading the way.

"C'mon, let's get going" says Preston.

"Yeah, we're gonna be late for social studies." Willie jumps off the top porch step and lands with a thud. The September air rustles the sycamore leaves. He squints into the noonday sun.

They fall in behind the kindergarteners for half a block before they pass them up. A group of boys cat-call Lucy from across the street.

"Woooo-hooo, Lucy! Ramma-lamma-ding-dong!"

"Shut up creeps!" She holds up her fist.

This is new. They'd been friends since kindergarten, but Willie has never thought of Lucy the way other sixth grade boys think of her. Recently, though, he has noticed her long, lush, dark brown hair and bright blue eyes.

Her smile and the dimple on her chin.

He'd asked Preston: "Do you think Lucy's pretty?"

"My God, man, are you nuts or something?"

Willie puffs himself up and glowers at the boys across the street.

"Oooo, we're shakin'," calls the ring leader.

"Morons," says Willie.

"Hey," says Lucy, nudging Willie in the ribs. "See that guy?"

"What guy?"

"The guy, that one over there crossing the street." She points.

"Yeah, so..."

A guy in a suit, white shirt and tie and walks into Scanlon's Service Station.

"Have you ever seen him before?"

"Naw. Why?"

"Nothing." Lucy watches the man in the suit as he exits the gas station. He stops, unwraps a pack of cigarettes and lights one up. He turns and looks right at Lucy. "Just seen him around a bunch of times."

By then, Preston is half a block ahead of them, running as fast as he can without stepping on any cracks.

The school yard is full of kids waiting for the bell to re-enter Wood Street Elementary for the afternoon session. Lucy lays her books on the grass. Willie leans against a tree. Preston chases a fifth grader who'd stuck his tongue out at him.

"Man, I hate those sirens" says Willie.

"The sirens?"

"Yeah, you know---the sirens. Didn't they bother you?"

"I don't know. I was making lunch for my mom and cleaning up the kitchen. So, no, I guess they didn't."

It was quiet for a moment. Is he the only one who pays attention to these things? Is he the only one who understands what's at stake?

"My mom says it's just a big nothing."

"Really?" says Willie.

The bell rings and everyone pours into the school, bees to the hive.

"I hope she's right."

Once in his seat by the window, Willie forces a smile as his classmates clamor in. Maybe if you put on a happy face, you won't feel so jumpy, Pop had told him. He waves to Preston. It helps that everyone is loud and boisterous, not a care in the world. He nods to Linda, Sally and Frank. He wonders if any of them were hiding behind their couches just a few minutes before.

Mr. Highmark enters the room, Mr. Clammerman close behind him.

Oh no, not this, thinks Willie.

Mr. Clammerman is wearing a civil defense badge on his sleeve and a broad smile on his even broader face.

"Good afternoon, kiddos!"

"Hi, Mr. Clammerman," several kids call out in sing-song rhythm.

"Good afternoon, gang!" Mr. Highmark is the new social studies teacher. He doesn't look much older than Willie's brother, Denny, although Mr. Highmark has a bushy moustache that looks like an upside-down U. Willie's brother can barely grow fuzz. Pop told Denny he didn't need to shave. He could just dust his lip.

"We have our friend Mr. Clammerman with us this afternoon. He's here to help us be aware, stay safe and---(he pauses for effect)---avoid the red menace. Mr. Clammerman, welcome!" He bows slightly and sweeps his arm out in a regal gesture. The class giggles.

"Thank you, Mr. Highmark." He faces the class; everything about him is paunchy. "As you young citizens of this great nation know, we are in a time of peril..."

Of my God, thinks Willie. He looks out the window, breathing as evenly as he can.

"...the Soviets are not our friends..."

A bead of perspiration drips from his forehead to the inside corner of his right eye. He doesn't touch it.

"...the threat of nuclear war, something we here in America won't tolerate..."

The words of Willie's neighbor, Mr. Ashwood, ring in his ears: "They don't just want to destroy our way of life, they want to destroy us. It's coming, I'm telling you." He snorted and hawked a loogie onto the sidewalk. Pop flicked his Camel into the street. "You think?" was all he said.

Later Willie asked Pop if there was going to be a nuclear war. Pop said, "Nothing for you to worry about," and walked away. He was like that. Didn't say much. Willie asked if he could call Denny. "No, you can't call him, it's long distance; I'm not made of money." said Pop. That was that.

He talked to Preston, but it didn't help much: "I'm telling you, man, America is like Popeye and the commies are like Bluto, you know? Popeye never loses to Bluto. He always finds his spinach. We'll kill the Soviets to death if they try anything!" His father had fought in World War II and Korea. "My dad says we should have bombed all our enemies to smithereens when we had a chance." He had a battery-operated toy machine gun on his front porch that was mounted on a tripod. He shot at any suspicious looking car or truck that passed by---RATTA-TAT-TAT! "They don't stand a chance, man."

Willie watches as two students struggle to set up the movie screen. Mr. Highmark finally steps in to hook the screen at the top. Mr. Clammerman attaches the movie reel and threads the film through the projector. There is a fifty-fifty chance the projector won't work. Willie crosses his fingers. No luck, though. Soon jaunty music fills the room as smiling children with bows in their hair and bright smiles on their faces appear on screen. A pretty young teacher, also smiling, talks to them when, suddenly, a loud bell rings. "What do we do?" she calls in a pleasant voice. All the kids say, "Duck and cover, Miss Woodson!" Their knees hit the floor. They slide under their desks and fold their arms over their heads. The camera, at floor level, films their fresh scrubbed faces. They all have freckles and happy grins. They remain perfectly still until the bell stops ringing. "Wonderful, boys and girls!" says the teacher.

With that, Clammerman stops the projector. Mr. Highmark leans against the wall, his arms folded.

"Okay, boys and girls, now it's your turn." Everyone claps and whoops. "Here we go. Mr. Highmark, please turn off the lights." Highmark pushes away from the wall and flicks the light switch.

"Here we go. I want you to imagine that the sirens are about to blast and we have to get as safe as we can as quickly as we can. Okay?" Everyone yells, Okay! "One, two, three----SIREN!"

There is a flurry of activity, kids pushing chairs aside, shoes scuffing the floor, some boys tripping and falling, one calling out that his nose is bleeding. Soon, though, everyone is under their desks. Mr. Clammerman keeps yelling "Siren! Siren!"

Willie is in a fetal position under his desk and can barely take a breath. He hopes the smaller he makes himself, the less likely he'll be incinerated.

He wants to raise his hand and ask Mr. Clammerman a question: If an atomic bomb was dropped near us and we were hiding under our school desks, would we be safe? But he is afraid of the answer.

By now, Willie is sweating "like a pig," as Pop would say. He feels light-headed and wishes he'd eaten more than a Clark Bar for lunch.

Mr. Clammerman stops yelling "Siren!" and tells the kids they can get up on their feet and stretch. Clammerman praises the students, as they stand by their desks like budding soldiers: "Take your seats. Good job young Americans! You have done your country proud!" And then he calls each student up to give them a civil defense patch. It is a blue circle with a white triangle in it. Inside the triangle are the letters 'C' and 'D'. Willie has ten civil defense patches at home in his underwear drawer.

When it's Willie's turn to go forward for his patch, he looks up at Clammerman but all he sees are cascading spots before his eyes. He tries to stand once, then twice, but when he does, the room whirls and his stomach whirls with it. He tilts back and forth like a top slowing down, about to fall. He calls out, "Help!" but the only thing his classmates hear is "OooooooUuuugh." Before he knows it, he's lying on the floor staring at the hissing radiator.

CHAPTER 2

Hal Mitchum crushes the stub of his cigarette on the blackened, cinderblock furnace room wall and tosses it into a battered metal trash can. As he moves through his basement sanctuary, dirt and dust puff and billow around him. He looks through the grate of the coal-fired boiler and then opens the iron door. Only cold ashes now, but in a month or so it will be roaring. The coal bin in the far corner is full of that beautiful, black sedimentary stone, ancient cousin of oil. Nearby is a cot where he sleeps on frosty winter nights to guard against the fire going out and the kids freezing the next day. He hopes his knee will feel better by the time snow shoveling season arrives.

"Take some days off now before the weather changes and you can't," the school nurse had said the day he wrenched it slipping off a step.

"It's just a sprain."

"It looks like the Hindenburg. Here, let's at least do this." She wrapped his knee with an Ace bandage.

Hal bends over and rubs his knee gently, but the ache doesn't recede. He shifts his weight to his other leg. He pulls a fresh pack of cigarettes from his pocket, taps one out, tucks it in the corner of his mouth, and flicks the end of a match with his thumbnail. He holds the match to his Camel and draws the smoke deep, firing the furnace of his lungs. He launches blue smoke into the air above his head. He coughs loud.

He lines his three mop buckets side-by-side in one corner where a dozen string mops are drying in a garbage can. Beside them are his brooms. Three standard brooms for everyday needs. Five push brooms for hallways. Two angle brooms for corners. Two water brooms. He takes a standard broom and sweeps shards of coal in front of the furnace and tosses them back into the bin. He returns the broom to its notch on the wall.

Near the back door, there's an old metal desk with one broken leg where he keeps paper work, order forms, pencils and coffee mugs. The coffee pot stands on a wooden stool beside his hot plate. This is his space. Here he sits and thinks. He makes plans for the day. He keeps things in order. From here he makes his building rounds. Collects the trash. Sweeps and mops the floors. Changes the light bulbs. Stocks the school supply shelves. Repairs whatever is broken. He works at his own pace. He completes his checklist each day. So different from the car business with its constant demands, its hustle, hustle. Everything was push, push. No neck ties here, no fake smiles, no constant jibber-jabber. And no money.

He straightens the picture of Mae on the wall. Beside it is a photo of Ruthie. And pictures of the boys.

There is a knock at the door.

"Yeah!"

A girl sticks her head in and looks around. "Mr. Mitchum, Nurse Correa wants you to come to her office when you have a minute."

The walk from the janitor's room to the nurse's office is a familiar one for Hal. He gets two, sometimes three calls a month, every time someone vomits in a hall or classroom. His box of sawdust is always at the ready. Nurse Correa sits beside an eighth-grade boy waiting to pull the thermometer from his mouth.

"Do you have a pop quiz today in algebra, James?"

The boy shrugs and mumbles "Mm-mm."

"Miss Jackel says you do." Nurse Correa pulls the thermometer. "You can go back to class now." The boy shuffles out of her office. "Hope you don't miss your quiz!"

She looks at Hal. "Rascals."

Hal leans against the door. He takes a deep breath and raises his eyebrows at nurse Correa.

"I think a certain young boy over at Wood Street School needs you. Again." They look at each other for several seconds.

"Okay."

Hal takes a final draw on his cigarette and tosses it onto the ground before getting into his pickup and heading across the river. He stops at the house to let Smoochy out. Then he walks to the school. Willie, back straight as a board, sits in the nurse's office, his face pale. He looks down when Pop enters.

"Hi Evelyn," said Pop.

Evelyn winks and tilts her head to one side, indicating he should follow her into an exam room. She closes the door. When they come out, Pop puts one hand on Willie's shoulder.

"Ready to go."

Willie walks out without saying a word.

They stand together at the crosswalk as a car passes. They will continue down the street for two blocks, then around the corner to the house. It is red brick with two front dormers and a small porch; two Japanese maples in the front yard. A weeping willow at the side. There's nothing green left in Pop's garden, just dirt, though the tomato cages are still in place.

It's Willie's job to tend the garden in the spring and summer. It had been a good year for leaf lettuce, peas, green beans, tomatoes, peppers and beets. When Willie would bring an arm full of vegetables into the kitchen, Pop would grab them in his hands, hold them under his bulbous nose, and close is eyes. Willie would do the same, although he wasn't sure why. "Smells like the earth," Pop would say. Willie would say, "Yeah."

"How was school?" Pop lights another cigarette.

"I don't know."

"Well, what did you do today?"

"Nothing."

"I'm sure you did something, boy."

"Just the usual stuff."

Willie watches from the corner of his eye as Pop drops ashes along the way. "What about social studies?"

Willie trots ahead to pick up a stick lying on the sidewalk. He breaks it into pieces and tosses them, one at a time, into the street. He picks at the tar that was drizzled onto the cracked pavement over the summer. Pop walks slowly, favoring his knee. Willie tries to stay a few paces ahead. He throws a stone at a starling that is yelling at him from a telephone pole. He misses, so he picks up another and tries again. Another miss. By then Pop catches up.

"Tell me about social studies."

"I didn't feel good, that's all."

Pop looks at the boy whose head is bowed, his rangy red hair parted by the wind.

"Didn't feel good."

"Yeah."

"Anything else? Did something happen?"

"Huh uh."

Pop doesn't know how to draw Willie out. It is always a dance, Willie stepping back as Pop steps forward.

"Okay, so...why don't you run ahead and get Smoochy. She needs a walk."

Willie runs as if he's been shot from a rifle. Pop catches up and sits on the front steps, smoking. Mr. Conner rakes his yard across the street, even though there is nothing to rake.

"Winter'll be here in no time," calls Mr. Conner.

"I'm sure it will."

Nothing more to say, Mr. Conner scratches his yard some more. Pop tilts his head back and blows smoke into the air. A squadron of geese cross the sky.

"Look at that, Mae," he says.

Smoochy jumps on Pop's back, and slobbers on his neck as Willie struggles to leash her. They walk slowly to the corner, letting Smoochy sniff every leaf, every blade of grass, every tree. Pop puts his hand on Willie's head as they wait out the traffic.

"Okay, go," says Pop. "I'll be at the pharmacy." Willie dashes across the street and into the expansive triangle-shaped field. He unleashes Smoochy who chases a squirrel up a tree and then advances on a robin that's jerking at a worm fifty yards away.

Pop ambles down the street to the Park Pharmacy. He stands at the entrance for several minutes, finishing his smoke and watching Willie. When he sees Preston hot-footing it down Haig St., Willie waving both arms at him, Pop disappears into the store.

"Hey Smooch," says Preston. He rolls on the ground, letting the dog attack him. "Whoa, girl, don't lick me to death."

"Come'ere girl." Smoochy runs past Willie, chasing leaves swirling in the middle of the field.

"Hey, man. You okay?"

"Yeah." His response has more edge than he intended.

"That was something, though, I mean, you know." Preston looks away and fires a stone at a tree, missing it.

"I slipped, that's all."

"I don't know, man, you just laid there for, like, a whole minute, which doesn't sound like much, but, I'm telling you, it was like forever. You shoulda seen Clammerman. His face got all red and his pits were all sweaty. He thought he killed you."

"I was fine."

"Mr. Highmark looked all worried and he ran out of the room. I've never seen Nurse Ansel run so fast. You could hear those rubber soles a mile away. I mean her cap flew right off and she didn't even stop to pick it up."

"Smoochy!" Willie walks toward his dog.

Preston grabs his arm.

Pop watches from the store window. An employee notices him. "Hi, Mr. Mitchum, how are you today. Can I help you?"

Pop walks up to the counter, browses a rack of Kodak film and a display of Brownie cameras.

"Hi Brenda, how are you?"

Brenda's smile makes her bounce. "I'm just fine. How about you?"

"I'll have a couple packs of Camels and a Clark bar." He looks out the window again. "Make that two Clark Bars."

Pop takes a seat on the bench in front of the pharmacy. The wind blows the dry leaves around his feet. He stuffs the Clark Bars into his blue work shirt pocket. He leans back, opens a pack of cigarettes and lights one up. He stretches his right leg out slowly, then back again. One car, then another pass by and blow their horns. He waves, takes a long, slow breath, and bends his head this way and that, trying to relax his shoulders.

"Fall's coming, Mae," he says to the wind. He blows some smoke. "Ruthie." He looks down and smiles at the sound of her name.

The boys are standing close together. Preston is gesturing and Willie stares while Smoochy, that long-haired streak, chases everything all at once.

Preston shows a wicked little smile. "They weren't the only ones that were all goofed up about you lying on the floor," he says in a sing-songy tone.

"Whadaya mean?"

"I'm just saying that a certain someone, not a teacher, not a nurse, not a civil defense guy, was pretty worried about Mr. Willie Blevin."

"I don't know what you're talking about, punk."

Preston sticks his arms out and quivers his hands. "Ooooooo." He doesn't get a rise out of Willie. "Okay for you, then. I'm not tellin' you who."

Willie shakes his head and forces a smile. "I could care less."

"Yeah, you wouldn't say that if you knew who I was talking about."

"Shut up." Willie whistles at Smoochy, who stops on a dime, looks around, and then runs in the opposite direction.

"Poor Smooch. Not a rocket scientist, is she?"

"Hey, don't say that. You'll hurt her feelings."

They both start laughing when Smoochy catches her tail between her choppers and yelps.

"You ever notice how small that cranium is?"

"Watch yourself."

"I'm just saying, whatever's inside there can't be much larger than a walnut...maybe a peanut."

"That's it!" Willie lights after Preston. Smoochy joins the chase, chomping on Willie's pant leg just as Preston is within his grasp. "Smoochy, for God's sake! Lemme go, girl." Preston sticks his thumbs in his ears and wiggles his fingers. "Who's the punk now, punk?" Willie leaps after him, tackling him to the ground.

"I'm gonna kill you," says Willie.

"Yeah, well, if you do, a certain someone won't like you anymore."

Willie rolls off his friend and sits cross-legged on the grass. "What are you talking about?"

"You said you 'could care less'."

"C'mon." Willie pushes him. "What's up?"

"Okay. But don't go nuts on me after I tell you. Cross your heart."

"My God, are you two years old or what?"

"Cross!"

Willie crosses. "G'boy," said Preston.

"So?"

"A certain girl got totally upset when she saw you 'trip' and 'fall' on the floor. You also need to know that you left a little pool of slobber on the floor. It was so—"

"Pres!"

"Anyway, she was so upset she began to..." Preston grins and raises his eyebrows.

"Began to what?"

He put his knuckles to his eyes. "Waa—waa—waa!"

"What are you talking about?"

"Her face got all red and she cried, like real tears, and then she just ran out of the room."

"C'mon."

"And no one saw her the rest of the day."

"Liar." Willie's face is getting pink around the ears.

"Suit yourself. But has any girl ever liked you before? I mean, liked you liked you?"

"Smoochy! Come'ere!" Smoochy stops, her head shoots up. "Over here, girl!" Smoochy wags her tail and goes back to sniffing a fire hydrant.

"Look, you can tell me if you want. It doesn't matter one way or the other."

"Geez, Willie. Look at you. Your face is all blotchy."

"Just tell me and get it over with."

"Guess."

Willie grabs Preston by the shirt and holds a fist to his face.

"Okay, okay already." Preston pulls away. He takes a deep breath. "You ready for this?"

Willie purses his lips and furrows his brow.

"It's Lucy."

"What?"

"You heard me."

CHAPTER 3

Lucy Hallowell lies on a cot in the nurse's office, exam room door closed tightly and curtains drawn. She holds her stomach with both hands and pulls her knees up. She hears murmuring coming from the office. It is a man, a loud man who is talking fast. Soon that voice is gone. Nurse Ansel is talking now, her voice a low steady hum, to someone who doesn't answer. She stops and then starts again. There is a long pause and then she speaks once more.

Finally, the student answers. It's a boy. She can't hear what he's saying, but the timbre of his voice, like someone strumming a guitar, is familiar. She sits up slowly, trying not to make a sound. After a few minutes, the nurse's voice goes up an octave and another voice, much deeper, fills the room.

Sharp stomach cramps return and she winces. She hopes no one will knock at the door, that no one will call to her or ask her how she's feeling. She turns to face the wall. She hears all three voices speaking at once. It's got to be Willie and Mr. Mitchum. She doesn't move a muscle. She breathes as evenly and as deeply as possible, just like Nurse Ansel suggested when she first arrived: "Good breathing is a cure for just about anything. I'll be right back," she'd said.

It was no surprise to her that Willie had trouble with Clammerman's movie. But she felt so sick at the time that his problems didn't matter. She had put her head on her desk in the dark. The cool surface felt soothing. The room was quiet except for Clammerman's voice and the clickety-clack of the projector. She closed her eyes.

Then there was a ruckus on the other side of the room. She raised her head and saw that Willie's seat was empty. Everyone got up and crowded around to see what had happened. That's when she darted out of the room and ran down the hall to the nurse's office. Otherwise, there would have been two kids lying on the classroom floor.

Lucy thinks of her mother. "I'm twelve, Mom."

"I know, honey, but trust me, something's coming that's gonna make you a woman and when it comes you'll know." Lucy's mom took her chin in her hand. "You'll know."

"You've been saying this forever."

Her mother, wrapped in a pink bathrobe, leaned forward and touched Lucy's chest.

"Things are changing, girlie." Lucy pulled away. "You're wearing that training bra, aren't you?"

Lucy folded her arms over her chest. Her mother laughed as Lucy walked away. "I didn't have nearly as much going on up-top when it happened to me. It's coming, young lady."

Is this it? Lucy wonders. She isn't even sure what "it" is.

Her friends, Jill and Linda, talked to her about it; how their mothers warned them; how they told them once it happens, their bodies will start changing drastically and boys will flit around them constantly, wanting to do what they want to do. The three of them looked at each other and shrugged. As far as they were concerned, the only thing boys wanted to do to girls was annoy them.

Her friends aren't wearing training bras yet. Lucy feels like a freak in her class. The boys whisper and point. Joey Kendall even tried to snap her bra at recess. She punched him and bloodied his nose.

Is this going to be a regular thing?

She wishes she had someone to talk to about all this stuff. Her mother talks about Lucy's body all the time, but when she does, she's edgy, even angry, like it's Lucy's fault she's growing up. Her mother pushes a wheelbarrow full of unhappiness wherever she goes. Every once in a while, she dumps the whole thing on Lucy.

"Why'd you even have me?" Lucy'd said once.

There was fire in her mother's eyes when she slapped her. Lucy ran to her bedroom, her mother close behind. "I'm so sorry, Luce...dammit..." There were tears in her eyes, but there were always tears in her eyes. "Please forgive me." Her mother laid her head in Lucy's lap. Lucy stroked her blonde hair, a blank stare on her face: "Okay, Mom."

There is a tap on the exam room door. Nurse Ansel tiptoes in.

"Is this your first time, Lucy?"

"Uh huh."

"Do you have anything with you?"

Lucy didn't know what she meant. She grabbed her book bag.

"No, no, dear, I meant for...you know." She dropped her eyes in the general direction of Lucy's lap.

"I don't think so." Lucy feels like she is joining a secret club that has rules no one shares and rituals no one explains.

"Okay. I have some things you can use."

Nurse Ansel swivels on her stool and rifles through a drawer until she finds what appears to be a slingshot of some sort.

"You wear this under your underpants."

Lucy puzzles over why she should wear a slingshot (that didn't even have a pouch) under her panties.

When Nurse Ansel turns around, she has a thick napkin in her hand. She drops a box full of them on the floor.

"Okay, this is what you do. See this short end sticking out? You put that in this front snap, like this." She is a pro. "Then you take the long end and you do the same thing in the back." She holds it up in front of Lucy's face. Now *there's* a slingshot, thinks Lucy.

Nurse Ansel stands up and holds the contraption in front of her waist. "It goes like this underneath." She hands it to Lucy. "I'll give you a few minutes to put it on and then I'll be back." She also leaves a baggy pair of cotton panties on the desk. "Just in case yours are soiled."

Lucy takes the slingshot and holds it tight. She rolls over on the cot again. The longer she lies there, the less certain she is about putting it on. Why do I need to do this? Whose idea is this? I can't imagine the other girls letting Nurse Ansel make them wear an elastic belt around their waste with a diaper between their legs. She can feel dampness down there. Her panties are dark red. She feels sick and then the cramps begin again. Why is this happening to me?

Lucy pulls her panties off with two fingers. She looks at them, but has to hold her nose. She drops her underwear into the wastebasket. Then she takes a tissue from the desk top, wipes herself, and disposes of the evidence. She grabs the slingshot, stretches it a few times, and then put it on. She pulls up Nurse Ansel's panties and slips her dress back on, hoping it will hide everything that's going on underneath.

There's another tap on the door. "Okay, that wasn't so bad, was it?" She puts the extra pads into a brown paper bag and hands it to her. Lucy's face goes scrunchy and she begins to cry again.

"There, there, sweetheart, there's nothing to be upset about. This is just nature's way." She hugs Lucy. "Everything will be okay."

"Yeah, but you're not the one walking home with a box of Kleenex between her legs."

CHAPTER 4

"It's Dennis, Dennis Blevin." No one ever calls him Dennis. He's always been Denny. Dennis sounds more adult. "Dennis Blevin, I'm Scott Prescott, your residency director here at Williams Hall. I'm looking forward to getting to know you," he says. He reaches for the hand of another freshman before Denny can respond.

Assembled on the front lawn, they are playing an orientation game in which each new freshman has to shake hands with at least ten other dorm newbies. When the game is over, each student will try to recite the names of everyone he's met. After the first handshake, Denny retreats to his dorm room where his roommate is lying on his bed, tossing wadded paper balls at a miniature basketball hoop taped to the wall. There is music blasting. Someone with a moaning, twangy voice who plays the harmonica.

"Hey," says Denny. He walks across the room and reaches for the kid's hand. "I'm Dennis, Dennis Blevin."

"And I'm desperate for a beer, son."

Denny drops his hand and stares. His roomie laughs, shoots one more ball and stands. He wipes his hands on his jeans and sticks one out. "I'm Jessie, Jessie Storm." Denny smiles and takes hold. "Dennis, huh? I'm surprised no one ever called you Denny. You look like a Denny; you know what I mean. And I'm not kidding about the beer."

"Sure." Pop made him drink three beers in rapid succession when he was fifteen. He got furiously sick. "Never forget what that was like, okay? There's a lesson here."

Jessie is a talker, which helps Denny, who is often at a loss for words. Once, when he was eight, he didn't talk at all for four months. His teachers tried to work with him. The doctor tried. Everyone took a crack at it. But Denny stayed mute. There was too much to say.

Denny was at the DQ with Pop and Willie when he found his voice. The kid at the window said, "What can I get you?" Pop stepped up to answer when Denny blurted out, "A Dilly." He never became a conversationalist, not even close, but he could talk after that whenever he felt the need.

"My parents are both teachers, can you believe that? I mean, what are the chances that I'd be stuck with a couple of bookworms for parents, but I am. I hated school, wanted to drop out but they threatened to disown me. We fought all the time about homework and grades and stuff. What a couple of drips. I wanted to go to New York or something and hit the coffee houses, maybe start a band, live out on the street, y'know. School was a complete drag. If it weren't for Doris, I wouldn't have made it to the finish line. She's my girl and I'm telling you (he growled a laugh) she's all girl, if you get my meaning..."

Denny sits on the bed, hands in his lap. Where do all the words come from?

Denny's first college class, bright and early on a Monday morning, is French. He'd taken it all four years in high school, so they put him in an advanced class. Little did he know his high school teacher had never been to France, Quebec or even a French restaurant; she spoke the language with an authentic American accent.

The professor, a tiny, bent over woman wearing horn-rimmed glasses, speaks nothing but French as soon as she enters the room. Everyone in the class responds and even laughs at what she says. Denny stares. What is this? To complicate matters, he's the only male. All the girls are giddily conversing like natives.

To kick-start things, she asks each student to stand and repeat the alphabet, something Denny was never asked to do in high school. He listens to each girl whiz through with near perfection. It sounds like all he has to do is add a long 'A' sound to everything. Everything except 'W'. He moves his lips as he listens to each recitation. 'Doobla-vey' is his best guess. When his turn comes he adds the 'A's, nails 'doobla-vey', skips 'X' and then sits down.

His teacher's face is solemn. She has him in her sights.

And so, college begins.

American Lit, Poli-Sci, Sociology, Humanities. English is spoken in all these classes. By the end of the first week, Denny lies exhausted in his dorm room. Jessie has gone home for the weekend to see his girlfriend. "I need some, son, if you get my meaning." Jessie's meaning about most things is easy to get. The weekend looms.

Denny looks out the window at the lake. There is an open-air amphitheater on the shore, its vaulted roof anchored by massive beams. A girl and boy are sitting on a wooden bench, embracing. He sees their heads swaying slowly back and forth as they kiss. He sees the boy's hand caressing the girl's breast. Gee. Then they get up and go behind the amphitheater, nearer the lake. She is on her knees. He pulls back from the window, embarrassed. Then he looks again. Only her head is moving.

He wonders if that's what Jessie is doing right now. Is he parked somewhere with his girlfriend, doing exactly the sort of thing most boys and girls do when left to their own devices? God. Jessie intimated he was having sex with Doris. "Doin' the deed, son." Just hearing his boast made Denny feel something unusual in his private parts. He wonders if he'll ever get the chance to be with a girl.

He missed his junior prom when Marsha Handleman backed out because she had a boyfriend in another school. Denny acted sad when she told him, though he felt nothing but relief. He hardly knew her. She sat behind him in English and one day he impetuously turned around and asked her. He was startled when she said yes. He didn't speak to her again for weeks. As prom neared, he screwed up the courage to call her and ask her out for dinner. That's when she told him about Nicky.

He asked Linda Harrison to the senior prom. They had known each other since grade school. It was a last-minute thing. Her boyfriend had an emergency tonsillectomy and Denny offered to step in for him. She hugged him; she was so appreciative. Who wants to miss their senior prom? They danced the first dance of the evening together, but then she spent the rest of the night with her friends. Denny found solace in the boys' lav. When he took her home, she kissed his cheek in a sisterly way, and said goodnight. His first kiss.

He looks out the window again. Now the boy is on *his* knees. What? Denny is startled by this but can't stop watching. How do people learn this? He can't imagine Pop explaining what to do to a girl while on your knees. How would he even ask the question? "Pop? Did you ever go down on your knees with Grandma and, if so, what was that all about?"

The cafeteria at Williams Hall is the saddest place in the world on a Friday night. There are twenty, maybe twenty-five, students sitting at separate tables. He's sure every kid has a pathetic story to tell: "Hi, I have six toes. Wanna see?" "My name is Bernard; yeah, I know, I smell." "In high school, everyone called me Skippy; I don't have an uvula." These are the left-behind. They don't have anyone on campus to hang out with; no girl or boyfriend; they only leave their dorm room to go to class or cafeteria or, worst of all, the library. On Friday, they open their door, look into the hall and discover that everyone is gone. No idea where or why.

Denny takes a tray from the stack. There are only two workers, gigantic serving spoons in their fists. He looks into each vat of food. He's seen most of it, in one form or another, earlier in the week. Some things have been mixed together to create new, exotic dishes. He gets two glops meat loaf marinara. Carrots, peas and corn. Two chocolate milk cartons. He looks around the room, big as a football field, and spies an empty table in the farthest corner by a window. He walks, head bowed, to his spot and takes a seat. He forgets his utensils and napkin ("Oh...no.") and walks back across the cafeteria to the utensil rack. A girl is standing alone deciding what to eat. She looks at him, a finger on her lip, as if she's unsure what to do next. Denny grins, she smiles, then he walks away.

He watches from his corner. Tray in hand, she hobbles slowly through the maze of tables. What is wrong with her? he thinks. A milk carton slips from her tray. He looks away as she bends awkwardly to pick it up. She steadies herself and starts again. She's homing in on his table. No, no... He buries his face in his entre. Ten seconds pass; he assumes it's safe to look up.

"Hi!"

She's wearing a plaid wrap around skirt and a Weston College t-shirt and big, clompy shoes. She smiles broadly. Buck seems like a harsh word to use, but it is the only one he can think of to describe her teeth. Not as buck as Nelson Diddle, who, in the fourth grade, could barely close his mouth. But, close. Nevertheless, she has a nice smile, a sparkling smile. Just big. Freckle-face would be the other term that comes to mind. Some people have lots of regular skin and a few freckles. She has lots of freckles and a little bit of regular skin. Her hair is short-ish, and tucked behind her ears. It isn't golden brown, or honey, or bronze or chestnut. It's brown. She has large hazel eyes, white all around.

"They're new," she says.

"What?"

"I thought you were looking at my eyes. Because I blink. A lot. My mother thought it would be good, like a fresh start, if I got contact lenses before I left for school. I'm not used to them. That's why I keep blinking like I'm a bug or something. The other night, I slept with them on and I couldn't open my eyes when I woke up. My roommate had already left for an 8 o'clock, so there I was."

Oh."

"It took a half-hour for me to figure things out, but now it's better." She closes her eyes tight and then pops them open. "See."

"That's good."

She bends over laughing. "And my hair, that's another thing. It used to go down below my waist. Never got it cut since third grade. I wore it in a braid. I was given the 'What's-Going-on-There?' award from my senior class. They made it up just for me. Like an honor, maybe. But my mom said no one wears their hair like that in college. So, she took me to her hair stylist and they cut it all off. I cried and cried. I still have all of it in a shopping bag at home." She pats her hair and fluffs it. "This is the latest thing. That's what Mom said. It's a 'flip-bob' just like Jackie Kennedy." She scrunches the ends of her straight hair. "But it's lost its flip and I don't know what else to do with it, so I put it behind my ears." She shrugs.

Denny exhales through his nose and smiles, except his smile looks more like he's baring his teeth.

"Anyway, is this seat taken?"

"No."

She puts her hand on the back of the chair, opens her eyes wide, and smiles, as if to say, 'Okay to sit here?'.

He gestures for her to take a seat.

For a moment it's quiet. She opens her milk and sticks in a paper straw. She divides her food into separate sections with her fork. She unfolds her napkin and places it on her lap. She crosses her legs and looks at Denny. "Bon appetit." She sips her milk.

Wait a minute, he thinks. That sounds...French. In fact, he's sure it's French for something. 'Bon' means 'good'. 'Appetit' means---context clues suggest 'appetite'. Good appetite; enjoy your meal.

"Same to you," he says. He takes another bite and sips his milk.

"You don't remember me, do you?"

How dumb can I be? he thinks. "Monday French class with the lady professor?" She witnessed his humiliating performance.

"Madame Cole, yes. You sit in the third row third seat. I'm in the fifth row fifth seat."

"Oh, sorry. I didn't see you. I guess I was preoccupied..."

"Trying to learn the alphabet." She says this without a hint of judgment.

"Guilty as charged...And I took French all through high school."

"You sure you weren't taking some other language, maybe German or Chinese?"

Denny's smooth forehead becomes furrowed. Then her eyebrows go up and down several times and she winks.

"Maybe Swahili," he says. Pretty good response, he thinks.

"Swahili, of course!" Her voice goes up two octaves and everyone within thirty feet turns to look. She doesn't seem to notice or care. So, he doesn't care either.

She asks him what he's majoring in. "I don't know" is the best he can do. "I'm business," she says. "My dad has an insurance business and he thinks it would be perfect for me. I'm not so sure."

"What would you like to do?"

"Oh my, what would I like to do? What wouldn't I like to do?" Her head goes back as if she's star-gazing. "Well, I'd like to backpack through Europe. That's the first thing I'd like to do."

Denny doesn't know what to say. College is the furthest he's ever been from home. Seven whole hours. He can't imagine going any further than that. Pop has lived in the same town his whole life. Except during the war when he was in San Diego. He's never mentioned wanting to go anywhere. Why would you backpack through Europe? How would you eat? Where would you stay? How would you talk? Where would you go to the bathroom? You'd get lost, for sure. Then what?

He looks at her as she takes tiny bites from each of her food sections. "Why would you want to go to Europe?"

"Because it's there."

"Wouldn't you be afraid? I mean, anything could happen, right?"

"I hope so. Otherwise, what's the point of going?"

Denny chews slowly.

"Could I ask you a personal question?"

Denny lays his fork down.

"Well, sure, okay."

"What's your name?"

He exhales. "Oh, it's Denny...Dennis...Blevin, Dennis Blevin."

She reaches across the table to shake Denny's hand. "Nice to meet you Denny Dennis Blevin Dennis Blevin. I'm Becky Hopewell."

Denny watches everything she does, as if he's never seen a girl before. The way she wags her head when she wants to emphasize something. The way she talks without stopping, even when she's eating. The way her hair moves and her eyes dart and her hands gesture. She is motion itself. It's almost too much to take in.

"So, my mom's a nurse, like in a doctor's office, a pediatrician. I go there but usually the other nurse sees me. Once in a while Mom has to be in the room and it's beyond weird. But it's okay. She's okay. Dad's okay, too, but different. He's higher energy, I guess; he's always psyched up like he's selling you the most amazing thing in the world even though it's only life insurance. He's funny, too, him and me. My older sister, I miss her a lot. She's, like, married and everything."

Denny is spellbound. He nods his head and tries to eat; he smiles when it's appropriate and says things like "Oh" and "That's something" but it isn't even necessary because she keeps talking no matter what. He's never had a girl talk to him before, not like this, not like he's someone, not an important someone, but, at least, someone.

When they get up and head back for dessert, he notices her shoes are different. Actually, it's her left shoe that's different, thicker heel and sole. And her left leg, it's much thinner than her right. She walks like she's on the side of a hill. He looks around, feeling embarrassed for her, but she doesn't seem to be aware there's a problem.

When they reach the dessert line, he says, "Hey, what's..." and then thinks better of it.

"What's what?" she says, grinning.

"Nothing. What do you want?" he points to the array of options. He settles on apple pie and she takes two Jell-O's, strawberry and cherry.

When they leave the cafeteria, the sun is setting. The air is balmy and the quad is empty. They circumnavigate the quad three times. This must be 'college life', he thinks. Meeting someone you would never meet anywhere else. Not going back to the dorm because you have something better to do. Staying outside for as long as you want. No adult to tell you it's late or that you need a jacket.

They head up the hill to Elmer Hall, the girl's dorm. She struggles and alters her gait to a stutter step.

"Do you...can I help?"

"No, no, really," she says, as if there's nothing wrong.

"Okay."

"So gallant of you to escort me back to my castle," she says.

"Well...I'm sure you would do the same."

She glances at the entrance where several girls are talking. Her face is pensive. Her eyes, her mouth, everything about her droops a little. She walks away, waving over her shoulder.

"Demain."

"Sure," he says as he leaves.

At the dormitory door she says "Hi" to the girls but they don't respond.

Denny treks back down the hill, across the quad, past the library, over the walking bridge and through a stand of trees to his red brick dorm. The air smells sweet and the moon, nearly full, sits atop the fieldhouse. He stops and turns a three-sixty, taking in the ivied buildings and lush green grass, the sports fields in the distance and the crisscrossing walkways all around; the clock on Hanley Hall, its chimes echoing across the empty campus.

A handful of dorm windows are lighted. Before pushing the elevator button, he goes into the lounge to check his mail slot. To his surprise, there is a letter waiting for him. The return address is 'Willie'. His chest aches. He opens the envelope and then decides to wait. He puts a dime in the candy machine, pushes the buttons and waits for his Necco Wafers. He opens the wrapper and searches for the chocolate flavored candies. He tosses the rest into the wastebasket.

Denny stands at his dorm window again, pulls back the faded yellow drapes and looks out across the lake, the moon reflected on its still surface. He lays the letter on his desk. "Give him time," Pop had said. "He needs to get used to you not being here. And you need to get used to being away." Willie had already written Denny a letter. He decided to wait before answering it. Give his brother time to settle into sixth grade. Feel his way. But now a second letter.

Denny remembers how his brother clung to him when he was little. How he slept with him, curled in a little ball. How he worried about things long before there were things to worry about. Why does it get dark? What would happen if the sun didn't come up in the morning? What would we do? Denny always reassured his brother, even when he was unsure himself.

Pop had decided it would be best for Denny to go by bus to college. It would be too hard on his brother if they drove him to Weston, harder to say goodbye, to drive away; Willie would brood for seven hours on the way home.

The morning Denny left, Willie brought Lucy to the bus depot with him. He didn't say much, but when Denny hugged him, Willie didn't want to let go. Denny slipped him five packs of baseball cards, which made him smile. "I hope Mays is in there, maybe Clemente, too." He got on the bus and didn't look back. In fact, he felt relieved as the bus pulled away. Then he started crying.

He undressed and got into bed, his reading light on. He opened the letter.

Dear Denny,

It's me, Willie. I hope you get this letter. How are things at college? Is it like high school? Have you made any friends? Do you have air-raid drills at college? We have them all the time. You know old man Ashwood? He's building a bomb shelter. Do you have bomb shelters at college? It's college, so you probably do. School is okay. Smoochy says hi. Remember when I used to sleep over in your room? I hope you can come home sometime.

Your brother,

Willie

PS I got an extra one, so I thought you'd like it.

Denny turned the baseball card over in his hand. Willie Mays.

CHAPTER 5

There is room enough for three cars in Preston's garage, even though they only have one. "Dad thought he would make a workshop or something, but he never did." In place of the shop, a ping-pong table is sprawled across the middle of the garage. Paddles hang on the wall--rubber coated, sandpaper coated, and soft foam to add terrific English. There is a box of balls on a table below them.

"Okay punk," he says. "This is it."

Best of five and Preston is already up two games to one. He bends over, hiding the ball in his palm. Willie shifts his weight back and forth and leans in, paddle ready. Preston slams one across the table but it dies in the net.

"Doggonit."

"Who's the punk now?" chirps Willie.

"Here she comes."

"I'm ready."

"No, here she comes." Preston stands up and points down the driveway. Lucy coasts into the garage on her Schwinn. Preston presses his tongue into his cheek, trying to hide a smile as he nods to Willie.

"Gentleman." Kickstand down, Lucy steps up to the table. "Got winner."

"That would be me," says Preston.

"Yeah, right," says Willie, not yet looking at Lucy.

Preston bounces at the knees. Willie is ready for another top spin across the table. But, no, Pres whacks the serve into the opposite corner. Willie waves a backhand to no avail.

"Game, set, match, my little tiny baby boy."

Willie slings his paddle into the net.

"Come on, buddy, we know you're a loser. But you don't have to be a sore loser."

Lucy gives Willie a soft shove. "Don't pay any attention to him. Remember he's the one who pooped his pants in kindergarten. Smelled so bad everyone had to leave the room for, like, an hour."

Willie forces a derisive laugh and sniffs the air.

"Old news, old news," says Preston. "We've been over this. I was sick."

"Yeah, yeah," says Willie .

"Stick with that story, Pres." Lucy crosses her eyes and sticks out her tongue. Willie smiles.

"You ready for me?" Lucy takes a foam-covered paddle from the wall. She rolls her sleeves up and takes her stance. She and Preston warm up.

"Hey, have you guys seen what old man Ashwood's doing in his backyard."

"I heard about it." Preston spikes the ball into the net. "C'mon." He slaps his thigh with the paddle.

"What about it?" With a sharp wrist snap, Lucy's serve ricochets off Preston's paddle and onto the floor. "Who's the little baby boy now?"

"That's nothing." Preston flips the ball into the air and twists his wrist as he hits it.

"He's got a gigantic hole in his backyard. He's had a backhoe guy there for about a week."

Lucy returns the ball into the corner. Preston backhands it to the middle of the table. Lucy snaps her wrist and the ball jumps. Preston reaches but misses.

"Who cares if he's got a giant hole in his yard?" says Lucy.

"It's what he's putting in it that's..."

"That's what?" says Lucy.

"Weird," says Preston. "Weird like old man Ashwood's weird. My dad remembers him when he was in high school. Everyone said he ate his cat." He and Lucy are counting strokes now. "Let's see how long we can keep this going."

"Anyway, like I said, it's what he's gonna do with the hole that's, well, let's say odd."

"What's he gonna do with the hole?" Lucy reaches and saves the streak.

"Yeah," says Preston.

"Pop says Ashwood is building---get this---a bomb shelter."

"Geez, man, not with the A-bomb stuff again!" Preston pops the table hard with his paddle.

Willie clams up. For a moment the only sound is the ping and the pong of the ball.

"I don't get it, I mean the A-bomb stuff," says Lucy.

"It's---"

"Remember when Khrushchev was here back when, like, we were in third grade and he pounded his shoe on a table and said he was going to bury us? Ever since then, young Mr. Blevin has been waiting for the world to end." Pres shakes his head and smiles.

Pop had laughed at all the news coverage the Soviet leader got at the time. "Idiot," was all he said. But Willie didn't sleep for several nights after that. He dreamed of mushroom clouds and Khrushchev clobbering him to death with a giant sneaker. Awake, he imagined everyone careening through the streets terrified, like in *The Day the Earth Stood Still*. This nuclear thing was inevitable, he thought. He never told Pop how worried he was, but he did tell Denny, and later, much to his regret, he told Preston, who said he was crazy, "No one can do anything to this country. No one."

When he lay in bed with his brother, Denny would tell him it was scary, but that he was sure things would turn out okay. He said Khrushchev was just "showing off." His voice was always so calm and matter-of-fact that Willie would believe him. It helped him sleep, although in the morning, he often didn't want to get up.

Time passed and he worried less. Soon there was a new president. He was young, maybe too young. Pop was a Nixon man, so Willie was, too.

There were many political arguments with his friends on the way to school that fall. Mostly, they made fun of the candidates' middle names---Milhouse and Fitzgerald. Even Willie knew his candidate's middle name was the worst. What's a Milhouse anyway?

Things settled down after the election. Not that bad stuff didn't happen, like the Bay of Pigs, whatever that was. Good stuff, too, like John Glenn and some other guys rocketing around the earth. Mainly, though, there wasn't much to worry about.

But this year has been worrying. So much talk about nuclear weapons, nuclear war, nuclear everything. Air-raid drills at school and sirens blaring all over town. Willie was sure it was on everyone's mind, even though you'd never know it when you went grocery shopping at Spoa's. People nodded and smiled and talked about the weather or sports or something. Everyone went about their business; everyone, that is, except old man Ashwood. He had a different understanding of things.

"Willie?" says Lucy, trying to keep her eye on the ball. "Are you waiting for the world to end?"

"I think things have gotten pretty...serious, I guess."

"You can't go by Ashwood."

"Why not? I mean, I know he's weird, but maybe he's onto something." He pulls a folded pamphlet from his back pocket. He lays it on the table. "Looky here."

Lucy and Preston squeeze in beside him. "Look, it says, 'Office of Civil and Defense Mobilization'. That's real stuff. And listen to this: 'Adequate shielding is the only effective means of preventing radiation casualties'. That's from the 'National Academy of Sciences'. Also, very real." All three of them look at each other. Willie licks his finger and turns the page. "Okay, so, listen to this: 'Let us take a look at the hard facts. In an atomic war, blast, heat, and initial radiation could kill millions close to ground zero of the nuclear bursts'." He reads on, skipping the descriptions of fallout shelters. "And then it says: 'There are means of protection. But that protection must be provided before, not after, the sirens sound'."

"Where'd you get this?" said Lucy.

"It doesn't matter where I got it." Stealing the pamphlet from Ashwood's construction site was a whole new thing for Willie. He never stole anything before. Maybe penny candy. Maybe baseball cards. Black Cows. A *Mad Magazine*. But nothing important. Pop would kill him. Anyway, he planned on sneaking back to Ashwood's and putting it on the table where he'd found it...stole it. "This is the government talking. This isn't some goofball standing on a corner somewhere. They are warning all of us; they wouldn't make this thing (he held up the pamphlet) if they didn't think a nuclear war was right around the corner. I'm telling you, if we don't get with it, we could all..." His voice trails off, not wanting to say it out loud.

"Bomb shelters are for chickens and crazy people," says Preston. "Do you think for a minute we would let some stupid missile penetrate our airspace? That's nuts! Not possible. My dad told me the Strategic Air Command has B-52s in the sky twenty-four hours a day. The Soviets know that. They're just trying to scare us. We don't scare." Preston's fists are clenched.

Willie's eyes are wide.

"You stole this, didn't you, Willie? From Mr. Ashwood," says Lucy.

Willie ignores her. "What if something unforeseen happens? What if, just what if one missile, just one missile slips through? I mean, you can't stop everything."

"We'd blow them to smithereens!" says Preston as he makes exploding noises with his mouth and runs for cover under the ping-pong table.

He doesn't get it, thinks Willie. The world is a balloon balancing on a straight pin.

Lucy grabs Willie's shirt and yanks it. "Hey, what's wrong with you? You don't steal stuff. Why would you do that? You could get in real trouble. I mean, that's government property. Maybe the government has asked Mr. Ashwood to make this thing."

Gosh no, he thinks. Mr. Ashwood? Could he really be working for the government?

"You better get that back to him as soon as you can, like right now," says Lucy, her fists planted on her hips.

"Better do what your girlfriend says," whines Preston.

"What?" says Lucy.

"Shut up, man!"

A car pulls into Preston's driveway. Lucy's mom steps out of the car, almost losing her balance. She holds onto the side view mirror to steady herself. Her bathrobe barely covers her thighs, and her hair is in curlers as big as coke cans. Lucy freezes.

"Who said you could go out and play? There's things to do at home and I can't do it all!" She leans against the car to maintain her balance. "You get home right now!" She pulls the draw string tighter around her waist and glares at the boys.

"What in the world...?" Preston laughs.

"Shut up." Lucy's eyes are moist, but her voice is razor sharp.

"What's wrong with your mom?" says Willie.

Lucy looks at Willie. She opens her mouth to answer and then closes it. She looks at the car. Her mom blasts the horn.

"I gotta go."

"Are you okay?"

Lucy walks her bike slowly up the driveway. Her mother backs into the street and waits for her, then follows close behind as Lucy rides away.

"She's really something, isn't she?"

"I don't understand what's going on," says Willie.

"Weird. Not weird like Ashwood's weird, but close behind."

CHAPTER 6

As Pop approaches, he sees Robert Ashwood bent over his wheelbarrow, shovel in hand, mixing concrete. No longer the skin and bones upperclassman he remembered from high school, Robert rests his ample belly on the rim of the wheelbarrow, his chest heaving as he gasps for air. He pulls a handkerchief from his back pocket and wipes his brow. He reaches for a beer on the ground beside him.

"Evening," says Pop.

Robert drops his shovel and turns, almost losing his balance. When he sees it's Hal, he smiles, his jowly face expanding. "Neighbor."

Pop surveys the hole. "That's something."

"Security."

"I imagine."

"Lot of work."

"Yes, I'm sure."

"You ought to consider it."

"You think?"

Ashwood crosses his arms, resting them on his belly shelf. "This isn't anything to fool with. There are dangers out there we know nothing about. You were in the service, right?"

"Yes. No combat, though." Being ashamed he had never engaged in combat, it is always the first thing Pop mentions when asked about his time in the service.

"Still. You understand the risks out there," says Ashwood.

"I suppose I do," he says, unsure of what Ashwood means. "How long will this take you?"

"Depends. Sometimes the work goes fast; sometimes it goes slow."

"Can I take a look?"

"Be my guest."

Pop comes forward to the edge of the hole. The concrete floor has been poured. There is a narrow hall between the exit and the rest of the shelter. Pop estimates the walls will be seven feet high, before being covered with earth.

"You're right. Lots of work."

Ashwood chuckles. "It's involved." He points to where the vents will go. How they will need special filters to protect against "radioactive particulate."

"I've been saving rations in my basement. Canned goods. Bottles of distilled water. Sand for waste disposal. Batteries. Transistor radios."

Hal raises his eyebrows and nods.

"This isn't something to mess with. Last year the Soviets said it would only take a few megaton bombs to destroy a country. Even Kennedy says everyone should have a fallout shelter. As quickly as possible. He knows what's at stake. No one's paying attention. No one's listening." The two men look at each other. "With everything you've gone through, Hal...I'm surprised you aren't planning ahead, even building a shelter of your own."

Hal swallows hard. Sometimes preparing is just pretending; it's pretending you can do something that you can't, that you have power that you don't. Once he believed he was prepared for anything life had to offer, but then he found out he wasn't.

"You're probably right, Robert. I should start digging. And digging and digging and digging...how stupid of me."

Hal takes a pack of cigarettes from his pocket. He sticks one in the corner of his mouth, lets it dangle for a moment, then lights it. They both listen to the sizzle and smell the sulfur. He draws long and tosses the match to the ground.

"Look, Hal, I'm sorry....I didn't mean nothing." Ashwood shuffles his feet and clears his throat. "I think you know I understand."

Hal collects himself so when he speaks, his voice is soft. "Yes...I know you do...Sorry I snapped..."

Both men look at their feet.

"We okay?" says Hal.

Robert shakes his head.

"Look, Hal, we go back a ways. We've seen things, you and me." Hal nods. Robert points at the hole. "When this is done, I'm gonna have room for six people. I'd be more than pleased to have you and the boy join me. Denny, too, if he's around."

Hal smiles at Ashwood. "That's good of you. It is."

Willie comes running around the corner of Ashwood's house and stops abruptly. What are they doing? thinks Willie. He pulls his shirt down over the pamphlet tucked in his back pocket. Both men are quiet as he approaches. Willie smiles.

"Hi."

Mr. Ashwood smiles and sticks out his hand. He takes Mr. Ashwood's hand in his. Ashwood shakes it vigorously. "Gettin' big," he says.

"I suppose he is." Pop looks into the hole again.

"You know what this is, son?" says Ashwood.

"I think so."

"I told your Pop there's plenty of room for you when the time comes."

Willie looks at Pop who is still staring into the hole.

"Okay." He kneads his palms with his finger-tips.

Ashwood raises his arms, like an evangelist about to announce the Apocalypse to a wayward heathen. "It's our future. The way things are going to be, I'm afraid. Bomb shelters will be in our backyards as regular as patios, but more comforting. That's the truth."

Pop places his hand on Willie's shoulder and squeezes gently. "Got homework?"

"Some."

"Maybe go on back and get a head start."

Supper is TV dinners, Salisbury steak, balanced on TV trays; they watch *Looney Tunes*. Willie side glances Pop, wondering if he will mention the hole in Mr. Ashwood's backyard. Pop watches the 'tube' as he calls it.

"Can you turn it to two?" says Pop.

Willie gets up and turns the dial to channel two where the news is just starting.

"Thanks."

"Can I have some ice cream?"

Pop scans Willie's plate. "Are you done?"

"Yeah."

"Okay then."

Willie scoops vanilla into a bowl. He opens a fresh can of Hershey's and drizzles chocolate syrup on top. "Heading up," he calls to Pop.

"Take your bath."

"Will do."

Willie swishes in the bathtub briefly while Smoochy, front paws on the edge, licks whatever she can reach. Brushes his teeth with water, deciding toothpaste is unnecessary. He lifts the toilet seat, but still manages to water the floor behind the john. Smoochy cocks her head, curiously.

Willie puts on his blue striped pajamas and slides into bed, shivering at first under the cool sheets. In a few minutes, though, he feels warm and safe. Smoochy sprawls at his feet. He pulls the curtains back from the window so he can breathe the cool night air. A neighboring willow is silhouetted against the fading light. He looks around his room as darkness accumulates. He closes his eyes but sleep is elusive. He looks out the window again admiring the gentle mountain range formed by rooftops along his street.

He gets out of bed one leg at a time, hoping not to awaken Smooch. When he tiptoes down the stairs, all he can hear is the television. He peeks into the living room. Pop is slumped in his easy chair, feet on the ottoman. The light from the TV flickers on his stubbled face. His ample head rests on his shoulder, his mouth open slightly, his work shirt unbuttoned; a framed picture lies on his chest. There are two empty bottles and an overflowing ashtray on the table beside him. Willie looks at the TV. Pop's favorite, *The*

Twilight Zone, is on; a man looks out an airplane window only to be startled by a gorilla-like creature tampering with the wing.

Willie goes to the back door and tiptoes into the night. The sky is star-speckled. The grass is damp on his bare feet. The air is windless and the tree limbs slumber. He heads across the neighbor's lawn and then across another and another until he reaches Mr. Ashwood's yard. There are no lights on in Ashwood's house.

He inches closer to the gaping crater and looks in. He squints to see the darkened bottom. Ashwood said he and Pop could live there when the time came. They could live in this hole in the ground, covered by dirt, a place to wait until everything is better. How would they breathe? How would they go to the bathroom? What if things didn't get better? His breaths quicken. He looks at the white smoke billowing from nearby chimneys. He thinks of his neighbors asleep inside, their backyards hole-less. Where would they go 'when the times comes'?

Willie pulls the pamphlet from the elastic waistband of his pajamas. He looks around for some place to put it. There is a pile of bricks nearby. He places it carefully on top where it will be easily found in the morning. He puts a stone on top to keep it from blowing away during the night, then turns to go back home.

"Thank you."

Willie gasps and holds his breath. He looks in every direction, hoping to find the voice. He is about to give up, when he hears a man clearing his throat. He looks at Ashwood's back door and sees a hulking shadow, darker than the night that surrounds it.

"Sleep well," the shadow says.

Willie nods, then runs back across the yards to his house. He pauses at the door and looks towards Ashwood's but can't see a thing. He opens his door as quietly as he can and disappears inside.

CHAPTER 7

Another Friday. Denny opens his eyes, then sits on the edge of his bed and looks at the blank walls. Jesse's bed is still unmade, just as it was when he left two weeks ago. No word from him since.

He pulls his chair up to the desk and rests his head on one hand. He studies the lake, how it shimmers in the morning sun. There are walkers and runners, even a few kayakers cutting its surface. Staff are setting up tables under the pavilion. What for, is anyone's guess. Bells chime the hour. Eight o'clock. He breathes a sigh of relief---no class until AmerLit at eleven.

Denny opens the letter from his brother. He looks at the note he'd started to write. He had stopped mid-sentence days ago, unsure of what to say. He had called home the day after he received the letter, but there was no answer. He planned to call again, but never did. My days are full, he reasons.

He loves his newish life, the energy of the campus, the constant movement, the sound of it, the future coursing through every student's veins. It is a far cry from life at home, where it felt like the sky hung lower, the sun shone dimmer, and the days crawled, snail-like. He would never have recognized this if he hadn't left for college. He feels sad, heavy hearted, when he thinks how much better it is to be here than there. When he thinks of his brother, his insides groan, he misses him so. Perhaps Willie will leave someday. Perhaps he will find another life. He thinks it's probably best that Pop has never left. Sadness fits him.

Classes are getting better. He's into a study routine, doing some work in the afternoons and leaving the rest for the library at night. The smell of the books, the hum of students, the hidden corners, the study carrels.

During the first few weeks, he felt afraid when he left the dorm and headed across campus to his classes. Who will be the first to laugh at me, to ask why in the world I think I belong here? He'd berate himself for this. There's no reason to be scared, he'd think. Toughen up. Don't be weak. He followed the same route each time---past the library, across the quad, down the hill to the lower campus, around the always buzzing Student Union and into Franklin Hall, where most of his classes were held. As it became familiar, he looked more and more like a student with purpose, someone who had places to go, things to do.

Eventually, he altered his route. Now he walks through the always busy, always crowded Union and realizes no one cares, no one looks at him any differently than they look at anyone else. In fact, everyone ignores each other, mostly.

. . .

Some days Becky heads the same way as him. Walking with another person elevates one's status, at least that's the way it seems to Denny. You aren't a loner. People see you talking and laughing like you are confident, like you belong.

He looks at his brother's letter and feels the weight of it, like an anvil balancing precariously on top of his head.

"He misses you. That's, like, so normal." Becky'd said. "He just needs to hear from you. No need to worry so much about what to say."

Denny wants to believe she's right. He wants to believe it's simpler than he thinks, that it's just a brother missing a brother who's left for college, something that will pass in a few weeks. Maybe a letter from Denny would help Willie with the process. But Denny doubts it. He knows this is not only about two brothers missing each other, but two brothers missing their parents, two brothers missing a life that was supposed to be but never was.

He remembers that the first night, after learning about their parents, his brother crawled into bed with him. Neither of them said a word about their mom and dad. They played with Willie's Lone Ranger and his horse, Silver. The Lone Ranger always got the bad guys, hiding, as they did, in the folds of Willie's blankets. They played for hours. They never slept. The only thing that mattered now was being together.

For several years, they remained as inseparable as they were that first night.

Pop tried to get Willie to sleep in his own room. "It's better that way," he said. Willie dutifully got into his bed each night and then, when Pop had gone downstairs or to bed himself, he'd come to Denny's room and crawl in beside him. Denny didn't even have to roll over. He knew to leave a space open.

Willie seldom asked questions. Which was good, because Denny didn't have any answers.

Pop worked hard all the time. He had to. At age ten, instead of playing with friends, Denny stayed home, making the lunches, taking his brother for walks, swinging him at the nearby park, teaching him his letters and numbers. Once Willie got used to going to school without Pop, Denny held his hand every day and waited for him after the final bell.

He listened to his brother's stories; he took interest in the things he did, the pictures he drew, the books he read and worries he had. It wasn't hard for Denny. He understood what it was like to be timid, to be unsure, to take every step like it was the very first one.

He bends over his note again, pen in hand: *I think you would like this place. It is so big. There's a lake and a cool store, called the Union. You can find almost anything you need. They sell records, sweatshirts, all kinds of stuff.* He looks out his window again. The tables are set in the pavilion. They are covering them with linen cloths now. *Maybe you can visit sometime.* He stops and re-reads what he's written. He erases the line about coming to visit. No chance Pop would let him travel alone on a bus.

Mr. Ashwood is a little crazy, I think. Here, everyone talks about 'banning the bomb' all the time. I don't think anything bad is going to happen. Recently, he'd listened to a senior give a speech in the Union. He'd come back from a meeting in some place called Port Huron where they talked about getting rid of nuclear weapons, about how America "oppresses other people" around the world, about how America is "racist."

He said America was sneaking into a war somewhere in Asia. He was pissed about everything. Some students yelled back at him and others cheered. Denny didn't know what to think. He knew Pop would have punched the kid in the nose. It was confusing. There were recruiters on campus trying to get students to join ROTC. They talked about the dangers of the Cold War and how it could become a Hot War.

Yes, they have air-raid practice on campus, but no one pays attention. As for the air raid sirens, no, we don't have them here. I don't think people are all that worried. If they aren't worried here, you don't need to be either. What else to say? He doesn't plan on coming home until Thanksgiving. *I hope school is going well. Sixth grade! Next stop---Junior High! Maybe I can come home to visit before Thanksgiving.*

Denny folds the letter, slips it into an envelope, addresses it---*Mr.* Willie Blevin---and slaps a four-cent stamp in the corner.

He dives into the steady current of freshmen streaming toward the main campus. He pulls up the collar on the jacket Pop bought him as a going away gift. He spies a gangly girl bobbing awkwardly along in the crowd ahead of him. He picks up his pace.

"Hey," he says, tapping Becky on the shoulder as he catches his breath.

"Bonjour, mon ami," she says, freckles glinting on her cheeks. "Did you go to language lab this morning?"

"Uh..."

"Madame Cole will not be pleased."

"Look, when I go to lab, it's like I'm listening to scrambled eggs. It's worse than class."

"Mon Dieu!"

"Yeah, I guess. I'll go next week."

She stops and stares at him.

"Promise."

Having a girl as a best friend---his only friend, actually---shocks Denny.

Each year in elementary school they had square dancing lessons, which meant boys and girls had to partner up. The boys stood on one side of the school basement and the girls stood on the other. For most of the boys, it was easy to walk across the room and ask a girl to dance. For Denny, it was like a forced march into enemy territory. Square dancing was supposed to help everyone feel more comfortable with each other. It didn't work. He felt nauseous and gassy and sweaty. Once he pretended he'd sprained his ankle and couldn't participate, leaving Alice Campbell, the last girl, without a partner. She had to double up with Corey Coogan and Belinda Bangle.

He skipped the seventh-grade dance; eighth grade, too.

He waited and waited for something to change, for his confidence to emerge, like a bird finally busting out of its egg. But he was never able to crack the shell. Instead, it hardened.

He liked Catherine Katoby throughout high school. The closest he ever got to her was in French Club playing a game where students passed an apple lodged under their chins from person to person. It was tough enough receiving the apple from Stanley Mandelbaum, but it was even more challenging passing it to the next person in line---Catherine Katoby. She had long strawberry blonde hair parted in the middle. A dazzling smile. The bluest eyes. She wore a white sweater with puffy sleeves, a pink poodle skirt, gleaming white tennis shoes and white ankle socks. And physically, well, what could he say? She was nice to everyone. Even Denny, although he felt certain she didn't know his name. When he leaned toward her, apple firmly in place, the feel of her breath on his cheek made him gasp. The apple fell from his neck and gouged her big toe, which started bleeding.

Denny didn't go to any other French Club meetings after that.

He drops the letter to Willie into the mailbox outside the Union. As they enter, Peter, Paul and Mary can be heard over the speakers...'If I had haaammer'. "I love these guys," says Becky.

"Uh huh."

"'Love between my brothers and my sisters, all-alll over this la-a-and'."

She closes her eyes and throws her head back. She sings confidently, creating sounds that have never been produced before.

"I didn't know you were a singer."

"Whenever the spirit hits me. Come on, let's take that booth."

Denny slides in and to his surprise Becky slides in beside him.

"What?"

"Nothing."

"It's not nothing. What is it?"

"Nothing."

"Afraid I'll bite you?"

He laughs, kind of.

"You're not so good around girls, are you?" She flashes her enormous smile.

"I guess..."

She loops her arm around his and moves closer. Their hips and thighs are touching.

"You'll have to get used to it." She kisses his cheek. He stops breathing.

"What's the matter?" she says.

"Nothing."

He tries to kiss her cheek but gets the corner of her mouth instead. He's never been this close to a girl's face...not since Catherine Katoby. He's never noticed the crinkle between Becky's eyes or how her nose flares slightly with each breath. He kisses her again, this time square on the lips. It is quick, dry, wonderful. I can't believe she let me kiss her, he thinks.

"That wasn't so hard, was it?"

"Huh uh," he says.

"Let's get something to eat."

He steps onto the quad after his eleven o'clock as the bell tower chimes noon. Everyone is scurrying, like bees to various hives. Some sit in circles on the grass. Others toss footballs. There are a few long hairs with earnest looks on their faces. Couples hold hands. A few lean against craggy hickory trees thinking Big Thoughts. Several nod or say "Hi" as they pass him. His resting face is a smile. He's not running back to hide in his dorm. Nothing is different although everything seems to have changed. It's him, he realizes. He is not afraid today.

CHAPTER 8

"Lucy!"

Her skin prickles at the sound of her mother's voice. She doesn't answer. Her mother mutters and stumbles through the house looking for something.

"Lucy!"

She waits. Soon her mother will find whatever she's lost and that will be that. Lucy sits on her bed, a Barbie in her lap. She smiles at Barbie and admires her sleek white one-piece bathing suit. Her face is bright and happy and perfect. Her tummy is flat, her legs are long and smooth, her toes pointed. Lucy looks at her own stomach, how it bulges slightly over her waistband; her own legs, short and thickish. If only her hair shown like Barbie's.

Lucy keeps a picture in the bottom drawer of her dresser. It's a man in a blue suit, white shirt and striped tie. He has a square jaw and wavy brown hair. He's looking right at the camera, a broad smile on his face. He is the handsomest man she can imagine. He looks happy and kind. She tore him out of a Sears catalogue. She dreams her real father is like this perfect man, at least a little, despite what her mother says.

When she was younger, Lucy often asked where her father was. "In the wind," was all her mother would say. "You're lucky he's gone. Believe me, he wasn't father material."

A father is a father, thought Lucy. Any father is better than no father at all.

Lucy loves to watch *The Beverly Hillbillies* with her mom. It's one of those rare times when they are happy together. "Where'd they come up with this idea?" her mother'd say with a laugh. They'd curl up on the couch and sing, "Come listen to a story 'bout a man named Jed, a poor mountaineer barely kept his family fed..." Sometimes, though, even Jed and his family couldn't keep the good times rolling. By the first commercial her mother would start to change. She'd gulp instead of sip her drink. She'd get another and another. She'd slump into one corner of the couch, her legs splayed. By the time the credits rolled, her mother was so sullen---"Why the hell do they call it a cement pond? How stupid are they?"---that Lucy would move by inches toward the other end of the couch. Her mother'd keep staring at the TV, no longer watching.

Was she ever happy? Lucy wonders. She doesn't have anyone in her life. She stopped speaking to Lucy's grandparents long ago, her uncle and aunt, too. "Trash," she calls them. The only person she has is Lucy.

"I'm leaving, okay!" her mother calls from downstairs. "I'll be back around two."

"Okay," calls Lucy, but the door has already closed. Lucy's fists unclench, her shoulders, her whole body relax. She picks up her Barbie and studies her from every vantage point, her perfection so obvious. Her mother has a new job as a typist at the mill. "The only good advice my mother ever gave me---take typing." For five consecutive days she's made it to work on time. She lost her last job because her boss was "an idiot." The one before that because she was late all the time, "which was a lie."

Lucy is happy her mother is working again. She is happy that she wears a nice dress, puts makeup on, and curls her hair. She even bought a new pair of heels, navy blue with a gold band across the toe.

She looks like an important person who has important places to go and important things to do. And for once, she looks like the other moms, the moms who come to school with their kids, or volunteer when there is a concert. Except she is younger than any of them. Preston's mother always says, "Your mom looks like she could be in school with you." She means it as a complement, but it makes Lucy feel uneasy, like her mom is different in a way that isn't good.

This morning she was in a hurry, because she got an early call to go in. Something about new orders that needed to be processed. "Double-time, Lucy! You be okay?"

Lucy hugs her Barbie and dresses her again and again, before getting dressed herself. She pulls her hair back on the sides with two sunflower barrettes, and smiles into the mirror.

"Heyyy, Luuucy!" She runs to her mother's room and pulls back the curtain. On the grass below are Willie and Preston. They are fighting with imaginary swords. She runs back to her room and makes the bed as quickly as possible. She kisses Barbie and places her carefully on her pillow.

"Heeyyyy, Luuucyyyy!" they call again.

She flies down the stairs and out the door.

"Did you forget?" says Preston.

"No, I didn't forget."

"Let's go," says Preston.

A few blocks away they disappear into the woods high above the Conoquenessing Creek. The hillside is thick with maples and elms and oaks and granite boulders loosely stacked, creating dark, inviting caves.

"I didn't think we had to do this until next year." Lucy steps over a rotting log as they follow the lane deeper into the woods, enjoying the smell of the cool, damp earth, the sound of squirrels skittering through dried leaves and the singing of birds perched high on the surrounding trees.

"My brother didn't have to do it until seventh grade." Willie kneels to examine a leaf. "What kind of locust tree do you think this is?"

"Who knows? Just keep it. We'll figure it out later." Preston yawns. "What do we gotta find anyway?"

Lucy pulls an orange leaf from a nearby limb.

Willie takes a paper from his back pocket. "Here's the list."

Lucy stops walking and studies the paper. "It says we have to get an 'alternate leaf' arrangement, a 'whorled leaf', a 'compound leaf' and a bunch of other kinds. Here, look." She shows the drawings to Preston.

"Are you kidding? They all look the same. Who cares anyway? A leaf is a leaf. For real."

Willie tosses a stone at a nearby tree, but misses. "Noodle arm," says Preston as he grabs a rock and hurls it at the same tree, hitting it dead center.

Lucy presses her palms to her cheeks dramatically. "Oh my, Preston, you are such a big strong boy." She bats her eyes.

"Better than your Mr. Loverboy."

"My what?" says Lucy.

Willie drops his leaves and glares at Preston.

"Nothin'," says Pres.

Lucy shoots a look at him, then at Willie, who's staring in the opposite direction.

"How 'bout that?" says Willie. Three deer scamper up the hillside, there white tails high. They turn and look back at the kids. Then they disappear into the brush.

"Something, huh?" he says. "I mean, they just live out here on their own, no help from anybody."

"Yeah," says Preston. "My dad says the woods are crawling with deer because they know you can't hunt 'em here."

"That's good," says Lucy. "I can't imagine shooting one."

"My dad likes the meat. He says venison is the best, better than steak. He'll kill as many as he wants when hunting season opens," says Preston. "He says he'll take me with him when I'm old enough for a license." He points a long stick in the general direction of the deer. "Pow!"

"My Pop used to hunt, but he doesn't anymore. My brother went once. Didn't get anything," says Willie.

"What about your dad? Do you know if he hunted?" says Pres.

Willie shrugs. He picks up a stone but doesn't throw it. He rolls it over in his hand several times and then drops it. "Don't know."

Lucy raises her eyebrows at Preston and shakes her head for him to shut up.

Preston frowns at Lucy. He clears his throat and pokes Willie with a stick. "Hey, looky there." He takes Willie by both the shoulders and turns him around.

"Yeah, so?" says Willie.

"I think that's 'bare ass beach' down there, isn't it?"

"Wha'd you say?" says Lucy.

"You heard me, Missy---Bare. Ass. Beach. My dad used to go there with his friends. They'd swim with no clothes on. So---bare ass, get it?"

Lucy heaves a sigh.

Willie looks down the hill toward the strip of sand at the river's edge. "Never been there." When Willie left the house, he told Pop they were going downtown to the five-and-ten-cent store. Pop warned him to be careful crossing Fountain Ave at Second Street. Willie answered in the affirmative.

The hair on Willie's neck stands up and his palms sweat when he bends the truth, especially when he bends it with Pop. But if he didn't, he'd never be allowed to do things, like exploring the woods with his friends. "Stay away from there, boy. It's too dangerous." As for the river, Pop was adamant.

"And never go near that river. The water can sweep you away like nothing."

"Let's go," says Preston, urging them forward with a wave of his arm as he abandons the trail and heads for the beach. In no time, Preston is standing on a rocky outcrop, like an explorer who's reached the highest peak.

Willie and Lucy are still on the path.

"C'mon!" calls Pres.

Willie takes a deep breath. What could go wrong, right? They both leave the path and head into the brush. Lucy holds a branch back so it won't hit Willie in the face.

"Thanks."

"Hey, guess what?"

"What?"

"I saw that guy again."

"What guy?"

"The guy I told you about."

"The suit guy?"

"Yeah."

"You saw him?"

"Yeah, down at Scanlon's drinking a soda."

"Do you know who he is?"

"Huh uh."

"Well, it's probably nothing. Coincidence. Tell your mom about him?"

"Why would I do that?" says Lucy with a scoff.

Willie continues on, ducking under low limbs and creating his own path as he goes. Lucy, lost in thought, doesn't move.

"You coming?" calls Willie.

"I'm coming, I'm coming!"

The Conoquenessing looks angry, its roiling waves crashing against vaulted granite boulders that look like gray whales breaching. It roars like a thunder cloud. The air smells wormy. Pres flips rocks, looking for critters. Willie and Lucy perch on a flat slab, a few feet from the current.

Lucy lies on her belly and dips her fingers into the frothy water. Willie holds her ankles.

"One a year," he says.

She turns on her side. "What?"

"One a year. That's what Pop says. Sometimes two."

"One a year, what?"

"One person drowns in the river every year."

Preston jumps on the slab and tosses a stone at nothing. "Maybe we should find that guy and tell him to be more careful."

"It's a dangerous place, that's all I mean."

"Willie, there's danger everywhere, if you think about it," says Preston. "Most bad accidents happen in your house. What're you supposed to do with that? And cars, geez, cars! And lightning and diseases and more cars and bridges that collapse and ships that sink in the ocean and hurricanes, and there's always a war or something. I mean..." He shrugs and tosses another stone. "You can't, like, get away from it. You just gotta close your eyes and keep going."

Willie finds a hefty stone and tosses, losing his balance as it flies. It plunks in the mud on the opposite shore.

The friends head back up the hill to the trail, Pres several strides ahead, smacking tree trunks with his stick. Willie and Lucy walk side-by-side. Lucy notices Willie is taller than her. From kindergarten on, they have always been the same, always side-by-side when they had to line up in PE by height. His hands seem bigger, too. Kids used to make fun of his baby cheeks, but they're gone now. His hair was nearly orange in first grade, but now it's red. His shoulders are still rounded, like a little old man. His face seems naturally sad, which makes his smile all the more striking, even when he's missing teeth.

She reaches out and pulls his earlobe.

"Ouch! What was that for?"

Lucy laughs. He grabs her arm and shakes it.

There are few constants, thinks Lucy. Things or people that will be there day in and day out; you don't have to worry about losing them or finding them. Each day, they're there. Kind of like the river. It's always going somewhere, that's for sure, but it's never going away. Willie is like the river, she thinks. She reaches for Willie's wrist and holds it tight.

Willie looks at her. "What?"

She lets go.

Willie looks back at the beach. He definitely won't tell Pop where he's been.

"Hey!" calls Pres. "Let's get a move on!"

CHAPTER 9
1953

Ruthie Blevin, her brown hair pulled up in a loose knot, stood on the porch watching her husband, Cliff, as he tried to push the mower through four inches of grass. "Should have done this two weeks ago."

Cliff looked up, wiped his brow on his shirt sleeve, stared at Ruthie and then gave the mower two more swift shoves before stopping. "I didn't really have a choice about when I could come over here and do it, did I? I'll finish this later. Let's get going."

"Willie!" called Ruthie. She crouched and watched her shining little star come running around the side of the house, his new puppy, Smoochy, close on his heels.

"Mama," he cried as he climbed the porch steps, one at a time, on his hands and knees. He collapsed into her arms, knocking her to the floor. Smoochy jumped on the pile and they began to laugh. Cliff leaned stiffly against the car.

"Where go, Mama?" Ruthie paused, lost in her son's sharp eyes and bright smile.

"C'mon, let's get going?" called Willie's dad.

Ruthie turned her head. "Just a minute."

Cliff huffed and folded his arms.

"You remember, Willie, we're going to the river for a picnic."

Willie clapped and said, "Smoochy go."

"No, Smoochy can't come with us this time."

Willie scrunched his face and pretended to cry. Ruthie's stern face began to crack. "Okay, he can come." Willie reached out with one finger and tapped his mother's nose.

"What do you mean, Smoochy can come? What did I tell you about dogs in the car?" said Cliff.

"It's fine. It'll make Willie happy."

"I'm telling you, you're spoiling that boy. Every day you spoil him more and more. How's he ever going to grow up and deal with the real world?"

Ruthie held her breath, then let it out slowly. "Speaking of growing up and dealing with the 'real world'. How many times has my father asked you to come by the dealership? How many times have you ignored him? How long can you go without getting a job?"

"I don't need any help from him. I can find a job on my own."

"But you never try."

"I don't want to be a used car salesman."

"You've gotta step up! Do something!" Her jaw jutting, she scowled at Cliff.

"Enough! Let's just get in the car and go, alright?" said Cliff.

Willie sat quietly in the back seat, hugging Smoochy.

CHAPTER 10

Trish Hallowell walks briskly across the Park Bridge, clutching her dress against the wind swirling up from the river below. She curls one big toe where a blister is starting to swell. She wishes she had bought a coat along with her new shoes and dress. The air feels more like November than September. Her head aches and her eyes are red from the night before. She stops in the middle of the bridge to catch her breath. The view is exactly how it was when she was a girl. The winding river, the towering trees, limbs bent to the water, the power house on the left bank with its rusting metal roof. The trees may be taller, fuller; the road down the hill to the power plant may have more potholes, aside from that, everything is the same. This could be the first day of junior high, walking to school, giggling with Mandy and Clarissa about boys and teachers and who's new clothes were sharpest. She smiles.

A car horn breaks her reverie. "Hey, chicky!" A teenage boy with a pompadour hangs out the window, waving and whistling. She's embarrassed because she wants to wave back.

"Beauty is your gift and, just as easily, it could be your curse," her mother had said. "Don't be afraid to use it. But don't be stupid about it."

Trish always had her choice of the cutest boys, the boys that all the other girls wanted but couldn't have. She was never alone on Friday or Saturday night. When she walked into the high school dances, everyone looked. That blonde hair. That figure. She presses her hand against her stomach and then pulls at her hips, trying to adjust her girdle.

She looks at her watch. At best, she'll be five minutes late. She clutches a fistful of her dress again and picks up the pace, her mother's words ringing in her ears: "Just remember, knees together or legs crossed."

Quietly, Trish opens the office door, glances at the other two girls at their desks and tiptoes to hers. Over clacking typewriter keys, a voice booms: "Thank you for joining us, Mrs. Hallowell!" Mr. Hopkinson stands at his office door, tapping his watch and grinning. "A cup of coffee, please."

"Yeah." Hopkinson turns and looks at her, eyebrows raised. "Yes, sir."

As she leaves the office, she hears tittering behind her. The other girls don't like her. They talk, talk, talk, but never to her. They go out for lunch, but never invite her. They complement each other, but never find anything to compliment about her. To them, she is there but not there all at the same time.

Elsa is married to "the most amazing" man who has "the most amazing" job at "the most amazing" place, US Steel. They go on "the most amazing" trips to "the most amazing places," like Acapulco and Miami Beach. And Donna's son is a "genius" tenth grader who's "going to be a lawyer, I just know it." Not only that, but his music teacher says he "sings like Sinatra."

Trish listens, nods, smiles and laughs when they laugh. But they never laugh together. Her laugh is an echo.

It's not hard to see what's going on. From the heaviness of their makeup to the girth of their hips, they must be in their late thirties. Maybe even forty. They look at her smooth skin and trim waistline, her curves, her straight legs and silky hair. Such youthfulness. Such attractiveness. No one's whistling at them on the bridge. They're envious, plain and simple.

Trish hates them and wishes she had their lives.

She takes her boss's mug from the rack. She remembers he likes two heaping spoonfuls of sugar. "That man is going to rot his teeth right out of his head," the girls say. She stirs, drops the spoon into the sink and heads for his office.

"Close the door," he says as she enters. She's greeted by dark paneling and plush gray wall-to-wall carpeting. Behind his desk is a framed portrait of his wife and three sons. She places the mug on his desk blotter as he pushes some blue prints to the side.

"Thank you," he says.

"Is there anything else, Mr. Hopkinson."

"Teddy---when you're in here, you can call me Teddy." He leans forward as if sharing a secret. "Just don't tell the other girls." Mr. Hopkinson is balding on top; a thick, brown ruffle from ear to ear across the back of his head. His wire-rimmed glasses make him look older, distinguished. He wears gold cufflinks with 'H' engraved on them.

Trish doesn't speak. She stands straight, her hands folded in front of her. He smiles as he looks at her. Is her bodice too tight? Dress too short?

"Why don't you have a seat for a minute," he says, pointing to a chair. Trish drags it from the corner and sits. She tries to look pleasant but not friendly; warm but not inviting. She holds one hand tightly in the other, her knuckles like snowcaps.

Hopkinson leans back in his chair and folds his hands behind his head. His shoes clunk when he drops his feet onto his desktop. "So, you've made it through your first week. How do you like it here?"

She takes a moment to think before she answers. "I like it fine."

"That's good." He looks at her, as if waiting for Trish to say more. "Well, I'm glad we could bring you on. We're hitting a boom right now; so much construction going on; so many machines to build, orders to be filled."

"That's good news, I'm sure."

"I know it's been a while for you..."

"Pardon?"

"Since you did some typing. It's been a while."

"Yes...Yes, it has."

"You're just a little slower than the other girls, you know, fewer words per minute."

"I'm---"

"No need to apologize. I'm sure you'll get the hang of it." He puts his feet back on the floor and leans across the desk. "I wouldn't want to lose someone as pretty as you. Makes it a lot easier to get up in the morning, knowing you'll be here."

His eyes meet hers. He grins. Her eyes drop.

"Looking at you, (he's scanning her now) it's hard to believe you have a twelve-year-old daughter." He gestures toward her body. "And you still look like that."

"Well..."

"You know, like I said, we're so busy I might need a little help in the evenings."

Trish freezes, her eyes dart back and forth.

"That's all for now...Trish."

She puts the chair back against the wall and leaves. She leans against the water cooler in the hall, feeling confused, exhausted, defeated.

Despite her dire warnings, Mother also encouraged Trish to "please" the boys. "You have to give them what they want before you get what you want. You understand?"

Del Hanahan was the first to uncross her legs. She was a few weeks shy of her fifteenth birthday. He was a senior, a much sought-after senior, who had walked her home a few times, had helped her with math a few times, who'd asked her out once, then twice, then a third time. He was polite, kind, handsome, the way all upper-class boys seemed handsome. She was flattered. Her mother even liked Del. "His mother was a year ahead of me in school. Very popular. He must get his charm from her."

One night they went to Johnny's for pizza and then he took her for a ride in his new Vette. His grandmother bought it for him on his eighteenth birthday---fire engine red, four bright eyes in the front, egg shaped grill, and sleek lines front to back. "Toughest car in town," he said, his head bobbing with pride. It hit ninety on the back roads; tree limbs waved and leaves rustled in its wake. She had never felt so excited. Hunkiest car. Hunkiest boy.

Streaking along the winding Wampum Road, he suddenly down-shifted and turned into a dark lane. He steered around holes and tree stumps, abandoned refrigerators and sofas, piles of worn tires and the carcasses of a few stripped cars, before parking in a clearing beside the railroad tracks. He turned on the radio---"Sherr-er-y, Sherry baby..." Turned up the volume.

"Love this song," he said as he put his arm around her. He pulled her closer and kissed her long. He cupped her breast, then squeezed.

"C'mon," he said. He reached into the back seat for a blanket. They got out of the car. He led her by the hand to a patch of grass under tree.

"What is this place?"

"It's nothing, Trish."

"But---"

"C'mon, it'll be fine, you'll see."

He spread the blanket on the ground and pulled her down beside him. He kissed her neck and whispered in her ear: "I think maybe I might kind of love you, Trish." Her heart leaped. She threw her arms around his neck and kissed him again and again. His hand was on her inner thigh now. Then higher. She flinched and tried to pull away.

"Just relax."

"But I don't know."

He sat up. "I thought you loved me, too."

"I do, it's just..."

He put one finger to her lips. "Trust me."

It was awkward and fast and painful. When they were done, he pulled on his pants and stood. She smiled up at him, but he was combing his hair. "We gotta go," he said. She grabbed her shoes and socks and panties. He was in the car by then. He played the radio loud on the way home. They didn't talk. Once in front of her house, she hugged him. "I love you," she said. "Right," he said.

It is nearly two o'clock and Trish has only completed four orders. She finds it hard to focus, hard to find the keys. The other girls' fingers fly like jazz pianists. They look at her, shake their heads. Hopkinson has come onto the floor a few times, always stopping by her desk or glancing at her, smiling. The room is quiet for a long moment after each visit. She feels eyes on her.

Walking home, she is hobbled by the burst blister on her foot. Approaching the bridge, she takes off her shoes and continues bare foot to the middle. She leans on the railing again.

Del never spoke to her during school. He said it would be odd to talk to an underclassman. But he showed up at her house every Saturday night, for weeks. When the weather got colder, he'd arrive in his father's big Buick. No blankets needed. The car was warm and the back seat was plenty big enough.

When he was inside her, his eyes warmed and his smile seemed genuine. He told her he wanted to be with her always. She knew he meant it. She closed her eyes and felt relieved, relieved she had a place in the world and someone to take care of her. While he grunted and moaned, she thought of a house, a dog in the yard, and kids on the porch. She floated through each day. "What's got you so happy?" her mother would chirp with a wink and a knowing grin.

After a couple of months, Del didn't show up on a Saturday night. She sat in her living room, hair bobbed, a hint of perfume, tight skirt and his favorite V-neck sweater. He called the next day to apologize. He came the following week, but then missed three weeks in a row. No phone calls.

One Monday, she saw him in the cafeteria with another girl. She ran to the lav and burst into tears. "I told you he was just using you," said her best friend, Suzie. "I mean, he's a crud." She cut her afternoon classes and went home. Her mother didn't need to ask what was wrong.

A week or two later, Del's best friend, Tommy, called to console her. He suggested they go out for a burger. He was attentive and understanding. He asked her out on a date. They planned on a movie but went to the railroad tracks instead. He said he understood why Del had loved her so much. He said he might love her, too. Trish was surprised someone would fall in love with her again so soon. "Can't you see what they're doing?" said Suzie. Trish figured Suzie was jealous; she never got this kind of attention. After several weeks, Tommy stopped coming by.

Then it was Craig, who didn't call to console her or to ask her out on a date. All he wanted was to go for "a ride" on Saturday night. In the middle of it all, she asked if he loved her and he said "Sure." They went for rides twice more.

Sometimes boys just stopped by the house unannounced and blew their horns. If she didn't recognize them, she didn't go out. There were times, though, she felt lonely enough that she went, hoping this would be the one.

Dallas Grove was different. He was the only boy in her typing class. His black hair glistened with Brylcreem. He wore the smartest clothes, dress shirts with bleached collars, buffed wing-tip shoes, a gold watch on his wrist. He was quiet. He had a bashful smile and long eyelashes. All the girls thought he was "dreamy," like Bobby Darin. They said "Hi" to each other when they passed in the hall, but little more.

That summer, after Dallas's graduation, they both volunteered at the Red Barn Theater. They painted sets and built scenery and got to know each other. When Dallas asked her out, Trish swallowed hard. "If it's okay with your mom," he added. "I know you're, well, you're a little younger." He blushed and Trish could feel herself falling again.

They went to a movie and when he dropped her off, he gave her a kiss on the cheek. She didn't know what to make of it. Didn't he like her after all? He asked her out again and again, though. They made out in the car in front of her house, Trish's mother peeking from an upstairs window. He was gentle. He made her laugh. He liked her. She could see it in his smile, how it was just for her.

Soon they were spending all their time together. "Are you having sex with him?" her mother asked. She demurred. They weren't "having sex," she thought; they were "making love." They flowed together effortlessly. She couldn't tell where she ended and he began.

In August, when it became clear his parents couldn't afford college, Dallas enlisted in the Marines without telling her. Her insides crumbled when she found out. He held her close and insisted they'd stay together no matter what. A week later, he left for basic training at Parris Island.

A week after that, she missed her period.

Trish leans on the railing and rubs her blistered foot. She looks at the tree limbs dipping into the water near the river bend. Below her there are hawks gliding on sweet, invisible updrafts. She wishes she could fly. She wishes she could stretch her arms out and catch that wind. She looks back across the bridge to the mill. She dangles her shoes from her finger tips as she looks down at the water. She lets go and watches them twist and turn in the breeze until they disappear in the rapids below.

CHAPTER 11

Becky Hopewell sits on the stone bench outside her dorm. Her eyes are closed. A smile lights her face as she listens to a bird perched in a nearby tree. She squints, intensifying her focus, wanting to identify the bird by its pure liquid tones. Five, sometimes six tweets every ten seconds; the arrangement, the rhythm differing slightly each time. She chuckles, thinking of the bird, how impressed he is with his own virtuosity. "Lord Baltimore," she whispers. Becky opens her eyes. Above her, the sturdy little oriole, its flaming orange and black coat glistening in the sunlight, whistles again and then takes flight.

"There you go!" She imagines what the bird sees, the checkerboard campus, the bug-like creatures below hurrying here and there, the brick buildings with their slate roofs and stone chimneys, the yellowing hillsides in the distance. How beautiful it must be. As she takes a deep breath and stretches her arms, she feels something slip off her lap. There is an envelope at her feet, placed there during her reverie.

She looks around, hoping to identify her benefactor. She assumes it's Denny hiding somewhere nearby, perhaps behind Lord Baltimore's tree. But when she takes a peek he's not there. She shrugs and sits down again. Becky eagerly opens the envelope. She looks up again, expecting someone to be standing there smiling.

She unfolds the note and stares at its contents, a tiny crutch made of toothpicks and the word "gimp" scrawled across the page in red crayon. Her hands fall into her lap. She takes a deep breath. She lets it out cautiously and turns slowly, scanning the long, green yard that reaches to the crosswalk at the bottom of the hill. Standing now, Becky looks up and down at the windows of her dorm. Is someone watching? She turns back toward her dorm, wanting to go to her room, to her bed where she can lie under the covers, eyes closed, in the hope that this is a dream. But she can't. Her legs aren't ready to go anywhere. She sits; she stands; she sits. She studies the note and the crutch again. Who? she wonders. I thought college would be different. She holds back her tears, not wanting to give anyone satisfaction.

"Hey."

She jerks.

"You okay?" says Denny.

Becky looks at his face, it's simpleness. She smiles and winks.

"I'm totally, what's the word? *Boss*."

"Boss?"

"C'mon---boss...fantastic. The fifties are over. It's 1962. Get with it."

Denny's face goes aw-shucks and she pokes his ribs.

"What?"

"Nothing. Let's get some breakfast."

Denny Blevin is like a book that has never been opened. His face says, What's going to happen next? Not in a curious or excited way, but anxiously. She is convinced that while everything he does say, I'm hiding, he doesn't want to hide at all. But he doesn't know how to come out in the open. She understands what it is to hide. She also understands what it is to open up, or at least try. Both are painful.

They decide French is expendable today and go off campus to Betty's. There is a row of booths along the left wall and a counter on the right. There are slow moving fans hanging from the tin ceiling and the floor is black and white checked tile. Each booth has a song selection dial for the juke box. They take the one farthest from the door.

"They make the best waffles in the world here. I mean, the best. Light, crispy on the outside, soft on the inside. Belgians. Great French toast, too. Real maple syrup." Becky smacks her lips. "Omelets, if you're an omelet kind of guy. My favorite, though, is the bagels."

"What's a bagel?"

"What's a bagel? Oh my. Hm. What's a bagel? It's heaven. Order one, you'll see."

"Is it some kind of toast; I like toast."

"Oh my, no. It's not toast. It puts toast to shame. You put a schmear of cream cheese on it, maybe some lox." She smacks her lips. "Good eatin'."

"Okay. I like cream cheese." Denny's face is hidden by the menu. "But what are lox?"

Becky laughs. "Salmon. Lox is salmon."

"The fish?"

"Yes, the fish."

Denny puts the menu down. "Salmon, the fish. I've never had salmon. I've had fish sticks. Is it like that?"

"Just get a bagel with the cream cheese. Tell you what, let's get bagels, waffles, pancakes, the whole deal. My treat." She claps her hands with satisfaction and waves at a gawking customer.

Plates full of food arrive. Coffee (also new to Denny), and juice. They dig in.

"Hear from your little brother?"

"No. But I saw Jesse."

"Jesse, your roommate Jesse?"

"Uh huh."

Denny takes a bite of his bagel. Becky puts down her utensils and waits.

"And?"

"And what?"

"And the bagel, what do you think?"

Denny swallows. "I like it."

"Fantastic, right?"

"It's good."

Becky chuckles. "I don't think you know 'fantastic'. What's with Jesse?"

Denny stops chewing and wipes his mouth with a napkin. He takes a drink of his apple juice. "He dropped out."

"He dropped out! Just like that! What was he, here for a week? A little quick, don't you think?"

"Yeah."

"So, what happened?"

Watching Denny prepare to speak is like watching her father get ready to mow the lawn. The first several yanks on the pull cord produce little more than a cough or two. Then he waits, hoping he hasn't flooded the engine. He tries again and after several more jerks it sputters into action. Then he crosses his fingers, hoping it won't stall out before the job is done.

"Well...I found him in the room... "

"And?"

"I asked how he was, what was up." Denny pours syrup over his pancakes.

"And..."

Denny reaches for his cup of coffee.

"I don't know. He said he wasn't coming back. I guess when he went home, his girlfriend had already found someone else."

"Ew."

"Yeah."

"So...that's no reason to drop out."

"It was for him."

"Wow. I mean, wow."

"Yeah."

A group of students crowds into a nearby booth. Two boys blow straws at each other. Denny studies his pancakes, cuts one piece with his fork and dips it in a pool of syrup.

"So. What's he going to do? Get a job at MacDonald's? The car wash?"

"He enlisted." Denny chews slowly.

"Really?"

"Yeah, the Army."

"You're kidding."

"Showed me his papers."

"You're kidding."

"No."

"What was he thinking?"

"Said it was something to do. Couldn't stay home. His parents bugged him constantly. And he couldn't be around his girlfriend. So, he joined up." Denny takes another bite of his bagel. "This is really different from bread."

"But the war."

"He didn't seem worried about that. I don't know, is it a war?"

"There's like ten thousand Americans over there. People are dying."

"He thought they'd teach him a trade."

"My God, a 'trade', like how to shoot guns at people?"

Denny shrugs. "I don't know what to tell you." He wipes his mouth again, drops the napkin on his plate and leans his elbows on the table. "What's this?" He reaches for the envelope dangling from her French book.

She wags her shoulders back and forth then takes another bite of her bagel, and slurps some coffee. "It's nothing."

He takes out the note. "What the..."

Becky puts her fork down.

"What the hell is this?"

"A joke...I think it's someone's idea of a joke."

"Who did this?"

"Who knows? They didn't exactly come up to me, face-to-face, and say, 'Here, this is from me'."

Denny holds up the miniature crutch.

"Put it down...please."

"This is the worst thing I've ever seen. I can't believe..." He's shaking his head back and forth vigorously. "Did you tell anyone about this?"

"Just got it."

"This is ridiculous...so let's tell someone. This isn't right."

Becky loves how Denny assumes clarifying right from wrong matters. She puts another spoonful of sugar in her coffee and stirs.

"I'm serious."

"I know you are. Who would you tell?"

"I don't know. The residency director."

Becky leans back and scoffs. "You know when this kind of thing happened to me for the first time?" She looks at the ceiling and taps her lip with her finger. "Yeah, I was three. Three years old. I'm in our front yard playing with something, maybe a doll, I don't know, and this neighbor boy, Cosmo, who was nine, maybe ten, comes down the street with one of his friends and he points at me and says, 'Hey cripple!', and they walk away laughing. I'd never heard the word, so I didn't understand. But my mother bursts through the front door and screams at the boys who haven't a clue why she's upset. Now she's crying and I'm crying and I didn't know why.

"When I started school and it kept happening, I still didn't understand. My second-grade teacher said, 'It must be hard for you, being different, I mean'. I think she was trying to be sympathetic, but really, I hadn't thought of myself as different. I thought the kids who made fun of me were different." Becky lifts her coffee cup, then puts it down before taking a sip. "Look, Denny, there's no one to tell because no one really cares."

Denny leans against the table, his arms outstretched. "Hey, I do."

"Denny, you've never even asked about my leg."

"It doesn't matter to me. I mean, I don't even see it. It's not a thing."

"It's 'a thing' to me. It's a part of me. If you don't see it, you don't see me."

Denny sits back and folds his arms. "Okay..."

"This is how I was born. It is my absolute 'normal'. It's like I'm a beautiful balloon but someone forgot to blow me up the whole way. So, I'm shorter, thinner, weaker on one side." She shrugs, but her face is taut.

"I'm sorry."

"And the shoe." She takes her shoe off and puts it on the table in front of Denny. "Where do you get shoes for shorter legs, right? Look at this. My father had them made special, with a lift in the heel that the shoemaker said wouldn't be noticeable. They're big and black and clunky. They say, 'Come look at me, I'm a freak'." Denny doesn't know what to say. "Worse, my feet kept growing. It cost my father a fortune." She holds the shoe in front of her face, studying it. "This is as much me as anything."

"I didn't---"

She leans forward, her face almost on the table top. "I think you like me. And I like you, Denny, Dennis, Blevin, Dennis Blevin. But for it to mean anything, you have to see me as I am and not overlook anything about me."

Denny swallows hard. He runs one hand through his hair and then leans forward on his elbows. "I don't know what to say."

"You don't have to say anything. You just have to listen. I'll be able to tell if you understand."

"Okay. I can do that." He watches Becky as she pushes her pancakes around the plate with a fork. "What keeps you going?"

"What?"

"Something must keep you going. I mean, you're the most positive person I've ever met. You could easily be the angriest person I've ever met, the bitterest person...why aren't you?"

Becky sees in his eyes that this is a real question, an honest question. "When I was little, I thought there were, like, angels or spirits or something all around, and everyone had one assigned to them. And these spirits cheered you on no matter what you did; they told you that you were wonderful and they helped you see how beautiful everything was if you just looked at it the right way, and they helped you not feel alone when you were all by yourself."

Denny clasps his hands behind his neck, a smile on his face.

"Don't laugh, there's more. I thought our job was to help others discover their angel, their spirit. Yes, this is crazy, I know, but I was a kid."

"And then what?"

"Well, the way I figured it, the more we could see each other's spirit side, the better off everyone would be. You know? Because everyone would understand how much alike we are no matter how different we appear to be." Becky's eyes bug out a little, as if to say, Sorry, but that's the way it works.

"But so many terrible things happen," says Denny.

"Yeah, they do. Terrible things happen. Because that's life. But there could still be a spirit side to all of us, something that links us up and helps us make it through. You never know."

"Sounds a little far-fetched. To me, anyway."

"Hey, everything people believe is far-fetched!"

Denny nods. Becky sips her coffee.

"You still believe this...the angels and spirits and stuff?"

"Maybe. Sometimes it feels like they're there; sometimes it doesn't." She takes another bite of her bagel. "They come and go, I guess. Maybe they have other things to do, besides looking after me."

"You're right."

"How's that?"

"You are crazy."

"Thank you!" She grabs Denny's hand and shakes it. "Maybe you'll be crazy someday, too."

CHAPTER 12

Pop sits at the breakfast table drinking coffee and smoking a cigarette. Willie, across from him, is reading a letter and scratching Smoochy behind her ears. The boy's eyes are wide and his lips are moving. His bowl of Cheerios is getting soggy. "Better eat something." Willie doesn't respond. "Boy?"

"Huh?" Willie keeps reading.

"Pick up your spoon and eat some of that cereal. You're gonna have to leave soon."

Willie takes one bite of his cereal, then another. He picks up the bowl and slurps some of the milk, then puts it on the floor for Smooch to finish.

"What's the letter say?" When Pop found it in the mail box, he almost left it there. But Willie was right behind him, on tiptoes, watching.

He had written to his brother twice. Since then, every morning he'd stand at the front door, watching for the mailman. "Anything from Denny?" was the daily mantra. "Brother could be busy, you know," Pop would warn. "What do they do at college?" Denny'd ask. "I don't know."

For a while after Denny left, Willie slept in his brother's bed, an old habit. And for a while after Denny left, Pop sat up at night wondering how Willie was doing, also an old habit.

It took a week, but Willie started sleeping through the night, sometimes having a nightmare, sometimes not. In his own bed, though, that was the big news. Then Cuba heated up, and he was an open nerve ending all over again.

He'd get out of bed at night and come down stairs to ask if Pop had heard anything on the news. "Did I just hear Cronkite?" he'd ask. "No bulletins, go back to bed; nothing to worry about." Willie would turn and walk back up the steps, then sit at the top for another half hour, just in case.

"Willie? What's Denny say?"

"They don't have sirens and stuff at college. No one's worried." Willie looks at Pop, his eyes unsure. "Does that make sense?"

"Yes, yes it does," he says, his voice sounding like it did when he'd sell a clunker to a naïve customer.

Willie puckers his lips and whistles low. "Good, that's good, don't you think?"

Pop nods in agreement. "Anything else?" Willie holds the letter in front of his face with both hands. As a little girl, Ruthie had the same look when she was concentrating. Pop sees Ruthie in the angle of Willie's face as he reads, how his cheek hides his nose and his chin dimples in the corner. As soon as he moves, it's gone.

"Willie?" he says, tapping him on his shoulder. "Any other news of note?"

Willie looks up, his face twinkling. "He says he's coming home before Thanksgiving?"

Pop hides his concern behind an enthusiastic voice. "Does he say when?"

The boy reads the second page of the letter again. "No." He grins at Pop, like the first day of summer vacation is just around the corner.

Pop had hoped if Denny stayed at school until Thanksgiving the gravitational pull of home and everything he'd left behind might finally be broken. But coming back sooner? Pop didn't know what to make of it. Denny never wanted to go away to college. He wanted to live at home, attend a nearby community college, maybe even get a job and forget about school. But Pop felt he should honor his mom's wishes.

Going away, being with different people, making some friends, seeing new things, was more important to Pop than the education he might receive.

Denny was eight when everything happened. The losses came so fast and there was so much to deal with, that Pop never talked to him about anything. He told himself they had to move forward, briskly. That was the only way they could avoid total collapse. He bought a smaller house in a different neighborhood. He changed jobs to be more available for the boys. He enrolled Denny in the Wood Street School. He found a neighbor lady to help with Willie. In time, they all got on with life.

Pop felt relief more than sadness when Denny left for college. If Denny succeeds in college, the door to his future will open wide; and he will point the way for Willie. Pop fears that if Denny comes home too soon, if he comes home before college life has taken hold of him, before it has turned his face toward tomorrow, he will never leave. He will settle in and never go back and all the doors will close.

. . .

Lucy lies in bed listening to a quiet house. When she looks at her alarm clock, she is startled by how late it is. She washes her face, brushes her teeth and gets dressed. She stands in front of the mirror for a long time trying to get her high pony tail perfectly centered. Soon she smells coffee, a hopeful sign; maybe Mom is getting ready, too.

She bounds down the stairs and into the kitchen. Her mom is at the table staring into a cup of black coffee. Her hair is tossled, her feet are bare. She sniffs and coughs. Lucy exhales hard.

"Are you sick, Mom?" Lucy steps closer. "Are you okay?"

"No, I'm not sick; no, I'm not okay."

"Oh."

Her mother looks at her, red-eyed, her face worn, like the thread bare rug in their living room. She reaches for Lucy and pulls her close. "It wasn't the right place for me."

Lucy pulls away, takes her books in her arms and heads for the front door.

"Don't you want something to eat?"

Lucy shakes her head.

"Okay, well, your lunch is in the bag there." But Lucy is gone.

Trish opens the morning paper and folds it back to the help wanted page. She scours the ads with the tip of one finger.

"Hey!" calls Willie. Lucy is a half block ahead, her arms full of books. She doesn't slow down. He picks up the pace to catch her. "Hey." Lucy's face looks like someone had crumpled it in their bare hands. He matches her stride for stride but doesn't say anything for another minute. Lucy struggles with an armload of books. She shifts them.

"Hey?" he says softly. "What's wrong?"

She slows down. "What isn't?"

"Something happen?"

"Mom."

"Already?"

"Yeah."

Lucy keeps walking.

"It'll work out, Luce."

She walks faster.

"Really."

"You don't know." She stops, shifts her books to her other arm and looks him dead in the eye. "Do things ever work out?"

Good question, he thinks. "Sure, they do," he says.

"When?"

"I don't know exactly."

She huffs and turns away.

"I'm sorry your mom does this. I'm sorry." He wishes he had something more comforting to say. Lucy shifts her books again. "Here, let me carry them."

Lucy pauses, then hands them to Willie. "Thanks."

"Things gotta get better, you know?"

They start walking, slowly this time. Kids pass them by. A block later, Willie stops again.

"What?" says Lucy

"Look at this, I got a letter from Denny." He opens it. She leans in, trying to see. "He says no one at college is worried about nuclear war; and he's coming home before Thanksgiving. Now we got evidence. Sometimes, things do get better. Right?"

Lucy's face goes from pale pink to deep rose to out-and-out red as she begins to cry. Willie balances the books in one arm. If this was third grade, maybe even fourth, he'd hug her without thinking. But now, he's not sure. What would she think? What would everyone think? Especially after Pres told him about Lucy's crush. He puts his arm around her shoulder.

. . .

There is always someone howling in the shower room. Someone snapping a towel at someone else. Someone stuffing a toilet with paper towels. The floors are always wet, sticky. No one flushes, no matter what. It always smells like a dank sulfuric sweaty stew.

The only thing worse about dorm living is not having a roommate. This surprises Denny. It's not like he and Jesse had become best friends. They spent little more than a week together. Jesse did take him to a roadhouse where they accepted anything as ID---Boy Scout membership, library card, whatever. He watched Jesse obliterate himself on a dozen brewskis. And after much harassment---"You fuckin' wimp!"---Denny sipped his way through one beer. He cleaned up the aforementioned shower room after Jesse spewed fermented pizza and sour beer across its pasty tile floor.

When that first Friday came and Jesse left for home, Denny was glad. He couldn't remember the last time he'd spent a night alone. After a week of monkish solitude, though, he started worrying about his roomie. He didn't have his phone number and the res director wouldn't divulge.

By the second week, his worries shifted. It was then that he noticed how small the room was; how the closets were barely a foot from the bottom of his tiny bed; how the side of his student desk pressed against his face when he slept. And the antique windows that opened barely six inches when he cranked them. Sometimes he felt like he was suffocating.

Is Jesse coming back? As the likelihood of Jesse's return grows bleak, he shows up.

"You what?"

"I signed up."

Jesse beams and punches him in the arm.

"You signed up."

"For the Marines, dimwit. Semper fi, man! My friend, Donnie, and me, we were out all night drinking and we thought---What the hell?---so we went straight to the recruiter's the next morning. I mean, we were there a half hour before it opened. We were psyched, man, I'm tellin' you. And the recruiter, Sergeant something, he was so cool, just a few years older than us and he said it was the best decision of his life." Jesse is cramming things into his brand-new Marine duffel.

"But what about, what about your girlfriend?"

"The skag broke up with me. Can you believe that? I mean, she dumped me. Never happened before in my life and, I'm tellin' you, I've had a lot of girlfriends. Says a lot about her."

Jesse is a whirling dervish. He doesn't hear a thing Willie has to say, including, "Are you sure about this?" His eyes are bulging, his face looks crazed.

"Man---a helmet, a rifle, I can shoot at just about anything I want. Me and Donnie asked if we could train together and the Sergeant wrote that down. It's gonna be so bitchin' cool!"

Willie can't imagine any scenario in which joining the Marines would be 'bitchin' cool'.

"I'm telling you, he said we'd be perfect for this 'adviser' program they have." He punctuates this with self-important air quotes. To hear him describe it, he'd be meeting with people "in, like, other countries" and giving them advice "about stuff." He likes the idea of helping others. "A few good men, y'know?"

Denny stands in the parking lot waving as Jesse peels out, blaring his horn the whole way. He looks up at his dorm window and can't bear the thought of going back in. He crosses the lot and heads toward the lake. No one is there. He sits on the cool grass, his knees up to his chin, spying minnows darting along the shore. Round stones shimmer in the sunlight. Gulls skim the surface and a lone blue heron keeps its solitary watch on the opposite shore. He leans back on his elbows.

Willie and Pop, Smoochy, too. He looks at his watch. What are they doing?

He thinks of his mother and father and their place in a hazy corner of his mind. It's been a year, maybe more, since he could conjure up their voices. Now, when he closes his eyes, he can't even picture their faces. But he feels them. Or pretends he does.

"Did they love us?" Willie would ask in those early years.

"Very much."

"That's good."

"Yes, that's good."

Becky wants to backpack across Europe. Jesse wants to serve his country. What does Denny want? He gets up and walks along the water. He bats the ground with a stick. A seagull takes flight.

. . .

Pop finishes his rounds, emptying wastebaskets, sweeping out the faculty room, changing a few bulbs. He holds onto the railing and single-steps it down to the basement. He exhales loudly when he reaches his room and tumbles into his desk chair.

"Dammit." He pulls his pantleg up and re-wraps his knee, this time even tighter. He reaches for the aspirin and pops a few into his mouth, washing them down with cold coffee. He takes the picture of Mae and holds it close to his face so he can make out her expression. She had an uneven smile, the right side of her mouth higher, her right eye closing slightly, like she was always about to wink.

Larry Kensington always knocks three times and then enters, whether invited in or not. He's been building and grounds supervisor for the district since Ruthie was in school. Hal sold Larry many a car. He liked his Buicks, sky-blue if possible. White side walls, just like in the brochures. He was such a good customer, that, when he could, Hal would work out special deals to sweeten each trade. Showing his appreciation, Larry referred most of his friends and family to Hal. It was a match made in automotive heaven.

It was odd having a former customer as his boss, but they worked things out. Larry let Hal run his school the way he wanted, and Hal worked hard so Larry wouldn't have to get too involved with daily matters.

"You know I never question anything you do. Heck, you're easily the best man I have, Hal. I think you know that."

Hal is sure another shoe's about to fall.

"And I know you like to work alone; don't want anyone bothering you."

It's coming.

"But, it's like this. Darn it, you can't do everything with that bum knee of yours."

"I'm fine."

Larry rubs his chin.

"No, you're not, Hal. You need help. At least for a while."

"Wait a minute."

"Now hear me out. We've got a problem at the West End School and you could use some help here in the junior high. We have enough work to hire a floater. They'd spend some time with you and some time at West End." He tapped the table with his knuckle.

Hal argues with him, even though he knows Larry's right. He hates the idea of needing help from anyone about anything. You deal with things on your own.

"This isn't negotiable, Hal. I'm sorry. If you can't work 'cause of that knee, what are you gonna do?"

Hal doesn't have an answer. It's not like the old days when he could take a day off here and there and it didn't matter. Now he needs to use every sick day for the boy.

"You wouldn't be talking to me if you didn't have someone in mind."

"True true," says Kensington.

CHAPTER 13

"No wonder she's mad at her mom." Preston leans over Willie's shoulder as he struggles with his algebra. "Look, you gotta figure out what 'x' is."

"What do you mean?"

"If 'x' is twenty-five, what is 2x; then you gotta divide it by five?"

"No, about Lucy's mom?"

Preston goes to the fridge, pulls out a quart of milk and takes a long drink. He wipes his mouth on his shirtsleeve.

"Your mom lets you drink out of the carton?"

"You kidding?" He takes another drink, offers it to Willie who declines, and puts the carton back on the shelf. "She doesn't seem to be here, does she?"

"So?"

"I live by my own rules." Pres flexes his measly muscles.

"No, I mean Lucy's mom."

"What can I say, she's messed up."

"What are you talking about?" Willie puts his pencil down on the tablet.

"I don't know if I should tell you this stuff. I heard my dad talking about it a few days ago, that's all."

"And?"

"Well, it's like this, according to my dad, Lucy's mom, like, has been a walking disaster all her life."

"How?"

"Like, when she was a teenager, she did it with everyone; it didn't matter who."

"Did what?"

"It. She did it."

A light goes on. "The big 'it'?"

"Yeah, doesn't get any bigger."

"That's not possible. I mean, she's a mom."

"Willie boy, you just get dumber and dumber. First of all, she wasn't always a mom. Second, she's like half as old as all the other moms. Third, so how old was she when she had Lucy? You get me? She must have been just a little older than us. I mean, he didn't say it right out loud, but he was kinda saying she was a slut."

"God."

"Have you ever taken a good look at Lucy's mom? I mean, she's more woman than you could possibly hope for. She's something. So, so tuff."

"C'mon."

"I'm sorry, maybe I like older women."

Willie does feel things when he's around Lucy's mom, but he never talks about it. Something in the way she moves. When he watches other moms, he never feels like he should look away. But with Lucy's mom, he does. There are parts of her body that move all by themselves, like they can't help it. He gawks and gawks until he feels embarrassed, then he turns away. But he always takes a second look, often a third. He hates himself for it, but that doesn't seem to matter. And the way she smells, he can't breathe deep enough to take it in. No, Mrs. Hallowell is not like the other moms. (None of the other moms have hair like Marilyn Monroe, either, God rest her soul.)

How could she be a slut and have a daughter like Lucy? It doesn't make sense, he thinks. Maybe someday parts of Lucy will move around like her mom. That doesn't mean she's going to be a slut, does it? He can't imagine Lucy being anything other than what she is---a plain old good person---no matter what she looks like.

"Do you think Lucy knows all that stuff about her mom?"

"You kiddin' me? Kids don't really know anything about their parents. My bet is she doesn't have a clue."

"Good."

"Well...I guess."

Willie picks up his pencil and leans over his algebra worksheet again. "I think she's just upset her mom lost her job."

"Who loses a job after five days?"

"It happens."

"She's a mess."

"Pop says she's 'fallen on hard times'."

Willie tackles another algebra problem, but his eyes glaze over. Why is he defending Mrs. Hallowell? Lucy is miserable all the time because of her. She comes to school in tears; she has to iron her own clothes, make her own breakfast, wake her mother up in the morning. She acts like she doesn't love Lucy at all.

But Willie hates to think Lucy has a crummy mother. He hates to think of any mother being crummy. If he still had a mother, he's sure she wouldn't be crummy, no matter what anyone said.

Pres slaps some peanut butter on two pieces of soft, mushy Wonder Bread and takes a bite. He tongues some Skippy's off the roof of his mouth and gulps.

"By the way." He swallows hard again.

"What?"

"Turns out I was wrong about Lucy."

"Wrong how?"

"She wasn't crying because she's madly in love with you. Mary Alice told me Lucy was on the rag."

"On what rag?"

"The rag, you know, the rag."

"What are you talking about?"

"Wow, you really, truly, don't know anything about women, do you?"

Willie pushes his chair back from the table. He folds his arms and waits.

"When you were across the room fainting, she was busy having her period. That's why she was crying. You know what a period is, don't you?"

"Of course." He's clueless.

"I guess it was her first time and she didn't have any stuff to put between her legs to stop the bleeding so she ran out of the room and down to the nurse's."

What the heck? Bleeding? "Mary Alice told you this?"

"Yeah."

"Why'd she tell you?"

Pres rolls his eyes. "Because they're keeping count of which girls get their period and which don't. It's like a contest."

"A contest?"

"Yeah, like who's turning into a woman and who isn't."

Willie's mouth falls open.

Pres laughs. "What. It's a big deal. Happens every month. Like for the rest of their lives. My mother gets her period and when she does, my dad stays away from her."

"Stays away from her?"

"Yeah, I heard my mom tell him, 'Just stay away from me'. After a bunch of days everything's okay again."

"Man, Lucy had her first period." He doesn't know what to make of this. Lucy doesn't look like a woman. She's a little different here and there, but that's all. Man-o-man, he thinks. That's why all the boys catcall her. What's happening? Why does she have to become a woman right now?

"Yeah, she's a woman. I mean, she can have babies and everything. If she wanted to, she could do The Big It all the time, just like her mother. Man, would she be popular."

Willie jumps out of his chair and shoves Pres, who topples to the floor.

"Geez-o-man! What's wrong with you?" says Preston.

Willie stands over him, his fists at the ready, unsure of what to say. He doesn't know why he attacked his friend. "Sorry, man." He grabs his school work and rushes out the back door, Pres still calling after him.

Willie sprints home, but runs out of gas near Mr. Ashwood's. He crumps to the ground. He closes his eyes and lies back on the grass, the sun pounding his face. For a moment, it's like he's standing outside himself, looking in. He sees himself huddled under a mushroom cloud, unable to breathe; he sees Lucy exploding with babies she doesn't want; he sees Denny, his back turned, just beyond Willie's reach; he sees Grandma Mae disappearing into a mist; he sees his mom and dad floating in a pall of smoke; he sees Pop limping, limping. No matter where he looks---up, down, back, forth---this is what he sees.

He stretches his arms out on the grass and crosses his legs at the ankles. "C'mon, man," he whispers. The inside of his eyelids go dark. He hears someone's raspy breathing. A hand presses his chest.

"Something wrong?"

Willie opens his eyes slowly. The fleshy face of Mr. Ashwood hangs over him, so close he can smell hotdogs on his breath. Ashwood is on his knees.

He shakes Willie harder.

"Hey, you okay?"

"Yes, I'm okay."

"I've been watching you. You don't seem okay."

Willie sits up and Ashwood leans back on his haunches.

"You seem not okay."

What is he supposed to say? A friend of mine had her first period, and it pushed me right over the edge? And I don't have parents and the world's coming to an end.

"I think I'm okay."

"Thinking you're okay and being okay are two different things. I think you think you're okay, but down deep, you know you're not okay. That's how everyone feels. That's how I feel. That's how the world feels. Everyone pretends otherwise, but that's the way it is. Everyone is going through something hard."

Mr. Ashwood says this without a hint of uncertainty or a pinch of doubt. He is self-assured, even content with his Kafkaesque slant on the world's condition. His eyes look warm, welcoming, but what lurks behind them?

"Would you like something to drink? I've got Royal Crown. Cold."

He doesn't wait for an answer. He skuttles towards the Styrofoam cooler on his back porch. Willie sits on the ground a moment longer, then follows him.

Mr. Ashwood pulls an RC from the ice, puts the cap end in his mouth and pops the top between his upper and lower molars.

"Here you go."

Willie takes the frosty bottle in his hands and chugs. "Thanks."

"You're welcome, Willie."

Ashwood pops a beer for himself and invites Willie to sit in the lawn chair nearest the hole in the ground. The walls are almost complete. The vents are going in. Pre-cast corrugated metal sheets lean against the garage. A dozen or more two-by-fours are stacked beside them. An enormous mound of dirt is ready and waiting to bury the whole thing.

"It won't be long," he says.

"Sure is something."

"Thank you. It's lookin' pretty good."

They both take swigs and wipe their mouths on their arms.

"Do you really think you're gonna need it?"

Ashwood places his bottle in his lap and looks at Willie cockeyed. "I wouldn't have spent the money and done all the work if I thought I didn't need it."

Willie puts his bottle on the ground beside him. Out on the street, cars are passing by, as always. Birds in the trees around the yard are singing, as always. Mrs. Jackson is on the back porch with Mrs. Herman laughing and talking, as always. Their toddlers are digging in a sandbox nearby, as always.

"All of this could disappear," says Mr. Ashwood. He takes another drink and then tosses the bottle toward the garbage can at the end of the driveway.

He thinks about his mom and dad. Why didn't 'as always' apply to them? He feels his face flush. Ashwood reaches for another bottle. He raises it to Willie as if to say, Another? Willie shakes his head. Ashwood is talking again, but he's not listening. Willie stands up and gets his bearings. He interrupts Mr. Ashwood. "When do you think you'll finish this?"

Ashwood belches. "Excuse me...Oh...I'd say a couple of weeks, maybe a little longer. Still waiting on a few things."

When Willie gets home, he lets Smoochy run crazy in the back yard for a few minutes. Pop has a doctor's appointment, so he won't be home until dinner time. Willie sets the table. Opens the fridge, takes out a spaghetti casserole, slides it onto the rack in the oven and turns the eat on low. He opens a can of green beans and dumps them in a pan on the stove. Smoochy whimpers and shimmies beside him. He tosses a few beans on the floor. "There you go." He pops a bean in his own mouth.

He stops chewing when the air raid sirens start screaming. He spits the bean into the wastebasket and heads for the couch in the living room. "C'mon, Smooch." But Smoochy is chasing a slippery bean that's skidding across the floor.

Willie kneels, about to crawl behind the couch. Smoochy catches up to him, a ball in her mouth. Willie hugs her and scratches her ears. He takes the ball from Smooch's mouth and tosses it into the dining room. Smooch chases after it and bounds back. Willie yanks the ball from her mouth again and throws it into the kitchen, Smoochy in hot pursuit. He takes the ball again and holds it over his head as Smooch jumps and yaps.

Willie is standing as the siren blares again. He listens for a moment and then takes Smoochy by the collar. He attaches the leash, sticks the ball in his pocket and heads toward the triangle park, Smooch loping along beside him. He stands in the middle of the field, siren blaring. People come and go from the Park Pharmacy. Kids are playing catch with a football in the opposite corner of the field. Willie waves. A semi crosses the Park Bridge, as several old guys watch from the pharmacy bench.

Willie closes his eyes, imagining the siren is summer cicadas, thousands of them, their high-pitched whine like scores of scissor blades pressed hard against a grinding wheel. He smiles to think of the empty shells he and Pop collected in July and August, shells left behind by the molting insects as they grew and changed, grew and changed. Will they collect shells next year?

Smoochy barks and jumps against Willie's chest. "Okay girl." He re-attaches Smoochy's leash and they turn for home.

CHAPTER 14

Becky drops the drawing of a wheelchair, and a napkin with 'cripple' scrawled on it, into the desk drawer. These are part of what she calls her 'Welcome Basket'. She no longer counts the thoughtful items she's received.

Everyone in her dorm is polite. They smile when they see her. They say "thank you" and "excuse me." Sometimes they say, "How are you?" Her roommate, Jeanie, laughs when Becky tells her what's going on: "There are silly girls in all the dorms. Don't take it too seriously." When Becky tells her residency director, she says "That's awful" and promises to look into it, but never writes the complaint down.

When she arrived at college, she felt ready, although she couldn't say the same for her parents, whose faces were hound doggish when they pulled away. "I'm sure everything will be fine," said her father. Until he'd said that, she had never thought things would be anything but fine. College would be different. College was full of smart people who don't do stupid things. "Just remember, honey, we are only a call away if anything comes up," her mother said. Did they know something she didn't?

It had taken almost four years, but many of her classmates in high school had accepted her, sort of. She didn't get invited to dances that often and sometimes the halls seemed lonely, but they appreciated her sense of humor and how positive she was. No one talked to her directly about her 'disability', a word she grew to hate. There were things she couldn't do in gym, like almost everything. When they did relay races, girls frowned if Mrs. Warneke assigned her to their team. Most days she said, "Have a seat today, Becky."

Over time her skin became turtle shell tough. Most things didn't penetrate her defenses. She joined chorus and played the flute, neither of which required any legs. She was smart and graduated with honors. She felt proud when she crossed the stage to get her diploma, despite some snickering.

But she was convinced college would be different. She assumed the idiots and morons would be left behind, and she would make her way easily among young adults who were eager and open-minded. Denny accepted her. She knew a few girls in her dorm. But none of it was solid. There was something in the air, a fog of condescension, dismissiveness. There was darkness behind the smiling faces looking past her. She felt invisible. She was not a person to most of them.

How much to tell Denny? She feels safe with him. She doesn't think he could hurt her, even if he wanted to. Their angels or spirits or whatever you wanted to call them, connect. Something flows between them.

When she first shows him her Welcome Basket, he says, "I don't get it. Are you collecting this stuff?"

"They are 'gifts'. From anonymous detractors."

Afterwards, they don't talk about it much. But then he starts showing up at her dorm at odd times. "How are you doing?" is his usual question. He appears each morning so he can walk her to class. He clutches her hand.

Finally, after her last class on a Thursday afternoon, she says, "Thank you."

"For what?"

"You know what I mean."

"Well...I guess I want to be around. Just in case."

"You know you can't protect me, don't you?"

"Yeah, I know."

She can't admit it to herself until days later, but she's fallen in love with him. "You will fall in love a hundred times," her mother had told her casually. "Don't make yourself crazy over any boy." She doesn't think she is making herself crazy over Denny, but how is she to know if this is love? Maybe if they were more intimate.

For Senior Night in high school, juniors decorated the gymnasium and cafeteria with streamers and balloons and crepe; they made signs---"Greatest Class Ever" "Yay, Class of '61"---that hung from the rafters; they stood outside as the senior class arrived and cheered them. It was a big deal. The unspoken biggest deal, though, was the tradition requiring kids who arrived at the party in a state of virginal innocence, to go home the next morning "devirginated," as class president, Oscar Swank, put so eloquently.

Becky had been friends with Calvin Klopper since first grade. For a while in fourth grade, they were an item. By eighth grade, they were merely acquaintances. But in ninth grade, when they both joined chorus, they became sort-of friends again. They both went to Senior Night as singletons and found themselves sitting at the same table. Despite a rash of acne on his neck, Calvin wasn't half bad looking. He'd had girlfriends along the way, which gave him credibility. And she knew for a fact he'd had sex with Carrie Fletcher, because she heard some girls talking about it in cafeteria. "Calvin and Carrie, really? They, like, did it."

The line between juicy rumor and actual fact was paper thin. Becky went all in with those who believed it was a fact. At Senior Night, she struck up a conversation with Calvin while classmates swirled around them to the sounds of Fats Domino. Becky tried to be discrete, whispering across the table to her would-be lover, but he didn't quite get it: "Do I want to have wax with you? What?" She scooted around to the other side just as Del Shannon started wailing "...a run, run, run, run, runaway!" She whispered her proposition into his ear. His response was music to hers: "Sure, what the heck." They finagled their way into one of the Athletic Department's offices and in less time than it takes to say "Yay, Class of '61" Becky was devirginated. She had crossed over from "Girls Only" line to the one marked "Women Only."

Denny stands on tiptoes, squinting across the south lawn to see if Becky is in front of her dorm. There is a cavalcade of coeds---all saddle shoes, pencil skirts, and gleaming smiles---coming toward him. Beyond them is a solitary figure standing on the base of an ornate lamppost. He scans the surrounding area, but sees nothing out of the ordinary, nothing threatening. He waits several minutes more before he strides down the walkway, waving to get her attention. She jumps off the lamppost flailing both arms over her head. He smiles.

"You looked like you were about to run yourself up a flagpole."

"If I could, I would." She tickles his arm with her fingertips.

Without saying a word, they head to the lake. Denny never anticipated being the guy other guys in his dorm would spy on. But there he is, Becky in his arms, lounging on the grass, body to body. He thinks of the first time he and Becky kissed. He was so clumsy, he could have broken one of her teeth.

All that changed in a few short weeks. He never thought the phrase "they were all over each other" would refer to him and any person of the opposite sex. But here he is, lips locked with the girl he feared didn't exist.

They come up for air and lean on their elbows, legs stretched out before them. Two swans drift by. The sun is hot and the air smells of burned autumn leaves.

"Any news about a new roommate?"

"I'm gonna be on my own for the rest of the semester, maybe the rest of the year."

"Really?"

Becky says girls are always sneaking their boyfriends into their dorm rooms. No one cares, not even the RAs (who also do it).

"Yeah, I've seen things you couldn't imagine."

"Aren't they afraid they'll get in trouble?"

"Who with? I mean, they're not going to report themselves to themselves."

Denny sits up and pulls his knees to his chest, clutching them with his arms.

"What?" says Becky.

"Nothing."

"No, don't do that. Look at you. You're curled up so tight, I could stuff you into a glove compartment."

She slides closer to Denny, kisses him, places her hand between his legs and rubs slowly. She gets a quick and enthusiastic rise out of him. No need for further discussion.

"Okay, so...?" she says.

Denny insists he enter the dorm first. When he gets to his room and waves from the window, she is to come up. When, after ten minutes, he doesn't appear at the window Becky enters. The lounge is full of freshmen eating potato chips and drinking beer. No one notices her.

She takes the elevator to the third floor which smells like days old sweaty underwear. She knocks on Denny's door.

"Who is it?"

My God, thinks Becky.

"It's Alice the goon."

"What?"

She leans against the opposite wall. When he opens the door, she glares at him.

He takes both of her hands in his. "I had to clean a little."

His room wreaks of Lysol. There are no posters on the wall. Nothing hanging from the ceiling. The sliding closet door is bulging with piles of clothes and books. His desk lamp is on and the curtains are drawn. He has pushed both beds together.

"Aw," she says.

"Well, I didn't know what..."

They undress and get into the beds. She hands Denny a wrapped condom she had stolen from her RA's room. He tears it open and looks at it this way and that. He removes it from the wrapper, spins it on his finger, places it on the tip of his nose, and finally, puts it on one eye, like a monocle. "Cheerio."

"It's a condom...a rubber. You know?"

"Of course, yeah, it's a rubber...just looks different from the ones I've seen before. More rubbery..."

"It's like putting a sock on a foot...except it's not a sock and it's not a foot."

He is gentle when he touches her, like an archeologist lightly brushing the soft earth away from a long sought-after treasure. She breathes hard. Denny kisses her lips. He kisses her breasts. Now he's breathing hard.

They kiss some more. Their hands explore. Their bodies moisten. And then the moment of truth. Denny's approach to penetration reminds her of parallel parking for the first time. Back and forth, back and forth, still too far from the spot; bump the curb, scrape a fender, then finally squeeze into place. There are brisk movements, and then it is done.

"I feel a little nauseous. Is that normal?" he says.

Becky turns on her side and dangles her arm over the edge of the bed. It was so bad, but she felt so good.

His appetite voracious after walking Becky back to her dorm, Denny hot foots it across campus to the Union where he buys not one, not two, but three cheeseburgers, a large order of fries and a double chocolate shake. He doesn't care what anyone thinks. Today he scaled the highest mountain, crossed the deepest ocean, ran the fastest mile, hit the longest homerun and scored the winning touchdown. Today he is the victor. Today he is a man. He gobbles one and a half burgers, most of the fries and half the shake. He has a belly ache, but feels triumphant nonetheless.

He leans back in the booth and relives the afternoon. The whole condom thing was the only bump on an otherwise smooth road to carnal bliss.

Denny sits up suddenly. He forgot to ask Becky if she liked it. Are girls supposed to like it? There was a point in the process where he kind of blacked out. He closed his eyes and for all he knew, he was riding a roller coaster on the moon. Nothing else mattered. Did he make noises? Yes, he did. Loud ones. Did she make any noises? He didn't know. That's not good. There should be noises.

He considers walking back to the dorm and asking her what she thought of the whole thing. After cleaning up his table and returning his tray, he heads that way, but then wonders, What do I say? Hey, did you like the sex today? What if she says no? What if she is offended that I'm even asking her such a question? Are there rules for talking about sex after sex?

Denny feels more confused about his relationship with Becky after the sex than before. Shouldn't this have made things simpler? Isn't this the sign at the end of the romance tunnel that says, "You've Made It!"

CHAPTER 15

"This is not possible." Willie stops at the bottom of the steps, refusing to enter the school.

"What?" says Lucy.

"Didn't you see him?"

"Who?"

"Clammerman."

"Yeah. It's Wednesday."

"This is Wednesday?"

For a few days, Willie does better. He ignores Cronkite's ominous daily reports about the American-Russian tit-for-tat. He ignores the banner headlines on the papers he's delivered.

To his surprise, Pop is paying more attention to the crisis than Willie. He's glued to the CBS news. When he reads the *Post-Gazette* each morning, his expression is dire. Usually, he smokes a cigarette while perusing the paper. Lately it's two.

Mr. Ashwood, though, has been positively giddy. He's whistling while he works. He seems as light on his feet as Jackie Gleason, twinkle-toeing in and out of his nearly completed bomb shelter. Neighbors, once derisive, are visiting more often, checking out his progress, hoping to get a spot.

Willie feels conflicted about all of it, especially about 'having a spot'. He's relieved, for sure, but he has doubts about the construction. He's seen Ashwood jerry-rig things that surely came with Official Instructions.

"Where's the glue?" When he found open space under the door, he stapled strips of rubber to the bottom and secured it with duct tape. That can't be right, Willie thinks. What to say? "It doesn't matter," says Pop. "We're not going near that thing. We won't have to."

Willie worries about his friends. What will happen to them? Will they have a safe place of their own? Could they hide in the caves by the river? The thought of them having no place to go brings tears to his eyes. If something happens to them, he hopes it's fast, like they don't even realize what hit them. Poof!

In school they learned a little bit about Japan and those cities that got bombed. How it was Japan's fault, how it was necessary, and how it shortened the war and saved lives. But for the people, what was it like? He imagines they were going about their daily routines, walking down sidewalks, going to schools, driving cars, eating in restaurants, sitting at home doing nothing at all. Maybe people were holding hands or laughing or exploring a river and upending giant rocks. Did it happen so fast that they were still holding hands when they died? Were they still smiling?

He hasn't told Lucy or Pres he's got a spot in Ashwood's shelter.

Dear Denny...Perhaps his last letter to his brother. *I hope you still like college. Are you having fun? Are you still friends with that girl? How hard would it be to come home? Sorry if I'm bothering you. But all this missile stuff is hard. I don't know what to do. I don't know what's going to happen. Mr. Ashwood is still building his bomb shelter. I hope I see you again. Please be careful. Thanks for everything.*

He folds the letter, puts it in a business envelope and writes his brother's address in his best cursive. He rifles through the kitchen junk drawer for a stamp. Just as he is about to lick the envelope, he stops. Willie reads and then re-reads his letter. He wrote one like this a couple weeks ago. Why send another one saying the same things?

Denny has done so much for him over the years, how much more can Willie ask? Denny has his own life. Willie can't run to him forever. He reads the letter one more time. He folds it up and puts it back in the envelope and tears it into tiny pieces. He pulls the trash can out from under the sink, moves the coffee grounds and wrappers and cigarette butts out of the way, scatters the pieces at the bottom, then lets everything fall back into place, burying what he's written.

. . .

"Well, Hal, you're not a kid anymore." Doc Helman teeters back in his well-worn leather desk chair. On the wall behind him are diplomas and awards and too many books to count. Helman's face is wizened, his glasses sit precariously on the tip of his nose. The air smells of pills and elixirs and anxiety.

Helman delivered Ruthie. It had been a long labor and Doc sat at Mae's side all night while Hal slept on two chairs in the waiting room. Near dawn, Ruthie slipped into the world. Mae barely knew what happened, she was completely exhausted. Doc came and went every few hours for the next several days as she slowly gained strength.

Hal leaned against the window of the nursery staring in amazement at his daughter. How do these things happen? he wondered.

"She'll make it." Helman said this three days after delivery, but he wasn't talking about Ruthie. "Mae's heart's never been strong. The rheumatic fever took some of it away when she was a girl." He clapped his hand on Hal's leg. "You have a healthy, beautiful daughter. Do everything you can to make sure Mae doesn't have to go through this again."

Hal brushes aside the memories of sitting in this same chair after Mae died. He'd avoided seeing Doc Helman since then, except for the boys' polio shots and vaccinations.

"What are you saying?"

"You're not an old man, but you have an old man's knee. Best solution's surgery." He tipped his head and raised his eyebrows. "What do you think, Hal?"

"I'm not made of money, Doc."

"I didn't think so."

Helman tells him to keep his knee wrapped, keep it raised when he can, avoid heavy lifting, and do some light exercise. He stands and demonstrates knee lifts and bends. He scribbles on his prescription pad. "This should help some with the pain." He takes his glasses off and tosses them onto the desk.

"And accept some help. I know you hate that, but..." He shrugged. "If they want to bring someone on at work, don't fight it."

Hal gets up to leave.

"And I want to see you back in my office in two months. Sooner if things get worse."

When Hal gets to his car, he tears up the prescription and throws it out the window. He hits the steering wheel with the palm of his hand. "Goddammit, Mae."

He rolls down the window and looks up the street toward his old dealership. He sees men in ties waving their arms and escorting would-be buyers around the lot. The service bays are open. Men in grimy clothes stand under elevated cars, drills in hand. He takes a deep breath, trying to remember the new car smell that filled the display room. He'd been promoted to sales manager just a few months before everything came to pass. Leaving seemed like the right thing to do. Anymore, though, he can't tell what's right, what's wrong. Everything just is.

Hal rolls up the window, stretches his leg, rubs his knee and checks the tightness of the Ace bandage. He puts the key in the ignition and heads back to work.

. . .

Willie deep-breathes his way through Clammerman's dire talk. "As you kiddos know, things are getting worse. The enemy is making a move. We must be diligent. We must be prepared." Willie watches Mr. Highmark. Although he never openly disagrees with Clammerman, his expressions often look like he's giving Clammerman the finger. It's like Clammerman is spouting his propaganda and Highmark is giving his silent commentary. This time, though, Highmark is listening closely, shaking his head, supporting everything he says.

This is not a good sign. Over the last few days, he's noticed everyone's eyes are downcast, faces are pensive. There is less friendly chatter. People are lumbering through their days waiting for the end to come.

"What are you talking about?" says Pres. "Nothing's different as far as I can tell." Willie seeks solace in Preston's take on things. "Like I said, my dad knows this stuff inside and out; he's been in wars and understands the enemy better than anyone. And he says the whole thing's just a bunch of 'malarky', that's his word for it, 'malarky'. And he's not kidding. I don't know why you worry about this. I never watch the news. They don't know what they're talking about. They're just a bunch of 'puppets', that's what Dad calls them."

Just as Willie warms to this perspective, Pres goes on: "My dad says, 'Let 'em try something. Let 'em drop a bomb on us. We'll blow them off the face of the earth. No one plays chicken with us and wins'."

Willie remembers how disastrous a game of chicken was in *Rebel Without a Cause*. He imagines Kennedy and Khrushchev in their hotrods racing toward a cliff. Who will flinch? Or will everyone go over the edge with them?

Willie rushes out the door at recess. Instead of tossing a football around, he sits under a nearby maple tree and digs at the dirt with a stick.

"You made it." Lucy sits beside him. "You didn't pass out."

"And you didn't have to..."

"No...I didn't. Big day for both of us."

Lucy's voice is light, melodic, bouncy even. The corners of her mouth are turned up a pinch which makes her whole face glow. If he looks at her too long, he finds it hard to speak. He looks away.

"What's up with you?"

"In case you haven't noticed, the world is coming to an end."

"Today?"

"No, not today?"

"Tomorrow?"

"No."

"The day after...the day after that?"

Willie looks away again.

"You don't have any idea what's going to happen. Nobody does."

"Yeah...so?"

"So, don't waste so much time on this. It's driving you crazy. You're gonna miss out on your whole sixth grade year."

"All of us may miss out---"

"Come on."

"Aren't you worried?"

"Some. But not like you. My mom says, 'Don't let the world keep you from your life, Lucy'."

Lucy quoting her mother? The only time she talks about her mother is to register a complaint. Given what Pres told Willie about Mrs. Hallowell, it's no wonder Lucy never has anything good to say about her.

"Your mom said that?"

"You don't know my mom."

"I thought you couldn't stand her, that's all."

"Sometimes, I can't. But she's my mom."

Lucy stretches her legs out on the cool grass.

"Here's why I'm happy today."

"Why's that?"

"My mom got up before me this morning." She turns her head to him and nods, as if her meaning is clear. "She never gets up before me. Never. Except if she looking for a job or has one."

"That's good, I guess."

Lucy's face looks quizzical.

"Every time she gets a job, well, it's like, I don't know, things fall apart and then you're miserable and I feel bad and I don't know how to help you." Willie wanted to stop after 'miserable' but the words kept coming. It sounded too much like what a boyfriend would say.

Lucy feels heat around her ears.

"Maybe this will be different," she says. "Things can change."

"Yeah, maybe this will be like, you know, a turning point." He hopes the tone of his voice doesn't bely his skepticism. He wants to believe in change. He wants to believe things can turn out different, at least once in a while. But that's not been his experience. Change came and it almost destroyed his whole family. Pop's done his best to avoid making changes ever since. Denny leaving for college was the first big exception to the rule. It's still feels like an amputation.

·　·　·

The nights are getting colder. Hal studies the furnace inside and out. He empties the pan and rakes the fireplace, dumping old ashes into a barrel. He looks for cracks in the pan and furnace walls. He reinforces the coal bin with two-by-fours. He takes a lump in his hand and breathes in its faintly sulfuric scent. How long did it take to make this? he wonders.

As the bell rings for afternoon recess, Hal grabs a push broom and guides it carefully up and down the first-floor hallways. He nods at Miss Fischer and Mr. Hollingsworth and Mrs. Angler as they chatter in the hall. "Don't work so hard," he says. Eye rolls and laughter follows.

He pops his head into the nurse's office. "Hi Ev."

Nurse Correa waves him in. "How's that knee of yours?"

"Couldn't be better."

"Couldn't be better, huh?"

Hal shuffles a dance step or two.

"Regular Fred Astaire."

"It's fine."

"You know they've hired that swing person, right?"

Hal shifts his weight off his bad knee.

He pushes his broom down the hall to the main office, hoping to spy who it is. He waves through the windows at the secretaries and pretends he's working on something by the door. He peers into the office several times, but doesn't see anyone new. The principal's office door is open, but Mr. Haverford is not at his desk. False alarm? Maybe Evelyn is pulling his chain, maybe there's no new person, no one to 'help' him, as if help is what he needs. He feels a wave of relief, then finishes his rounds, dumping the accumulated waste into a closet barrel at the end of the seventh-grade hall. In one short year, Willie will be on that hall, room 106, probably, Mrs. Finney.

When Denny moved up to junior high, he felt relieved. He could keep an eye on the boy, make sure he had friends, protect him if needed, keep him from fading into the deep background, becoming one of the invisible kids, the vulnerable ones, the shy and anxious kids, kids with braces, kids with limps, girls that are too tall, and boys that are too chubby; all of them doomed to slink from room to room, heads bowed, arms wrapped around their books, trying to avoid the predators who were always lurking.

It didn't work. Three weeks into seventh grade, Hal found Denny crammed into his locker for the first time. Denny made a few friends, but it was a struggle. He was relieved when Denny went to ninth grade, not because things improved but because he didn't have to witness it on a daily basis.

He wants to be a launch pad for the boys, nothing more. He wants to be their solid ground, the place where they can thrust their engines and spread their wings, where they can lift off and fly away.

Maybe it will go better for Willie. At least he has friends. At least he seems to fit in at school. But he is so afraid. Hal had hoped he would grow out of it, that he would become confident, self-assured, that he would smile more often and enjoy his young life.

In time, he gave up on the idea that Willie's fear would dissipate, that it would drift away like a mist, that the joys of childhood would replace it, that the darkness in his eyes would finally brighten. Hal hopes Willie can harness his fear, rather than be harnessed by it. He hopes Willie can make room for other things, other feelings, maybe even happiness.

This is the first year he feels comfortable leaving Willie alone for longer than an hour, the first year no one has walked with him to school, the first year Pop hasn't called the Wood Street School each day. Willie is learning how to walk even though the ground still feels shaky.

He was finding his way until the damn missile thing. None of the other kids are worried. None of them. Willie caught the atomic-bomb-virus and can't get rid of it. Damn Ashwood and his shelter. Damn TV news. Damn newspapers. Damn gossip. Hal wishes Mae were here; she'd take the boy in her arms and all would be well, just like she did with Ruthie when she'd wake up crying from a nightmare. There, there, and a hug; there, there, and a kiss.

Hal has none of her softness, none of her warmth. He can feel Willie's pain, but it paralyzes him.

When Hal opens the door to the furnace room, he sees someone standing in the slanted sunlight, someone who is not wearing work boots or overalls. Who is this? wonders Hal, until he notices the hair.

"Can I help you?"

She turns and smiles. "Hi, Mr. Mitchum."

Hal closes his door and leans on his broom.

"Do you remember me? Your daughter taught me in school. I was a sophomore and her English class was the only one---"

"Yes, I remember you." Ruthie was heart sick over 'that pretty girl', as she called her. So much potential, she would say, shaking her head.

"You don't really know me, but I have to tell you, I loved your daughter, I did; she was so nice to me; I don't know why, but she was." Trish looks up, trying to catch his eye. "I don't think I ever got over the shock---"

"Your Lucy is friends with my Willie...have been for a long while."

Trish clears her throat and tries to cover her embarrassment at being so forward, so prematurely familiar. "Yes, they have. I think she really likes your Willie."

"He's a good boy." Hal and Trish look at the floor, hiding their uncertain smiles. "Well...it's very nice to meet you, Mrs. Hallowell---"

"Please, you can call me Trish."

"Is there something I can do for you? Are you lost?"

Trish's chest feels hollow. "Well, I guess you could say I'm kinda lost." She forces a chuckle. "But, actually, it's more, like, what can I do for you?" She exhales a breathy laugh and grabs her right arm with her left hand behind her back. She shifts back and forth. "I'm the new swing...man...girl...woman."

Hal loses the grip on his broom but catches it before it hits the floor.

CHAPTER 16

Becky stands in the middle of Denny's room, naked. He turns on his side and watches as she reads the letter. Her skin is taut and white and smooth. Her back curves, gently arching at the base, just above the tailbone, lifting her firm, round, ample behind as it slopes to one thick, long leg, slightly bent, and one short, thin leg. When he runs his finger along the course of her back, she shivers and gooseflesh rises on her legs. When he kisses her there, she sighs and moans softly.

After the first time they had sex, the next day he went to the local pharmacy, bought a Snickers, some peanut butter cups, chips, a coke and, feigning an afterthought, asked for some condoms.

"Trojans?"

"Big fan," he said, thinking the pharmacist was referring to the USC Trojan football team.

The pharmacist, his gray face wrinkled and dour, tossed a three pack into the bag and said, in monotone, "Go Trojans."

Denny returned the next day. He didn't buy any candy or soda or chips. He asked for a box of Trojans.

"Going for a national championship?" said the pharmacist as he tapped on the register keys.

When Denny left the store, his face was as cardinal red as a USC Trojan helmet. But his step was lively as he scurried back to his dorm room where Becky awaited.

Of late, Denny smiles all the time. He wakes up smiling, goes to his classes smiling, studies at the library smiling, and probably sleeps smiling. At least that's what Becky says. She's been staying with him for a week or so, ever since receiving another note, another slur, that someone slipped under her door. Denny went with her to the Dean of Student's office, Becky clutching a single-spaced, typed list of complaints. The secretary took it into the Dean's office. Five minutes later she returned, telling Becky the Dean would "definitely look into this."

"When?" said Becky.

"Soon," said the secretary, as she hunched over her typewriter.

"How soon is 'soon'?"

The typewriter platen clicked as the secretary scrolled a sheet of letterhead into place. "Soon," she said with a hard 'n'. Where'd the spirits and angels go? thought Becky.

Becky finds solace in Denny's sweet gentleness, his soft soul. Some days, it feels so good that she never leaves his room. She stays in bed. She doesn't dress. He brings her food from the Union. He washes her clothes. He listens. She's tempted to stop doing her work, but she can't. Doing well, asserting her intelligence, is her best revenge.

And they make "sweet love," as Denny insists on calling it. It took some doing, but now she gets as much pleasure as she gives, sometimes more. When they are together, everything disappears, nothing matters. Closed eyes, arms entwined, legs stretching, skin to skin, lips to lips.

She turns and holds out the letter. "When did you get this?"

Denny sits up in bed. "I've had it for a bit."

"He sounds...scared. I mean, genuinely afraid about the Cuba thing."

Denny shakes his head. What is he supposed to say? That's my brother's normal state?

Some kids stand at the door afraid to enter kindergarten for the first time. They cry and call for their mommies. Then, after a few minutes in class---meeting their teacher, playing with new friends, locating their cubby---they get over it. Not so with Willie. He slept with Denny the night before school started. In the morning the sheets were wet from perspiration, and his little brother was curled in a ball, shaking like he had spiked a fever.

Denny called Pop who was already standing outside his door. Pop was wearing the same clothes he'd worn the day before.

"Something's wrong with Willie."

Pop didn't answer. He walked slowly to the bed, placed a hand on Willie's shoulder and asked, "Are you okay?" Denny remembers this because he'd never heard Pop's voice be so gentle; it was soft as a kitten's breath. He stretched out beside Willie and patted his hair. Willie stopped shaking. His wide eyes were locked onto Pop's face. Smoochy bounded in and jumped on the bed, tail flopping. She laid on her side wheeling her legs, which made everyone laugh.

Pop told Willie Smooch was excited because she was going to walk to school with them. Willie smiled through tears. Didn't eat any breakfast. He stretched out on the couch, one of Grandma Mae's afghans pulled up to his chin, hoping eight o'clock would never come. Pop turned on cartoons and made chocolate milk, but Willie's fog never lifted.

Pop carried Willie to school that first morning, Smooch at their side. He carried Willie to school every day for two weeks, Smooch dragging her leash behind.

Once Willie agreed to use his legs, to walk under his own power, Pop still held his hand the whole way. Willie spent his school days with his head on the desk. He watched other kids at recess, but seldom joined in. "No, thank you," he'd say when his teacher, Miss Marcus, invited him to take walks around the school yard. He was a frequent flyer at the nurse's office, always complaining of a stomach ache. The nurse let him sit on her lap pretending to type until he felt well-enough to go back to his room.

Things changed when Lucy Hallowell joined the class in late October. They found shelter in each other's shyness. They were alone together. Soon, Denny was walking him to school, Pop watching from the front door until they disappeared around the corner. Later each morning, he'd call school to make sure Willie was okay.

At home, no one mentioned Willie's difficulties. No conversations around the dinner table. No family meetings. Something wasn't quite right, but, nevertheless, they depended on their daily routine to get them through, to move them forward.

When it became clear Willie's disquiet, his trepidation about life, wasn't like a lingering cold that would leave in due course, no one knew what to do. Getting him to school, getting him engaged with classmates, getting him to sleep soundly, to eat, to poop, to stop crying, to smile, were major accomplishments, skirmishes won in a much larger, yet invisible, war. Too much time had passed, it seemed, to address the underlying 'why' of Willie's struggles. Pop had inadvertently committed to a strategy that landed them all in an emotional quagmire without an exit strategy. It was as if Willie and Denny's parents had never died.

"Has he always been anxious, afraid?" Becky knows what it's like to be unsure of your footing every time you leave the house.

How much does Denny want to say? It's been so long since everything happened that the words, the precise words he needs to explain it all have, like his parents, disappeared without a trace; the syllables, the letters, the alphabet of his grief is gone.

"Mostly, yeah." Denny can't look at her.

Becky frowns and reaches for his hand. "Denny, are you okay?"

"Why would you ask that?"

"Well, I don't know. It's like you've disappeared."

"It's nothing."

He pulls her close and tries to kiss her.

"Don't do that. I'm serious. Is there something you're not telling me about him? Has something gone wrong? He sounds so forlorn."

Denny sits back against the wall. Becky's eyes do not accuse, they don't criticize. They wait, they wait for what he doesn't want to say. His chest tightens and his breathing shallows. She watches but doesn't speak.

"It's my parents...what happened to them."

"I know they died---"

"Willie was the only one there. He saw everything. But remembers nothing."

CHAPTER 17

Muriel Ashwood sits slumped in a metal hospital chair, two pillows at her back, one behind her tilted head. Her chin rests on her concave chest; the room fills with her raspy breath. A strap is knotted behind the chair, holding her in place while an aide changes her bed. A second bed lies empty.

"Yeah, her neighbor died the other night," says the aide in a stage whisper. "My gosh, it was awful. She screamed and screamed and no matter what they did, she, well it was awful, that's all. Choked to death is what it looked like to me. I wouldn't want to go like that," she said, as if it were a choice. Robert Ashwood imagines the poor deceased woman, just before she was born, being asked how she wanted to die. Thinking it was too far off to matter, the woman says, 'I don't care,' to which the administrator says, 'We need to fill the choking quota, is that okay?'.

"Your mother has accidents, but they all do. She seems happy enough, I think. She likes her puzzles and word find books. She's still all there, pretty much. Forgetful, a little confused at times, but aren't we all." The aide tosses the soiled sheet onto the floor and unfurls another. She tucks it quickly and covers it with a tattered comforter. She fluffs the pillow. "There."

"Is she eating?" says Robert Ashwood.

"She had some cream of wheat this morning. Didn't want her juice. She drank some tea. None of them eat all that much, you know. It's just being old, y'know? Sweet Jesus, deliver me from old age."

Robert Ashwood pulls his chair near to his mother. He leans close. "Mom? Are you awake?"

"This is nap time you know. She likes her naps. Don't expect her to respond much." The aide pours cold water into a glass and leaves the plastic pitcher. She drops two packs of Saltines onto the tray. "I like your mom, Mr. Ashwood. She's a fine lady." She marches out, her arms full of dirty linens.

His mother snorts. "Robby?"

"Yeah."

"Is she gone?"

"Yes, she's gone."

Muriel Ashwood opens one filmy eye and closes it again. A grin percolates in the corners of her mouth. Her skin in the light of day is like pale, translucent gauze. Her wispy hair floats. She sighs and opens both of her eyes.

She chuckles. "Am I alive again today, Robby?"

"Yes, very."

"That's good. Better to be very alive than very dead."

When her face lights up, he sees his mother as she once was. Her pointed chin, her scolding eyes, the way she tweaked everything with a raised eyebrow. Her hands and fingers, once so quick to discipline, are mere twigs on thinning branches now; her feet, cat quick when a boy was trying to get away, are permanently parked in saggy slippers. Straight back bent, squared shoulders round. Where once there was fire, an ember remains.

"Why didn't you come yesterday?"

"I did come yesterday, Ma. In the morning. Remember?"

"If you say so. Untie me."

Robert hesitates. "I don't know, Ma. You know what happened."

"For chrissakes, Robby."

"You fell, remember."

"I never fell and you know it."

Robert stands over his mother.

"You gotta lose some weight, Robby. You'll be dead before me."

He reaches behind her and unties the strap while holding her in place. He steps back and lets go slowly.

"That's better." She stretches her back and tries to sit straight. "Don't get old, Robby. You're not strong enough. Better you should die young."

He drags a lounge chair from her neighbor's side of the room and lifts her by both arms to a standing position. They shuffle together to the chair and he lowers her into place.

"Thank you, son. Let's keep that chair on our side. She won't need it anymore." She winks at him.

Robert Ashwood regrets putting his mother in the county nursing home. They had been a twosome for nearly twenty-five years, ever since the day his father died of a heart attack on 'C' shift. It took hours to retrieve him from his crane high above the mill floor. "Such a waste," his mother had said, never shedding a tear.

By then Robert's older brothers had scattered to the west coast, California, Oregon and Washington. Robert was working as a carpenter at Blaw-Knox Manufacturing. Marriage to his high school sweet heart had collapsed after their baby son, Bruce, died of pneumonia. Any love they'd had for each was buried with him.

After the divorce, Robert lived on his own for a few years. But when his father died, his mother asked him to move back "for a while." He never left. "Why waste money on an apartment, you can live here for free," his mother said. He dated a little after that, but nothing serious. Eventually, he stopped trying.

Living with his mother, he never felt entirely 'free'. As her knees became useless, he shopped for her, cooked for her, cleaned house for her, dressed her from time to time and even bathed her. In the beginning, he kept his eyes closed, but, in time, it didn't matter. All privacy disappeared under the crushing demands of an aging parent. His only source of relaxation was food and drink. He packed the freezer with half-gallon containers of ice cream, never letting his stash fall below six. The local beer distributorship made regular drops at the house on Fridays and Mondays.

"You're gonna end up dead," his mother would say.

"I'm gonna end up dead no matter how thin or fat I am. That's a plain fact."

"You have to take better care of yourself."

"No, I don't. It's my choice. That's the beauty part."

Robert retired comfortably at age fifty-five, thanks to the United Brotherhood of Carpenters. He was lucky to reach fifty-five. His weight, and budding congestive heart failure, made it impossible for him to do much work at all toward the end. Thanks to the Brotherhood, he spent his last few years as an informal 'supervisor', which involved being on the job and watching what others did.

Only after he retired did he realize his mother's concerns about his health were as much about her welfare as his. Would he be able to take care of her? She watched him as closely as he watched her.

"Did you take your pills, Robby?"

"Ma! Stop!"

"You're a young man---"

"I know what I am, Ma. Let it go."

It was a Thursday night. He'd put her to bed around eleven. He watched Carson for an hour and then hit the sack. He was sound asleep at three when he heard her calling---"Robby!" Sometimes if he waited, she would fall back to sleep, but not tonight. She called again and then again. "What?" She didn't answer. "What's wrong?" She was in tears when he got to her room.

"Ma, what's the matter?"

"I gotta go." She tried to lift her head. Tears puddled in the corners of her eyes.

"It's okay, Ma. Don't get upset." He bent over to help her out of bed and felt his face go flush and his stomach roll over. He raised her to a sitting position and then stopped. Once he caught his breath, he tried to hoist her to her feet. By then, he was slippery with sweat, his heart was pounding, pain bunched between his shoulder blades, and his legs had turned into mashed potatoes.

"No, oh no!" cried his mother. The floor was wet with pee. "I'm so sorry, I'm sorry."

Robert's socks were sopping. The pain along his shoulder blades had migrated to his chest. He was sucking air and feeling faint.

They both toppled to the floor, two old growth trees finally falling.

Robert did not remember two ambulances arriving. He did not remember sirens and flashing lights and the heavy breathing of EMTs as they struggled to carry him down the stairs on a stretcher. When he asked about his mother, they said she'd been taken to the hospital. Then he passed out again.

When he woke up, a monitor was staring at him, lights blinking, numbers changing, his bed surrounded by curtains. His stay in the emergency room was brief. More sirens as they rushed him off to a Pittsburgh hospital for bypass surgery. When he woke up in recovery, the nurses told him he'd had a heart attack and several of his arteries were blocked, so they Roto-Rootered them back to health.

They also told him his mother had had a successful surgery to repair her broken hip and that she would be transferred to a rehab hospital in Zelienople. He slipped into a deep sleep and dreamed he and his mother were endlessly falling through darkness. He woke up with a start. The nurse told him the story about his mother's hip again, and again he slept away. He would hear the story three more times before he understood what they were telling him.

Robert had one visitor during his stay in the hospital. His neighbor, Hal Mitchum, stood at the bottom of his bed, fumbling with his belt buckle and smiling sheepishly. They had the kind of relationship long-standing neighbors have, forged with greetings shouted across the yards, weather talk, and respect for privacy.

Robert tied the back of his gown closed and they walked slowly down the hall, stopping every twenty feet or so until they reached the visitors' lounge where he fell onto a couch and tried to catch his breath. Hal stood over him, statue still, fearing he was about to witness Robert's demise. He went to the sink and got Robert a paper cup full of water.

Needing no encouragement, Robert spilled his story in one lengthy narrative with details that made Hal squeamish. He went again for water, this time for himself. "The only thing that confuses me is how we got to the hospital. Who called the ambulance?"

Turns out Hal was wrestling with sleep that night and when he finally accepted defeat, he got up and went outside to have a smoke. He didn't tell

Robert this part, but he was convinced that in the dead of night, he heard his wife, Mae, speak to him. She assured him that everyone was doing fine in heaven, that they were at peace and there were no hard feelings. This didn't make any sense to Hal, considering the terrible problems they'd left behind, two young boys without parents and him without a wife. Easy for her to say all's well. Being there was better than being here.

Hal was about to raise a few questions, when he heard other voices, muffled voices. At first he thought---"Could it be Ruthie?" Could she be near her mother but too far from the microphone (or whatever they use in heaven) for him to hear her?

Soon it became obvious the voices were earthbound, actually neighborhood bound. There was screeching and then moaning and finally a deafening thud that echoed through the night, like a barn collapsing in a wind storm. He looked at the Ashwood house.

He entered through the back door and called for Robert, but there was no response. He almost left but something felt odd; there was an eerie stillness that made the hair on the back of his neck stand. He called again. Then he walked slowly up the staircase where he found both Ashwoods in a heap, her legs in odd tinker-toy positions and him like a sleeping walrus.

He shortened the story for Robert. "I was outside for a smoke and thought I heard something. Turns out I did, so I called the ambulance."

Robert held Hal Mitchum in high esteem from then on. Hal'd been through hard times and he'd saved Robert's life, but more important, he'd saved his mother's life. Perhaps he and Hal were even now.

His mother had been in rehab for a few weeks before Robert was well enough to visit her. She wasn't the same person. She was as thin and shriveled as a worn-out paper straw. She seemed indifferent about getting well again. She wore out her time in rehab and they encouraged Hal to transfer her to the county nursing home until she was well-enough to return home. How long will this take? he'd asked. A month, maybe two.

Five years later she was strapped in her nursing home chair because it was the most convenient way for staff to keep her safe. "If you're asking, sometimes I think she throws herself on the floor, just to make me crazy," one of the LPNs had said.

In the last year, especially the last few months, as Armageddon cast a shadow on everyone's life, Robert had become more philosophical about his situation. In high school math he learned that adding one negative to another negative resulted in a positive. Maybe that worked with people, too. Maybe they should be together again. Maybe it was time to bring Ma home. Maybe both of them would benefit from a reunion. Also, the thought of her being incinerated in an atomic blast while he ate yummy canned foods in his bunker seemed not only unfair but immoral.

Muriel Ashwood feels comfortable once she's nestled into the chair Robert's confiscated from her dead roommate's side of the room.

"Gladys won't mind. Actually, she won't know. Now that I think of it, if she knew, she'd mind. She was that kind, you know what I mean, Robby? Like your Aunt Gert. Remember her, your dad's sister? She wouldn't share a piece of bread with an orphan. She was a hoarder, that's what she was. Inside her heart, that's what she was. So was Gladys. Mind you, we got along, but that was only because I'm an easy-going type, I'm always willing to give in to make peace...Have you gained weight, Robby? You have, haven't you?"

Robert reconsiders the wisdom of his lofty plan. But he holds fast to the unsubstantiated notion that something good can come from combining two things that are, well, not so good.

"Ma, I've got an idea."

"An idea? How did that happen."

"I was thinking---"

"Always good to try new things."

"C'mon, Ma."

"What?"

"I'm trying to talk to you about something...something important."

She blinks twice and smiles.

"Look, Ma, you've been in this place, like---"

"Five years. It's been five goddam years."

"Yes. Five years."

"And it's killing me! I don't know why you put me in here to begin with. What were you thinking?"

"Ma, remember? You broke your hip. I had a heart attack..." Robert rubs his palms on his pantlegs.

"I know, I know...But that was five years ago, Robby. That's a long time. I mean, you know how many roommates I've had? Ten. They're all dead now." Muriel looks out the window and scratches her cheek.

"I'm sorry, Ma, I am. I mean...look, that's what I want to talk to you about." He swallows hard. "Like I was saying, I got this idea...What if you come home?"

"What?" She squints and carefully lifts her left arm with her right hand and places it in her lap. She straightens her back as best she can. "What are you saying, Robby?"

"I guess I'm saying maybe you should come home, you know?"

"You want me to come home?"

"Do you want to come home?"

They hold their breath.

The nurse's aide breezes into the room. "How you doin' in here, Miss Muriel? You need anything? Hey, Mr. Ashwood, good seein' you. How you doin'?" Robert nods. "Beautiful day out there, Miss Muriel. I'll take you out this afternoon. We'll get you some wheels, okay? Sit by the garden for a while. Get out of this place, you know, honey." Her melodic laugh fills the room.

"That would be nice, Kat."

"Great! It's a date." Kat circles the room, empties the trash can and waves as she sweeps out of the room.

Weather conversation ensues. It's been a warm fall, not much rain, leaves turning, there's conjecture about winter, and hope that it doesn't come soon. Then silence. This is usually when Robert heaves a sigh, puts his hands on his knees and says, "Well, better head out." Maybe that's what he should do today, as well. Maybe he should get up, kiss his mother's cheek, tell her not to do anything he wouldn't do and hit the road.

"Well, Ma...what do you think? Do you want to come home?"

"Who would take care of me?"

"Well---"

"What about my pills? Who would give me my pills?"

"I guess---"

"And the stairs, I can't go up and down stairs anymore." There is fear in her eyes. "Who would take care of me, Robby?"

There is no reason for Muriel to assume Robby can do the job. The events that brought her to the nursing home have bruised her modest confidence in her son. She knows he had a heart attack and had to recover, but she still feels he abandoned her; he didn't show up for weeks. What would happen if she goes home?

"Well, Ma, I'll take care of those things. Your bedroom and the bath are on the first floor. Remember? I'm upstairs in the attic. I mean, I'm always there. I can run the errands. I already cook all the meals. I mean...you've told me a thousand times how much you hate this place; how much you wish you could come home."

She is confused. "Why are you suggesting this, Robby? Why now?"

What is he supposed to say? Look, Ma, there's going to be a nuclear war; the Russians are going to attack us; the world's coming to an end. It's the kind of thing that makes you think. Maybe we should be together when it happens.

"Look, Ma...I miss you. You're alone, I'm alone. Maybe it makes sense to be together. Who knows what the future will bring?" Another huffing sigh.

Muriel looks past his fleshy cheeks and bushy eyebrows to his pea-sized eyes. Even when he was a little boy, his eyes hid under his brows, like tiny brown birds in a nest. She has to look hard to see them at all. But when she does, she can see all of him. All of him is afraid, she thinks. He is more alone than me.

"Okay, Robby, let's get me out of here." She forces a chortling laugh.

"Good. That's good, Ma. I'll get the ball rolling."

His heart skips with thankfulness and his stomach knots with anxiety.

"I should tell you about the bomb shelter."

"The what?"

CHAPTER 18

Richie Caplan is a year older than Willie. He's been delivering the *Pittsburgh Press* for two years. "I make good money. I can make like twenty bucks every couple weeks. And it's all mine. I don't have to beg money from my parents, you know what I mean?"

Richie folds a paper over three times and then tucks it in. He drops it in his newspaper bag. He has forty-five customers. "You'll get strong doing this work. I mean the Wednesday Press weighs like a ton with all the extra junk in it. Sometimes I take half the route, get a Klondike, and then come back for the rest."

Willie sits on the sidewalk outside the Newsstand, his elbow on is knee, his chin on his hand. He listens to Richie's steady jabber. "Some people, like the Wilsons or the Foxwallers, they tip good, so you make more; but then there are others, like old lady Herman, she gives me eighty-five cents and waits for the penny change. I mean, really?"

Willie shifts his chin to his other hand. If he lived to be, say thirty, he'd never ever think of getting a paper route. But Pop thinks it would be good for him: "You need a job, it's good to have an important responsibility, and you can make money." What Pop wants to say is, 'You need to grow up a little, you need to see something other than this neighborhood, you need to meet people and get used to being out there in the world'. Willie lives in Ewing Park and Richie's route is across town in North Side, a whole mile and a half away.

"How am I gonna get there?"

"You got feet don't you? This kid will be gone for three months. Three months, that's all. You can help him out and make some money. That's that."

Pop had a friend, one of the higher-ups at the tube mill, who knew Richie's father. He's going to who-knows-where on a "special assignment" and taking the family with him. Why his decision to drag his family to Timbuktu has to mess up Willie's life is anyone's guess.

"You carry 'em and I'll toss 'em," says Richie.

Willie stares at him, then hoists the bag over one shoulder and adjusts the strap. The weight of forty-five folded and tucked papers nearly topples him.

"Wha'd I tell ya, heavy ain't it?"

"Let's just go."

Richie hands Willie a large metal ring with forty-five tickets on it. All the customers' names and addresses as well as dots he has to punch every time he collects. They cross back and forth on Maple Terrace and Richie tosses a paper onto a porch, sticks one into a mailbox, then drops one between a screen door and an inner door. "Gotta remember this stuff. People get nutty and then you don't get tipped."

When they finish, Willie thinks, An hour and a half of my life, gone forever. He thanks Richie who is as excited at the end of the route as he was at the beginning. "See you tomorrow, buddy!"

Willie follows Richie for one week. By the end he's folding and tucking and tossing on his own without missing a house. He feels proud of himself. People smile and say thank you and ask who he is and even shake his hand.

The Handelbaker's dog is the only problem. He's a German shepherd who's always pissed off about something. He snarls and growls and pulls on his rope whenever Willie approaches. "His bark is worse than his bite." Mrs. Handelbaker smiles while her dog snarls.

The first day on his own, Mrs. Handelbaker isn't home. But her dog, Rocko, is. She likes her paper on the back porch which is right in Rocko's wheelhouse. Richie suggested Willie bring dog biscuits with him to make friends with some of the mutts on the route. Today his pocket is bulging.

Doesn't matter. Rocko wants meat. His teeth are bared and a ridge of fur stands stiff down his back.

"Hi, Rocko. Good boy." Willie makes kissing noises which always work with Smooch. She wags her tail and rolls on her back and then wiggles up to Willie hoping to be scratched. Not so much with Rocko. It seems to infuriate him. Willie can almost hear him thinking, Don't try that bullshit on me, punk. What to do? He snaps his fingers, makes more kissing noises and then smiles as Rocko inches closer. Rocko launches from the porch like a Russian missile and snaps the rope like it was thread off a spool. Willie stops with the kissing and snapping. He high-tails it across three yards and down an alley, Rocko hot on his trail. Willie flies across another yard and lurches to a screeching halt on someone's porch. Rocko the Rocket is ready to leap. Maybe screaming unintelligibly will be a successful strategy. When Rocko wraps his jaws around Willie's ankle, his screams go up two octaves, well into dog-hearing range. Rocko hesitates, then steps back and whimpers.

By then Mrs. Handelbaker pulls into her driveway, jumps out of the car and follows the growls and screams to the scene of the crime.

"Rocko, goddammit, get over here right this minute!"

Willie, frozen with terror, stands by the door. Rocko has hungry eyes, but centuries of domestication win out. His obedience to his owner overrides his instincts, and he dashes victoriously back to Mrs. Handelbaker's loving arms. She waves and calls, "I'm sorry."

"That's okay," he calls back. He sits on the concrete steps and looks at his ankle. Blood oozes onto his sock. He pulls off his shoe and sock. He wipes the blood away with his hand, revealing two teeth marks. He looks at them indifferently. Just another day at the office. He feels relieved, like he's gone to war and survived his first major battle. Maybe he's invincible. Maybe there will be a parade.

Feeling exhilarated, he spits on his ankle and rubs it with his sock; he spits again and lets the air dry it. The bleeding stops. He puts his sock and shoe back on. Hoists his bag over his shoulder, ready to venture out again.

Willie reaches for the banister and stands, but something stops him. He looks at the dirty white railing and its curlicue end. He slides his feet across the step, noticing the tiny pebbles ingrained in the cement. The porch floor has long uneven planks, holes here and there. He walks back and forth across the porch then jumps onto the boxy wood railing, grabbing hold of the pillars.

Standing there, he feels an odd sensation. Tingling maybe or prickling. His breathing becomes shallow. He studies the porch from his perch. He imagines green Adirondack chairs, the paint chipping. Maybe a swing hanging from the ceiling at the far end. Three rhododendrons in front of the porch, no longer in bloom. Willie closes his eyes and imagines purple flowers. In the corner, beside the steps, a peony. White, maybe.

Willie peaks through the front door window. There is a small vestibule and another door with leaded glass. It is hard for him to see beyond, but he thinks the staircase may be on the left and the living room on the right. There's no furniture, no sign of life.

Back on the front walk, he surveys the house, with its missing shingles, peeling white paint and dipping gutters. His nose fills with the smell of dust and old cardboard boxes. He looks down the driveway to the garage at the back end of the property, part of its roof falling. Grass and weeds and wildflowers have grown through the cracks in the cement.

The house, so dark, so lifeless, stands out like a rotting tooth in an otherwise brilliant smile. There is nothing like it on this block or the next one or the one after that. It's still standing, but what's holding it up?

There's no for sale sign. No one wants it.

Willie's eyes begin to well up. He turns and trots back down the street, then breaks into a run. His breath fails him after two blocks and he leans against a tree to settle himself. He looks back but can't see the house.

CHAPTER 19
1953

Ruthie Blevin held the picnic basket in the crook of her arm. Willie stood beside her, a new ballcap sitting askew on his head. "Are you ready for this adventure?" Willie jumped up and down. She took his hand and they went down the front porch steps.

Cliff Blevin yanked the garage door handle, backed the Nash Rambler down the driveway to pick up Ruthie. He saw Willie and the dog, Smoochy, running back and forth on the porch as Ruthie tried to corrale them. He blared the horn and they all jumped.

Ruthie helped Willie and Smoochy get in the back where Willie stood on the hump and leaned over the front seat. Ruthie got in the front and slammed the door. She glared at Cliff. "No need for the horn."

Cliff gripped the steering wheel, his knuckles white. He looked at his wife, her face turned to the window. Willie threw himself backward onto the seat; Smoochy piled on. He hopped back onto his feet and rammed against the front seat.

"Careful there, young man," said his mother.

"Dada," he said as he patted his father's head.

Cliff tickled his son's hand. "We're going to have fun, little man. This is gonna be a whole new beginning."

Ruthie shot a disapproving look at him. "Don't say that. It'll confuse him."

Willie squealed and jumped up and down.

"Whoa, be careful. Don't want you to bump your noggin."

Willie put his arms over his head, fell back again into his seat and started bouncing. Smoochy jumped on him and started barking.

"Stop it!" said Cliff.

"Don't yell," said Ruthie, her face still turned to the window.

Cliff leaned toward her and spoke in a harsh whisper. "I told you not to bring that dog home."

"The boy needs something right about now. He's happy, for once."

"He wouldn't need a dog if you'd let me come home."

Willie stood and looked out the window. Smoochy tried to stand beside him, but kept slipping to the floor. Willie squealed. "Cuckoo, 'moochy, cuckoo, 'moochy."

Ruthie turned to watch them. "That Smoochy is cuckoo, isn't she? I think you are, too."

Willie screeched and placed his tiny hand over his mouth. "No, Mama, you cuckoo."

"I think there's a lot of cuckoo going around," said Cliff, with stiffened grin.

CHAPTER 20

"So, how you liking it?" says Pres as he leaps and swats at a tree branch.

"Okay, it's okay."

"Getting rich, huh."

"Yeah, right."

"So, how long's it gonna take to deliver them? I gotta be home for dinner at, like, six."

"Not a problem."

Willie, his bag over his shoulder, and Pres walk slowly, crossing the Park Bridge, traversing Fountain Ave., then turning right onto the Fifth Street Bridge, which is even higher than Park. They stop and fill their pockets with stones, which are soon bulging like a squirrel's cheeks. They feel the bridge shudder with each speeding car or truck. Finally in the middle, Willie drops his bag. Pres is standing on the bottom rung of the fence, leaning over for a bird's eye view of the river one hundred and seventy feet below. He tips forward, balancing only on his stomach, half his body in thin air. He sticks his arms out.

"Looky here."

"Man-o-man, Pres, are you crazy?"

Pres screams like a banshee, his head tilted toward the sky. Willie steps back and looks away.

"C'mon, man."

Pres tips back and lands on his feet beside is friend. "Try it."

"No way."

"It's fun, I'm tellin' you."

"No chance, man."

"Too much for you, huh? Maybe my grandma could teach you how to knit. Maybe that fits you better." He shadow boxes around Willie who is emptying the stones onto the sidewalk.

"That's funny. Too bad I forgot to laugh."

Pres takes a stone from his pocket, steps back, lurches forward and rips the stone into the air. They both lean over the fence, watching, watching, as the stone becomes a pebble and then a dot and then the tiniest splash.

Willie follows, hurling his stone up as high as he can. They watch it pass in front of them at breakneck speed. Then the wind takes hold of it. "Look at that," says Willie. They lose it for a second and then see it just as it careens off a boulder and into the water.

"Very cool," says Pres.

"Yeah...Better get a move on, don't want you to get in trouble with your Mama."

Pres adds his stones to Willie's pile and they kick them over the edge.

"Bombs away!" says Pres, making exploding noises when the stones reach their target. "Kaboom!"

Pres insists on carrying the paper bag. "It's nothin'." When they reach the first few houses on Willie's route, Pres hands the bag back to Willie and asks if he can toss one.

Willie hesitates, then gives Pres a rolled paper. "They want it on their porch by the door, so let's get a little closer."

Pres stops in his tracks, estimates the distance and hurls the paper, which clips a rose bush and settles in a sandbox.

"Like I said, let's get a little closer."

They're in sync after about twenty deliveries. Pres regales him with tales of his father's glory. "Yeah, he shot tons of Japs and then, when he went to Korea, he shot tons more gooks."

"That's something."

"He's a real patriot, you know, a modern-day hero."

"Yeah."

"Did your dad, like, do you know if he went to war?"

Willie doesn't skip a beat. "Yeah, sure. Europe somewhere. Fighting the Nazis."

"A hero, too."

It's tiring to always answer "I don't know" when kids ask about his father; sometimes it's easier to make things up. Some kids think his dad's a boxer who had to leave the country after killing a guy in the ring. Others think he's an explorer at the North Pole who can't come home because his work is too important. A few think he's a spy stationed in Russia. He can't remember how any different things he's told Pres and Lucy.

Pres gets better at tossing papers. Other than almost breaking a window, there've been no mishaps.

Willie falls silent as they approach Handelbaker's. Not because of Rocko, who's become a pussycat now that he knows Willie. It's that house, that old, worn-out house that's on his mind. He's avoided it for days. But he's dreamed about the place twice. He thought of talking to Pop about it, but didn't. It seemed too weird, too out of bounds for a conversation with his grandfather. If Denny were home, that's who he'd talk to. He almost told Lucy a couple of times, but she has her own troubles. So, Pres. He's not a great listener, but that's okay. More than anything, Willie wants to hear what it sounds like when he talks about it; whether he sounds nutty or not.

"That's the dog? Geez, he's nothin'. I was expecting a monster." Rocko barks and lunges. Pres gulps and shuts his mouth.

Rocko bares his teeth. Pres steps back. "Do you really want me to throw the paper onto the porch. I mean…"

Willie takes the paper from Pres and tosses it onto the porch where is slides to a halt at Rocko's front paws. Rocko growls.

"How do you do this every day. I mean, geez, you could get eaten alive." Willie isn't listening; he staring in a different direction.

"C'mon, I want to show you something."

They cross several yards, walk up the narrow alley, cross another street and there it is.

"Look at that place over there," says Willie. "The dumpy place with the overgrown grass."

Together they size up the house with its rickety porch and dirty white trim, its grimy oval window on the rotting front door, its cracked steps and uneven sidewalk, its fir trees that overwhelm the gutters. There is a gable on the second floor with two widows, one missing glass. The chimney, tilted like Pisa, is held in place with a metal rod. The long driveway leads to a one car garage, its roof caved in.

"It's creepy. What about it?"

"I don't know exactly. That's where I went when Rocko attacked me. And, it felt weird."

"What do you mean, weird?"

"I can't explain it. It just felt like something was wrong."

Pres's face brightens. "Maybe it's haunted, y'know. My dad told me there's lots of haunted houses around town, but no one wants to admit it. They're afraid of what might happen if word gets out."

Before Willie can say anything, Pres is half way across the yard. Willie drops his bag and follows. They stand in the shadow of the empty, creaky house. Pres trudges across the yard and stops at the bottom of the front steps, fists on his hips.

"So, what do you think?" says Willie.

"It's haunted, for sure, no doubt. Look at it. You can almost hear the poltergeists and demons and stuff." He sniffs the air. "They have an odor." He takes another deep sniff, while Willie stands back. "Yeah, my dad told me all about this stuff. He's had first-hand experience with this kind of thing. Like sometimes in the middle of the night, with my mom fast asleep beside him, he sits up, all scared, and he sees them, the ghosts."

"Ghosts?"

"Yeah, mostly the ghosts of guys he knew in the war, guys who got killed. He says they won't leave him alone. How's that for creepy? Have you seen anything?"

"I haven't seen anything." says Willie. "Should I?"

"You must not be looking hard enough. There's gotta be stuff going on in there. C'mon."

He tiptoes onto the porch, Willie a few feet behind. Pres peers through the front door again, then through the front window, but can't see anything. "Maybe they're there, but they don't want us to see them, you know?"

Willie wants to say, There's something there, whether we can see it or not. Thinking about this house has kept him awake at night; but he doesn't see ghosts like Preston's dad. It's more like he's trying to put a puzzle together, but he can't because too many pieces have fallen under the table and no matter what he does, he can't reach them.

He'd like to say something, but Pres has moved on from poltergeists and demons to Casper the Friendly Ghost and what he wants to be for Halloween. "A hobo, that's what I'll be. Doesn't cost a dime, just get some of my dad's old stuff, smudge up my face..."

Willie heads down the driveway to the backyard. He wades through the grass and looks up at the corner window. He feels cool air on his back and warmth on his face. What is this? he thinks.

"There you are," says Pres as he comes around the corner. "I thought you ditched me."

Willie's head is cast down, his hands cover his face.

"Hey, man?" Pres steps closer, then stops. "Are you okay, Willie?"

Willie's palms are moist, his face is ashen, his knees are buckling. He tries to walk; he tries to speak; he sees Pres, who appears to be moving in slow motion, speaking without a voice. Pres reaches for Willie, but not in time. Willie falls slowly, like a folding chair.

In less than a minute he's awake and trying to stand.

"No, man, just sit there." Pres's hand is on Willie's chest. His own face is pale; dried saliva is in the corners of his mouth.

"What happened?"

"Well, it was like, you know, it was like the school thing, only this time you didn't hit so hard. It was weird. You kind of bent over and I thought you'd make it but then your knees gave way and you were down for the count." Pres looks at Willie, waiting for a response. Willie is sitting now, his legs outstretched. He wipes perspiration from his face and neck.

"You know, maybe you're hungry or something. My dad gets dizzy if he doesn't eat at five o'clock, I mean right on the dot. Drives my mom crazy." Willie stands slowly, trying to get his bearings. "Willie, it's probably nothing, right?" says Pres, his hand on his friend's shoulder.

"I don't know."

CHAPTER 21

A stiff breeze ruffles the makeshift curtains. He turns his desk chair to face Becky who is lying on the bed reading Camus. "Look at this," says Denny.

Becky drops *The Plague*.

"Okay, what?"

"See the handwriting, I mean, printing?"

"Uh huh."

"That's not my brother. That's Pop."

"So?"

Denny sits on his bed, Becky sprawled beside him. "You don't get it. I don't think my grandfather has ever written a letter."

Becky sits up and places her hands on his shoulders. "Well, that makes it extra special, right?"

"I don't know."

"What do you mean?"

"Pop doesn't talk much and when he does, it's only because he has to, like something's so important he can't help himself. And what he has to say may not be something you want to hear. I think that might be the same with letters." He holds the envelope up to the window and squints, wishing he had x-ray vision.

"Are you going to open it or wait for it to open itself?"

She takes it out of his hands, but he yanks it back. "Whoa, what could be so bad?" she says.

"That's just it, I don't know." In his heart, though, Denny knows. It has to be Willie. Why else would Pop write to him? He opens the envelope and takes out the lined paper. It is filled with Pop's scribbles. Becky kneels on the bed and looks over his shoulder.

. . .

A day or so after Pres went with Willie on his paper route, Max, Preston's father, calls Pop.

"So, I wanted to tell you about what happened on Willie's route the other day." There is a lengthy pause.

"Okay." Pop doesn't know Preston's father, though he's heard the stories, how he dropped out of high school and joined the army, served with distinction, then re-upped for the Korean War, leaving his pregnant wife behind. He was in his early twenties when he returned the second time, yet he was a veteran of two wars. He was treated like a hero at the VFW. It was a year or more before he found steady work, but the jobs didn't last.

"My Preston said something happened, something that sort of scared him." He describes Willie's "spell." Pop holds the receiver like it's a hand grenade. Mr. Stapleton explains that Pres had begged his father not to tell anyone, but he thought Pop should know. "I'd want to know," he says, faintly. "I mean, things happen and sometimes you don't think they mean anything, but then more things happen and before you know it…well, that's why I'm calling you." He stops abruptly. Pop, pacing the room, has stretched the phone cord as far as it could go.

"I thought you oughta know. He's a good boy. I hope everything is okay." Pop thanks him. "And, well, Pres doesn't know I'm calling you, so if you don't mind, could you keep that part quiet?"

Pop looks at the receiver for a moment before putting it back in its cradle. He goes to the fridge for a beer and then sits at the kitchen table. He presses his fingertips to his temple and slowly massages his forehead, eyes closed. He pops the top and drains half the bottle. He stretches out his bum leg and rubs his knee. Smoochy slinks into the kitchen and sits at his feet, chin resting on Pop's leg. "Hey, girl." He scratches Smoochy's ears and tries to clear his cluttered mind. "Mae." He hisses. "Why did you have to go?" He tosses back the rest of his IC. He puts the bottle on the table with a thud and pats Smoochy one more time.

He thinks of twelve different ways to draw Willie out about what happened without divulging his source. As he rehearses them in his mind, each one falters, each one ends with Willie walking away and Pop saying something like, "Come on, talk to me!"

He goes to the kitchen junk drawer looking for a pencil or pen. He tears a sheet of paper from Willie's school tablet. He sits bent over the kitchen table, trying to find words. When he's done, he folds the letter and puts it in his pocket for safe-keeping. Two days later he goes to the post office during lunch and drops the letter in the slot. As soon as it leaves his fingertips, he wishes he could get it back.

He promised himself when Denny left for college, he'd make sure he wouldn't have to come home early because of his brother. He'd take care of everything. It turns out he couldn't keep that promise.

I don't like the idea of you coming home before Thanksgiving, but I'm worried... He goes on to talk about the paper route *"incident"* and how Willie sits awake every night worrying there's going to be a war and how Pop's unsure what to do. *Come sooner, if you can.*

"Your poor brother," says Becky. "He's just lost."

"I'm not sure about going home."

Becky puts her arms around Denny. "Why?"

"I don't know; it's just a feeling."

Becky rubs his back and shoulders. "Well, if you can do it, I think it would be good."

Denny holds her. "I'll go if you come with me."

"Of course."

CHAPTER 22

Lucy Hallowell stands in front of her mother's full-length mirror which is propped in the corner of her bedroom. Her mother hasn't worn this dress in years. She smiles at what she sees. The dress is soft pink with a thin belt, a gold buckle, and tiny pearl buttons from her neckline to her waist. The pleated bottom flairs like an accordion. Lucy stops to listen, thinking she hears her mother. When she doesn't, she twirls slowly this way and that, self-consciously enjoying the swishing sound of the dress. She reaches behind herself and pinches the dress tighter across her bodice. She is developing a shape all her own. She turns and looks over her shoulder, admiring the hemline.

Lucy searches through her mother's messy closet and finds a pair of white pumps, worn a little on the toes. She slides her feet into them and is surprised they almost fit. With them on, she's nearly as tall as her mom. She takes a deep breath and exhales exultantly. "You are a pretty girl, Miss Lucy Hallowell," her mother had said the night before. She'd had a few beers and was giddy and full of herself. Lucy loved when her mother was carefree and happy, it happened so infrequently. "Yes you are---A. Pretty. Girl. Don't ever forget that."

Lucy pulls her hair back on both sides, takes bobby pins from the corner of her mouth and sets her hair in place. Voila! She looks thirteen, maybe even fourteen, if she uses her imagination. "Stay a girl as long as you can." Her mother was pointing at her with one hand and dangling a cigarette in the other. "Watch out for those horny teenage boys. Watch out for them, I'm telling you." It wasn't hard to figure out what "horny" meant.

She opens her mother's silver compact and removes the tiny brush. She feels the bristles with her finger. She dabs the brush into the powdery blush and fans it across her cheeks. When she finds a gold tube of lipstick called "Roses are Red," she smiles so broadly her eyes close. She pulls the makeup mirror close and leans to within a few inches of the mirror. She guides the tube awkwardly across her upper lip and then her bottom, coloring only a little outside the lines. She smacks her lips and studies herself top to bottom, her mother's words from the night before still echoing in her mind.

"I think this is as good a time as any," her mother had said, trying to conceal a smirk. She lit her cigarette and opened another can of beer. She raised it to her mouth, but didn't drink.

Lucy waited anxiously. "For what?"

"The Talk. T-h-e T-a-l-k, little girl."

Not this, thought Lucy. Her mom had been threatening her with The Talk since she was eight. "Why now, Mom?"

"'Cause you recently became a women or did you forget?" She threw her head back and cackled. "Soooo, we're going to talk about sex, s-e-x. And count yourself lucky, because no one ever gave me The Talk. Not my mother, for sure. I learned it all lying on my back in an old Chevy. I don't want that for you."

Lucy sniffed. Her armpits were already damp. She looked for the nearest exit.

"Once upon a time, there was a little girl named Lucy. And Lucy didn't know nothin' about nothin'. Then one day, completely out of the blue, she had a bleeding spell down there in that place that didn't seem to serve any purpose."

"Mom, do we have to---"

"And she found out! She found out that even though she still looked like a girl, she wasn't one anymore. She was a woman. Not a fully grown-up woman, but a woman, nonetheless."

"Mom, really---"

"Just listen, this is important." Her jovial veneer was wearing off as it always did. Her eyes grew darker, matching her changing mood. She sucked her drink and her cigarette. "Nothing's more important than this, this sex thing. That little place down there can make or break your life." She opened her eyes as wide as possible and stuck her neck out for emphasis. "That little place is your power and your weakness. And it is the one thing every boy wants. And he'll do anything to get you to let him...come visit. You know what I mean?"

Lucy squirmed in her chair and looked everywhere but at her mother.

"Here, let me get you something to drink."

"Mom, I don't want---"

"I want you to be at ease about all this." She went to the fridge for a bottle of Crown Cola. She put it down in front of Lucy with a thud. Then she filled a bowl with Snyder's potato chips. "There." Lucy didn't move.

"Okay, where was I? Right, do you know what I was trying to tell you?"

"I think so."

"You think so. Well, let's go over it. Have you ever seen how a garden hose screws right into a spigot so they fit together perfectly?"

Lucy swallowed hard.

"That's what a boy wants to do with his...peepee."

"Oh, my God."

"He wants to screw it right into your...special place." Wide eyes and jutting neck again. "Do you get it?"

"Yes, Mom."

"Yes, Mom, what?"

"Yes, Mom, I know what you're saying." Her girlfriends speculated about where a boy's thing went. For a couple of years, the belly button was the consensus choice. It made most sense. Some thought the 'bum hole' was possible. Too gross for most of the girls to even consider. A few thought there was magic involved; that sex happened as soon as you married and you knew it happened because a baby showed up nine months later.

At least now she knew. She wasn't sure why a boy would want to do that or why a girl would let him, but maybe that was for another time.

"Now, the one thing to remember is what I told you at the beginning. You must *wait*. You must wait for the right time before let a boy in; if you wait, everything will be good. Be in a hurry, be careless, let boys in willy-nilly and your life will be ruined." She flicked ashes into her empty beer can. "Trust me, I know. It ruined my life. I don't want that to happen to you."

When Lucy went to bed that night, the main thing she remembered was that having sex had ruined her mother's life. Having sex had ruined her life because she got pregnant. Having sex had ruined her life because Lucy was the result. Sex, Lucy, life ruined. She cried herself to sleep.

The next morning, her mother was up early, though she was dragging a little.

"You want breakfast," she said.

Lucy looked at her, noncommittal.

"What's the matter, Luce? Do you want breakfast or not?"

Lucy's brow furrowed. She sat down in the same chair she sat in the night before.

"How 'bout pancakes? How 'bout that?" Her mom raised her eyebrows and smiled. "I got time before work."

"Okay."

"Great, that's my sweet girl." She took a couple of aspirins with a full glass of water and then got the Aunt Jemima's out. Her mother whistled and turned up the radio. The last time she made pancakes on a school day was...never. What was going on? She seemed completely unaffected by the excruciating heart-to-heart she'd force fed Lucy the night before. Then it dawned on her: Lucy's mother didn't remember any of it. She didn't remember 'The Talk'; she didn't remember her dire warnings; she didn't remember suggesting that getting pregnant with Lucy had ruined her life.

Lucy decided if her mother didn't remember what she had said, then maybe she didn't mean it. She ate three pancakes with butter and maple syrup and decided that breakfast was her mother's way of saying she loved her. She was walking a thin line, one that would take all the balance she had, but believing her mother loved her was too important; if she didn't believe it, she would fall into such a deep hole that she'd never make it back up.

Now standing in front of the mirror, her mother's clothes hanging off her, Lucy understands she isn't a woman at all. She may wear a napkin between her legs several days a month, but she is still a young girl. And though she loves dressing up and looking pretty, she is in no hurry to be a woman. Especially if being one too soon, means your life could be ruined.

Lucy wipes the lipstick and makeup off her face, hangs her mother's dress up and puts her jewelry back in the box. She leaves the bobby pins in, though. She likes the look.

CHAPTER 23

"You did something with your hair." Willie looks closer. "Right?"

"I guess," says Lucy. None of her girlfriends had noticed. She replaced the bobby pins with white barrettes her mother never wore.

"It looks nice."

They sit together on the ground in front of the school and open their lunch bags.

Willie wishes it were Friday, the best day of the week. On Friday, there's gym class and if the weather is good they play football. On Friday, he can luxuriate knowing he won't have school again until Monday. He can stay up and watch *Twilight Zone* with Pop. Maybe even get a pizza from Johnny's. He doesn't have to set an alarm; he can sleep as long as he wants or until Pop calls him.

Willie needs it to be Friday, a day of peaceful refuge in a week of turmoil. He got Pres to pinky-swear that he wouldn't tell anybody about what happened. So far, the promise has been kept, as far as he can tell. No one is snickering at him or staring at him, always good signs.

He lies back, resting his head on dry leaves, gazing up at the branches above, listening to babbling second graders eat their lunch with their teacher. Lucy sits cross-legged beside him, looking at a teen magazine.

"Hey, so how about my mom's new job? Cool, huh."

Willie doesn't know what's she's talking about. The last 'new job' Mrs. Hallowell had ended three weeks ago. He smiles and nods. Lucy beams.

"Has your grandfather said anything about it?"

Why would Pop tell him anything about her new job? He gets pinch-faced.

"Willie, is something wrong. You look...I don't know."

"Uh...I was thinking how nice it is that your mom is working..."

"With your grandfather," Lucy says emphatically.

Why hadn't Pop told him this? Willie heard him complaining to Mr. Ashwood about the school hiring a 'swing' person, but nothing more.

Lucy is bursting with excitement. "Yeah, she said at first he was a little reserved, but now he's pretty friendly. She likes him because he doesn't treat her different. She's just a person trying to do her job."

"That's good."

"Yeah, bosses have always been a problem for her. But not your grandfather."

Why don't I know any of this? thinks Willie.

"You remember, don't you, that your mom taught my mom in high school. I've told you this before, like, way back in kindergarten."

Willie doesn't remember much about kindergarten except he was so afraid to go that Pop had to carry him to school every day at the beginning. That's not something you want to talk about. The rest is a blur.

"My mom? My mom taught your mom? Are you sure?" Willie feels like he's playing catchup in a game he never knew existed.

"Yeah, she loved your mom. She said your mom was smart and funny, not like a real teacher, more like a person. I mean, my mom was only fifteen, and they were, like, friends."

Willie thinks, Mrs. Hallowell, who is very much alive, used to be friends with my mom when she was still very much alive. It doesn't seem possible. It was like his mom was still alive by association.

"Really?"

"My mom said sometimes your mom was the only person she could talk to."

"About what?"

"She didn't say. She did say it broke her heart when your mom died. I mean, she hadn't seen her in a while, I don't think, but still."

"Huh." He looks at Lucy and then looks away, unsure of what to say.

"I'm sorry, I shouldn't---"

"We don't talk about my mom and dad."

"Never?"

"Huh uh."

Willie wonders whether his family's way of dealing with his parents' deaths, the silence that has always seemed normal, wasn't normal at all, that, in fact, it was out of the ordinary, odd, maybe wrong.

"I ask about my dad all the time. I never get good answers, but I ask. Do you ask about your parents...sometimes?"

Willie can't remember the last time he asked Pop about his mom and dad. He was so little when they died, he didn't know what to ask or how to ask it. Denny told Willie he would call out 'Mama?' or 'Dada?' in the middle of the night. When he did, Pop would mumble and stutter and run his fingers through his hair and walk away.

He was six years old when Denny told him they died in an accident. But he refused to say more. Maybe it was a car or a plane, thought Willie. He heard about accidents on TV all the time. They were awful. He hoped his parents died quickly.

"It was an accident."

"That's terrible." Lucy catches her breath. "What kind of accident?"

"I'm not sure."

"You're not?" says Lucy, her face still puzzled.

Willie's gut knots and then twists. "Car, I think; maybe like a car accident."

"I'm so sorry, Willie." Lucy reaches for his hand and rubs his palm with her thumb. "You must miss them so much."

Do I? thinks Willie. Do I miss them? I must. What kid wouldn't miss his parents? And yet, he feels other things too, things that make him angry, things that keep him awake at night. Why did they have to die? Why did they have to go away without saying anything to me? What were they thinking? He hates these questions. He hates himself for asking them.

"Can I ask what their names were?"

"Pop called my mom Ruthie. And Dad was Cliff." Saying their names feels strange, like he'd never spoken those words before.

"I bet they were nice." says Lucy, quietly.

"I don't know."

Kids scurry into the room, sweaty and giggly from lunch break. Pres sees Lucy and Willie sitting together; Lucy removes her hand from Willie's. Pres covers his mouth and raises his eyebrows in delight.

"Dumb dope," she whispers.

"Yeah," says Willie.

Friday is not in sight. It's Wednesday again. Hammerman enters the room, wearing an arm band, and for the first time, a safety helmet. That should send me over the edge, thinks Willie.

CHAPTER 24

Hal and Trish, along with other district janitors, were enlisted to remove all the books from the high school library so they could paint the walls.

Trish Hallowell hasn't been back to Hartman High School in almost thirteen years. She remembers the building having a few more stories, its sidewalks uneven and cracked, its halls wider, its ceilings higher. There is a new entrance, all glass, framed with two pillars fifteen feet tall or more.

The kids look so young. She never felt young at Hartman. Walking the halls was like walking a gauntlet, boys leering at her, girls shunning her. While Hal checks in at the main office, she stands in the hall watching a clutch of girls, all wearing pastel skirts and fluffy sweaters, looking like parasols forming a rainbow, giggling, whispering. She wishes she was one of them; she wishes she had a do-over. "You got one chance at life, not two," her mother often said.

She has no recollection of the library, a place she rarely visited. She cut classes often, left school to go to the soda shop on the corner, smoked on the catwalk above the stage, hid in the school's dark room with whoever she wanted. It was fun until it wasn't. Her friends came and went depending on the tide of rumors that washed over her. The boys, like bees to honey, buzzed around her constantly, making promises, flattering her, cajoling her, using her, leaving her. Standing in the hall again makes her feel small, insignificant, dirty.

Two junior class boys were enlisted to help her box all the fiction. They are scrawny, pimply, smelly and every bit as inexperienced with life as the sixteen-year-old boys she'd known. They smile at her and do what she asks; they watch her every move, sometimes nudging each other. When she smiles at them, they blush.

She always felt pressure to look like the newest, shiniest, most dazzling car that ever came off the assembly line, all chrome and polish. But no matter how hard she tried to maintain the façade, the paint chipped and the shine faded, and when it was gone, there was nothing left.

"Hello, Trish." Miss Hosenfelder, a librarian now, had been Lucy's gym teacher her last year of school.

Trish forces a smile. "Hi, Miss H."

"It's been a long time, hasn't it?"

"Yes, yes it has, a very long time." She looks at the boys and points at some boxes in the corner. Miss Hosenfelder scans Trish top to bottom. Back then, she had been the first to notice.

"And how are you doing, dear?" Miss Hosenfelder's face seems to crack as she forces a grin, her glasses hanging off the tip of her nose so she can make a thorough assessment.

Trish remembers several sophomore girls were crowded into Miss H's gymnasium office, a gaggle of gleaming faces, their voices hushed, their bodies surrounding Miss H. Trish watched from the bench in front of her locker. For the third time she had come to gym wearing a baggy sweatshirt over her mandatory white blouse and shorts. She insisted to Miss H that the drafty gym was too cold, that her mother forced her to wear something warm and that this was all she had. When the bell rang, the girls scattered, but Miss H's eyes remained glued to Trish.

"Fine," says Trish, wanting to avoid Miss Hosenfelder's snaky eyes.

"I see you have a new job."

Trish wrings her hands and shifts her weight. "Yes, I do."

"You like it?"

"Yes, I like it fine. It's good for me..."

After gym class the following Monday, Miss H had asked Trish to stay behind. She found Miss H in her office, feet on the desk.

"What's going on with you?" Miss H had said.

"Nothing."

"Why do you keep wearing that sweatshirt?"

"It's cold---"

"I have one hundred fifty girls and not one of them, except for you, thinks this place is cold." The only cold thing about the gym was Miss H's icy stare.

"I guess I'm different from the other girls."

"From what I hear, yes, you *are* different from the other girls." She took a deep breath and stood, her eyebrows crowding the lines on her forehead.

Miss H reached across her desk and pulled Trish's sweatshirt up, revealing a modest bulge. Trish grabbed her sweatshirt out of Miss H's fisted hand and flattened it back into place. She opened her mouth, but Miss H lifted a finger of warning.

"What do you think you're doing? Really. When I was a girl, this would never happen. We were dignified; we were modest. We didn't throw ourselves at every boy that came into view. You'll find out what the price is. By the looks of you, you'll find out in about seven months."

Studying Miss Hosenfelder's creased face and clustered age spots, Trish is happy she has not aged gracefully. She is stooped shouldered now, perhaps from the burden of bitterness she seems to carry. She smells musty and moldy as a museum piece. Did she ever marry? Did anyone love her? Did she remember what she'd said?

"I suppose that little girl of yours is almost grown."

"Sixth grade at Wood St."

"Wow, sixth grade. She must be twelve. If memory serves, you were about fifteen. Am I right?" Miss Hosenfelder crosses her arms and looks down her nose at Trish, her eyes narrowing, a grin on her face. Trish doesn't answer. She turns and walks toward the boys, directing them to keep moving the boxes.

"Be well, Trish," Miss Hosenfelder calls.

Trish turns but she is gone. She places a hand on her stomach and reaches for the book shelves to regain her balance.

Their task complete, Hal and Trish cross the parking lot and get into Hal's car. He looks at Trish's wintery face. He starts the truck, checks the rearview mirror and shifts into reverse. "I heard you were working with Miss Hosenfelder today?" Trish doesn't move, she doesn't answer. He looks over his shoulder as he eases the car out of its parking spot. "I've known her for many years. Sold her a car back when I was at the dealership." He faces forward, steps on the gas again and leaves the lot. "Denny mentioned her often when he was in school. More often than any teacher." He slows as the traffic light turns red. His wrist wresting on top of the steering wheel, he peeks at Trish, whose head is bowed. "As far as I can tell, Miss Hosenfelder is still full of shit." The light changes and the car lurches forward. "Excuse my language." Trish raises her head, and takes a deep breath.

CHAPTER 25

"My God, it's finally happened."

"Ma---"

"You have lost your goddam mind, Robby! Your father, God rest his heartless soul, always worried you would, how did he put it, 'cross over'."

"Cross over? What?"

"You know what I'm talking about! There is a line. On one side are almost all the people in the world, people who get up and go to work, cook and eat and sleep; they talk like anybody talks; they read the paper, or if they're fancy, they read a book; they're plain and they're regular. On the other side of the line are people who don't know here from there, who laugh when there's no reason to laugh, who cry when there's no reason to cry, whose ideas are always left of center, who are lost as lost can be, but don't know it.

"I had a cousin who got up in the middle of the night and walked naked to the top of a hill and sat down. When we found him and asked him what the hell he was doing, he said 'God told me to come here and wait'. Jesus Christ, I said, why in the hell would God do that? Now, Robby, he had crossed over, no doubt about it. And once he took that step, he never came back." She closes one eye and looks at him hard with the other. "I'm telling you, you've got at least one foot on the other side. And the rest of you is just itching to follow. Who in their right mind..." Muriel, rocking as hard as she can, is breathing like a locomotive. She's shaking her head and waving her stick-like arms in every direction.

"Ma---"

"Don't 'Ma' me, Robby. Where did you get this idea? Did you get naked in the middle of the night and go up top some strip-mine where God said, 'Hey, let's do something stupid?' Is that what happened?"

Robby leans forward in his lounger, the leather squeaking like worn brake pads. Mom is back, he thinks. Mom is back in full force. He can hardly believe that recently she was tethered to a chair, raggedy clothes hanging off her back, eyes closed tight as a banker's wallet, passive as Jesus about to be mounted on the cross. He smiled to himself; her fire, he thought, it's still there.

And that's the problem. Mom's persistent, grating ire, and all the days ahead. Can I do this again? Will I end up sprawled on the floor, just like last time, clutching my chest, Ma beside me, this time dead? His goal in bringing her home is to be the son he'd always hoped to be, a success, the one that saved them both, a hero. "My God, Robby, you've turned out to be a big nothing, high school dropout working at the mill, living with his mommy and daddy," were among the last things his father said to him before he left for his final shift at the mill. His mother concurred: "Listen to what your father is saying, Robby, he's trying to help you."

Robert thinks he's no different than a lot of guys his age. Everyone got jobs at one mill or another, worked hard, paid their bills, didn't expect much from life. Some got wives and children and their very own home, but not everyone. Some lived at home, sacrificing their own well-being for the well-being of a parent. In some countries, this is considered a noble life choice, he often tells himself. He wishes he lived in one of those places.

"Son, can you hear me? I'm talking to you."

Robert gets up from his chair. He looks at his mother and then at the Philco, balanced on a nearby TV table, rabbit ears wrapped in aluminum foil. He turns down the volume on *The Guiding Light*.

He takes a breath and smiles. He rubs his forehead, thinking of what to say. He speaks slowly, calmly. "Okay, I haven't crossed the line. I'm not nuts. I have not run naked anywhere. I have not heard God tell me anything, ever.

But I do watch Cronkite. I do read the *Post-Gazette* every morning. I do listen to what the president is saying."

"You mean what the president's daddy tells him to say---"

Robert's palm goes up. "I listen to what our military is saying. And the simple fact is---Russia is arming Cuba with missiles that can travel two thousand miles." He pauses for emphasis. "Do you know how far it is from Cuba to Pittsburgh?"

"Don't be so---"

"Do you?"

"No, I do not know," she says, wagging her head.

"Twelve hundred miles."

"That's not---"

"Twelve hundred miles. Which puts us in range."

"Well...that's..."

"If I hadn't pulled you out of the home, you'd be a goner. Simple as that."

Muriel's head is bowed. She sneaks a look at her son. She still sees the little boy inside the massive cream puff that has become his face. His lids droop over sunken brown eyes, eyes that seemed sad from birth. He was a colicky baby; his father stayed away most nights because he couldn't stand the screeching. Later he stayed away because Robert was always one step behind everyone. He was held back in kindergarten, for "social reasons," which, as far as she could tell, meant he couldn't make friends. Muriel tried to double her love, encircling him with her protective affection, while hiding her disappointment. She wanted so much more for him, but it never happened. Unwilling to blame him, she blamed herself. She was the failed mother, he the innocent son.

Gradually, almost invisibly, her love, her regret, her sadness for Robert soured into displeasure and resentment, and self-loathing, which, like a razor stropped to a fine edge, slashed everything that came near, especially her only son, her only love. She always hoped Robert didn't know, that he was oblivious, that her anger was so global he might think it had little to do with him. But she knew otherwise.

She raises her head to her son. Sweat drips from his forehead, his mouth lies open, his eyes barely visible. "Can you show me this hole in the ground?"

Buoyed by this blunted show of interest, Robert straightens his back, wipes his face dry, and stands. He reaches out for both of her hands and gently steadies her as she gets to her feet. She half-smiles and squeezes one of his hands. He reaches for her cane.

"I don't like that thing. Makes me look old."

"Ma, the backyard is uneven. I almost fall every day."

She takes the plane wooden cane from his hand. Together they head to the back door; together they shuffle onto the porch and down four steps to the yard. They both stop, nearly out of breath.

"We're a goddam pair," she says.

"Look at this."

She stares at what looks like a concrete block garage (minus a peeked roof), sunk halfway into the ground. There is a hatch-like door and two pipes that look like chimneys. All around are mounds of dirt, a few shovels. It reminds her of her husband's funeral. The grave diggers waiting just barely out of sight, eager to finish their job so they could go home to their families.

She pulls a tissue from her sleeve as the dam behind her eyes, so stalwart for so long, begins to leak. She sniffs and wipes her nose.

Robert huffs quietly and tries not to look at his mother for fear of embarrassing her. He steps closer without saying a word and pulls her to his side. She leans on him as a chilly breeze arrives from the western hills. He wants to speak, he wants to tell her how glad he is to have her home, how sorry he is that it has taken so long, how happy he is she understands, that she sees what he is trying to do. For the first time in a long while, he feels full.

What in the world? thinks Muriel.

CHAPTER 26

"C'mon man, you know you're not supposed to be doing this. No women. That's the rule." Scott Prescott, the residence director, clothed only in his underwear, stands in the middle of Denny's dorm room tossing a football from one hand to the other. He smirks. "Of course, if it were up to me, I'd give you a medal. You are the talk of the dorm, man. I don't think a freshman has ever pulled this off so early in their first semester. I mean, I was in the second semester of my sophomore year before I had a girl in my room. But you, I mean, you've got this girl living with you." He shakes his head and studies Denny's face, his arms, his body. He shakes his head some more. "You don't exactly look like a lady killer, no offense, but maybe you got something going on in the groinal area."

The thought of anyone, let alone the whole dorm, talking about him behind his back, is horrifying. If there is one thing he doesn't want from his college career is attention. The first day of French class was still an open, seeping wound.

"And, the girl, well, she's no Gina Lollobrigida, being a gimp and all, but who cares, you know? When you're in bed, every girl's the same, right?" Scott Prescott winks, the kind of wink that suggests you are in the same club, you are brothers.

Denny stands, his back straight, his head high. "Get out."

"What?"

"Please get out of my room."

"Are you serious? Do you know who you're talking to? You could get into a shitload of trouble, dweeb."

"That's fine. Just get out."

Scott Prescott takes a step forward. He reaches out with his football and bounces it off Denny's forehead. "How's that?"

"Get. Out. Of. My. Room." He goes to the door and opens it, then gestures for him to leave. In the hall, Prescott turns, his lips curled, his face a snarl. Before he can speak, though, Denny says, "I know where you hide all the booze. I even know about the weed." There is a brief stare-off, before Prescott turns and retreats in stunned silence. Denny exhales from head to toe. He doesn't know anything about stashed liquor and he's never even said 'weed' before. But his bluff works. He doesn't hear another word from Prescott. Becky comes and goes as she pleases.

Denny fumes for days over one word---'gimp'. Slurring people isn't new to him. There'd been three Negroes in his senior class and he heard what some guys, even girls, called them. They tried to demean them, to erase them. Denny never talked that way, not because he was enlightened, but because if he did Pop would give him that look, that hard stare that said, 'I am disappointed in you'. There was nothing worse than that.

But Denny never gave a moment's thought to what it was like to be on the receiving end of a slur, to be the 'it', no longer a person, just a piece of nothing. Scott Prescott had been so casual about it. There wasn't any malice in his voice. To him, the word was descriptive, nothing more, a word that explained, that defined, a word spoken without thought. Sticks and stones will break my bones, but words?

There is no doubt Becky is different. Different by one-inch. In the eyes of the world, though, the difference is ten miles, maybe more.

Becky sits on the grass in front of the Union listening to a campus folk group singing some Pete Seeger. Her French book nestled in her lap, her mind wanders. She watches trees swaying and imagines they are moving on their own, independent of the wind, creating a random, graceful dance. She breathes in the smell of fresh cut grass and exhales a smile. All around her students flit and dash and dart, like balls in a pinball machine. Each the center of their own universe, they all shine their own light.

Her reverie is interrupted by someone in the distance, someone coming round the bend from Old Main, someone walking carefully, awkwardly, stumbling toward the Union in a posture of determination. Others around him part, like the sea opening for Moses, as he passes by. She squints but can't make him out. She watches this halting procession, now a football field away. The top of his head is red. It can't be, she thinks.

As Denny gets closer, she notes the odd hitch in his get-along. His arms flair out this way and that as he looks up then down, up then down, trying to stay the course. She sits up on her knees. Students are stopping now, watching, pointing, laughing. He doesn't seem to notice. As he passes nearby, Becky sees something on the bottom of his right shoe. She stands to get a better look. Is that...? she wonders.

There is a block of wood on the bottom of Denny's shoe, cut crudely to match his size nine and a half foot and held in place with reams of masking tape. There is an earnest look on his face, the look of a bemused explorer.

Becky grabs her book and runs up to Denny, catching him before he enters the Union.

"Denny!" Her voice matches the scowl on her face.

"What are you doing here?"

She grabs his arm and pulls him out of the student flow. She looks down at his foot.

"What are you doing?"

"I'm trying something."

Becky steps back, bends over, hands on her knees, as if she's completed a marathon and is about to throw up.

"Becky? You okay?"

Becky's eyes are slits, her glare intense. An expression of incredulity crosses Denny's face. He takes several steps toward her, but she steps back. The usual Indy 500 pace of students passing by slows to a buggy's tempo, as their attention is glued to the unfolding scene. Tears fill her eyes, but her lower lids, like Hoover Dam, keep them in check.

"Becky?" Denny reaches for her, but Becky steps back. "What's wrong?"

"Is that a serious question? I mean, do you not understand what you're doing?"

Denny's arm falls to his side. He looks down at his Gerry-rigged footwear. "I thought..."

"What? You thought what? That my feelings don't matter? That everything I've told you about this...this thing at the end of my leg, that everything I've told you was, was, I don't know..."

Becky turns and walks away.

Denny is dumbstruck as he watches her, his heart sinking. He looks at his foot, masking tape trailing behind his shoe, like toilet paper. The students gathered round him smirk. He wants to explain, he wants to tell them he isn't being thoughtless, and that he knows exactly what he's doing.

"Becky, wait!" She slows but doesn't stop. He tears at the tape and yanks the wood from the bottom of his shoe. He runs after her, "Becky, please."

She stops but doesn't look at him. She's heard the apologies before. He reaches for her but she pulls her arm away.

"Becky." He bends his knees and leans forward, hoping to catch her eye. "You hurt me."

He puts his hands in his pockets. His breathing feels labored, his legs weak. "I'm so sorry. I am. I'm sorry." Denny struggles for words. "I was trying to, you know, *listen to* you, like you wanted me to. I thought I could listen better if I...if I experienced what it's like to...you know."

Becky looks squarely into Denny's eyes, her face blank. Denny reaches for her hand. "No." She points at his foot, her hand shaking. "Don't ever do that again. Understand?"

Denny shakes his head.

A car horn sounds in the distance. The quad is empty now, except for a few stragglers, arms full of books, running to class.

Becky's face is still cloud-covered. "Let's get something to eat."

CHAPTER 27

Willie pours himself a cup of coffee. He adds three teaspoons of sugar and an inch of milk so he won't taste it. He sips it and breathes, "Ahh."

Pop smirks, folds the morning paper, and slides it across the table so Willie can read the sports page. "When did you start drinking coffee?"

"A while ago." Willie takes another sip and tries not to scrunch his face at the nastiness.

"Like it, do you?"

"Like it fine." He lifts the cup to his mouth but keeps his lips shut, hoping Pop won't notice he's fake-sipping.

"I guess you're growing up, huh?" Pop wobbles the table back and forth, then folds a napkin into a thick square and puts it under the short leg. He tests the table again and is satisfied.

"What are you up to this morning?"

"School stuff."

"It's Saturday."

"Yeah, but we still got to get one more leaf for our science project."

Willie can't bring himself to drink any more coffee. Pop tunes the radio dial to KDKA, so Willie gets up quietly and pours the rest down the drain. He takes the Frosted Flakes from the cupboard, fills a bowl and adds milk. He carries it back to the table, only dripping once. He wipes coffee off his spoon and digs in.

"Lucy told me her mom was working for you."

Pop turns the volume up as he listens to Rege Cordic's morning show. "Uh huh."

"She says she really likes it."

"Uh huh." The news comes on, so Pop turns the volume down.

"She knew my mom, I guess."

Pop is silent.

"She was her teacher way back."

Pop gets up and pours himself a fresh cup. "Yes, she was."

"You knew that?"

"Yes, I did."

Willie feels like he's trying to open a clam with his bare hands.

"I knew Mom was a teacher. I didn't know she taught Lucy's mother.""

It's rare for Willie to say 'Mom'. It's usually 'my mom' or 'my mother'. Pop closes his eyes and Ruthie's voice, lilting, melodic, fills him. He sees glimpses of her, a smile, a slender hand, her hair so long. She always smelled like vanilla.

"I guess not."

It is hard to believe nine years have passed, and that his grandson is twelve. His neck is long, his face narrow, all the baby fat gone. His arms aren't sticks anymore and his legs pump hard as pistons when he runs. He's whip smart. And kind. Like his mother.

"We don't talk about Mom that much, do we? Or Dad?"

"It was a long time ago."

Pop's neck feels like his shirt collar is two sizes too small. He turns off the radio.

"Your mom, she had a hard time birthing you. Your brother came easy, but you were a different matter. Problem was you weren't in the right position to come out, so the doctor had to kind of reach inside and turn you. That way you'd come out head first, which is better.

"Your father paced around the waiting room like a caged animal, he was so worried something would go wrong. Grandma Mae was with your mom. She rubbed her back and her legs. She sang little songs to distract her from the pain. And when your mom had to push you out, your grandma got in the bed behind her and made grunting sounds like she was birthing you, too." Pop chuckles though his eyes look sad. "The doctor laid you on your mom's chest. Your grandma said she cried and cried and laughed and laughed. She held you up in front of her face and you looked at her, eyes steady, like you had a secret, like somehow you knew your mom from before. Like you were old friends. She was happy. So was your dad. He cuddled you in the rocker. Everybody was happy."

Pop and Willie look at each other, faint grins puckering their mouths.

He reaches for the newspaper again, opens the sports page, then lays it in his lap. "That was your mom. She loved you right then, and never stopped loving you." Pop thinks for a moment. "Your dad, too. Their love never went away. Their love for you, at least." The paper goes up in front of Pop's face, like a curtain, or a shroud.

Willie is still. He looks at his grandfather's quivering hands crinkling the paper. Willie isn't hungry now. He dumps the remaining cereal into the sink and runs some water. He wants to say something. He wants to thank Pop for telling him this story. He also wants to thank Pop for giving him a home when no one was left; he wants to thank him for never changing, for always being there. He wants to throw his arms around Pop's neck and hold on.

"I'm gonna go now, Pop."

"Okay, just be careful."

The trees are nearly bare. The ground is covered with brown-tipped leftover leaves. The gingko is the crown jewel they are looking for. If they don't find it, their grade will automatically be lowered from an 'A' to a 'C'. "How much does this really matter?" says Pres. "Do I care? Not really." But both Willie and Lucy have a streak of 'A's going back to first grade that they don't want to break. "Look for a leaf that looks like little fan," their teacher had said.

A light rain had fallen overnight, creating a morning fog. The river, rejuvenated by the storm, roars at the bottom of the hill. All three wear jeans and boots and double sweatshirts. Lucy and Willie walk together. Preston lags behind, talking to himself and kicking tree stumps.

Willie side-eyes Lucy; something is different; her hair? her nose? He can't tell, so he looks away, blinks a few times and then looks at her again, this time with fresh eyes. And then he sees. It's her jaw line, that's what it is, no longer soft and rounded, but straight and firm; it lifts her smile, lengthens her neck, and gives her face a look of confidence and even...beauty.

"What do you think?"

"About what?" Lucy picks up a long stick, breaks off one end, and holds it in her fist, tapping the ground as she walks along.

"The Cuba thing."

"I stopped thinking about it."

"What do you mean?"

"What I said---I don't think about it."

"How's that possible?"

"It's like, my mom has been happy for almost two weeks." She stops and holds up two fingers. "Do you know the last time she was happy for two weeks? One week?" A half smile crosses her face. "Not in my lifetime, she hasn't. Yesterday she came home with a stack of new 45s and we danced for, like a half hour, *He's a Rebel, Loco-Motion*, everything." Lucy flips her hair behind her ears. "I wake up every morning, wondering which mother will be sitting at the table when I go downstairs for breakfast. And for two whole weeks, it's been a new mother, one I've never seen before." She swats a tree with her stick. "So, Cuba? I'm like Alfred E. Newman ---'What, me worry?'"

Willie wants to say, But all of that could disappear. All your happiness, gone in an instant. Poof! You could disappear. Your mom could disappear. All of us could disappear. These trees and that river down there could be sucked into a nuclear cloud. Everything. And there's nothing we can do about it. He takes a deep breath, ready to speak, but just as he is about to open his mouth, she speaks again.

"And you know what?" says Lucy.

"What?"

"Your grandfather is one of the reasons she's so happy. At least that's what I think."

Willie exhales, his balloon of doom burst, his curiosity peaked.

"You're kidding, right?"

"Surprising, I know. Your Pop has always seemed kind of, I don't know, don't take this the wrong way, hard isn't the right word, but...well, hard, I guess. He says 'hi' once in a while, but I don't think I've ever seen him smile. He's kind of gloomy, don't you think?"

"I've seen him smile."

"No, I'm sure. He's so good to you. Like, the best." She nods rapidly in agreement. "I'm just saying, I don't get to see what you see." She pauses, gathering her thoughts. "Anyway. My mother says he's kinda funny; he's thoughtful; he's teaching her things; he took her out to lunch; they did some big something at the high school; and he helps her with stuff."

"What stuff?"

"He helped her get a car for almost nothing. I mean, it's like a thousand years old, but it's a car and it runs." She tilts her head, and a soft smile, like a swipe of chalk, crosses on her face.

"And they talk about your mom." Lucy stops again and takes hold of his arm. She explains that they were more than teacher and student; they were friends. "Yeah, isn't that kind of crazy when you think about it. I mean, crazy in a good way. Like unbelievable that they were friends and you and I are friends. I don't know, it's just neat."

"Yeah, neat," murmurs Willie. It's hard for him to appreciate the neatness when something so basic is missing---his mother. What's so neat about everyone but him knowing her?

"Did your mom say anything else?"

"Like?"

"Well, like, did she say anything about how my mother died?"

Willie's eyes look deep and dark, like someone has taken their thumbs and pushed them back so far that no one can read them.

"What you said, an accident."

"Did she say what kind?"

"She told me the details were a 'private matter'. I don't really know what that means." She shrugs. "Do you?"

"No. I don't know what anything means."

"C'mon you guys!"

They both turn. Pres is waving wildly at them, three gingko leaves in his hand.

CHAPTER 28
1953

Cliff eased the car through the park entrance, drove past the empty shelters, the basketball court, the public pool that was being cleaned, and arrived at the far end of the park where the river trail began. The late September air was brisk, like melting ice against their skin. A weak sun glowed through pale clouds. They looked up at the hulking trees; the white, black and red oaks; the sugar, silver, and Norway maples; the tulips, chestnuts, hickory and the occasional gingko; gold, red, rust and orange leaves everywhere.

"Look, Willie, look at all the leaves on the ground," said Cliff. He kneeled and pointed at a leaf. "What color is this one? Do you remember?"

Willie kneeled beside his father. "Wed," he said.

"That's right. Good boy."

Ruthie leashed Smoochy, who stretched it to the limit, stood on his hind legs, and barked at Willie. Cliff waved Ruthie to come. She grabbed the picnic basket with a free hand.

"Watch this. Willie, what color is this leaf?"

Willie studied the leaf for a moment. "'ellow."

"That's right," said Cliff. He turned to Ruthie. "When I get to see him, we've been working on colors."

"Great," she said grudgingly then turned her attention to Willie. "Hey buddy, that's fantastic."

As they walked down the path, they could hear the whoosh of the river in the distance. Squirrels, their mouths full of nuts, skittered to the nearest burrows. Squawking crows circled above. The air smelled of damp moss, rotting tree stumps and curled, crunchy leaves. The earth was rich and dark as chocolate syrup. Across the river, the steep hillside was lined at the top with small houses, each one the same as the next, built by the tube mill that loomed behind them.

Smoochy leaped over a tree that had fallen across the path. Willie followed, grunting as he grabbed the tree's bark and tried to pull himself up. His mother gently pushed his behind. He stood atop the tree. "Me, me, me!" Mama and Dada clapped. He slid down the other side and ran after Smoochy.

He stopped and pointed at the massive rocks buried in the hillside, dark openings inviting any passer-by. "Up, up!" called Willie.

"Not today, buddy; we're going this way." Ruthie pointed to a narrower, steeper path that led directly to the riverside. Cliff hoisted Willie onto his shoulders and stepped carefully onto the slick path, avoiding tree stumps and muddy patches as best he could.

The river was white with foam; churlish waves swept over hidden boulders. Massive slabs of granite covered the shore like so many beached whales. Rock formations, like smokestacks, rose into the air. The sound of water rushing, the constancy of it, the never-ending movement was hypnotic.

"Bare ass beach," Cliff whispered to himself. He put Willie down. He stood on a long, slanted rock with a smooth surface where generations of kids had come to sunbathe, among other things. He smiled. Beside the rock was tiny beach, no longer than fifteen feet.

"Don't get too close," called Ruthie as Smoochy yanked her forward. "Smoochy, ease up." Smoochy, up on her hind legs, howled and whimpered until Willie looked her way. Willie slid from his father's hand and ran across the rock to Smoochy. "Willie, be careful." Ruthie glared at her husband who was still standing on the edge of the rock, hands on his hips, staring at the water.

"Wish Denny was here," said Cliff.

"You know how he loves my father. A day at the lumber yard was too good to pass."

Cliff frowned. "I guess."

Ruthie sat Willie beside her as she opened the basket. Willie took one end of the checkered blanket while his mom took the other. Willie screamed with delight when it billowed like a parachute. He helped his father find four rocks to hold the blanket in place.

Ruthie had packed leftover fried chicken, potato salad, bottles of Verner's ginger ale and a bag of chocolate chip cookies from Straw's Bakery. Willie reached for the cookies. "Hey, you!" Ruthie pretended to be shocked and Willie giggled. She gave him half a cookie. Willie shoved the whole thing in his mouth and chewed voraciously, leaving only one chocolate chip on his cheek. "You and Smoochy sit here, okay, far away from the water. Don't move."

"He's fine. Don't be a mother hen." Cliff unleashed Smoochy who'd fallen asleep. "Let's just enjoy ourselves, okay?" He etched a line on the rock. "Willie, don't go past that line and you'll be fine."

Willie walked to the line and pointed. "Yine, Mama," he said and shook his head no.

"Come back here, honey." Willie scampered across the rock and grabbed his mother's leg. "That's a good boy."

Willie plopped down beside Smoochy, who was stirring, and kissed her. "I yove you," he said.

Cliff touched Ruthie's shoulder and nodded toward their son. She grinned and leaned over to pat Willie's head.

"The boys, best thing we've ever done," said Cliff.

"Yes." Her grin was gone.

CHAPTER 29

Denny watches Becky, warily, as she sits at his desk reading *The Scarlet Letter* for AmerLit. They have fallen into a silent truce since Denny's foolhardy act. To anyone else, Becky would appear unphased by what had occurred. But Denny sees something else, how her eyes rarely meet his. He wonders if he is now on the long list of people who have broken her trust. His repeated apologies are merely noise at this point. To his knowledge, she is the first person he has ever hurt, which is not to say he's never angered friends or said things he regrets. But this is different. It's like he pried her open, revealing her most tender parts, and then put on his winter galoshes and tramped around inside her, indifferent to her vulnerability, her pain. He feels guilt down to his toes.

On top of this is Pop's note. The more he's gotten into college life, the more he has spent time with Becky, the more he's spread his wings, the less he's felt the gnawing ache that has been his faithful companion for years. But getting the note from Pop brought it all back. What to do? Pop is asking for help. Unprecedented. He's stuck. Denny hasn't yet written a return letter.

He yanks the pillow from his bed and stuffs it behind his back as he leans against the wall. Becky hasn't looked up from the book in an hour, maybe more. His books are closed and stacked on the floor, work completed. He clears his throat, hoping she will glance his way. She doesn't. "I'll be back," he says. She grunts.

He leaves the room and walks slowly up and down the hall for ten minutes. He checks the shower room where a breeze blows through an open window. He rests his arms on the sill and watches guys and girls leaving their respective dorms, heading for the lake, where blankets are strewn on the lawn. It seems like a year since he spied the couple doing things behind the amphitheater that he didn't understand. How things have changed.

He walks slowly back down the hall, unsure whether he should return to his room. He hesitates at the door and then enters. Becky sighs heavily and slams the book closed. Her face is red; fury is in her eyes. *I wasn't here, but I'm sure I did something wrong*, thinks Denny.

"Damn Hawthorne!"

"Okay..."

"I mean, yes, it's a radical book for its time, but in the end it's one more story about a woman bearing all the guilt and shame, and protecting the guy."

"I thought Dimmesdale finally admits---"

"Right before he dies! She suffers for their adultery, actually their love, all her life, while he hides! He fesses up just as he's about to exit. 'So sorry, now I have to go'."

"Didn't Professor Stagg say he had some inner guilt or shame or something?" She glares at him. "I mean, I think that's what he said, but what does he know?"

"Hester wears the scarlet 'A'. It's there for everyone to see. There's no way she can hide it." Finally, she looks directly at Denny, her eyes narrow, her eyebrows pointed like spears. "All eyes are on her; and they are judging her; telling her she's sinful, bad, and will never be good enough. How else is she supposed to feel but ashamed? For her, shame is everywhere." As Becky stands, she leans on her short leg and folds her arms. "Do you understand, Denny?"

He doesn't. "Yes. I do."

Becky unfolds her arms. "I know you've been trying, trying hard, trying the way someone who wants to understand would try. Wanting not only to be empathic, but to be seen as empathic, seen as someone who gets it." Becky touches her forehead with her hand, as if feeling for the right words. "We've known each other for what, five maybe six weeks? I've been trying to understand myself for eighteen years and I haven't gotten there yet. There's no shortcut, no 'experiment' that will get you there. There's no final piece to the puzzle; trust me, the pieces are endless. Can you handle that?"

Denny feels his body shrink a little, his arms go limp, his eyes close to half mast. He looks past Becky to the wall. She is right. There is no final piece to her puzzle. Nor his. He has no outer mark, no physical sign, no scarlet letter for others to see, for others to pity, or misunderstand. His scars are under the skin, close to the heart. Neither he nor Becky can understand the whole of each other, the complete picture, because it doesn't exist. The best they can do is share their incomplete pictures, acknowledge their lack of understanding, and watch for the puzzle pieces as they come.

He understands. "Yes...yes, I can handle that."

"That's my hope." Becky takes Denny's hand in both of hers. She stands on tiptoes and kisses his cheek. Denny feels shaken. Can he live up to his words? Can he do what needs to be done, whatever that may be?

Becky returns to her work. Denny lies on his bed, hands folded behind his head. He looks at the ceiling light, its dull glow filling the room. He closes his eyes and thinks about what Becky said. Can he be patient enough to let the pieces reveal themselves in their own time?

And what of his own family's scattered pieces? Will they reveal themselves? Will the rest be found? Will anyone ever put them together?

He remembers the day his parents died. He had gone with Pop to the lumber yard to buy paneling for a home project of some sort, nails and a new hammer, too. Why is this so clear? Pop talked to the owner, Zack, while Denny roamed the yard, breathing in the smell of pine, watching men on forklifts load wood onto a tractor trailer. Then Pop called him, his voice sharp and jagged as a saw blade. Denny ran back fast. Pop sped home, horn blaring. Denny held the arm rest with both hands, he was so frightened. Everything else an agonizing blur. He's certain someone told him his parents were dead. Was it Grandma Mae? But the whole story was never told. How did they die? What actually happened to them?

It's a Pandora's box, thinks Denny. And Pop is sitting on the lid.

The trip home is a week away. Will he be able to help Willie overcome his fear of being consumed by a mushroom cloud? Will he be able to overcome his own fear of being consumed by a different, perhaps darker, cloud?

Denny opens his eyes. "Becky?"

She turns in her chair. "Uh huh."

"We're leaving in about a week. Are you still planning to come with me? I mean, after everything."

Becky gets up from her chair, kneels on the floor beside Denny and kisses him lightly on the forehead. "Sure."

CHAPTER 30

Trish leans on her broom and watches Hal, pushing a barrel of garbage down the hall toward her. His sleeves are rolled up and his sinewy arms are flexed. He looks back and forth, checking each room for stray waste paper, toppled desks, and deep scuffs. The round toes of his work boots peek out from under his cuffed denims. He has the face of an old lion.

She feels her forehead and neck unclench, her shoulders sag into comfort, as she watches him. She finds being near him a comfort.

Hal stops at 211 and knocks on the door. When no one answers, he enters, then returns with a wastebasket full to the brim. He dumps it into his barrel.

Hal often sits at his desk, looking at his pictures of Mae and Ruthie, Denny and Willie, while Trish pretends to work. The picture of Ruthie is exactly as Trish remembers her---broad, careless smile, hair blown by the wind, back and legs perfectly straight, longish nose, narrow, bright eyes. She's standing on the front steps of their house in North Side. Her head is tilted slightly, as if she is looking at something far off, perhaps the future, forever delayed.

Hal enters another classroom and then another. Students are gone and the four o'clock sun inches slowly down the hall with him.

Over lunch recently, as Trish studied Hal's pictures and they ate their peanut butter sandwiches and potato chips, and drank the Cokes Hal had brought back from Scanlon's, she said, "You know, Hal, you know, I was thinking."

Hal chewed, swallowed and said, "Uh huh."

"I don't know if I should bring this up..." She hesitated, hoping he would say, 'Go ahead', but his mouth was full again. He raised his Fanta and gulped while she watched his Adam's apple bob.

Hal wiped his mouth. "Yeah."

"Looking at your pictures brought something to mind, something I've been thinking about. And it's, well, it's...you know, isn't it a little amazing how your Ruthie and me were pregnant at the same time; how we got to know each other and how our babies, Lucy and Willie, they grew up together and are best friends today; and how you and me are sitting here, you know, friends, too. It all kind of fits together, don't you think? It's just...well, I was thinking, I'll bet Ruthie would be pleased." She smiled at Hal and waited.

Hal had been startled by Trish's question. He'd looked at Trish and her bright expectant smile. He wanted to believe her, he wanted to believe that somewhere, somehow, Ruthie was watching and that she was pleased. He wanted it more than anything.

But Hal felt certain Ruthie, rather than being pleased from afar, would have wanted desperately to be here in person, alive, able to hold her sons every day, able to show them her love.

That being impossible, who's to say whether she'd be pleased? Or whether she'd still be grieving, still heartbroken over leaving far too soon?

A sad smile had crossed his face. "Yes, I'm sure she'd be pleased."

When their talk was over, Trish felt different, like everything she'd endured over the years had meaning---the deaths, the births, the overlapping histories---and that going through it all, despite the pain, had made her better, stronger. At least that's what she hoped.

Hal comes out of yet another room; they wave to each other. He picks up the pace, and pushes the barrel hard, making it glide on down the hall ahead of him. They laugh. He walks a little faster to catch up.

Something is different about him, she thinks, but she can't put her finger on it. She watches him intently as he gets closer and closer. Then she sees it. He's not limping. His stride is normal again.

· · ·

Willie chases Smooch across the field, Hal watching, enjoying his grandson. Willie throws Smoochy's ball in Pop's direction. They run toward him, Willie laughing, Smoochy barking.

"You're getting faster than Smooch," says Pop. "I never thought that day would come."

"Well, what can I say?"

As they walk home, Willie spies Mr. Ashwood and his mother coming out onto their front porch. He's not sure he wants to face the Ashwoods and more talk about the bomb shelter. It's finally complete, stocked with can goods and batteries and flashlights and everything Mr. Ashwood thinks he'll need to survive an attack by the Russians.

His backyard is now an imposing mound, like the Indian burial mounds Willie learned about in social studies. Some tribes filled their mounds with utensils and colorful pottery and carved pipes, stone knives and copper axes, as if the afterlife was no different than the life they'd lived, only in a different, a better place. Willie's pretty sure Pop believes in an afterlife; that's why he talks to Grandma Mae, sometimes right out loud. He thinks she's still out there, a living spirit, watching over the family. Willie wonders if people believe in an afterlife because they can't stomach the idea of life just ending, full stop, like a car crashing into a brick wall.

Willie doesn't know what to think about the afterlife. He's talked about it with Lucy and Preston, who both believe. Preston is Catholic so there are all kinds of sins that could land you in hell. It's quite complicated for Catholics to get into heaven, he'd explained; even good people don't get a direct flight. Everyone has a layover in Purgatory, hoping loved ones will pray them out of their captivity. On the other hand, Lucy believes there's a place where everyone goes, a place where you reconnect with loved ones and everyone is happy. This is much simpler than the Catholics. This is the one Willie would choose, if there were options.

Willie worries there won't be a happy ending to Ashwood's burial mound, that, despite all hope, there will be no life thereafter.

Ashwood is standing in his front yard clapping his hands and making kissing noises, hoping to get Smoochy's attention. Smooch whimpers and tugs as Willie holds onto the leash with both hands.

"You can let her go," says Pop.

Willie looks at Pop, consternation in his eyes. "You sure?"

"Yeah, I'm sure."

"But---"

"But what?"

"Will he be safe?"

"Yes, he'll be safe."

Reluctantly, Willie lets go of the leash and Smooch hightails it toward Ashwood's front yard, his leash flapping in the breeze. Mr. Ashwood slowly kneels on one knee, then the other. Smooch slouches the last few feet, his tail wagging rapidly. Ashwood holds his hand out for Smooch to smell. Having passed the smell test, Smoochy rolls over on her back, her tongue hanging sideways, while Mr. Ashwood scratches her belly.

"Are you one of Ruthie's boys?" calls Mrs. Ashwood.

Unsure what to do, Willie ignores her. Maybe she'll give up before she gets started.

"Hey!"

Mr. Ashwood looks at his mother, grim-faced. "I'm talking with Hal. What is it, Ma?"

"That boy right there with the red hair, is he one of Ruthie's boys?" Then she points at Willie like she is selecting a pork loin at the butcher shop. "You can see me, can't you boy?"

Pop clears his throat and pastes a smile on his face. "Hi there Mrs. Ashwood. It's me, Hal Mitchum."

"I know who you are, but I'm not sure who he is." She's pointing again. "Is he one of Ruthie's boys?"

"Yes, he is," says Pop.

"Which one?"

"It's Willie, the younger one."

"My God, you have grown like a damn weed." She chuckles as if satisfied with her discovery. "That mother of yours, I'll tell you, the sweetest person in the world and I wouldn't lie about someone's sweetness."

Pop nudges Willie. "Thank you."

"I can't hear you boy, speak up."

"Thank you!" his voice is as shrill as the fanbelt on Pop's truck.

"It's been a long time since I seen you; long time since I seen your mother and father, and the other boy, too, what's his name?"

Pop puts his arm around Willie's shoulder. "That would be Denny, Muriel; he's the older one."

"Ma, maybe you should go inside; you might get a chill."

Muriel looks at Pop. "Can you feature that---my Robby telling me what to do on my very own property."

"Ma..."

She turns her attention to Willie, who is shuffling his feet and trying to hide behind Pop. "I'll bet your parents are very proud of you, young man."

"Thank you?" Willie still has the jitters. As far as he can recall, he's never met the woman before. But there is something about the way she talks; Mom and Dad "are" proud of you, not "were" proud of you, like his parents are still alive, and we're still living together down the street and Mom is busy at school and Dad is considering a job at Pop's dealership and everything is so normal it's almost boring. Move along folks, there's nothing unusual to see here. Wouldn't that be something? thinks Willie.

"And how's your beautiful wife, Mr. Mitchum."

"Mom, don't---"

"Don't 'don't' me, Robby. I'm being neighborly and that includes asking about family."

No one has asked about Mae in a long time. Except, that is, Pop himself. She is the kite and he holds the string; she's far aloft now, above the trees, the clouds, beyond the moon and all the stars, so far that Pop doesn't know if he's holding onto anything anymore. And yet he holds on.

The night before she died, Mae lingered longer than usual in her bath, a source of calm and solace. He left the light on, though, not wanting to fall asleep until she'd joined him, until they'd hugged and kissed and said 'I love you'. When she finally came to bed, she sat on the edge for a long moment.

Hal asked, "Are you okay?"

To which Mae said, "Just so tired."

Hal awoke with a start in the dead of night and looked at his clock; it was three o'clock. Mae was unsettled; her legs were moving like she was pedaling a bicycle. He nudged her. "Mae?" She stopped and her breathing fell back into a familiar rhythm. He put his hand on her side and kept it there while he fell back to sleep.

With the deaths of Ruthie and Cliff a few months earlier, Mae seemed exhausted every minute of every day. Usually talkative, she didn't speak for long periods and, when she did, she'd stop mid-sentence, like a train that had reached the end of the tracks. Hal thought, Give her time; more than anything, that's what she needs.

He awoke the next morning before Mae, tiptoed down the stairs and brewed some coffee. He cut her a slice of whole wheat, then toasted and buttered it; he got a fancy tray from the hutch, added a linen napkin, a dish filled with strawberry preserves to sweeten her toast and some sugar to sweeten her coffee. When he got to the bedroom, she was still on her side, facing the window. In a low, whispery voice, he said, "Wake up, sleepy head." She didn't budge, so he went around the bed to her side, laid the tray on the dresser and kneeled down beside her. Her eyes had as much life as two of Willie's marbles; her skin was ghostly and when he touched her cheek it was cold as stone. Still, he called to her and shook her gently at first, but then insistently, as if she had not yet left the room and might be coaxed back to life.

Muriel narrowed her gaze on Robby while asking again, "How's Mae?"

Willie watched Pop intently, wondering what he would say.

"She's gone, Muriel."

"Gone where?"

"Away forever."

"Dead? Why didn't you tell me, Robby? She was such a delight, such a good soul. Did this just happen? I'm so sorry I missed it."

"It's been a little over eight years."

"That can't be true! I've been here all that time---"

"Ma, remember you were away, you were in the home for a long while. Hal, I'm sorry. Sometimes she gets like this."

Muriel could not be deterred. "What happened?" Willie's ears perked.

Hal speaks as if no one is there. "She died in her sleep. She'd been a little tired, but she seemed fine when she came to bed. In the morning, I was up first and I decided to let her sleep. After a while, I went back up and called to her, but she didn't answer. When I saw her face, I knew."

To this day, Hal wonders how this could have happened on his watch, how he could have missed her leave-taking. But he did, and she is gone. So sudden, so permanent. No goodbye.

It was clear to him Mae's death began the day Ruthie slipped away. She had a good heart, but not a strong one.

"It was her heart," says Pop. "Weak since she was a child. It just couldn't keep going, no matter how much she wanted it to."

Willie's heart breaks for his grandfather, whose arms hang limp as a little boy's.

"Well, I'm so sorry for your loss, but that's definitely the way to go; cash out while you're asleep. None of that slow, dragged out dying. I can only hope I go the same way." She looks at Robby, who sits on the steps, his beefy shoulders overwhelming his tiny head. "Did you hear me, Robby?"

"Nothing I can do about that, Ma."

Muriel cackled with laughter so loud it sounded like a smack in the face.

Willie grabs his grandfather's arm. "Should we be going, Pop?" Pop's face looks like crumpled newspaper, dark lines on a pale background. "Pop?"

Pop startles, looks at Willie and then at the Ashwoods. He takes a hard, deep breath and lets it out through his nose. Robby can tell his mother is about to speak again. "Shush," he says.

"Let's go, Pop."

Pop squeezes the back of Willie's neck gently. "Yeah. We should...getting close to dinner..."

Willie steps on Smoochy's leash preventing her from chasing an errant leaf. "C'mon girl."

Robby stands and reaches for Pop's hand. "I'm sorry about this, I never---"

"No need to apologize," says Pop as he takes Ashwood's hand in his.

Willie and Pop are quiet as they walk down the block to their house, Smoochy yanking her leash the whole way. Willie wants to say something; he wants to ask Pop for more. He wants to ask about his mother and father, what actually happened to them. But Pop's face, its dark eyes, jutting chin, and reddened cheeks tell him not to.

They eat their beans and franks and corn bread in silence. They skip Cronkite. Pop opens a beer and sits in his chair, newspaper hiding his face. Willie pretends to do his homework.

Once in bed, Willie thinks about his Grandma Mae. She died in the room right beside him. Perhaps her bed was against his wall, nearest his bed. What is it like to die? he thinks. Once someone dies, do they know they've died? Was she in the middle of a dream and then suddenly the lights went out and the show was over, like when a movie reel snaps at the Majestic Theater and all that's left is darkness? He pulls his covers up and calls for Smoochy, who curls up at the bottom of his bed.

A third empty beer can sits on the end table beside Pop's chair. He opens a fourth, leans back, puts his feet on the ottoman and watches as the TV picture dissolves into a single dot and then is gone. He wasn't going to say anything when Muriel asked. Before he could stop himself, though, words came. It had been years since he'd talked to anyone about what happened that final night, although he thought about it every day. It was different, having to put it all together again so it made sense to anyone who listened. As he feared, it brought her death back to life, the words like a scalpel uncovering the lingering disease below.

CHAPTER 31

Trish Hallowell, still in her nightgown, leans on the kitchen table, cold coffee in her cup and a cigarette dangling from the corner of her mouth. She studies the *Daily Ledger* for jobs, circling one after another. Waitress, baby-sitter, secretary, office manager, nurse, teacher, cleaning lady, crane operator. She is qualified for all the jobs that don't pay enough to live, and not qualified for the jobs that do. Why she never finished school, why she never planned for the future, why she wasn't more careful along the way, these are the questions gnawing at her.

Since noticing Hal's knee was better, she's been holding her breath, hoping the ax wouldn't fall.

"It's hard to tell," said Hal. "You're a terrific worker, that should count for something." 'That should count for something' seems like a thin thread to hold on to.

She doesn't want to tell Lucy any of this. She wants to protect her, especially since she has been happier in recent days. Lucy smiles for no apparent reason; she laughs like she doesn't have a care in the world, like her only job is to be twelve.

She drops her cigarette into her cup of coffee and listens to it sizzle. She reaches for her pack of Virginia Slims, shaking her head derisively at their trademark slogan---"You've come a long way, baby." Her pack should read, You've come an inch or so, baby. She lights up again and blows blue smoke into the air.

Lucy floats down the stairs from her bedroom, happy it's Sunday. Earlier in the week they had talked about going to Mena's for lunch today. She can almost smell hotdogs on the grill, chili in the pot. She takes a deep breath and lets it out slowly, savoring the moment.

As she turns the corner at the bottom of the stairs and looks into the kitchen, she sees her mother, a circle of smoke hovering over her; she has bed head and is wearing her faded pink night gown. There is a newspaper sprawled across the table.

Lucy's smile wanes; her arms and legs feel heavy and her feet feel flat. She doesn't want to go into the kitchen. She doesn't want to ask her mom what she's doing for fear of the answer. Maybe if she stays away, if she goes back up the stairs and comes down again, maybe everything will be okay, maybe her mom will be dressed and smiling and standing over a griddle of pancakes, maybe saying 'Good morning' in a sing-song voice.

"You're up finally."

"Yeah."

"There's Rice Krispies in the pantry and I think we still have some milk." She remains glued to the want ads, circling, circling.

Lucy takes a bowl from the cupboard and fills it half full with cereal.

"What are you doing?"

"Nothing that concerns you."

Lucy opens the carton of milk and smells the contents. She pours it on her Rice Krispies. The 'snap, crackle and pop' sound more like 'oh, no, stop'. She sprinkles a heaping spoonful of sugar onto the cereal, looks at her mother, then adds another.

There is nothing worse than facing Lucy with another failure, another job loss, another dead end, thinks Trish.

"Just thinking about getting a better job. You know, so we can have a better life."

"What happened to the job you got?"

"What makes you think something happened to my job? It's fine. Nothing for you to worry about." She turns in her chair, draws on her cigarette and blows smoke again. "This is normal, I'm telling you. Successful people are always looking for new opportunities."

She feels her daughter's piercing eyes, but doesn't look up.

Lucy thinks, The really successful people don't sit in their kitchen scanning the want ads every month; they get something and they keep it. She looks at her mother. All she can feel is sad. And afraid.

"We aren't going to Mena's, are we?"

"What?"

"Mena's?"

"I don't think so, honey."

Lucy picks up her bowl of cereal and goes back to her room. Unable to eat, she dumps the cereal into the toilet, gets dressed and heads out the door without a word.

Trish hears the door slam shut. She holds her head in one hand and rubs her face with the other.

. . .

"No, Pop hasn't said anything about your mom." Willie pulls his sweatshirt on as he and Lucy head down the street to Scanlon's Service Station to get some cherry Fantas. "Why, what's wrong?"

"Nothing."

"I can tell it's not 'nothing'."

Lucy kicks a stone. "She's looking at want ads again."

"Really?" Willie picks some bark off a sycamore and throws it at a parked car.

"Yeah, really."

"Well...maybe she's just interested in seeing what's out there."

"That's what she says."

"Okay."

"But I don't believe her."

"Why's that?"

"Your Pop, how's his knee, is he limping anymore?"

"What?"

"Your Pop's knee, is it better."

"I guess so."

Lucy curls the corner of her mouth. "If he's better, she's out of a job."

Willie doesn't know what to say. They pass under the Texaco sign at Scanlon's and drop dimes into the pop machine. They sit on the island between the pumps and watch the traffic go by. A Buick pulls up to the stop sign. Lucy notices the car behind it; at first she's not sure, but then the driver looks at her. It's him, the man in the suit. She nudges Willie just as Pres jumps out of his car and heads their way.

"I saw that man," says Lucy.

"What man?"

"You know, the man I've been telling you about."

Pres sits down between them. "Hi guys," he says with a sigh.

"How's it going?" says Willie.

Lucy looks again, but the car is gone.

"I don't know," says Pres.

"Coming back from seeing your dad?"

"Yeah." Pres takes out his pocket knife and digs at the dirt between the cracks.

"Any news?" says Willie.

"No, nothing, zip."

"Sorry, man," says Willie.

"Awful," says Lucy.

"It's like he doesn't even know who we are." Lucy and Willie shake their heads. "I mean, he says my name and everything, but it's like I could be anyone. He's very, like, excitable, like he's waiting for orders to go back to the front. He calls his doctor, 'General, sir'."

Lucy says, "What's your mom think?"

"She cries a lot. She doesn't think I know, but I hear her every night. When I'm around, she smiles all the time, like her smile is glued onto her face." Pres jabs the sole of his sneaker with his knife. "This is different than the other times. He just seemed sad and nervous back then. This time, he, well, he's crazy, that's the only word for it."

"I'm so sorry," says Lucy.

"He's gonna bounce back, man," says Willie, not believing a word he's saying.

"I don't know. I don't know anything about anything anymore."

Willie buys Pres a Fanta. "Here you go, man."

"When do you go back again?" says Lucy.

"We go once during the week and then on the weekend; who knows if it matters."

"I'm sure it does," says Lucy.

"I don't know if I can do it anymore."

Not knowing what else to say, they drink of their Fantas. The wind picks up, and the Texaco star atop the white pole sways. Pres steps on the rubber tubing in front of the pumps and the service bell rings. He jumps on it over and over, a crisp ding-a-ling filling the air. He removes a gas pump from its cradle and pretends to spurt it onto his head. Lucy glances at Willie, who shrugs. They put their hands in their pockets and squeeze their knees together for warmth.

"We are a sorry lot," says Pres as he slumps to the ground beside them.

"How's that?" says Lucy.

"Willie's parents are dead, your mom can't keep a job, and my dad's nuts."

They all laugh in that way adults laugh when something isn't funny. Willie rocks back and forth; Lucy's turns her feet in, then out, in, then out; Pres opens and closes his pocket knife repeatedly. A semi rolls up to the stop sign. They all chug their arms up and down; the driver nods and blows his horn long and loud. They wave their thanks and then go back to their various squirms and fidgets.

Willie finally breaks the silence. "Guess what? Mr. Ashwood's bomb shelter is all done."

"You're kidding," says Lucy.

"No, I've seen it. I mean, all you can see is this giant mound of dirt, but underneath it there's a room with all kinds of food and water and stuff."

"Bathroom?" says Lucy.

"Let's just say, you'd have to go like a cat."

"My God."

"I thought my dad was loco but old man Ashwood is nuttier than a bag of Planters. Everyone calls his bomb shelter the ash-hole."

"No!" says Lucy.

"Honest to God," says Pres, crossing his heart with his pointer.

"Ash-hole. That is too funny."

Willie doesn't laugh. He doesn't seem to hear them.

"What's with you?" says Pres.

"I've talked to him. I don't think he's crazy."

"For real?" says Pres. "I don't know---"

"He's given a lot of thought to this thing. He just wants to be prepared. No one knows what's gonna happen. He doesn't want to wake up some morning to a blinding flash of light and think, 'Gee, I wish I woulda built that shelter'." He looks at his friends, their mouths hanging open. "It's not stupid or crazy. If you watch the news, you know what I'm talking about. Everyone's gonna need some kind of shelter, some kind of protection."

"I don't have any shelter," says Lucy.

"Neither do it," says Pres. "Neither do you."

Willie shuffles his feet, takes a drink and clears his throat.

"So, what are you going to do?" says Lucy.

"Yeah," says Pres.

"Well, it's like...there might be a chance...maybe, I'm saying maybe I might have a shelter."

"How's that?"

"Well, Mr. Ashwood told my dad he would have enough room for us. My brother too."

"Oh." Pres looks at Lucy. "How much room is there in this thing?"

"It's big enough for six people."

"Six. Hm." Lucy counts on her fingers. "Mr. Ashwood, you, your Pop, Denny, if he's home. That's four. Room for two more." Pres and Lucy look at each other and then at Willie, their faces beckoning.

"There's Mr. Ashwood's mother, too. That's five."

"Room for one more," says Lucy.

"But who?" says Pres.

"Wait a minute---"

"Who've you known longer?" says Lucy.

"Us guys have to stay together," says Pres.

"Whoa, back it up a little. Who said I could pick someone, it's not my shelter."

"Old man Ashwood likes you. I can tell," says Pres.

"Back to my question---Who have you known longer?"

"I can't pick between you two. You're equal friends."

"So, you're gonna let both of us die, because we're 'equal friends'."

"No, that's not---"

"Very harsh, man," says Pres.

"Look, how about this---I won't go in the shelter. I'll stay with you guys. We'll face the end together. How's that sound?" says Willie.

"If you don't go in, then there's two spots left, one for me and one for Lucy," says Pres.

"So, it would be okay if I died and you two were saved. It wouldn't bother you."

Lucy and Pres nod their heads. "We'd build a statue in your honor."

Lucy grins in agreement.

Pres stands, a smile on his face, and puts his hands in his pockets. He takes a long breath and honks it back out through his nose. "Thanks, guys, I didn't think it was possible, but I feel better, a little."

Willie's brow is furrowed, his eyes are narrowed, his palms are sweaty.

· · ·

Hal stands at the kitchen sink washing three days' worth of dishes. He swirls the dish cloth around each plate and holds them under the faucet for at least ten seconds before putting them in the drainer. "You never want to have soap on your dishes," Mae always insisted. "It'll make you sick, sure as anything." This bit of wisdom always befuddled Hal. He could've cared less how clean the dishes were. He rinses another plate, watching every bubble of soap disappear down the drain. "How about that, Mae?" he said. "Satisfied?"

He still misses the little things. How she massaged his head when he had a thumper. The way she twitched her nose in the springtime air. The cinnamon toast, the chocolate milkshakes, the chicken pot pie, everyone the best. How her singing voice could clear a room. How, even with a ball of tissues in her hands, she'd never admit she had a cold. How soft her lips were, the nape of her neck, the skin behind her knees.

He closes his eyes, his wrinkled hands still in the soapy water. "My God, Mae, things are hard." What would she say about Willie? His spells? His curiosity about his mother and father? "He's tender, like you." Would he blame his grandfather for the way things turned out? "If you were here, Mae..."

He looks at the pots and pans stacked high on the counter, bound together by the crust of dinners past. She would be appalled. "What in the world, Hal Mitchum!" He wishes he could hear her say his name one more time.

Before tackling the ovenware, which is stacked against the cupboard, he dries his hands, tosses the towel onto the counter and opens the fridge. On the bottom shelf, he finds a six-pack of Carling's Black Label. He is refreshed by one can, calmed by two, happy by three, indifferent by four, sullen by five, but by six, he feels Mae's presence, he knows she's there, not just in his heart, but in the room itself; she's there and she is telling him it isn't his fault, none of it. "Is that true?" he mumbles as he tumbles sideways into his favorite chair, his favorite picture of Mae clutched to his chest. "Is it?" he whispers.

The pots and pans will have to wait. Hal's raspy breathing settles into a deep snore. Mae's picture slides off his lap to the floor, the last beer can still in his hand.

Hal wakes up with a start. "What?" he calls. "Who is it?" He rubs his eyes and holds his thumping head. Then he hears it. Someone is at the door. Hal ignores it. Ten seconds pass; he's in the clear. He struggles to get out of his deep cushioned chair. He looks at the wall clock through slit eyes. "Jesus." Two hours have passed. He puts his hands on the armrests and hoists himself to a standing position.

The knocker raps on the window panes, the sound of it like a nail being pounded into his temple. "Coming," says Hal. The knocking persists. "Coming!" He buttons his flannel shirt, ending up with an extra hole at the top. The knocking stops. He reaches for the knob, takes a deep breath and opens the door.

Trish stands on the porch step, her hands folded, her face streaked with tears.

"Why...hello," says Hal, as if startled by an apparition.

"I'm sorry...I shouldn't..."

"No, no, it's fine. I just didn't expect..."

"I can leave; actually, I should leave. I don't know what I was thinking." She backs down the steps.

"No, no, no, please come in."

Trish sits at the kitchen table, her jacket still on, her feet crossed at the ankles, her face downcast.

"Coffee?"

"Please."

What am I doing here? thinks Trish. She scans the room without moving her head. Her eyes linger on the pots and pans. She sees wood flooring peeking through the worn linoleum, a shopping bag in the corner full of waste paper, a set of stainless-steel canisters, an empty milk carton on the counter, Hal's work boots in the middle of the floor, one on its side. The walls are white, pale yellow showing through in places.

"Sorry for the wait."

"Thank you," says Trish. "I mean...for letting me visit. I'm sure it's not---"

"No need to thank me." Hal shifts his weight to one leg, then the other. He looks in the coffee pot to see if the grounds have collected on the bottom, then pours the coffee back into the first pot through a strainer. Hal turns up the burner to re-heat it. He takes two mugs from the cupboard, wipes them out with a dish towel and fills them up.

Trish watches Hal's slow, methodical process, so similar to how he swept halls and washed walls. Sitting in his kitchen, she feels oddly comforted. Being in her own kitchen, her own house, though, felt suffocating. When she couldn't take it any longer, she threw on her spring jacket and started walking. Across the Park Bridge, down Fountain Ave., up Fourth St. and over the railroad tracks, then up Lawrence Ave. past Oswald's, Blocher's, Edmin's and back down Fifth to the Fifth Street Bridge. Back in the neighborhood again, she found herself standing on Hal's porch, not knowing exactly why.

Hal sits in the chair opposite Trish, his arms resting on the table top. Trish looks so small, her hands like a little girl's, barrettes in her hair, her jacket falling off one shoulder. She's lived too much life in too little time, he thinks.

Trish sips her coffee. "Strong," she says.

"Maybe some milk?"

"No, I need it."

They stare into their cups.

"I didn't plan on coming to your house. I know...it's a little over the line."

"Good to see you."

She meets his eyes, deep set like Ruthie's, then looks at her cup again.

"I think you know I'm going to lose my job."

Hal wraps both hands around his mug. "I always hoped you wouldn't."

"I knew it was temporary."

"Yeah---"

"But it felt so permanent, you know? Such a good fit. It's been a long time since I felt like that...anywhere. Or with anyone."

Hal's mouth is dusty. He tips his coffee mug again.

"Look, Trish---"

"I know you can't do anything; I know that..."

Hal shifts his weight. His chair creaks.

"I've already talked to Larry." He cocks his head and raises an eyebrow. "I'm sorry. If it were up to me..."

"No need for you to apologize."

The room feels like a funeral parlor after everyone has left. Trish looks at the tiny pool of brown water at the bottom of her mug. Should she drink it? If she does, would she have to leave immediately?

"Look Trish, it's been a lot of years since I worked at the dealership, but I still know a few guys there. Maybe I could talk to them. Would that be okay with you?"

"Yes...yes."

"I can't promise---"

"I know. I just appreciate...everything."

"It's nothing, really."

Trish takes another sip.

"Can I warm it up for you?"

"No, it's fine…well…maybe I should get…"

"Trish." He looks directly at her, his eyes sharp. "Let me see what I can do."

There are no more tears for Trish to shed; her ducts have nothing more to give. Nevertheless, the corners of her mouth sag and a knot clogs her throat. Her shoulders quake as she stands. She puts her arms around Hal.

His back stiffens at first, then softens as he embraces her.

"Now I know where your daughter got her kindness," says Trish.

CHAPTER 32

Frost crystals glisten in the morning sun as Willie, wearing only his pajama bottoms and a T-shirt, runs barefoot to the mailbox. He stops to blow warm air into his hands.

It's been a good week. On Monday, they played softball during recess and Willie hit the ball so far it broke the McKelvey's living room window across the street. There was an arithmetic test on Tuesday. Even though it was only a times table review, Willie got one hundred percent, including the twelves. On Wednesday, Mr. Clammerman was ill and couldn't be there for ducking and rolling. Thursday, Lucy lost a molar on the playground and no one could find it. The whole class was on their knees searching, even Miss Loss. In the end, Willie found the tooth, which still had some blood and goo on it. The whole class cheered and Lucy gave him a hug.

Willie felt embarrassed, and a little proud, when some of the boys cried "Whooooa!" Later Lucy told Willie she didn't mean to cause any problems; that the urge to hug showed up without any prior notice. Willie felt a tingle everywhere in his body, but kept it to himself.

As for Friday, all Friday has to do is show up at the end of every week. That's enough cause for celebration no matter what's happened during the day. But this Friday had a cherry on top. It was the sixth-grade spelling bee and, wonder of wonder, Willie won. There'd be an asterisk by his name, though, because Calvin Kingfisher was absent. Calvin had won every spelling bee since the first grade. One year, Willie made it to the final round before losing. Who knew there was a 'W' in wrinkle. What was the point?

This year was more like a sandlot competition, rather than the World Series. It lasted only four rounds. In the end, Willie and Spence Klinger were still standing. Everyone laughed when Spence spelled "island" "eyeland." He smacked his leg hard, "Geeeez!" All Willie had to do was spell the next word and he'd be the champ. His word was "vault." He closed his eyes, searching for the letters. He moved his lips silently---v-a-l-t. Lucy must have been watching, because when he looked her way, she wide-eyed him, always a signal something was coming, and then sneezed, "Aaa-chu-u." That sealed the deal. "Vault, v-a-u-l-t, vault." Applause again from his adoring peers.

After a week like this, it doesn't matter that his toes are curling into little ice cubes and Pop is calling from the front door---"You'll catch your death of cold." Life's been good to him for the first time in a while. Granted he hasn't watched Cronkite all week and he's avoided reading the papers he delivers, but still, a pretty good week is a pretty good week, even if you have to ignore the world to get it.

• • •

"Watch your head," says Robert Ashwood, as he and Hal navigate into his bomb shelter. They maintain their Groucho Marx posture once they've entered. "The ceiling is lower than I wanted, but you can't have everything." He smiles and stretches his arms out, as if to say "Voila!"

Everyone who knows about the bomb shelter makes fun of it. Teenage boys routinely drive by his house yelling, "Ash-hole! Ash-hole." The *Daily Ledger* interviewed him for an article, pictures and everything. The interviewer jokingly asked if the structure would protect him from outer space aliens. Robert had laughed and said, "Sure, why not." The headline the next day read, "Local Man Prepares for Martian Invasion."

There are a few other souls in town like Robert who fear for their future, fear that a nuclear holocaust is not beyond the realm of possibility. Many among them also believe their shelters will protect them from Martians when they arrive. And Venusians.

Building the shelter was a challenging, solitary endeavor from the beginning, but as he said to Hal on numerous occasions, "Better safe than dead."

It is difficult to argue with such reasoning. And Hal doesn't. He keeps his befuddlement about the bomb shelter to himself. He doesn't question the cost (even though the money could be better spent replacing fallen roof tiles); he doesn't challenge the notion that it is "hermetically sealed" (despite noticing a one inch crack under the door). And he doesn't doubt his intentions, which as far as Hal can tell, are pure and good. That should count for something, he thinks.

And much to his surprise, the interior is impressive. There are six cots folded in one corner, shelving built into the walls for food, three radios and a slim antenna poking through the soft ground above. "We gotta maintain contact with the outside," Robert explains. He is particularly proud of the lighting: "That there is a 4-cell hot-shot battery and, see there, its wired to a 150-milliampere flashlight battery. The Office of Civil Defense Mobilization says it can stay lit continuously for ten days." He hooks his thumbs on his waistband, sucks in his belly, pushes out his chest and beams like a boy who's just won best sheep at the county fair.

"That pot there is for toileting; we'd have to turn our backs or cover our eyes so whoever's going can have privacy. Turn up the radio if you need noise to...you know. And that giant can over there is for waste. We should count on being in here for about four days, so I don't think the smell will get too much out of hand." His voice seems uncertain about this critical detail.

It is easy to ridicule Robert and his project, but Hal is struck instead by his sincerity and his desire not only to save himself but others, too. 'Others' such as Hal, Willie and Denny (if he happens to be home when the end of time comes), and his mother (if he can convince her to enter what she calls, "the dungeon of death"). Tall order.

Although Hal has not yet committed himself and his family to the bomb shelter, he is painfully aware Robert assumes he will. "Not everyone is like you, Hal, most of 'em don't give a rat's ass about what might happen; they don't give their family's welfare a second thought." Hal is betting hard there won't be a nuclear war, that the brinkmanship will end in a tie, giving both sides the opportunity to declare victory. And yet, could Robert be right?

. . .

Willie opens the mailbox and peeks in. He's pleased to see that it is full. He grabs a pile of envelopes and bright colored advertisements. There is going to be a sale on snow shovels at Yahn and Jones Hardware Store. Luciano's grocery store is having a sale on chicken, twenty-five cents a pound; on ground chuck, as well, forty cents a pound. "Wow," says Willie, as he peruses the flyers for the new models coming out of Detroit---Cadillac Seville, Chevy Impala and the Thunderbird. "Man-o-man." How cool would it be to drive a T-bird around town, people stopping in their tracks, their mouths falling open at the sight of Willie Blevin driving the hottest car in town.

He shuffles through the other envelopes---water bill, electric bill, car insurance bill, license renewal notice, letter from Denny. Wait, what? A letter from Denny? He looks at the envelope again. The return address is Weston College. He rubs his eyes and holds the envelope up to the light. It's Denny's handwriting for sure, all scribbly and slanted like it might run off the edge of the envelope and onto the ground. He tosses the other mail back into the box, slips a finger nail under one corner, and runs it across the top of the envelope. Willie unfolds the letter, which is written on lined paper Denny must have yanked from a three-ring binder.

Dear Pop it begins. He looks again at the address: Hal Mitchum. He's surprised. He's the one who's written to Denny, not Pop. In fact, he's never known Pop to write a letter to anyone in his life. He shakes his head and goes back to the letter. He almost jumps out of his skin when he reads the first sentence: *I'm planning to come home for a visit over mid-term break; ten days from now.* The second sentence is a modest surprise. He's bringing Becky with him. Denny's mentioned her, but bringing her home seems like a big step. Where will she sleep?

As he reads on, Willie is ready to jump out of his skin again, but for a different reason. Turns out Pop knows what happened on the paper route with Preston, how he got a little dizzy, or as Denny puts it, *So sorry he passed out on the ground.* How did Pop find out? His eyebrows are touching now. Had to be Pres, he thinks. He crumples the letter, but then smooths it out and keeps reading. Sounds like Pop doesn't know what to do. Willie slumps and his feet go numb. What in the world is going on? Pop isn't concerned at all about an imminent nuclear war, but he's so concerned about Willie he writes a letter (perhaps his first) to Denny asking for help.

Willie's legs feel rubbery; he grabs hold of the mailbox. No, he can't let it happen again. He breathes slowly, deeply; he counts to twenty; he looks at five different things, naming each of them, so his mind can get unstuck---sidewalk, mailbox, squirrel, potato chip delivery truck, Mr. Connor. He waves at Mr. Connor, but pretends not to hear when he starts talking; if he has to answer "What grade are you in now?" one more time, he might do something unfortunate to Mr. Connor.

This ritual over, Willie has his wits about him again. But the anger and sadness remain; anger at Pres for blabbing; sad for Pop, who doesn't know what to do. He can't stay mad at Pres for long because his dad's in the bin. But the sadness he feels for Pop cuts deep. If his mom and dad were alive, Pop would never have had to write this letter. He wouldn't be raising Willie. He wouldn't have to cook him meals, or come to school when he's having problems, or buy him clothes, or anything; he wouldn't have had to move, or give up a job he loved, or clean up when Smoochy pees on the carpet. His life would be, at a minimum, okay, maybe even good.

Up the street, Pop is finishing his conversation with Mr. Ashwood. They both laugh and shake hands. Ashwood holds on a little longer, and Pop nods his head 'Yes'. Robert claps him on the back. Before Pop sees him, Willie goes into the house, tosses the letter onto the kitchen table and retreats to his room, Smoochy on his tail.

A spring in his step as he returns home, Pop feels like the heathen at a Billy Graham crusade who suddenly sees the light, scrambles down the aisle, drops to his knees, and makes his conversion known to the world. Like those who come forward for Billy, it's hard to know how long this conversion will last, but for now, Pop is a believer; Ashwood has convinced him the risks are too high to squander a chance for safe shelter for himself and the boys.

CHAPTER 33

"Willie!" The front room is quiet and the kitchen is empty. Pop stands at the bottom of the stairs listening. There is a scratch against a door and a whimper. Smoochy must be closed in one of the bedrooms. More than once, Pop has opened his bedroom door at night, turned on the light, and found Smoochy, silent as a statue, sitting in the middle of the bed.

He trudges up the stairs and lets Smooch out. Pop notices light under Willie's door. He taps lightly, not wanting to wake him up if he's asleep. At first there's no answer. He taps again; he hears a rustling sound and then springs creaking.

Willie isn't sure he wants to answer the door or talk to Pop. More than once, he's heard him say Grandma Mae died of a broken heart. Willie doesn't want to be the one who breaks Pop's.

Pop is surprised Willie doesn't open the door. Has he interrupted something, something young boys like to do as often as is humanly possible?

"Is everything okay?"

"Yeah."

"Can I come in?"

"I guess." How can he face Pop after reading Denny's letter? Is it enough to say, I'm sorry? I'll try to do better?

Pop opens the door and Smooch races to Willie's side as he sits on the edge of his bed. His face looks pale as chalk board dust.

"Willie? Are you sick?"

"No," says Willie without looking.

"Okay," says Pop, ready to retreat. "I'm going back down. Lunch is ready."

Before he reaches the hall, Willie clears his throat. Pop stops and turns around.

"Did you read Denny's letter?" says Willie.

"There's a letter from Denny?"

Willie shakes his head and combs his hair back with his fingers.

"Uh huh," he says.

"No, I didn't see it."

Pop tries to read Willie's face, so stern, so fixed.

"What did it say?"

"You can read it."

Why this stand-off? "Just tell me."

Willie unfolds his arms and puts his hands in his pockets. He must know what it says, thinks Willie.

"Well, he's coming home soon. For break."

"That's good news. Isn't it?"

"And Becky, the girl he knows, she's coming too."

"Okay...well..."

"Yeah, and he got the message."

"The message? What message?" Willie rolls onto his bed and opens his window. "Willie, c'mon, what message?"

"About me...the message about me."

Pop blanches, his fingers go limp. What did Denny say?

"What do you mean, Willie?"

"I hope he gets here before you have to take me to Dixmont." Willie's knees buckle. He tries not to cry, but the tears come. Pop takes him in his arms and holds him tight, then tighter still. When Willie was a little boy, sometimes that was the only thing that calmed him; Pop would meld them together, like a shoe matching the contours of a foot.

"You're okay, you're okay," says Pop. Willie is limp in his arms. "Maybe take some breaths." After a moment, Willie starts to move and Pop lets go.

Willie wipes his face with the sleeve of his shirt.

Pop leaves the room, goes downstairs and returns with Denny's letter. His head goes back and forth as he reads. When he's done, his arm drops, the letter with it, and he sits on Willie's bed. Willie stares straight ahead as if he's looking at an eyechart. Pop props his arm on his thigh, and says, "Willie, I have always needed help. You just never knew it. When you and your brother came to live with me, I hadn't been a real father in years. I'd never had sons. I didn't know what I was doing. Sometimes I still don't. Not knowing what to do scares me because you two came...well...you two came from your mom, just like your mom came from Grandma."

Pop looks at Willie and sees questions in his eyes.

"When I got you boys, it was like having two babies...I mean, you weren't babies...but you were babies to me...you needed, well...so much had happened, you were lost, you didn't know what to do, you needed someone to give you shelter, to be the one you could count on, the one who'd be there for you. Bad things had happened...fast...awful." Pop takes a deep breath. "You didn't deserve that." He frowns and shakes his head. "I wanted you to have regular lives, regular lives like other kids."

Willie wants to ask what really happened to his mom and dad. Saying it was "an accident" doesn't work anymore. There has to be more. But when he looks at Pop, all he sees is a well that has gone dry. Pop wipes his hands on his pant legs. His back forms a question mark. His head hangs and his round face sags. Of course, he needs help, thinks Willie. Maybe more for himself than anyone else.

"So, when Preston's father called, I didn't know what to do. That's why I wrote the letter. You've always been close to your brother." He turns his head to Willie. "Should I have talked to you? Would you have told me what happened?"

"No, probably not."

Pop puts his hand on Willie's back.

"That's what I thought."

"If Pres hadn't been right there with me, he wouldn't know either."

"What about now? Do you think you can tell me about it?"

Getting into the whole house thing is too unsettling for Willie.

"You've seen me, Pop. You know what happens. I get all hot, and I feel like I'm going to throw up, and it's like I'm dizzy or something, and my legs don't work right." Willie is expressionless.

Pop rubs Willie's back. "I wish I could get rid of this thing for you, Willie."

"Me, too."

CHAPTER 34

Denny stands at his dorm window, his eyes closed, his lips moving, but making no sound. Madame Cole gave the class one week to write a five-hundred-word essay about anything they want, but it has to be written in French. Worse yet, each student will have to recite the essay in class by memory.

During the first several weeks of the semester, Madame Cole treated Denny like he was a special student. "You have needs that are unlike any other student," she said brightly when meeting with him after class. "So, you will have my special attention." Even though he's made progress, his language skills are no better than a two-year-old French child. She stopped calling on him in class because the other students could not bear the sound of his mutilated French.

Given his language limitations, Denny assumed he wouldn't have to do the same assignment as everyone else. Instead, maybe he could recite the alphabet again (this time including 'X'), or read a sentence or two from *Les Miserables*, or bring in a few bottles of French wine (made in France with real French words on the label) for the class to sample.

He leaves his dorm and high-tails it across campus to Madame Cole's office which is tucked in the far end of the basement level. He holds his breath and then, as confidently as possible, he makes his suggestions to Madame Cole. She drops her wire rims on the desk, looks up at him with squinted eyes and says, "You and I both know you will never be able to speak French, not in my lifetime, or anyone else's."

"But---"

"Not a word please. Mr. Blevin, sadly, I must admit I saw in you potential; I thought I would be your Professor Higgins and you would be my Eliza Doolittle. Alas, I was wrong; I fear if we go further with this charade, our story will end up mimicking Mary Shelley's wonderful novel---*Frankenstein*. I apologize for not having recognized this sooner, because it is now too late for you to drop this course. And having you in class, while sometimes a humorous distraction, is holding everyone back; I am afraid you have become our ball and our chain."

"Okay?" Denny is still trying to figure out the Eliza Doolittle reference.

"So..."

"So?"

"I have discussed this at length with the chair of our department and we have decided a fair option would be to assign you a grade of C- in exchange for you not attending class again. A passing grade for you and a welcome reprieve for the class."

Could the news be any better? thinks Denny. "So, I don't have to attend class anymore. And I get a C-."

"I knew if I explained it in English, you would likely understand. Farewell, Mr. Blevin, I wish you all the best in whatever you do."

"Wait, what did she say?" Becky cocks her head to one side.

Denny rehashes the entire story as Becky, her mouth gaping at times, swallows and digests the news.

"You're off the hook. I mean, like, you are free." She smiles at Denny and wraps her arms around him. "There are spirits and angels at work here."

They hold hands and lean against each other as they walk back to Becky's dorm.

"You know, you could stay over."

"Yes, I am totally aware of that." Becky nudges him in the side. "But I have things..."

"What things?"

"Thingy things, I don't know. I just need the time."

Becky leans on the wall outside her dorm room, waiting for her roommate to finish doing "homework" with her boyfriend. Eventually, they leave without a word, and the room, thankfully, is hers and hers alone. She undresses and puts on her flannel jammies. She opens her political science text and closes it, her American lit, intro to sociology and humanities books as well, and closes them all. The smell of her laundry bag urges her to wash a load, but she doesn't. She lies down to rest but can't close her eyes.

She stands up again and wobbles back and forth on her uneven legs. She sits back down and softly caresses the "afflicted" one, as her doctor had called it. Compared to her other leg, it is noodle thin. She crosses her noodle over her "good" leg, as another doctor had called it, and massages it slowly, gently, bending her foot back and forth and side to side, to lessen the ache. "It's only an inch, that's all. No big deal," her father would say. But it might as well have been twelve or eighteen inches; the effect was the same. "Everyone has something that makes them different," her mother would say. "Look at your Uncle Ned, he's bald as a cue ball." Are his legs the same length? Becky would think.

In high school, where friendships were few and far between, her English teacher, Miss Hewitt, was always encouraging. "Becky, you have such flare, such flamboyance; these are gifts." Of course, they weren't gifts. They were finely crafted adornments developed over many years to draw attention away from what was most visibly notable about her. Perhaps starting a roaring fire over there would distract everyone from the long smoldering fire over here. It worked and it didn't work. Everyone knew Becky; she refused to hide; but the combination of her shortened leg and her overwrought exuberance made her seem odd to her peers, rather than unique.

She grew crocodile skin with a top layer of armadillo hide, which served her well. Most hurts bounced off, while other parts of her quietly flourished. She was smarter than the other kids, funnier and bolder, too.

But in every new situation she still hears that boy's voice, the one who called her 'gimp' as she innocently played in her front yard. Soon she will meet Denny's family. What will they think? What will they do?

CHAPTER 35

Lucy and her mother park their sputtering car in front of Edmin's for Women. Lucy looks at the manikins in the window, sophisticated poses, long fingers in the air, heads high, waves of satin adorning their legs and feet. From the corners, spotlights accent dresses, suits, slacks, and coats in the fabrics of the day, tweed and gabardine, crepe and gingham, serge and velour, silk, of course. The store is so far out of their league, that even the manikins know they should be home leafing through their Montgomery Ward or Sears catalogues.

"Mom, why are we stopping here?"

"Just because. Please be good." Her face is more beckoning than stern.

Chimes ring out as they open the door. The store is empty, except for a lady who walks briskly toward them, hands out, face rigid from hours of smiling. Her name is GraceAnne, she's the owner, and she'd like "nothing better" than to help them find their "heart's desire." Quite a promise, thinks Lucy.

She leads them to a wall of clothing that stretches from one end of the store to the other. There are dresses and skirts and suits and, farther down, blouses and sweaters and coats, all hung neatly on wooden hangers.

"You look like a six...no, a four."

"It's been so long, I don't know."

"That's fine, dear."

Lucy turns slowly, breathing in the freshness of stylish, yet to be worn clothing. GraceAnne laughs. "Don't worry, honey, before you know it, you'll be wearing these. You and your mom will be able to share each other's clothes. Soon enough, believe me."

"Please, don't even think that; it's all coming too fast," says Trish, who is pulling skirt after skirt off the racks. "If I could stop the clock I would." She and GraceAnne laugh politely.

While GraceAnne pitches the newest lines, Lucy checks some price tags and gasps---twenty-five dollars, thirty dollars, forty-dollars, even fifty. She looks at her mother, who's moving swiftly from rack to rack, like a water bug skipping across a pond. She is bursting with the kind of energy you'd expect from, well, a twelve-year old.

Lucy is sure she doesn't know how much these dresses cost. She notices a display in the far corner of the store. The sign says, "Marked Down 50%!" Hands on her hips, she looks at the dizzying array of dresses that are packed together tight as sardines, some even lying on the floor. She thumbs through them, hangers scraping. Perfect, she thinks. Some of the dresses are only seven, eight dollars. She looks closer. They have short sleeves or no sleeves at all. What? They're trying to get rid of all their summer stuff, dresses nobody wanted when the days were long and the sun was hot. She looks at some of the patterns---giant parrots, random geometrical shapes, red, white and blue stars and stripes. She sighs, disappointed.

Lucy stands on her tiptoes trying to spy her mother on the other side of the store, but she is nowhere to be found. GraceAnne waves to Lucy from the check-out counter.

"She's in the dressing room," she calls, pointing a well-manicured finger.

Lucy walks into the dressing room where she finds curtains pulled shut on what appear to be three tiny closets.

"Mom?"

"I'm in here, honey."

Lucy pulls back the curtain on door number three.

"Come in here and close the curtain. I don't want to put on a show."

Lucy's mom is wearing only a bra and panties. Although she's seen her mom unclothed, being in a dressing room with her feels different, like they are lady friends out on shopping spree, not a care in the world. Kind of.

"Look at these." Her mom points to three dresses hanging on a hook, waiting to be modeled. One dress is peach with a wide collar, half sleeves, and a skirt that flares like fireworks on the Fourth of July. Her mom tries it on and twirls in front of the mirror.

"What do you think?"

"I don't know. It's nice." Words fail. Her mother could be one of those starlets in a movie magazine with a crinoline dress and cinched waist. She looks ten years younger, her smile is so broad and her neck so long. Will I look like this someday? thinks Lucy.

"I don't think this is the one, though. It's too...I don't know, just not right."

Lucy breathes a sigh of relief, having noted the thirty-five-dollar price tag. This whole shopping trip is confusing. Usually, they go to the Penny's store up the street. Her mom always finds something, although what she finds never makes her face beam. Since she's been out of work for two weeks, they hardly have enough money for Penny's, let alone thirty-five dollars for a fancy dress (she doesn't need).

Trish puts on the second dress, which has the same A-line as the first, but is green with a leaf pattern. Again, she looks like a movie star. But this one's not right either. So, she tries on the third one which is a pencil dress to her mid-calf with a tight bodice, half-sleeves, and cinched waist. It is indigo blue and shimmers in the light, like a full moon reflecting on a pond. Her mother stands in front of the mirror for several minutes checking the hem, the cuff on the sleeves, the spaghetti thin belt and the shape of her hips. She doesn't even ask for Lucy's opinion.

"Come on, let's see what GraceAnne thinks."

When her mother steps out of the dressing room, there are three women about to enter. They step back as Trish floats by, like a dream come to life. They watch a moment longer, nodding their approval.

"Oh my, I don't mean to be forward, but that dress was made for you. I mean, your figure, I would kill for a figure like yours," says one the admirers.

Lucy blushes, but her mom's eyes sparkle. She says "Thank you," her voice quiet, dignified.

"She's right, look at you!" says GraceAnne, guiding her in a slow turn with her hand. "You look, well, the only word for it is elegant." She then rests her chin in her hand and studies Trish's face. "What do you think? Take it home?" Trish opens her mouth but doesn't answer. She looks into the mirror again. "Why don't I give you a moment." GraceAnne returns to the cash register.

Lucy sneaks a peek at the tag hanging from the sleeve---thirty-eight-dollars. Her mother stands in front of the three-sided mirror, her bare toes curled, checking every angle. Lucy can't believe her mother hasn't already taken off the dress. She could get five at Penny's for that price. Lucy looks over her mother's shoulder at GraceAnne, who is occupied with another customer. She taps her mother's arm.

"What is it, Luce?"

Lucy clears her throat and speaks in a near whisper. "I checked the price tag. It's thirty-eight-dollars. I mean...thirty...eight...dollars."

Without looking at Lucy, her mother says, "I know it costs thirty-eight dollars."

"You do?"

"Yes, I do."

"Then why are we still here?"

Trish leans close to Lucy's ear. "I think I'm going to buy it, that's why we're still here."

What's happened to her? thinks Lucy.

"Okay...where are you going to get the money?"

Trish cups her mouth and whispers into her daughter's ear again. "I broke open the piggy bank."

"Piggy bank? What piggy bank?"

Trish admires herself in the mirror. "You know that flour cannister I keep on top of the fridge?"

"Uh huh."

"That piggy bank."

"But...I don't get it..."

Trish puts her hands on Lucy's shoulders. "I been putting pennies and nickels and dimes in there for a year, maybe more."

"I didn't know you had---"

"I promised I wouldn't use it until something important came along."

Lucy makes a mental list---dresses that cost less than thirty-eight-dollars, pizza more than once a month, a movie now and again, premium ice cream, all the little things that would make each day less bad; but certainly not dresses that cost thirty-eight-dollars.

"What's so important?"

"I've got a job interview."

A job interview? That's all? thinks Lucy. How many has she had in the last year? Four? Five? Who knows? How many of them have been worth thirty-eight-dollars? That would be---zero. Has she lost her mind? Is she really going to waste thirty-eight-dollars on a job that may last two weeks, three weeks tops?

"A job interview where?" says Lucy, her upper lip curled.

"At Scutters." Lucy's concerned face awakens doubts in Trish. She looks again into the mirror. What am I doing?

Lucy's arms are folded as she stares out the store window at traffic on Lawrence Ave. "The car place?"

"Yeah, the car place."

"Another secretary thing? I thought you hated that."

Trish's lips are taut as she searches for the right words. "This time is different because I'm different. I took those other jobs, but I never wanted them. I knew I was just going through the motions; I knew they weren't going to last. But now...now I want a job, I want to work, I want to succeed at something...for both of us, and to do that, I need to look the part. I guess I want to, I don't know, be better."

On some level Trish always knew that how she adorns her body would determine how she would be seen by the world, meaning---men. She remembers her mother carefully guiding her clothing choices, making sure she was appealing to all the teenaged boys; low cut sweaters, tight capris; she even hemmed her Bermuda shorts so a little more leg showed.

Her mother's message about her body was meant to encourage her, but in the end, it only added to Trish's confusion: "show the body, but don't show the body." She felt like she was always playing peekaboo, always being deceptive, like a con artist running a shell game.

There was no doubt, though, it worked.

When she left the house on a date, her mother would say, with a wink, "Have a good time." But when she returned, her mother would say, with a scowl, "You didn't have too good a time, did you?" There was only one way to play the game, but there was never a way to win. "You don't have to like it, Trish girl, you just have to make your peace with it." Trish could feel herself withering inside.

What she learned was simple: How she was wrapped, her packaging, was more important than what was inside.

It was time to make a change.

Trish was no fool, though. There was still a game to be played. Self-confidence might give her the courage to knock on the door, but there was no doubt how she looked would get her inside. This time would be different.

Be better? thinks Lucy. I have a mother who wants to be better. That's something a kid would say to her mother after she's been reprimanded: "I'll be better, I will." Words from someone who feels desperate or frightened. I'll be better so you will...what? Care for me? Protect me? Love me? Lucy hears the words over and over in her head, and when she does, she feels sad; sad for her mother; sad for reasons that are unclear.

As her mother walks to the front of the store with GraceAnne, her dress draped over her arm, there is something different about her. She's my mom, for sure, thinks Lucy. But she's someone else, too. It's like she's a mom-most-of-the-time, for sure, but she's also not-a-mom. There is a not-a-mom world inside her; it's called 'Patricia Louise Hallowell', a world beyond Lucy's reach right now, a world she can only hope to know one day.

Lucy's mom waves to her. Lucy leaves the rack of blouses behind and heads to the checkout. She doesn't notice the man in the suit standing outside, window shopping.

CHAPTER 36

Muriel Ashwood is wearing her best floral dress, a little bit of rouge and lipstick, some of which has wandered off the corner of her mouth and onto her cheek. She is making her first trip uptown since coming home; her destination is Edelman's shoe store where she hopes to find a reasonably priced, and exceedingly comfortable pair of slippers, preferably brown or beige. She rolls the window down, despite the chilly air.

"Ma, what are you doin'? You're gonna catch pneumonia or something." Robby is her chauffeur today. His bunker completed, he's helping his mother get out and about a little more often, despite her difficulty walking and her faulty memory.

"You know, they never opened the windows at that damn place. For safety, they said. 'It's for your own good, honey'. What? My room was on the first floor. How far would I fall? Two feet? What could happen?"

"Maybe they were afraid someone would break in."

"And what, steal my cane? Snag my slippers?" Muriel shakes her head and opens the window a little further.

Worry that his mother's homecoming was a horrible mistake is never far from Robert's mind. He fights it with every fiber of his ample being, but it will not be denied. She berates him constantly. And when she thinks Robert is his father, she berates him even more.

She is at her most appealing when she's asleep. Robby sits and watches her in the afternoon while their shows are on. That's when he sees a different face, empty of invective.

For reasons that escape Robby, his father never left his mother. He must have wanted to, though. He stayed away from the house most of the time. And when he did come home, the fireworks began as soon as he turned the knob on the front door. Some nights the back seat of his Hudson was a more comfortable option than sleeping beside his wife.

If Robby wanted to see him, he'd go up Lawrence Ave. to the Bucket of Blood, his father's favorite watering hole. His father would hug him and give him a dime. Robby could never bring himself to ask the obvious question: "Why do you keep leaving me?"

"Looks like rain, Robby. See them clouds there, black as dirt they are. Did you bring an umbrella for once?"

"Yeah, Ma, I brought an umbrella."

"The blue one or the red one?"

"Red, I think."

"I love that blue one."

Robby has explained numerous times how his mother ended up in the county home, but his explanations don't hold a drop of water as far as Muriel is concerned. She can't believe he abandoned her to those devils. And that's what they were, devils. They'd get her up at night to take a pill she didn't ask for, a pill she was certain she didn't need. She'd tell them to get the hell out and they'd call for the aides, who'd hold her down until they put the pill in her mouth.

Where was Robby then? Visiting once a week was no help at all. How could a son treat his mother like that? Must be his father's influence, that sonofabitch. Maybe he'll grow out of it if he ever becomes a man.

"Let's get ice cream, Robby."

"Ice cream?"

"Yeah, ever heard of it?"

"I don't know if J&T is open."

"Jesus, why wouldn't they be open?"

"It's almost fall, Ma."

Robby turns onto Fourth Street and heads out of town to J&T.

"Where are we going?" Muriel leans forward and looks at the road ahead. "I want to get out. I'm not going back to that place. I'm not!" She shakes her fist at Robby and reaches for the door.

"Don't, Ma," says Robby.

J&T is open and Robby gets his mom a vanilla custard cone. He orders a large chocolate milkshake for himself. He smiles at the server when she puts a spoon and a straw in the middle of his shake and they just stand there at attention, the shake is so thick.

The best thing about an ice cream outing is that for fifteen minutes his mother doesn't speak. Robby reaches across the seat to put a napkin on her lap.

She finishes her ice cream and chomps the cone. "Thank you, Robby," she says with a smile.

"You're welcome, Mom." He smiles in return.

"I hope the Russians don't bomb *this* place." She points out the window at a farmhouse down the road. "They could hit *that* place, that would be okay, but not J&T."

When they get back into town, the shoe store is closed. "That's the way my life goes, Robby, in case you haven't noticed. I'm like Scarlet O'Hara. The world collapsing around me. No one to help."

"I'm here to help you, Ma. Just ask." Robby frowns and pulls a U-turn in the middle of Lawrence Ave., cars honking like crazy. Instead of going home, he takes the back road to New Castle, through rolling hills and farm land, where the leaves are turning in a hurry. His mother's favorite ride.

By now, she is fast asleep, her head on the headrest and her mouth open wide, like she was setting a trap for a small animal. Robert takes a deep, scratchy breath and lets it out. He takes another and another as slowly as possible. Doc Helman told him deep breathing pumps additional oxygen into his body and can also help calm him down when he's nervous. He takes several more breaths in rapid succession, but then he feels light-headed, spots appearing in the corners of his eyes. He pulls over to the side of the road and shifts into park. He closes his eyes until he's sure the spots are gone.

His heart is tap dancing. He rubs his chest.

The first time this happened, several months after his heart attack, he rushed to Helman's office, hoping for some reassurance. But Helman, his glasses in his hand, his eyes gauzy blue, shook his head slowly. He told Robert his heart was trying to warn him, trying to tell him that if he didn't take better care of himself, he might end up in the hospital, or worse. Robert tried to hold his stomach in, but there was no place for it to go. Helman urged him to lose weight and get some exercise.

"You've got an extra hundred fifty pounds hanging over your belt. I'm sorry to put it that way, Robert, but it's true. Put down your fork, take a walk, for God's sake."

Robert squirmed in his seat and folded his hands in his lap. He assured Dr. Helman this was the first time this had happened. Nevertheless, Helman wanted to get an EKG.

"If that goes on for a long time, you can get blood clots. Trust me, you don't want blood clots."

His face looked grim, like he smelled something vile, maybe limburger cheese. Robert shook his head, but didn't ask why clots were bad. He also never went to the hospital for an EKG and he canceled his next appointment, telling the nurse his mother was ill and he needed to go to the county home.

As for his heart, it skipped and fluttered through the next six months. Robert tried not to think about clots. He got the flu just as his irregular heart beat went on hiatus. Perfect timing, because he could go to the doctor's confident that Helman would find nothing wrong.

When Helman asked why he didn't get the EKG, Robert told him his heart beat returned to normal a day or so after the last visit. "Just seeing you must have done the trick," said Robert, forcing both a joke and a laugh. Helman didn't see the humor. And he didn't believe Robert, that was clear from his expression. But what was he to do? Call Robert a liar? Not a physicianly thing to do.

After a lengthy pause, Helman said, "Okay," in a tone that meant "Not okay, but it's your life." Robert fairly floated out of the office, medicine for his flu symptoms in hand, minus any additional admonitions about his heart and its wayward beat. Two days later, his heart beat became erratic again, and continued, with only fleeting pauses, until, well, this very moment. He hadn't seen Dr. Helman in over a year.

Robert is practiced at ignoring things---fire engines and police cars, children playing, bills that are overdue, the phone ringing, thunder crashing, his mother talking. Ignoring his heart isn't a heavy lift. There are times, particularly when he is lying motionless in bed at night, when he can almost hear it, pounding away like a Gene Krupa drum solo.

When his galloping heart wins the battle over sleep, Robert gets up, goes downstairs, fixes a bowl of chocolate ice cream and watches Johnny Carson. Maybe two bowls. Likely, three. When he goes back upstairs to his bedroom, not only does he have his heart to contend with, but now he's got indigestion, too.

On rare occasions, his mother will notice him rubbing his chest. Never a good thing:

"Robby, what are you doing?"

"Nothing."

"You're not doing nothing; you're messing with your chest, aren't you?"

"It's nothing, Ma, really. Just an itch."

"Itch, my ass. You've got that heart thing going on again, don't you? Bdumpity-bdipidy-bdumpity-bdop."

"Doc said there's nothing to worry about. It's just the way my heart works." Lies are so much easier than telling the truth.

"You're gonna die if you don't watch out."

"Whether I watch out or not, I'm going to die, Ma."

"Yeah, with that attitude, you're probably right. And then what will I do?"

There you go. All roads lead to this question. Robert thought bringing her home would put an end to her worries. Much to the contrary, her worries about where she'll go if something happens have doubled. When he asked Doc Helman about it, he said, "Your mother has always been a worrier. She will be to the end...maybe longer."

His mother opens her eyes and her brows flex hard. She's puzzled. Where am I? Trees fly by, the sun warms her arm, birds perch on telephone wires, and Robby holds the steering wheel with both hands, his eyes gripping the road ahead. She blinks slowly a few times and licks her lips, trying to stir up some saliva. At least I'm not at that damn county jail, she thinks.

"Ma?"

Muriel nods.

"Are you okay?"

"Well, I'm alive, right?"

And here we are, thinks Robert, an aging fat guy and a crazy old woman.

"Yes, you are."

"I guess that's the good news."

Robert is unsure that 'good' is the right adjective. "This is true."

When he turns into their driveway, the air raid sirens begin to scream. These drills are so routine now, that most people don't even pay attention. They think of the president as the little boy who's crying wolf. Robert isn't so sure. There was a report on the radio suggesting the military already knew there were missiles in Cuba, but didn't want to tell the American people.

"Why do they keep doing those sirens?" says Muriel, as she struggles to get out of the car. Robert extends a hand.

"Because we might be in danger."

"Don't be ridiculous."

"The rumor is the president may address the nation any day now."

"I like his wife. Very pretty. Too bad her voice sounds like she works in one of those high-class brothels."

CHAPTER 37

"That time again," says John.

Hal runs his hand through his hair. "I guess so. Starting to look like a bum."

John Milner, now in his seventies, has been cutting Hal's hair for at least thirty years. His shop has a black tiled floor with four barbers' chairs and a room length mirror behind them. There's only ever been one barber, who uses only one chair.

Hal had dated his daughter, Rosalie, briefly when they were in high school. Eventually she married, but died in childbirth. She was John's only child. The shop was closed for almost a year afterwards. He never spoke of it, but you could see it on his weather-beaten face.

Ralph Kramer is in the chair when Hal enters. He settles into his regular seat and opens a copy of *Field and Stream*. John tilts back the chair, grabs his tongs, takes a hot towel from the steamer, then wraps Ralph's face. Hal watches as Ralph's hands go limp and his legs fall open. When John removes the towel, Ralph, fast asleep, looks like a fully ripened beefsteak tomato. John works the lather in his cup and brushes it on Ralph's face quickly, efficiently.

He opens his straight razor, strops it, then puts it to Ralph's face and neck. With each pass of the razor, John wipes a mound of lather onto the towel hanging over his shoulder. When he's done, John taps Ralph's shoulder. Ralph gasps, sits up and looks around like he's on another planet.

Each time Hal gets shaved, he reminds John about the mole on his neck so he won't nick it accidentally. John always says, "Don't worry," as if he's offended. But a minute or so later, Hal feels a shooting pain in his neck like he's been stung by a hornet. John never apologizes or says a word. He dabs Hal's neck with the styptic pencil a half dozen times, sometimes more, and then moves on to complete the rest of the job. Today, when it is Hal's turn in the chair, he's going to take a pass on the shave.

Ralph greets Hal as he gets out of the chair. They have become friends over the years primarily because they are on the exact same haircut schedule. When Gordon "Gordo" Bannister enters, Ralph decides to stay a while and chew the fat.

They talk about the Wolverines, Ellwood's high school football team, and whether they will beat New Castle, their archrivals. The consensus is no. They shake their heads over the Pirates disappointing season, just two years after Maz beat the Yankees in the World Series. They each take a turn predicting the weather, agreeing that the Farmer's Almanac is more accurate than the TV weathermen. "I think they use a dart board." Even John laughs at this.

His turn now, Hal sits quietly, listening, as John shakes out the chair cloth, lets it float onto Hal's lap and chest, then ties it tight around his neck. The topic of discussion has changed.

"So, what do you think about this Cuba thing?" Gordo's eyebrows are raised.

"It's a damn mess and I don't know if our president has the balls to stand up to those Soviets," says Ralph. "Castro and the damn commie Cubans, for God's sake, what can you say?"

"Our guy already screwed the pooch on the Bay of Pigs," says John, trimming a little too close to Hal's ear.

They went on from there, excoriating Castro some more, then Khrushchev, and, finally, Kennedy and "his whole clan."

"My God, the pope has a direct line to the Oval, I'm telling you; and that Catholic, nothing against Catholics, you're a Catholic, aren't you John?" Gordo reels it in a little, waiting for John to answer.

"Lapsed," said John.

"Good for you," says Gordo. "We are a Protestant country through and through; always have been, always will be. Anyway, that Kennedy can't make any decisions without the pope sticking his nose into our business."

About then, Hal closes his eyes, hoping to nap.

Their rants complete, the room goes quiet, except for the soft whir of the ceiling fan and the rhythmic sound of John's scissors. Hal starts drifting off, until Gordo mentions Ted Hopkinson, a vice president at the tube mill, and "his latest conquest, you might say."

"From what Ted said, she was really something, quite a *willing* employee," Gordo says with a snicker. "He said she was willing every day."

Ralph and John snort and guffaw at this.

"He does have his ways, doesn't he?" says Ralph.

"He claims he didn't even have to try. She was on her knees, begging him, if you get my drift." Ooos and aaahs this time. "You might know her, Trish something, blonde, with a great set of bongos, very pretty in a trashy way. She musta had her daughter when she was about twelve, because they look the same age." Gordo's head's bobbing, like he's found his rhythm. "Man, I'll tell you, I can't blame him. If I was a few years younger, I'd take a run at her, too."

"Yeah, yeah, I know who she is. I think I mighta seen her a few times at the Oasis, dancing very, well, let's just say when she danced everyone watched."

They continue to bluster and boast about what they'd do with her. Sneers and laughter ensue as Hal's body recoils in disgust. "Whoa Hal, gotta sit still," says John. "Don't want to lose an ear do you?"

There is sweat on Hal's forehead and underarms. His fists are curled around the armrests. He wants to beat the crap out of all of them.

Hal removes the towel and stands.

"Wait, I'm not done. You got half a cut." said John.

Hal folds the cloth neatly and places it on the seat. He reaches into his pocket for money to pay John, including a substantial tip. He puts on his coat and then stands in the middle of the room looking at Ralph and Gordo. His voice is even but tense; his breathing shallow. "John, if you're going to allow men like this into your establishment, then I will not be coming back. Ever."

He reaches for the door knob, John close on his heels. "Hal, Hal, what are you talking about, 'men like this'?"

"Didn't you hear them, the things they said about someone they don't know at all?"

"They didn't mean nothing."

"Hal, come on," says Ralph, while Gordo frowns and waves a dismissive hand at Hal.

"Hal, really, we go back, what, thirty years, right? I mean thirty years I been cutting your hair, shaving your face."

"I know, John, I know." Hal shakes John's hands, says goodbye, opens the door and walks away.

He touches his hair. John wasn't lying. He stops and sits on the bench in front of the pharmacy.

"Mae, Mae, Mae, what am I doing?" He behaved like he was better than them.

· · ·

Trish Hallowell, in her Edmin's dress, faux pearl necklace, and patent leather shoes, enters the dealership showroom, with all the energy of a pinball machine. The floor's been cleared and men are parading new models into place while salesmen, broad smiles on their faces, gape at Detroit's latest and best. She steps back against the front window as a silver Riviera, tires squeaking on the linoleum, eases into place, its white sidewalls gleaming. Behind it comes a sprightly Corvair, black with a double racing strip; then a haughty Corvette, fire engine red with black leather interior that takes Trish's breath away.

This grand exhibition fills Trish with hope. She could be a part of a proud tradition at Scutters, Ellwood's automotive zenith. She looks around for Mr. Kleinman's office and sees a man waving to her from a doorway. He puts his suit coat on, straightens his tie and comes out to greet her. Trish crosses the showroom, taking care not to touch or scrape the glittering cars, posing like fashion models on a Parisian runway.

"I'm so sorry for all the confusion. I wasn't thinking when I set up this interview. It's usually a lot calmer here." Kleinman laughs and extends his hand. His face looks as familiar and welcoming as the father on *Leave it to Beaver*. Nevertheless, Trish is cautious; she shakes his hand.

Kleinman takes her to his office. "Please have a seat."

"Thank you." She sits, her back ramrod straight, hands in her lap, legs together and resting to one side. She straightens her dress, making sure the hem is well below her knee. She watches Mr. Kleinman, his eyes, his mouth. How long will it take before he mentions her looks, how pretty she is or how she lights up the room?

But Mr. Kleinman doesn't look, doesn't comment, doesn't sneer. He doesn't loosen his tie to 'be more comfortable'; he doesn't suggest she call him by his first name, whatever that may be. Trish feels disarmed.

He mentions knowing Hal from long ago, then moves on to the job, presenting a list of responsibilities, performance expectations, pay range, hours, so much information Trish feels like she should have studied for what feels like a test. He wants to start the new hire in billing, but then move her up from there, including into sales or marketing.

"I know that's a lot to digest." Kleinman smiles sympathetically.

"Well...it is...You know, I don't have any experience in this."

"I know you don't have any experience. I didn't think you would. Hal praised you up and down, though, and, well, that's not like him, not like him at all. If he believes in you, then I am willing to, as well. We can teach you everything you need to know while you're doing the job."

Kleinman leans forward on his desk, looks her in the eyes, and smiles.

Trish takes a deep breath. Here it comes. "Is there a catch?"

"A catch."

"Yeah, a catch, you know, like something I should know but don't."

• • •

Lucy opens the refrigerator, grabs a bottle of milk and pours some into a glass. She puts it on the kitchen table, a napkin beside it. "Thanks," says Willie. She stands on her tiptoes and grabs a box of ginger snaps from the top of the fridge. "Is there something I can do?" says Willie. The kettle shrieks and steam rages from its spout. "Nope," says Lucy. She turns the burner off, opens the metal canister on the back ledge of the stove and pulls out a bag of Tetley. She searches through their hutch for her favorite tea cup and saucer. "Be careful with that," her mother always says.

Lucy was permitted to use it for the first time on her tenth birthday. "This was your great grandmother's." Lucy admires the delicate gold filigree around the lip of the cup, on the saucer's rim, as well. The flowers, daisies and coneflowers and black-eyed Susans, all hand-painted. "This cup was painted by your Great Aunt Amelia, as a gift to her sister, my grandmother." Lucy often wonders at the steady hand, keen eye and delicate brush her great aunt must have used.

She puts the bag in the cup and adds water, a puff of vapor rising quickly and disappearing. She dunks the tea bag several times. Then, because she hates the taste of tea, Lucy adds milk and three teaspoons of sugar. She raises it to her mouth, blows and sips.

"Here." Willie puts three ginger snaps on Lucy's saucer.

Then he dunks one and takes a bite. Lucy laughs when half of the cookie falls into the milk.

"Spoons are over there." She points at the top drawer of the cabinet. While Willie looks for a spoon, Lucy dunks and consumes one whole ginger snap without dropping so much as a crumb. "Ta-da!" she says as Willie takes his seat, a so-what grin on his face.

"I thought Pres was coming over."

"Me, too," says Lucy.

Pres missed a whole week of school. Willie picked up his homework every day and dropped it off. Pres's mother always intercepted him before he could even get a look at Pres. On Friday, though, his mother wasn't home. Pres answered the door, wearing a terry cloth robe and moccasins. Pres looked chicken bone thin and his face was as white as the screen Clammerman used to show his drop and roll movies.

"Are you sick?" Willie asked.

"No," Pres mumbled.

"You aren't?"

"No," he said.

"So---"

"I guess, I don't know, I kept telling my mom I had a stomach ache. By Wednesday she didn't even ask anymore." Pres didn't invite him in. Willie could see blankets and pillows on the couch; there were baseball cards strewn on the floor.

"*Did* you have a stomach ache?"

Pres shook his head no.

"What do you do all day?"

"Nothing, watch TV, that's about it."

"Well, Lucy and me, we wish you'd come back. Not seeing you at school is a real drag."

Pres's face remained expressionless as tears flooded his cheeks.

"Look man, I'm sorry you're not, you're not feeling good."

"Thanks. I better do my homework." Pres closed the door.

He did return to school that Monday. He was quiet all day, but he was there, that's what mattered. This little get together at Lucy's was supposed to be a celebration.

"Where's your mom?"

"She's got another job interview." Lucy is embarrassed by her mother's frequent interviews, countless it seems, in the last few months. She hates even saying 'job interview' because she imagines Willie will laugh.

"That's good, isn't it?"

"Hard to say."

"What's the job?"

Lucy takes another sip and tries to speak matter-of-factly. "At the dealership, I think. Your grandfather set it up for her."

Willie's nose crinkles. "He did?"

"Yeah. Didn't you know?"

Willie lays his fifth cookie on the napkin and gulps his milk. "No. Didn't know a thing."

"Yeah, he's helped her a lot."

"What would your mom do at a car dealership?"

"I don't know, but she spent every penny we have on some fancy dress. She'll probably wear it, like, once or twice before she either loses the job or just gives up on it."

Willie's been through this with Lucy before. When her mother gets a job, a blanket of gloom hangs over the house, as if disaster awaits. "I don't know, Luce, if Pop set it up, it must be something good, you know, like a better than usual job, one your mom will like; the new dress and everything, it sounds like she really wants it; I'll bet it works out this time."

Lucy loves Willie's face, how his freckles splash across the bridge of his nose, how his cheeks shine, how his eyes flash, how he smiles with every word, as if what he's saying, without a doubt, is as true as the sunrise. It lifts her spirits, if only for a day or an hour or a moment.

"Crossing my fingers," she says.

"There you go."

"Hi, Mr. Mitchum."

Hal turns around and there's Brenda behind the counter waving. He nods and waves back. The barber shop confrontation is still on his mind. He passes the magazines, *Look* and *Life* featured prominently. Razor blades and shaving creams, perfumes and nail polish, Band-Aids and mercurochrome, Aspirin, Preparation-H in the new large economy size, candy, gum, Topps baseball cards, eye glass kits, Q-tips, just about anything you'd need and even more you wouldn't. He's not looking for anything.

There is a debate raging in his head---should he go back to John's and apologize or should he stand his ground? The standing-his-ground option is appealing. It makes him feel like Gary Cooper in *High Noon*, the good guy single-handedly beating the bad guys. Right beating wrong; good victorious over bad.

But it isn't nearly so black and white as that, is it? The go-back-to-John's-and-apologize option is mostly about friendship, not so much friendship with Ralph and Gordo, but with John. He gave the boys free haircuts for a year after their parents died. Never said he was going to do it, just did it. And when Mae died, he came to the funeral parlor and sat in the back crying, then left, unable to come forward and speak to Hal.

"So, you've completed your tour of our store," said Brenda. "Was it as exciting as you hoped."

"It took my breath away." He plants a bottle of Listerine in the middle of the counter.

"If not, maybe *this* will take my breath away."

"You're too much," says Brenda, chuckling.

"Add a couple packs of Camels and I'll be good to go."

John is sitting on his barber chair reading the paper, the day nearly over, all his customers gone. Hal opens the door quietly. John doesn't notice, so Hal taps on the wall a few times. John folds his paper and drops it on the floor.

"Look, John, I didn't mean to---"

"Your hair looks awful. Come over here."

John gets out of the chair and Hal gets in. John covers him up again and reaches for his scissors and comb without saying a word. Hal stares straight ahead, not knowing what to say. John's scissors sing as he combs and cuts, combs and cuts.

"How 'bout I throw in a shave, too."

"Sure. Thanks, John."

"You are very welcome, Hal."

John nicks Hal's mole and Hal flinches. John dabs it several times. Hal smiles.

"I stand by what I said---"

"I know."

"But afterwards I felt---"

"I know, I know. Pull your top lip down so I can get in there." Hal obliges. "There you go. Perfect."

"Thanks."

"Sure."

Outside on the sidewalk, Hal sticks the bottle of Listerine under his arm, opens a pack of cigarettes, lights up and puts his cigarettes and matches back in his pocket.

He hears a familiar rattling sound. Sure enough, coming off the bridge is an old, beat-up Rambler the color of a used baby diaper, smoke spiraling from the exhaust pipe. He grins, raises his arm high and waves, but the driver doesn't look. The driver's face is steely, cold; body leaning forward, hands locked on the wheel, like a child on a roller coaster. He follows the car with his eyes, hand still in the air.

Hal lowers his hand and flicks his cigarette into the street. What's up with Trish? he thinks.

. . .

Before they see her, Lucy and Willie smell the oily stench of her mother's car.

"Better clean up," says Lucy.

They grab dishes and stack them in the sink. Willie puts one more ginger snap in his mouth before dumping the rest back into the box and putting it on top of the refrigerator. Lucy wipes the table with a dish cloth. They look at each other as if to say, 'Good enough'. The front door opens and Trish bursts in, looking like she's not sure she's in the right place.

"Hi Mom," says Lucy, as her mother disappears up the stairs. She looks at Willie. "Hi Mom, how was the interview? Did you get the job? Oh, great. When do you start? Wonderful. How much money? Terrific. Good talk, Mom. Thanks."

"Sorry," says Willie.

CHAPTER 38

A squint-inducing sun warms their faces as Denny and Becky cross Old Main St. into the town of Weston. A flood of parents, alumni, and students flow past them, heading for Granger Stadium and the Homecoming game against nearby Westminster College.

Becky and Denny relinquished their free student passes to more worthy fans and, instead, used Saturday afternoons for other things. Today's main event---buying bus tickets to Ellwood City.

If you want tickets, you go to Buster Grimmus's house at 5 South Main St. and knock on the door. As often as not, Buster's wife, Gladiola, will answer. She'll invite you in and seat you in the front room. Soon Buster will bluster in, napkin still tucked in his shirt collar. He'll clear his throat, open his roll top desk, remove a shoe box where he keeps the tickets, and then sit down, smile, and ask where you're going. And so it was with Denny and Becky.

"Ellwood City, huh." Buster digs through his box. "Let me see, let me see...I don't get many requests for Ellwood City." He looks up and smiles. "Pittsburgh usually...but...Ellwood City...not so much. You from there?" Denny answers in the affirmative. "Okay...then..."

Finally, Buster finds two Greyhound tickets for their chosen destination, only fifteen stops along the way, seventeen hours all together.

"It only took me seven hours to get here," says Denny.

"Must be a bit farther going back."

Denny frowns, digs into his pocket for some cash, and plunks down twenty dollars. As they turn to go, Becky trips on a table leg and tumbles to the floor. As she gets up, Buster notices.

"I am so sorry. I didn't realize you were crippled," he says, a painfully sympathetic look in his eyes.

Denny helps Becky up and whispers, "Ignore him."

"Thank you for your concern. I wondered how long it would take," says Becky.

"What?" says Buster, a puzzled look on his face.

"Usually, people show concern almost immediately. They carry things for me, help me up and down stairs. They let me go to the head of any line because they know I can't stand up very long."

Denny pokes her ribs. "Let's go."

"They pick me up when I fall. I was in New York once and a man picked me right up and carried me across the street. I didn't even have to ask him. They understand I can't do things like regular people. But you, you and your wife. Your wife didn't even notice a thing. And you only reacted to my gimpy leg when I fell." She scrunches her face as if she is about to cry. "Is that the only way you can tell someone is needy, someone isn't as normal as other people; they have to fall down or get hurt or maybe even die before you---"

"I didn't mean nothing," says Buster. "I'm so, so sorry, miss, I didn't..."

Becky has already turned and is limping toward the front door. Denny holds her arm. He wants to say something to Buster, something that will clear the air, but he is too embarrassed to speak.

As they exit the house, Buster calls after them. "I didn't mean nothing!" Denny is puzzled. He waits for an explanation.

"You hungry?" she says, a blank look on her face.

"What?"

"Hungry. Are you hungry? I'm starving. How 'bout we go to Betty's, huh?"

Before he can answer, Becky is ten paces ahead of him. She stops, turns and waves for him to hurry up. He quick steps it to her side. "What's wrong?"

"Nothing's wrong."

"What were you doing back there? I mean, I really don't think he meant anything."

"No one means anything. Everyone gets a pass."

Denny stops. "What?"

Becky stops, but doesn't turn around.

"Becky?"

She doesn't answer. He walks up behind her, puts his hands gently on her shoulders, and turns Becky around. Her lips are taut, her eyes are downcast. "Becky?" he says, bending over so his face is in her line of sight.

Becky blinks several times to moisten her dry eyes. She looks at Denny, then raises her shoulders and lets them drop.

"This morning someone put an ad for wheelchairs in my mailbox."

"Shit."

"Yeah."

"Do you know who did it?"

She shakes her head. He puts his arms around her. "Let's go to Betty's."

Betty's is alive with the chatter of parents prying information from their college sons or daughters. For their part, the students resist the urge to regress into the pouty, slumpy, moody, needy children they were, with mixed results. A father tells his daughter to "get that thing out of your mouth," as his daughter slowly lights up a cigarette and blows smoke across the table. A son slips and calls his mother "Mommy." Most, though, do well; they smile and joke and tell funny stories about college life and their parents marvel at who their child has become in a few short weeks.

Denny and Becky take the booth in the back corner, far from the fresh-scrubbed feel of families reuniting. Cups of coffee come quickly. Soon thereafter, pancakes and bacon. And bagels. They eat in silence, Denny gobbling, Becky picking.

Denny waves for another cup of coffee, pushes his plate away, and pulls the bus tickets out of his back pocket. He runs his finger over the edges and tries to figure out where they'll be stopping. He expects Becky to show interest in the trip, ask questions, make plans for what to pack. But, no. The waitress pours him another cup and tops Becky's off.

"So, how was breakfast?" Denny uses a friendly, inquisitive tone, like he is conducting a survey.

"Good."

"Yeah, mine was great, too." What to say next? Denny is more tentative with Becky since his experiment in empathy.

"You know, I'm so sorry about what I did?"

Becky finally looks up from her plate, her forehead tensed. "What you did?"

"Yeah, you know, the whole shoe experiment. I'm sorry."

"Okay."

"It was so dumb."

Becky watches him, unsure why he's bringing this up now.

"I won't make that mistake again."

"Why are you talking about this?"

"Because it's important."

"Not anymore."

Denny tries to hide a sigh of relief. He feels like he could eat another stack of pancakes.

"This isn't about you or anything you did."

"Is it about the idiot ticket guy?"

"It's partly about the idiot ticket guy, but it's more than that."

Denny decides not to speak, but to listen.

"It's...it's everything really. I mean, even though it's only one part of me, a part of me that I can't change, and maybe don't want to change, it consumes all my energy. And it's how others define me. I can't do anything about that, but it drives me batshit crazy. I'm other things, too. It may be the starting place for everyone else, but I don't want it to be my starting place."

Denny vacates his seat and slides in beside Becky. He puts his arm around her. She puts both elbows on the table and rests her chin in her hands.

"I'm scared."

"Scared of what?"

"Your family. What will they think of me?"

"They'll think what I think. You're the most amazing person in the world."

Becky sits up and rests her hand on Denny's thigh.

"How could they be sure I'm the most amazing person? Do they know everyone in the world?"

"As a matter of fact, they do."

CHAPTER 39

Preston Stapleton sits on the curb watching cars speed up and down Jefferson Ave. He tosses a stone into the storm drain. Why is life hard? It's like a rope with knots that can't be untied. He thinks and thinks and when no answer comes, his head begins to ache.

His mom is working as a secretary at a bank, something she's never done before. She's home when he gets up, but has to leave before he goes to school. She makes his lunch sandwich and leaves it in the refrigerator for when he comes home at noon. Sometimes he throws it away and lies on the couch.

When she comes home after work, Pres has already set the table. Their meals are simple, hotdogs and chips, eggs and toast, tomato soup and grilled cheese. When he looks disappointed, his mother says, "This is plenty enough for us, Preston. We'll get back to normal." In recent days, she's stopped using the word "soon," as in "Soon, we'll get back to normal" or "Soon your dad will come home." Nothing, it seems, will be "soon."

"Hey, punk!" Willie runs down the block toward him. At the sight of his friend, Preston half-smiles.

"Did you call me punk, punk?"

"You looked up when I said it, didn't you? Must have gotten it right, right?"

Willie is breathing hard. He socks Pres's arm and almost hugs him.

"Hey, man, been a while," says Willie.

"Yeah...How's it going?"

"What can I say? It's going the way it's going. Guess what? Denny's coming home in a couple days."

"That's cool."

"Yeah, and you won't believe it, but he's bringing some girl with him."

"You're kidding."

"I know."

"Wow. Your brother with a girl. What are the chances? Is he, like, paying her to do this?"

Willie's head shoots back as he guffaws. Pres points and winks. Willie sits down beside him.

"How's Lucy? You two get married yet?"

Willie pushes him. "C'mon man." He catches Pres up about Lucy's mother's job, how Lucy's going nuts with worry, how she feels certain her mom will lose the job and, once again, the sky will fall.

"Speaking of the sky falling," says Willie. Preston is surprised to hear that old man Ashwood has finished his bomb shelter.

"I thought old man Ashwood's mother was dead," says Pres.

"Doesn't seem to be," says Willie.

Willie talks about the bomb shelter and how he thinks Mr. Ashwood brought his mother home because he didn't want her to die in a nuclear holocaust, which, to Willie, is pretty thoughtful.

Pres isn't listening.

Willie nudges his knee. "Hey man, you okay?"

"I guess." Pres looks at Willie and tries to force a smile, then looks down at the pavement.

"What's that---'I guess'? What's up?"

"My dad. It's always my dad."

"What's going on?"

"They're telling us he has, like, an illness or disease."

"Like he's sick?"

"Something like that, they aren't sure..."

Pres thinks about the day he came home from school and his father had locked himself in the basement. Each time Pres called to him, all he'd say was, "Sergeant Stapleton reporting for duty, sir!" When his mother came home from grocery shopping, he was sitting on the floor in front of the basement door, calling "It's okay, Dad, it's okay." His mother told him to go to his room. A half hour later, his father was in bed crying. Pres's mom explained his father was "not feeling well" and that "sometimes the memories are too overwhelming." Preston's mouth gaped open. "It's going to be okay; this has happened before. Your dad just needs rest."

Willie thinks this is odd. "Geez. I'm sorry, Pres." Willie picks up a twig and tosses it into the street. Pres does the same. A robin lands in the yard beside them and pulls hard on a worm.

"Did you ever think it would be so hard?"

"So hard? What?"

"Everything....you know, like...I mean, everything was fun, every day...and then...I don't know."

Willie wants to say that everything hasn't been fun; we just do our best to ignore stuff, but instead he says, "I know what you mean."

Pres takes a deep breath and blows out hard as a bellows.

"What if it's never any different than this?"

"Look, Pres, this is just a bad patch, that's all; bad stuff never lasts forever. Soon things will swing back to the way it was and we'll be laughing about how worried we were."

Pres can tell by Willie's halting voice he doesn't believe what he's saying.

And yet, it sounds so good.

"You think?" says Pres.

Willie looks at his friend, raises his eyebrows and grins, trying to show confidence. "Yeah, absolutely."

Willie slaps his hands on his thighs, and stands up.

"C'mon, let's get a Fanta."

Pres stays seated on the curb.

• • •

Muriel Ashwood sits on the front porch in the rocking chair she pulled from the living room. Scraps of wood are cradled in her lap. She retrieved them from the pile left behind when Robby finished his subterranean dream house. There's a pile of shavings on the floor around her feet. She holds a piece of wood with her left hand and steadily presses the knife blade to the wood with her right. The pieces curl and fall to the floor.

"Why don't you take up something like knitting or...crocheting?" asks Robby.

"'Cause I'm not an old lady."

Muriel rests the knife in her palm. It was her grandfather's. Her father had given the knife to her brother, Jerome, but Muriel commandeered it, hid it in her dresser until she moved out, and, for years, carried it everywhere she went. Except the county home. "Muriel, dear, what would you want with a knife? We'll just keep it in a safe place."

Her father said her grandfather made the handle from a bear's hip bone. He'd killed the bear as it was about to attack him. So, the story goes. Then he jigged the bone and dyed it black and tan. The single blade was three inches long. She folds it and opens it, folds it and opens it. Muriel picks up the wood again and continues whittling.

She hears young voices approaching. Two boys. She rocks and waits. Who are they? she wonders. Could it be Robby and that friend of his, what was his name, never trusted him. No, it's not Robby, too skinny.

As they get closer, she hollers, "Hey, who are you?"

"It's me, Mrs. Ashwood, Willie, Willie Blevin."

"Do you live around here, boy?"

Willie points to his house three doors down. "Right there."

"Are you related to Hal Mitchum?"

"He's my grandfather, yes."

"Grandfather, huh. You must be the boy with the dead parents."

"Geez," says Pres.

Willie gulps. "Yes, that would be me."

They try to move on, but Muriel has more to say.

"That was the awfulest of awful things, wasn't it? You were there, weren't you?"

Willie puts his hands in his pocket and kicks at a crack in the sidewalk. Pres suggests he not answer her, because she's looney. Willie shakes his head, as if to say no, she isn't, although he's pretty sure she is. Pres wonders if she's ever been in Dixmont. Willie says he thinks she's just old and that's what happens to old people. They agree getting old is not a good life plan.

"Did you hear me, boy?"

"Yes, ma'am. No, I don't think I was there, wherever it was. I don't really know that much---"

"That don't make no sense. My boy, Robby, the one who lives here with me, my boy, Robby, told me all about what happened and I'm pretty sure he said you was there. It was in the papers and everything."

Willie walks toward her porch, Pres close behind. "What did you say, Mrs. Ashwood?"

"Don't you come any closer, mister! I got a knife here and I'll use it." She points it at them. Pres laughs.

"I wouldn't hurt you, Mrs. Ashwood. I just want to know about the accident."

"What accident? Was there another accident? I'm telling you those hot rods come round that bend like bats out of hell, and end up in Conners' front yard. Why, in my day, cars couldn't go fast enough to end up in someone's---"

"Mrs. Ashwood, Mrs. Ashwood, really, can you tell me more about my mom and dad and what happened to them?"

Muriel's face goes blank and she smiles absently. Then her face scrunches and tears puddle in her eyes. "I don't remember what happened to my mother and father. I was just a girl. Maybe consumption, I don't remember."

"No, Mrs. Ashwood, I meant..."

Mrs. Ashwood is mumbling to herself now. She looks up and is startled to see them.

"Who are you?"

Willie and Pres look at each other.

CHAPTER 40

When Trish comes back down stairs, Lucy and Willie are gone. She looks around the kitchen until she finds her car keys. Once behind the wheel, she sits motionless, thinking about the interview, thinking about what Mr. Kleinman had said, thinking about what to do. She backs out of the driveway and goes.

Trish presses the door bell and waits. She pulls a tissue from her purse and wipes her eyes and nose. She forces herself to breathe slowly and deeply, the only way to regain her voice. No one comes, so she rings again.

Hal gets out of his chair, goes to the TV and turns the sound down. He listens for a moment and the doorbell rings. His left leg having fallen asleep, he walks slowly to the front door, shaking his leg every step of the way. He opens the door, ready to get rid of whoever's on the other side. But it's Trish again, standing on the front stoop looking like she's lost her dog.

Trish apologizes profusely. Hal tries to sound welcoming, but instead, he sounds screechy, like an angry owl. "Come in, come in."

Hal hurriedly picks up the beer cans and the newspaper. He puts pillows back on the sofa and punches them, hoping their puffy softness will return.

Trish watches as Hal tries to bring order to the room. His graying face is unshaven and his work pants look like they've never been acquainted with an iron. One side of his red checked shirt hangs on his hip like a hound dog's tongue. The wrinkles on his face have turned to trenches. She asks if she's come at a bad time. He tries to act surprised by the question and, although his face says 'yes', he shakes his head adamantly 'no'.

"Sorry the place is such a..." He shrugs.

"It's fine. I'm sorry that I didn't call---"

"Nonsense."

It's only been a week since they last spoke, yet it feels like ages to both of them. Hal insists coffee is called for. She follows him into the kitchen and takes a seat at the table. Having something to do, loosens Hal's tongue. He talks in excruciating detail about the leaf project Willie and Lucy are working on. "I'm telling you, those gingko leaves, right?" Trish agrees and then falls silent.

Hal pours two cups and puts a carton of milk and a bowl of sugar on the table. He sits, then gets up for the spoons. Her cup sits on the table untouched, while Hal sips his.

"Trish, it's good to see you. It is."

Hal rarely uses her first name in conversation. He feels like he's being too familiar, too forward.

Hearing "Trish" on his gravelly voice, makes her feel good, like she was right to come.

"It's good to see you, too. I'm sorry to crash in here like this."

"No, really, its fine. You are always welcome."

Hal has never seen Trish dress so formally. She must have had the interview today, he thinks. He looks at her drawn face, her slumping posture, and fears the worst.

Trish sees expectancy in Hal's eyes, like he's placed his bet and is hoping for a return. She reruns the interview in her mind over and over. She sees the tiny replica of the Statue of Liberty on his desk, the pen in its golden holder, the desk blotter full of scribbles and scratches. She sees his smile, though his eyes are hidden by the glare of sunlight on his glasses.

"I met with Mr. Kleinman this morning, actually about an hour ago. He told me to say 'Hi' to you."

"Yes, he started about six months before I left."

Trish's fingers are fidgeting, like spiders in a wrestling match.

"How did it go?" Hal shifts forward on the edge of his chair. He reaches for his coffee, but doesn't drink. "What did he say?"

"Well, he was nice, polite, and he explained a lot about the job and what they were looking for, what kind of person, that sort of thing."

"That's good."

"And well, I guess he offered it to me."

Ready to congratulate her, Hal sees the weariness on her face and hesitates, unsure of what to say. "Well, that's something," he says, with a middling kind of enthusiasm. "I mean, he must have been impressed."

"Yeah, I guess." Trish rests both arms on the table. "He talked about all the opportunities, that sort of thing."

"So...did you accept the offer?"

Trish begins to cry, her chest heaving and her face contorting.

Hal is befuddled. Faced with the best news possible, Trish looks like she's melting away. Should he hug her? Should he shake her? He does neither. He gets up, takes a box of tissue from the counter and places it in front of her. He rests his hand on her shoulder, squeezes once, then returns to his seat and waits.

The only promise Trish made to herself on the way to Hal's was she wouldn't cry.

"I'm so sorry, I really am---"

"No need---"

"It's just..."

"Take your time. Good news can be as hard as---"

"I took it."

Hal gasps. "Wonderful! That's great news."

She takes a tissue from the box and balls it in her hand.

"It's just that I don't know if I can do it."

Kleinman explained that in the beginning hers would be a jack-of-all trades position. It would include learning how to do billing, handling calls for the service department, some clerking, following up on customer concerns and complaints. This way she could learn the automobile business. Along the way, they would train her to work in sales, probably the used car lot across the street first, then the new cars. It would take a few years and a lot of hard work, but the opportunities were there for her. He said a few other things, but by then she couldn't listen anymore. All these opportunities felt like a mountain, a mountain that could fall on her if she wasn't careful.

She didn't remember saying 'yes', but Kleinman stood at his desk, a broad, triumphant smile on his face, his hand outstretched for her to shake.

"I mean, I knew I couldn't walk away from this offer. It's more money than I've ever seen. Lucy's life would be so much better."

"Why don't you think you can do it? I don't understand."

Trish is calmer now; she wipes her nose, gets up from her chair and throws the tissue away in the corner wastebasket. She leans against the sink, folds her arms and looks at Hal.

"Every job I've ever had, I got because of how I look."

"That's not---"

"It's true Hal, it is. The men who hired me could have cared less about how well I did the work. That didn't matter at all. What mattered was (she gestures to herself) all of this. I was always the pretty high school dropout. I was a decorative piece. And sometimes they expected...well...they expected things from me."

Hal is at a loss for words. He thinks of the barber shop.

"Here's the thing. Maybe I hated what they expected, but I knew how to do it. It was easy. I been doing it all my life. I'm good at it. My mother taught me and I learned quick, believe me. That's how I got in the mess I was in. Your Ruthie tried to convince me I had more to offer than that. But I knew what I had to offer. I knew it good."

Hal pushes his mug aside.

"I resented it, but I accepted it. I accepted that the outside parts of me were the only things that mattered." Trish, exhausted, turns her half-mast eyes to Hal.

"Look, Trish...No one should treat you like that. No one. Never. It's, it's..."

Trish lowers her head.

"It's like all the good stuff, the very best parts of you, have been, I don't know, hidden away somewhere. Hidden so good that even *you* can't see them. But *I* can." Hal rubs his chin. "Give yourself a chance."

From the color in Hal's cheeks and the earnestness in his eyes, Trish knows he means what he's saying. That he cares for her. And she loves him for that.

But is he right? Has the best of her been hidden away all these years? Is it as simple as giving yourself a chance? Is there more to be discovered? Or is she exactly what she appears to be?

CHAPTER 41

Their first stop in Pennsylvania is Gettysburg. They get out of the bus to stretch their legs and eat the sandwiches they packed. They walk around the expansive square, looking for a bench in the late afternoon sun. When they find one, Becky notices a plaque on the building adjacent to them. It says the room above them is where Lincoln slept the night before he gave the Gettysburg Address.

"Can you believe it?" says Becky.

"Unbelievable." Denny reads the plaque again and shakes his head. "Wow, can you imagine being here? You know, to see the man himself just walking around like, I don't know, a regular person."

"Yeah, really. He didn't know what was coming, that's for sure."

"Nobody did. Who'd've thought someone would kill him, you know?"

"They get way more protection now. I mean, have you seen those guys running alongside the president's car? There's always someone around, watching." Becky takes a bite of her ham and cheese sandwich. "It could never happen again. There are too many safeguards in place."

Denny chews and swallows a bite. "I don't know."

"What do you mean?"

"I don't know if you can make anything safe, like one hundred percent. Look at the whole Cuba thing. Are we safe?"

"No, we're not, but that's a whole international thing, it's different. If we're just talking about the president, one person, I think for sure, he's totally safe."

"Hope you're right." He takes another bite of his egg salad sandwich. "I think we tell ourselves everything's okay, you know what I mean, that nothing bad can happen to one of our presidents, but there's always a chance; I don't know, I just think we can never be one hundred percent safe. Maybe ninety percent, if we're lucky. But then we get so used to things working out ninety percent of the time, we ignore the other ten percent, you know, the risk that's always there; we start believing that ninety percent is *really* one hundred percent. And then we're shocked when it isn't."

"What about us, what about regular people?" Becky balls her bag and tosses it into a nearby receptacle.

"I don't know, maybe ninety-five percent." Denny drops the rest of his sandwich into his bag. "But that five percent may be enough, it may be enough to cause trouble. Like my parents. When they got up that morning, if you'd have asked one hundred people if they thought my parents would be dead by the end of the day, I bet all of them would have said no. One hundred percent. My parents would have said no, too. And they'd have been wrong. They'd have overlooked that five percent."

Becky stares at Denny for a moment longer, then takes another bite of her sandwich. Denny looks across the square at nothing.

Their next stop is Chambersburg, little more than a half hour west of Gettysburg. No one gets off, but four get on. The driver waits until the official departure time, and then pulls the handle, closing the door. He releases the brake and presses the gas. Everyone holds their breath as black smoke spews from the exhaust. They pull out of the bus station just as the sun is going to sleep.

Between Chambersburg and Somerset, Becky pulls a warm Coke from their bag. She nudges Denny and he gives her the opener. Denny closes his eyes and tries to get some rest. Becky opens her copy of *To Kill a Mockingbird* and continues reading. But she can't get her mind off what is ahead. Will the ninety-five percent prevail or the five percent?

When Denny first invited her to meet his family, she felt compelled to say yes. Just moments earlier, she had criticized him harshly about whether he could fully understand her predicament. Maybe by saying yes, she was trying to soften that blow.

Only later did the magnitude of her agreement sink in. Backpacking through Europe would be much less daunting than going to Ellwood City to meet Denny's family. How will they react to her "gimpiness," the name most recently given to her by a passing jock: "Hey, Miss Gimpiness."

She looks at her book again. How long have I been staring at page 156?

Denny's eyes have been closed for fifty miles. He's slept for the first two. The rest of the time, he's been treading emotional water. Ruminations about his family are pulling him down, like an anchor tied to his ankle. He imagines arriving to find Pop and Willie standing at the front door, Smoochy sitting obediently beside them. Pop is waving a copy of the letter he sent to Denny. As he walks up the porch steps, they greet him with a single question---"What are we supposed to do next?"---to which he shrugs and says "What we always do. Nothing." With this, his eyes shoot open, he gasps for air, like he's surfaced from the water with nothing left in his lungs.

He looks out the darkened window at the humble lights flickering in distant farmhouses. How can they see, he thinks, with so little light?

He looks at Becky who is immersed in her novel. He reaches for her hand and she half-smiles, though her eyes never leave the book. He squeezes and she squeezes back. He is relieved she is with him, that she agreed to meet his family and to provide him some support. She is the strong one, he thinks.

There are two dozen towering light standards at the Somerset stop. Each with several spotlights that turn the night into day. It is what Denny imagines a prison yard looks like when inmates try to escape. There are three truck stops with semis growling and grinding. Six gas stations with signs so tall you can see them miles away. There is a half dozen fast food joints and a couple of train car diners.

The truckers wear flannel and have scraggly beards and hair like straw sticking out from under their Harvester ball caps. Sleepy families tumble out of their cars, D.C. souvenir hats and shirts and flags drooping.

There are shaggy haired boys and long-haired girls outside the Howard Johnson's, bandanas around their heads, sleeping bags on their backs, thumbs up, hoping for a ride to who knows where. Becky wishes she was one of them, heading to some yet unknown adventure...other than the one she's on. Denny worries about how the hitchhikers bathe and whether their parents know where they are.

"Something, huh?" says Becky, reverence in her voice.

"I'll say," says Denny, a frown on his face.

Becky closes *To Kill a Mockingbird*, her thumb marking the page. She stretches her arms and legs, then massages her thigh while slowly swinging her leg back and forth.

"Everything okay?"

"Yeah. Just a cramp." She opens the book again.

"We could get out and stretch, take a little walk."

She closes the book. "Everything's fine." She opens the book.

"Okay," he says.

She begins to read, but she feels his eyes boring into her.

"What?"

"We've been on the road for a while now."

"Uh huh."

"And we haven't talked much at all."

Apart from the initial days of awkwardness when they were getting to know each other, they've never had problems talking. They are magpies. People stare at them bewildered by their constant chatter. Talking takes no thought, no effort, it just happens, like breathing. Until you have something to say.

Since the *Scarlet Letter* conversation, Becky has been preoccupied with her leg, her own flesh-bound scarlet letter. She wonders: Is this leg and all the energy it takes to bear it greater than the sum of my parts? Is it a whole unto itself, and the rest of me, merely scattered pieces clinging to it?

She thinks about Denny's family. Can she bear having new eyes on her?

The stern, unapproachable look on Becky's face frightens Denny. Where has my Becky gone? he thinks. She is faraway even as she sits shoulder to shoulder with him on this bus. This is not the time to ask her to listen, he thinks, this is not the time to ask her for anything.

Denny's comment hovers in the air as they sit together inside each other's silence.

. . .

"Is it time to go yet?" The weeks since Denny left for college feel like years. Now, suddenly, he is coming home. Even though he's coming because of Pop's beckoning, because of his worry about Willie, none of that matters. Willie feels only excitement and gratitude.

Pop doesn't have to look at the kitchen wall clock. "No, it's not time. They left late yesterday afternoon. It's a long trip. Won't get here until later this morning. Go back to bed."

"Naw."

"Eat something."

Pop didn't sleep all night. He sat in his chair until Carson was over, then watched Chilly Billy Cardilly who was showing back-to-back Lon Chaney films. Then he adjourned to the front steps with a pack of cigarettes and Smoochy by his side. He blew smoke into the darkness. Smoochy whimpered a little, then curled up at Pop's feet and promptly fell asleep.

In time, soft light descended through thick cloud cover. Pop heard the first robin chirp. Then the milkman making his rounds, pristine bottles clanging; pickup trucks racing across the bridge trying to make the 'A' shift; a *Post-Gazette* paper boy whistling while he tosses; and a new day settling into place.

Willie takes a soup bowl from the cupboard and fills it to overflowing with Sugar Smacks. He pours milk onto the cereal, grabs a spoon, and tries to balance the bowl by walking stiff legged to the table. He leaves a milk trail behind him. Smoochy cleans it up and waits for more.

Pop brews the morning coffee and watches Willie eat. The questions that filled his mind throughout the night still remain. What was I thinking? Was it a mistake to write the letter? Should I have kept everything to myself?

What's going on with Willie? What will happen when Denny talks to him? What will get stirred up?

He watches Willie slurp sugary milk from the bowl, then put the bowl on the floor so Smooch can finish it off. Ruthie would laugh; she would be so proud. He's so big, she'd say. Where did my little boy go?

He remembers the day. He and Denny were at the lumber yard. Denny was running toward the loading dock when Pop noticed his left shoe was untied. Denny didn't want to, but Pop made him stop dead in his tracks and tie them. "What did I say about safety?" he called. It seems silly now, tie your shoes and you'll be safe. The phone rang and when Zack picked it up, all he said was "No, please no"; then he looked at Pop who said "What is it?" Life was never the same again.

Willie is on the floor wrestling with Smoochy. Pop hasn't seen him this animated in weeks. Smooch leaps on him, barking and licking. Willie laughs, rolls over and tries to push Smooch away. Pop leans against the counter, pours a cup of coffee and watches with quiet satisfaction.

In the back of his mind, though, he can hear Mae: You've got to tell him. He should know what happened to his mom and dad; it's the right thing. He's still so young, thinks Pop. Willie worries about things, like the world coming to an end. What twelve-year-old worries about that? Sometimes he can't go to school, he's so worried. When I ask him, he can't say why. Mae, did you know he passed out? Twice. And the year's just getting started. Who passes out at his age? He is just a kid, Mae, and the world is too much with him. Does he have to know?

He can see Mae shaking her head and saying: What you should know but don't, can hurt you more.

·   ·   ·

Denny and Becky are waking up as the bus approaches Pittsburgh. They rub their eyes and look at the confluence of rivers that births the Ohio each day. Coal barges, like skulking sea monsters, navigate past one another, sounding their horns hello. The water is as murky as the sky. Inclines, like inch worms, crawl up the side of the mountain. Flakes of soot float through the bus windows as passengers rush to close them.

"Look at that paddle wheel boat," says Becky.

"That's the Good Ship Lollipop."

"That's really what it's called?"

"Yep."

"Ever been on it?"

"Yep."

"How cool is that."

Becky bounces in her seat and throws her arms around his neck. Denny is buoyed by her exuberance. Maybe things will go well when he gets home. Maybe talking to Willie won't be a big deal. Maybe Pop has already figured things out and he's already doing better. The maybe-not part of Denny shrinks, but it doesn't disappear.

They hug the Ohio River briefly on their way to Aliquippa, Beaver Falls and eventually Ellwood. On the opposite shore there are red flames shooting and smoke stacks belching and furnaces blasting and the smell of sulfur and sweat for miles and miles, as W&J forges the world's steel in what looks like the gates of hell.

"Is there anything I should know before I meet your family?"

Denny looks into his lap, thinking. "I don't know."

"Like some families hug and others don't; some take their shoes off when they enter the house, others don't; some families still dress up for dinner, others don't; some keep the doors closed, others don't."

He doesn't know what to say. He's never given a thought to what kind of family they are. Who does?

"I don't know. I think we're mostly an 'others don't' kind of family."

. . .

Pop relents and agrees to let Pres and Lucy come with them to the bus stop. They are eager to meet Becky.

Metz's Filling and Way Station has proudly fulfilled the dual role of service station and bus depot for upwards of twenty years. Some

Ellwoodians think it's unseemly that the first glimpse newcomers get of Ellwood is a broken-down, greasy pumping station with junked cars piled beside it. The issue comes before the town board once a year. Each time, it's put aside for later consideration.

There are two benches at the bus stop. Willie, Lucy and Pres occupy one, while Pop stands by the curb watching and smoking.

"What's she look like?" says Pres.

Willie raises his eyebrows and shrugs. "I don't know."

"You don't know?" says Lucy.

"That's what I said."

"Didn't you ask?" says Pres.

"No, why would I?"

Lucy tosses up her hands in disbelief.

"What?"

"A complete stranger is coming to stay in your house for, what, three, four days and you don't know anything about her?" says Lucy.

Willie has given little thought to Becky. He is focused exclusively on Denny. His initial worry about having The Big Talk with his brother has been muted by the relief and satisfaction of having him back.

Pop taps his pack of cigarettes against the palm of his hand, pulls one out and lights up. He looks at Willie, how excited he is. Pop smiles and wonders if he'd been right to send Denny to a college far away. Would Willie be doing better if his brother were nearby? But what of Denny? Would he ever be able to make a life for himself if he didn't go away? These questions whittle away at him day in and day out.

. . .

"Zelienople. What kind of name is that for a town?" Becky asks. "It sounds very outer spacey."

"It's not far from Mars."

Becky pinches his leg softly. "C'mon."

"Really, there's a Mars, Pa. a short drive from here."

"Enough, enough," says Becky.

In twenty minutes, the bus will pull into Ellwood. Pop and Willie will be waiting. Denny imagines their smiling faces, so different from the sagging faces he left behind just weeks before. He is excited to see them, though his stomach is fluttering. Does Willie have any idea about Pop's concerns? About Pop's request? What if he can't help Willie? What if he makes things worse?

He squeezes Becky's hand.

She looks at him. "What?"

"We're okay, right? I mean...you and me, we're okay," says Denny.

Denny looks like a little boy, his eyes wide and blinky. A little boy who is searching for something to hold on to, something that will steady him. She pulls his hand to her lips and kisses it.

"Of course," she says.

Her words, her kiss, change nothing and everything.

There are hills and farms and woodlots, Amish buggies, a radar station, an airport, and a manmade lake between Zelienople and Ellwood.

Becky leans back in her seat trying to rein in her anxiety. She feels it in her arms and hands and fingers, her legs and feet and toes; she feels it in her toothy smile, her freckled face and her enormous eyes. Be calm, she says to her body. Her body replies, You're kidding, right?

They pass a sign. Only six miles to go. In less than ten minutes she will be in Ellwood.

. . .

"Here it comes," says Pop, pointing at a distant bus clambering in their direction. He doesn't take his eyes off the bus, as if he is guiding it safely home.

Willie can't stand still, his legs shake and his arms flap, like he's a baby bird on the edge of his nest. What will Denny be like? A friend in school said that when his brother came back from college at Christmas, he had an accent; no one knew why. He seemed indifferent to everything around him and dismissive of his parents, as if they were dinosaur fossils. Willie tries to imagine Denny speaking with an accent.

The Greyhound finally pulls into the station. Willie spots Denny and the girl waving from the window. He doesn't look any different, thinks Willie. Either Willie's pants are too short or he's grown, thinks Denny. Pop holds his breath, eager to see the boys together again.

The bus door opens, the bus driver gets out in a rush and heads into the gas station. Behind him is the girl, Becky, and, behind her, Denny.

Becky stands briefly at the door, before taking one step down, then another. She turns to make sure Denny is behind her before she takes the final step. She wobbles and Denny reaches for her. She regains her balance just in time to miss the third step completely. When she hits the pavement, her leg buckles and she crumples to the ground in agony. "Becky," calls Denny. He bounds down the steps and kneels at her side. "Are you okay?" Becky grimaces and rocks side to side, unable to speak. Pop is beside them now. Even with their help, Becky can't stand. He gets up, goes to the pay phone near the air pump, and calls for an ambulance.

And so, the visit begins.

CHAPTER 42

Pop and Willie sit in the hospital waiting room, their heads resting against the wall, their legs outstretched on the threadbare rug.

Willie opens his eyes, sits up and listens. My God, he thinks. It's the air raid siren, its mournful scream gobbling up the air. He looks at Pop, who doesn't bat an eye. His arms are folded across his chest and an unlit cigarette between his fingers. The siren continues to wail.

Behind the door marked "Hospital Employees Only," there are four cubicles divided by thin curtains. Each has a bed, one chair, a tiny desk and a stool on wheels. Two of the cubicles are empty. One is occupied by a woman who is either in labor or being tortured. Becky, her battered leg, and Denny are in the fourth room.

There is a nasty bulge on Becky's left shin that's pressing against her jeans. At first there's no pain. Blessed shock has kept it at bay. But now, the pain is coming in tidal waves. She tries to stop crying, but can't. Denny sits on the side of the bed, holding her hand. "It's okay, everything's going to be okay. Okay?"

As yet, they have not seen a doctor. The nurse who saw them briefly, said, "Yeah, that's a busted leg, for sure."

The nurse returns: "Here's something for your pain. The doctor should be here anytime." Becky, not a fan of medicines after so many surgeries, gobbles the pills gratefully. In a short while, the pain devolves into an annoying, yet bearable, ache.

Eventually, a youngish woman in a white coat arrives. She introduces herself as doctor someone. Denny studies her diminutive stature, her pitch-black hair pulled back in a pony tail, and her horn-rimmed glasses.

"Is some other doctor going to come?" he says.

Doctor Someone doesn't skip a beat. "Are you the husband, boyfriend, friend, brother?"

"Boyfriend."

"Are you in college?"

"Yeah, freshman."

"Do you remember what grade you were in when you were nine."

"Yeah, fourth."

"You were in fourth grade. I was graduating medical school at the top of my class and being recruited by practices all over the northeast."

"Oh."

She pivots to Becky, asks what happened, examines the leg. She is certain it is a tibial shaft fracture---broken shin bone---but wants to confirm it with an X-ray before "casting."

"Have you ever broken that leg before?"

"Actually, yes."

"Not a surprise, unfortunately."

Pop is reading *Life* magazine while Willie fiddles and shifts and sniffs repeatedly. "Take a walk up and down the hall a few times."

Willie walks past the administrator's office, the gift shop, the visitor's cafe, the social work office. He stops at each of the old timey pictures of Ellwood, including one of the Park Bridge half finished. At the end of the first hall, Willie turns left and walks to the end of the next one where a "No Admittance Sign" convinces him to go no further. He heads to the other end of the hall where he finds a sign that says: "Maternity." No signs forbidding him from going further, so he opens the door and enters. There are rooms on the right side of the hall full of mothers-to-be in various stages of distress.

On the left side is a long viewing window. Several fathers are leaning against the glass, eyes agog as, for the first time, they see the tiny humans they helped bring into the world.

Willie steps forward, leans on the glass and watches six babies, wrapped tighter than an Ace bandage on a swollen knee, kicking and scrunching and crying. The fathers are all smiles. There are four pink blankets and two blue ones.

One father notices Willie. "Hey, do you have a little brother or sister in there? How's your mother doing?"

Willie doesn't know what to say. No, my mother's dead; so is my dad. He looks up at the man who is listening eagerly. "Not yet," he says.

"Oh, your mom in labor?"

"Yeah. But my dad's with her and she's doing fine."

"How's the pain?"

"No complaints."

"That's good. Maybe you'll be a big brother before the night is over."

"Uh huh."

"What are you hoping for?"

Willie furrows his brow, unsure what the man is referring to. "I guess, I hope the Russians don't do anything stupid."

The father laughs. "No, no, no; I meant do you want a little brother or a little sister?"

"Oh. I don't know. Either, I guess."

"What do your parents want?"

He would love to know the answer. Did they get what they wanted the second time around? And what would they want now? "I think they're partial to boys."

"Well, with a son like you, I understand why." Willie wishes the man was his father and that it was his mother who had given birth. He would be a big brother.

The man oohs and awws at his baby again. The man's hand is large, with squared fingers, raised veins, blunted nails. The man puts his hand on the window and fog forms all around it. Willie wants to take the man's hand in his own, just to feel what a father's hand is like.

Both of them turn when a squeak, squeak, squeak echoes through the hall. A nurse approaches at full speed, her arms chugging hard. She's pointing now. Willie points at his own chest and she shakes her head vigorously, a vein about to burst on her temple.

"What do you think you're doing?" Her fists are pressed against her hips and her lips are so tight they've disappeared. "Is this your son? Don't you know the---"

"He's not my son," says the man. Willie feels a pang in his chest. The man turns back to his newborn baby.

"Where are your parents, young man?"

"They're...dead," he whispers.

The nurse's pursed lips soften and her hands fall to her side. Nevertheless, she is undeterred. "I'm sure they'd want you to obey the rules---children are not allowed beyond the waiting area."

Willie doesn't respond. She bends over and whispers, "Do you know how to get back to the waiting room? Is anyone there for you?"

Willie shakes his head and walks away.

CHAPTER 43

Mr. Conner is standing in his driveway across the street. He waves to Robert Ashwood and Muriel who are on the front sidewalk in their bare feet. "Looks like rain," he calls. Robert waves and nods in agreement. Several other neighbors join them, eager to see why an ambulance has pulled into Hal's driveway.

Becky argued that an ambulance wasn't necessary, but the hospital said it was policy.

The mini-parade comes down hospital hill to Lawrence Ave., Ellwood's main drag. Shoppers gather in clumps and watch it pass, each, no doubt, theorizing about what's going on.

Denny sits with Becky in the back of the ambulance, not knowing how to comfort her. Becky runs her hand down her cast.

"God, look at that thing," she says.

"Yeah."

"Looks like someone stuck a muffler on it, a big white muffler from my knee to my toes."

"Yeah." Denny reaches for the pair of crutches lying on the floor. He stands them on their rubber tips. He fondles the grip. "We can wrap, like, a towel or something around this so it doesn't kill your pits."

"You incurable romantic, you."

She'd worried for two weeks that Denny's family's eyes would never wander far from her leg. She was right, but for an entirely different reason--

-her spindly leg had been replaced by a broken one; a broken leg encased in plaster heavy enough to break her other leg if she wasn't careful. The benefit? The true form of her leg is far less distinguishable. And the clunky bottom of her cast makes her short leg just as long as her fully formed, altogether normal one. Different angels at work, she thinks.

Pop is quiet in the car. Willie's shoulders are rounded and his face is a deep shade of sullenness. He never liked the idea of this Becky person coming to their house. It will be impossible to act normal in front of some stranger. Worse than that. She broke her leg and Denny will have to spend all his time catering to her every need. What in the world does he see in her? Let's face it, Becky isn't, well, she isn't much to look at. He imagines them married with kids and everything.

"Well, what did you think of her?"

Is this a trick question? Does Pop really want to know what he thinks or does he want Willie to be polite, which would make everything easier?

"I don't know. I mean, I just met her and most of that time was spent messing with her stupid broken leg." He doesn't want to show his hand, but there it is.

It's sprinkling when the ambulance pulls into the driveway. Neighbors, not to be denied, have their umbrellas now. The EMTs get out of the ambulance first. They look around, unsure of where to go next. Pop parks on the street, then hurries to them, indicating that the front door should give them enough room. Willie stands beside Pop, hands in his pocket, a modest amount of concern on his face. Denny slides out of the ambulance first, holding the crutches under his arms. Willie moves to his side.

The EMTs' voices echo from the ambulance which is rocking back and forth. Soon they back out of the vehicle, frustration written on their faces. "Miss, may I remind you this isn't the way it's done."

Becky suggests the EMTs back off and then she calls for Denny, who dutifully responds. He slides the crutches into the ambulance and, immediately, Becky's casted leg appears and then the rest of her. She arranges the crutches and waves Denny off when he offers a helping hand.

I'm not an invalid, thinks Becky. I'll do this by myself or I won't do it at all. She steps onto the driveway with her good leg. Hand clenched around the grips, Becky swings forward almost losing her balance. She stops, rearranges the crutches and adjusts her grip. She takes a deep breath and takes another step toward to the porch. Pop and Willie and Denny, the EMTs, too, walk slowly beside her, arms out to form a human safety net as she continues her balancing act in the rain.

"Look at that," says Robert, huddled under an umbrella with Ma. "She broke her leg."

"Looks like."

"Must be Denny's girl, the one Hal's been talking about. Wonder how it happened."

"She fell, how else would she break her damn leg?" says Muriel.

The men and boys surrounding Becky are squatting, their arms locked together forming a human sling to carry her up the front steps. Becky ignores them then sits on the bottom step and scoots on her bum until she is sitting on the porch. Denny rushes up the steps, crutches in hand, and Becky grabs the banister, pulls herself to a standing position, and takes the crutches from him.

"Determined, ain't she?" says Robby, a grin on his face.

Shortly, everyone but the EMTs enter the door and disappear into the house.

"She is something, huh?"

"'Something' is right," says Muriel.

Ma grabs the umbrella from Robby and heads for the house, leaving him standing in the rain.

CHAPTER 44

Pop tears open the bag of charcoal and dumps all of it in his brand-new grill. Saturates it with lighter fluid, warns Willie to step back, then flicks a lighted match into the burner and watches the eruption. In fifteen minutes, the charcoal is turning white. Willie opens a pack of dogs. "Wait a little longer," says Pop. He leaves for the grocery store to buy more hotdog buns, potato salad and a can of baked beans, maybe a half gallon of ice cream.

Willie takes the hot dogs back into the kitchen and puts them in the Frigidaire. He goes into the living room to watch TV, but stops dead in his tracks when he sees Becky sprawled on his couch, her broken leg sticking out like a piece of lumber. Willie considers retreating, but when he sees her struggling to reach her book on the floor, he walks across the room and retrieves it.

"Here." Willie extends his arm, book in hand.

"Thank you so much," says Becky, with a broad smile.

Does she go to a reverse dentist? he thinks. One who is known for putting teeth in rather than taking them out? "How's it going? Does it hurt a lot?"

As she turns on her side, Willie sees her thigh, above the cast where her jeans are folded back. Something's wrong, he thinks. Smoochy's legs are thicker than that.

"To answer your question, yes, it hurts. But I've had pain before. And I'll probably have it again. So…"

"Oh." Willie tries not to stare at her leg. He wonders if the doctor at the emergency room mentioned anything about it.

Willie isn't what Becky expected. She had envisioned a shrinking, passive, sweaty-headed, weepy little thing that was helpless as a baby bird. But here's this red-haired boy brushing his hair back from his deep brown eyes; tallish, thin but sturdy, roundish face, narrow set eyes. He looks like your average twelve-year-old boy. A little shy, a little anxious.

"Have you ever broken a leg?" says Becky.

Becky is one of those people who looks right into your eyes when she's listening.

"Not really. Pop says I fell out of a tree when I was about four. He took me to the doctor's because I was holding my arm and wouldn't let anyone touch it. Turns out I had something called 'nursemaid's elbow'. I don't know. But the doctor turned my arm just a little and it was all better. Pop said my mother had the same thing. I'll probably break something sometime."

"And I'm sure that when you do, you'll handle it just fine."

Becky laughs and snorts. He can't help but smile. Big teeth, gigantic eyes, a gazillion more freckles than he has, skin and bone leg. Separately, these things would be freaky, like a Halloween costume. Taken together, though, they're in balance, like a mobile, and they look okay, even nice.

Denny romps down the stairs and bursts into the living room. "Are you okay?" he says, barely breathing.

She laughs her laugh again. "If I weren't okay, what could you possibly do about it?"

"I'd move heaven and earth for you...or I'd get you an aspirin...or put a pillow under your leg."

They both laugh riotously, even though the humor eludes Willie. Denny has gotten taller or gained weight or something. He doesn't have an accent, but he's different, somehow. He always seemed a little flimsy, but now he's more solid, more substantial, if that makes sense. He's noisier, he laughs loudly, he actually talks, he stands closer, he touches without hesitation. He sits on the sofa beside Becky, his hip against her; he puts his hand on her leg; she puts hers on his arm.

It's her, thinks Willie. She's what's made him different. Denny leans over Becky and gives her a gentle kiss.

"Willie!" Pop's back from the store. "Charcoal's past ready. Better put the dogs on." Willie turns to go.

"Hey, Willie, hold up a second." Denny puts his hands on Willie's shoulders and leans in close. "I was thinking. How about I go with you tomorrow on your paper route? What do you think?"

"Yeah, sure, that would be great," says Willie.

"Excellent."

Willie heads for the kitchen, a smile on his face, a bounce in his step.

Pop is stirring the beans. Willie grabs the pack of dogs and heads outside again. He holds the door open for Smoochy, who bounds down the steps. "'Atta girl." He reaches for the grid that's leaning against the house and puts it carefully on the grill. He tears open the pack of hotdogs while Smooch rests on her haunches, hoping for a handout. "Relax."

Heat waves rise from the charcoal as he drops each dog into place and tries to avoid singeing his fingers. He reaches for the tongs and clicks them several times. He watches leaves, like helicopters, swirl to the ground. He pulls up his sleeves.

He rolls the hotdogs and looks around the neighborhood. Lawn furniture is packed on back porches, covered in tarp until the return of spring.

"Hey!" Mr. Ashwood approaches from his yard. "Beautiful day, ain't it? Won't get many more of these, will we?" Smoochy bounds toward him and Ashwood stoops to scratch her ears. "Good pooch."

Willie studies his dogs, intently, picking them up, turning them over, putting them down. Mr. Ashwood is on the patio now, hands on hips, heaving breath after breath. He wipes his brow with a handkerchief and tucks it into his back pocket. "Yeah, it's coming, alright."

"Uh huh."

"And I don't just mean winter."

He waits a beat, hoping Willie will ask what he talking about. Willie pretends the hotdogs are the only thing in the world that matter to him.

"Yeah, something more than winter is on the way...I'm telling you."

Willie looks up and smiles sheepishly.

"Maybe you've heard."

"No, I haven't."

"Well, let me tell you. There's a lot of people, people who know what they're talking about, who think there are Russian soldiers on Cuba. Maybe even Khrushchev, too." He raises his eyebrows for emphasis. "Less than a hundred miles from our shores." He shakes his head slowly and rubs his jaw. "Well...your Pop had told me to save some room in the shelter, but then I heard he mighta changed his mind. Maybe you and your Pop are still thinking it over. I hope so, because the offer stands. If you need a safe place, just let me know, because the storm's on its way."

"Okay."

Mr. Ashwood wanders back across the yards. He picks up the pace when he hears his mother calling, "Robby, goddammit!"

The dogs are done. Willie forgot a plate so he goes back into the house.

Pop is reaching for plastic glasses in the cupboard when Willie comes into the kitchen. "Ready to go, chef?" he says. When he doesn't answer, Pop turns. Willie's face looks like it's been doused in bleach. His hand is wrapped around the refrigerator handle. "What's the matter?"

"Nothing."

"You don't look---"

"I'm fine...just need a plate for the hotdogs."

Pop reaches into the cupboard for a platter. "Here you go."

Willie lets go of the handle and takes the platter from Pop's hand. Color is returning to his face. "Thanks." Before he starts to perspire, he exits, heading for the patio to fetch the dogs.

Pop stands in the middle of the kitchen, hands on his hips.

CHAPTER 45

Trish studiously enters sales data onto the ledger. Additional ledgers are stacked at her side, forming a veritable wall of numbers so boring that drinking gallons of black coffee each day is the only way to keep one's lids open. There's a reason the other women in the office call it scut work. The sound of the word---*scut*---mimics the feeling one gets doing it.

But for Trish, the ledgers, with their lines and rows and columns and minute notations, are like sacred texts. She is the scribe whose entries will be referenced for years to come. To have so many numbers under her guardianship is both an honor and a grave responsibility.

It doesn't matter that she threw her math book away in sixth grade and told Miss Weganstout a robber had stolen it, along with her mother's jewelry. It doesn't matter she didn't complete Algebra I, having failed it convincingly after one semester. Turns out she's good with numbers.

The past, as it turns out, is the past. Today and tomorrow are hers to mold. You only have to set sail in the right direction. Hal was right. Trish believes this about three out of five work days per week.

Mr. Kleinman has already given her a quarter bump in her hourly wage. To celebrate, she took Lucy to Kaufman's in Pittsburgh where they shopped and had lunch at a restaurant right there in the store. Lucy was so agog at seeing the tall buildings that Trish feared she might walk headlong into oncoming traffic. They traversed the city's golden triangle with its glistening silver skyscrapers and inviting park. They rode the incline up Mt. Washington where Lucy swore she could see their house in Ellwood City.

They laughed and laughed and laughed some more. They stayed up late and had pizza from and slept together in Trish's room. In all her twenty-seven years, that was Trish's first perfect day.

· · ·

There is a knock at the door. Her mother has warned her never to open the door to a stranger. Lucy always obeys this, with a few exceptions, like Mr. Post, the mailman, Mr. Derrey, the milk man, and Frankie, the paper boy.

There is another knock; she peeks through the lace curtain.

It's the man in the suit.

She lets go of the doorknob and steps back.

"Hello," he calls. The man in the suit is leaning forward so he can see better. He's taller than she'd thought. His face is all sharp angles, his hair is slick and his part is crisp; he has a thin moustache. She's seen him many times, so many, she didn't think much of it anymore. But seeing him on their porch, seeing him so close, hearing him knocking sends shock waves through Lucy. She holds her breath and squeezes her hands together.

"I was wondering if your mother's home?"

When she doesn't answer, he calls to her again. "Hello! Can you hear me? I can see you."

Frightened, Lucy goes into the living room, out of sight. His voice sounds friendly. She peeks again at the door. It's not locked. She creeps on her knees across the hallway until she can reach the latch. She turns it slowly then retreats.

"I know your name," he says. "It's Lucy, a very pretty name."

Lucy crouches behind the loveseat. How does he know my name? What does he want from me? What's he going to do? She wants to run, but there's no place to go. She wants to scream but there's no one to hear.

"Please come to the door. I know your mother. There's nothing to worry about."

He says this with a laugh, as if he knows Lucy somehow, and is confused by her reaction.

He knocks again, more insistently. "C'mon!"

Lucy's toes curl, her every muscle clenches.

"Okay then," he says, sounding defeated. Then, nothing. Where is he? What is he doing? She waits, huddled on the floor, a minute or two, then five, ten. She gets up, tiptoes to the door. He's gone.

. . .

Trish pulls into the driveway, her car coughing and sputtering. When she reaches the front door, it's locked. What? she wonders. Who locks their doors? She tries her key again and when it doesn't work, she tries another key, even though she knows it's the key to her car. She tries the first key yet again, this time shaking and rattling the door as hard as she can. When it doesn't open, she kicks it.

She peers through the beveled glass, but sees nothing. Where's Lucy, for God's sake? She looks through the living room window. Lights are on. She cups her hands against the window, trying to see into the kitchen. The lights are on in there, as well. She taps the window gently at first, but when there is no response, she bangs with her knuckles.

What to do? Standing on the front walk, she looks at the second-floor windows, but the curtains are pulled. She takes off her heels and runs to the back of the house, tries the back door, to no avail. She shades her eyes against the sun and looks at the bedroom windows. Nothing. She tries the back door again.

Frantic now, she grabs the handle on the outside basement door. She yanks it with both hands repeatedly until there's a loud crack and the door flies open. She dashes down the stone steps and kicks the basement door in. She's scared, scared of what she might find. "Lucy!" she cries.

She runs up the steps to the first floor, bursts through the door, then stops. She listens but doesn't hear a thing. Trish grabs a paring knife from the kitchen drawer and tiptoes up the stairs to the second floor. "Lucy?" Her door is closed. "Lucy, it's Mama. Are you okay?" She opens the door and finds Lucy under her covers sucking her thumb.

"Lucy, honey, what in the world...?"

CHAPTER 46

Pop hears the clomp slide clomp slide of crutches in the hall. Becky carefully navigates the narrow passageway to the kitchen. She struggles to maintain her balance.

"Need help?" says Pop.

"No thank you," she says, while banging one crutch against the wall and the other against the closet door.

Pop holds a pot of coffee and watches. Becky hobbles into the kitchen, smiles and says, "Ta-da!"

"Well done," says Pop. "Can I get you a cup of coffee?"

Becky plops into a chair and lays her crutches under the table. "That would be great."

He pours her a cup, then takes a seat. "When you're ready, I'll make you some eggs."

"Thank you so much, but I'm not hungry this morning." She pours milk into her coffee and lifts it to her mouth with both hands. She closes her eyes as she takes a sip. "Mmm, strong, I like it strong." She doesn't like it strong. It gives her indigestion. She adds a little more milk.

It was a long night. She slept in Denny's room amidst all his model airplanes and posters of World War II fighters. Denny slept with Willie. Her leg throbbed throughout the night. Sleep was a wish unfulfilled. Around 3:00am, Denny sneaked into the room and slipped into bed beside her. He was in an amorous mood, something that wasn't even in the top one hundred things she wanted to do. He fell asleep, woke up an hour later and went back to Willie's room.

By then Becky had to pee like she'd never had to pee before. But the thought of wending her way to the bathroom in the pitch dark, steadied only by her crutches, convinced her to cross her legs and stay the course.

At the first bird chirp and the first hint of light, she shuffles to the bathroom for the most satisfying visit in recent memory. By then, she hears rumblings downstairs and knows sleep would have to wait.

"How'd you sleep?" says Pop.

"Like a baby."

"Like a baby, that's good."

They both chuckle. A fly pounds the ceiling light.

"More?" he says.

"Sure."

Pop tops her off. He sits down again, crosses his legs, and turns on one hip. He asks about her family, how she likes college, what she's studying.

"How's your leg doing?"

"It's 'doing', I guess. Will take time, I suppose. No big deal, really."

"Uh huh." He drinks his lukewarm coffee. "Having a bum leg makes things hard, that's for sure. I racked up my knee a while back and it was near impossible to do my work. They had to hire a helper and everything. Took a good while before I stopped limping." He rubs his knee.

He knows, thinks Becky.

Looking out the Greyhound bus window, seeing the little band awaiting their arrival, she felt panic race through her, top to bottom. Calm down, she said to herself. Calm down, it will be fine. But her comforting words didn't make any difference.

As she stood, steadied herself, then walked to the front of the bus, an idea formed quickly. When she reached the steps, she hesitated, reconsidering, then closed her eyes and took the step, tripping and collapsing onto the pavement her ankle in a mangled twist just as she expected. Everyone gathered round her offering sympathy and support. She felt calm.

"I'm gimpy when I wake up, too. Ask your son." She forces a laugh and Pop returns one. "But I'm also gimpy when I walk to class, when I sit down for lunch, when I, well, when I do anything and everything, I guess."

"So, I understand." Pop draws his cup to his mouth, his eyes still focused on her.

"So, you understand?"

"Denny and I talked last night. You had fallen asleep. We needed to put our heads together about his brother, as, I'm sure, you understand. But he also talked about you. Turns out you are the sun and the moon and the stars; you are the reason he gets up in the morning and the reason he goes to bed at night." His looks away as he says this, so he doesn't see her face light up. "He told me other things, too."

"Oh."

"You know, I had an uncle, my mother's little brother, Hudson. I've seen pictures of Hudson, but I never met him. He barely went to school; the kids were so mean to him. Finally dropped out. Never went anywhere, really. Just stayed at home with my grandparents. Even that was hard. Grandpa wasn't, well, let's say he wasn't a sympathetic type. He didn't take to Hudson at all, which put a wedge between him and Grandma."

Pop stops to gather his thoughts.

"When he was born, one of his legs wasn't, what did my grandmother say, 'matured' enough. The doctor called it his 'noodle' which always made my grandparents laugh, well, at least Grandpa. And his foot, it was curled at the ankle so the bottom was up, if that makes sense.

"I guess what I'm trying to say, Becky, if I can call you Becky." He glances at her and she nods. "I guess what I'm trying to say is my uncle never went face-to-face with the world; he never made friends; he was scared to death of school; he never graduated; of course, he never went away on his own to college; he never had a close relationship, a loving relationship, you could say; and he never road on a train for seventeen hours so he could meet a bunch of people he didn't know from Adam's second cousin. Poor man, he felt like he never had a chance. Who knows, maybe the problem was that he never took a chance."

His hip going numb, Pop shifts his weight and crosses his legs the other way.

Becky looks at him, but is silent. Tears fill her eyes. Pop reaches for a napkin and lays it on the table in front of her. He shuffles for a minute, then leaves the room, pretending he has something else to do.

CHAPTER 47

The morning sun gives way to a cloudy, breezy afternoon. The newspapers have been dropped at the Newsstand and are awaiting Willie's arrival. He puts his new navy-blue sweatshirt on. It says Weston at the top and College across the bottom, all in white with a red boarder; between the words is the college insignia, olive branches with a red and white shield in the middle. The shield has words in some other language.

He stands in front of his mirror admiring it. He parts his hair with his finger-tips, and juts out his jaw a little to look like a college man. He goes down the stairs two steps at a time. Denny is waiting.

"Here comes our BMOC," says Denny.

"B-what?"

"Big Man On Campus."

"Alright."

"Time to go?"

There is no doubt in Denny's mind that his brother is no longer a little boy. He is on the verge of his teenage years, a time of promise and experimentation for some, but for others, like Denny, the most frightening years of one's life. Good luck, Willie, he thinks.

Denny will stay as focused as possible on Pop's concerns: Why did Willie pass out when he was delivering papers with Pres?

"I don't expect you to solve anything, Denny, I don't," said Pop during their late-night confab. "I'd just like to know what's bothering him."

Pop's urgency, though, suggested he did hope Denny's seventeen years of accumulated wisdom (and more than six weeks of college) might make a difference; that he might hold the key to unlocking his brother's door.

Pop also said Willie's been mostly okay recently, except for his fear of a nuclear holocaust. To his credit, Denny feels no obligation to solve the nuclear problem that hangs precariously over Willie's (and everyone else's) head.

The brothers stop in the middle of the Fifth Street Bridge and lean on the rusted railing. The Conoquenessing is whooshing far below.

"Geez, look at that." Denny points at a tiny strip of sand near the river's bend.

"Yep."

" I think that's bare ass beach." Denny gulps and turns to his brother. "I'm sorry, I didn't mean to say, you know, a-s-s."

"You mean ass."

"Uh huh."

"Bare ass beach."

"Yeah...I didn't say 'ass' until I was in eighth grade."

"We're more advanced. Ass, cock, shit. There, how's that?"

Willie strikes his BMOC pose. Denny shakes his head. "Wow, my brother..."

At the Newsstand, Willie teaches Denny how to fold papers. In no time, the bag is full. "Looks like a giant pack of cigarettes." Willie reaches for the bag, but his brother grabs it first and slings it over his own shoulder.

Willie shows his brother how to throw overhand for long distance, underhand for a soft landing, and sideways so it'll look like a UFO in flight. "Very cool."

"Most people don't appreciate the intricacies of delivering newspapers."

Denny's first toss ends up on a porch roof. They walk on quickly and quietly.

They take turns after that, accumulating points for distance, accuracy and speed. By the halfway mark, Willie is ahead by a wide margin. The game ends when they turn onto Rocko's street. Rocko is off his leash today. He glares at them, his head down, a ridge of spiked fir from his neck to his tail.

His growl sounds like a beefy '57 Chevy revving up at the start line.

"Will he kill us?" says Denny.

"Maybe you, but not me. Watch and learn."

Willie crouches, bares his teeth and walks slowly across the street toward Rocko. Then raises his arms and he curls his fingers like they are talons. Rocko's head goes up; he claws the dirt and wags his tail. Willie eases up as he gets closer, finally patting Rocko's head---"G'boy"---and tossing the paper gently onto the porch.

Denny applauds. Willie bows.

His boisterous, devil-may-care mood belies Willie's growing anxiety. Before they left the house, Denny asked if Willie could show him where he'd had his episode.

Willie tosses another paper, then another. "Okay...follow me," he says.

They cross several backyards, slip by a row of garages and down a long driveway to another sidewalk. They've left his route behind and are standing on the street where it happened, the street he's avoided for weeks. Willie slows down, halts, takes a breath, and is about to explain everything.

Denny begins to laugh.

"How 'bout that?" he says, as he looks down the street.

"How about what?"

"Wow, it's been such a long time."

"What are you talking about?"

"That...the house...the one that looks like it's been abandoned."

"What about it?"

"You don't remember, do you?"

"Remember what?"

"That house...Take a good look," says Denny.

"I have. Several times, whether I wanted to or not. It gives me the creeps."

"Why?"

"I don't know why...it just does."

Denny puts his arm around his brother. "Willie, that was our house. That's the house where we all lived when you were little...Back before everything happened."

Willie steps back. "What do you mean that was our house?"

"Like I'm telling you. Mom and Dad, Pop and Grandma Mae, you and me, we all lived there. Pop and Grandma had the third floor to themselves, but we all ate together, watched TV, and stuff." Denny's face beams. "I haven't been by the place since, well, I don't know. Pop discouraged it. How'd you find it?"

"I didn't. One day when I was on the route, Rocko attacked me. I ran like crazy trying to get away from him, but he wouldn't give up. Finally, I ran onto a porch just as Mrs. Handelbaker showed up and took Rocko away. Turns out that was the porch."

"That's when you fainted, huh?"

"Well, I don't know if that's the word, but yeah." Willie looks everywhere except at his brother. "Sorry Pop dragged you into this."

"Look, Willie, Pop was worried. So was I. Don't forget---I'm your brother; if you got problems, worries, whatever, then I do, too."

He walks toward the house. Willie lags behind. Denny waits for his brother. "It'll be okay, I promise."

"Why didn't Pop tell me? I mean, it's almost on my route."

Denny shakes his head. "He never said a word to me about where your route was, nothing about our house; I think he's clueless, I do. When Mom and Dad died and then Grandma died right in that house, he decided we needed to move. It happened fast. I don't think he ever looked back."

"Why does it look like such a dump?"

"Pop tried to sell it, but I guess the inspector found tons of problems with the foundation. Something like that."

"So..."

"Well, he was supposed to fix it up, then sell. Never did. Eventually, I think the bank took it. And there it sits. It's crazy."

The brothers sit on the front steps. Denny looks at Willie, remembering how little he was, how innocent. Pop and Denny did everything to protect him from the fallout of those deaths. Maybe what they did was the right thing, maybe it was the wrong thing; whichever, it was done out of love.

"I was just thinking," says Denny. "You and me used to play this game. I'd stand in the bushes and you'd be up on the porch. I'd roll a ball under the front rail and you'd chase after it, laughing and screaming like it was the most hilarious thing you'd ever seen. Then you'd say, 'Mo, mo…'. 'Mo' was your word for 'more'. I mean you were maybe two. So, you'd say, 'Mo, mo ba'. 'Ba' for ball. And I'd roll it again and again and again. You never got tired of it."

"Huh…"

"Yeah, we had some fun. You used to sleep with me all the time after Mom and Dad died. Followed me everywhere."

The brothers walk down the driveway to the backyard; a downspout is lying in the grass. "Geez," says Denny. "This used to be really nice. Dad mowed the lawn all the time and took care of the flowers and bushes. This is so bad. He'd go nuts."

Denny points at the corner window on the second-floor, the one that caught Willie's attention weeks before. "That's my room. Sometimes when you couldn't sleep, we'd sit on the edge of the bed, open the window and look at the stars. You thought the moon was a real person with a real face."

"Were you the one that sang 'The Big Rock Candy Mountain' to me?"

"We all sang it. Mom, Dad, me, Grandma. Even Pop, sometimes."

"Huh."

"When we sang it, you'd try to whistle while we sang. Thing was, you couldn't whistle, so you'd make this high-pitched screeching noise instead. We'd try not to laugh. You were very serious about your whistling."

"Pop talks a lot about Mom and Grandma, but doesn't say much at all about Dad, and when he does, he gets this odd look on his face, like he smells something bad."

"Probably 'cause they didn't get along. I don't know what that was about but sometimes they argued and then they wouldn't talk to each other for days."

"What was Dad like?"

"Hard to remember much now. He was tall, taller than Pop. And he had short hair, and a big laugh. He liked to work with his hands and do things outside. Sometimes he and Mom would dance together in the kitchen and we'd laugh, even Pop. He played ball with us and wrestled with us, even when you were little. He carried you around on his shoulders. I know there's more, but, I don't know, they were gone so quick."

"Sometimes I feel like I remember Mom, I get a warm feeling....but I don't know..."

"Yeah, well, that's how Mom made you feel. She'd bring pots and pans out back and sit with us forever, playing in the sandbox; she baked cookies with us, and this stuff she called 'boobyshingle' which was left over dough she rolled out and baked with cinnamon and sugar on it. That was our favorite. She'd hold you on her lap and kiss you over and over until you were breathless with laughter."

Willie peeks through the back door. Denny joins him.

"You know, Willie, Mom and Dad loved you. They did. They just weren't here long enough for you to remember it."

The brothers explore the garage. Denny talks about the turtle they kept in the back corner and how they played hide and seek, and how Willie cried if he couldn't find his brother. Denny points out where the swing was. It all seems impossible to Willie. This was their home. And then it wasn't.

"Denny, what happened to Mom and Dad? I mean, really?"

Denny takes a deep breath and looks up at his old room. "All I can tell you is what I know. We were at the lumber yard; I heard Pop screaming for me to come. Next thing I know we're in the car driving so fast, it scared me to death. Grandma Mae was home and they whispered back and forth. Pop left and I stayed with her---"

"So, where was I?" says Willie, needing verification.

"You were with Mom and Dad. On a picnic with Mom and Dad. Pop must have picked you up at some point. I don't really know."

"So..."

"So, next thing I know, we're sitting on couch, you on Grandma's lap and me beside her. Pop's kneeling on the floor in front of us. I never saw Pop cry before, but he's crying so hard that I start to cry. Grandma was hugging you and rocking back and forth. You didn't cry, at least I don't think so. Grandma said, 'It's okay,' to Pop. Pop caught his breath and tried to compose himself. He looked at you and then he looked at me and he said, I'll never forget this, he said, 'There's been an accident' and then he looked down and I could see him swallowing hard. He tried to speak, but he couldn't. Then Grandma Mae, in her tiny voice, said, 'Mommy and Daddy won't be coming home'."

Denny slumps over, and like Pop long ago, gulps hard. Willie watches his brother's hands tremble. His own mouth is bone dry and slack. He rubs his brother's back. Then Willie's tears, like a gentle rain, begin. They sit together in their old back yard bonded by a great silence, a deep and befuddling remorse.

"Do you know why Pop never talks to me about this?"

"Not just you. He never talked to me about it either. I just got used to it."

"I guess I can't get used to it."

CHAPTER 48
1953

Cliff kneeled on the beach and dug for flat stones while Ruthie cleaned up from lunch. "Willie, come here, son." Willie sat on the edge of the rock and slid onto the sandy surface below. Smoochy paced back and forth, whining, unable to figure out how to get to Willie.

"C'mon Ruthie," said Cliff.

Ruthie finished cleaning up, walked to the other side of the rock where it was easier to get down, then came round to the tiny beach. Cliff was helping Willie hold a paper-thin stone between his thumb and forefinger.

"Lean over and just fling it."

Willie leaned over, moved his arm back and forth and the stone fell to the sand.

"That's okay, buddy."

Willie sat down hard on the sand and started digging with a stick.

"You remember the last time we came here?" said Cliff.

Ruthie looked at him and sighed.

"I remember, Cliff."

"That's why I wanted us to come here today. We were in love, right?"

"I suppose we were."

Smoochy jumped on Willie's back. Willie fell forward, trying to reach his pup.

"You said you forgot your protection."

"Jesus, Ruthie, I did." He looked away as he said this. "Anyway, if I hadn't forgot, we wouldn't have Denny; and we wouldn't have this little fella, either."

They both looked at Willie rolling over and over in the sand as Smoochy barked and jumped and nipped at his feet.

"True. I love them more than I've ever loved anything. Or anyone," said Ruthie.

Cliff ignored her last comment. "So, we'll be okay, right?"

"It's not that simple, Cliff."

Cliff sighed and tossed another stone, this one screamed over the river and landed with a thud on the opposite bank. "It's simpler than you think; you're just stubborn, that's all."

CHAPTER 49

"Lucy, Lucy, what's wrong, honey?" She doesn't answer. "Lucy?" her mom says gently. She pulls back the cover slowly and curls up beside her daughter. "Is something wrong? Do you feel sick?" Lucy shakes her head. "Then what's..." Lucy releases her wrinkled thumb and turns over to face her mother. Trish puts her arm around her. "Come here," says Trish, pulling her closer. They lay together for a long time. "That's okay." Trish caresses her daughter's hair.

For Trish, this is all too familiar, the fear, the need to hide. She closes her eyes tight and hears her own parents---her mom screams, her dad roars and swings, her mother falls, gets up, runs to her bedroom and slams the door. She hears the lock click just as her father pounds with all his might.

She'd lie in her bed staring at the ceiling, hoping someone would come, hoping a whistle would blow or a siren would blare, signaling the all clear.

When she'd go downstairs again, her mother, face drawn and weary, would pour a glass of milk and put it on the kitchen table; she'd take a cookie from the cookie jar. "Here." Trish would sit, but leave her milk and cookie untouched. She'd lay her head on the table. "What's wrong with you? Huh?" Trish wouldn't know what to say.

"Lucy, please talk to me. Did something happen at school?"

Lucy shakes her head.

"Nothing happened at school and you're not sick? I don't get it. What's bothering you?" she says, struggling to remain patient.

"I don't know," she says.

"Honey, you must know something. Are you afraid to talk about it?"

Lucy turns over and sits up. She wipes the corners of her eyes.

"Look, I don't care what it is, I won't get upset. I just want to know. You hear me?"

Lucy looks at her mother, trying to read her face. Will she listen? Will she get mad?

"There was this man, he came to the door after school. He was a tall man and he wore a suit and he was friendly. He asked about you, if you were home and stuff. I didn't say anything, but he knocked and knocked and he wouldn't go away. And I crawled to the door so I could lock it. And he was right there. I think he saw me."

"Oh, honey, I'm so sorry, I'm so sorry." She cuddles Lucy closer. "That is scary, it is. But you don't have to worry. I'm sure it was some kind of mistake. And now it's all over." She rocks Lucy gently.

"I've seen him before."

Trish stops rocking. "You what?"

"Many times."

"Where?" Trish says, confused, concerned.

"All over."

"All over? You mean around here, in the neighborhood?"

"Yeah."

"Are you sure it was always the same man?"

"Yeah."

"You're sure?"

"Yeah."

"Has he ever come up on the porch before this?"

"No."

"Has he ever approached you when you were out?"

"No."

"Good." Trish still wonders if Lucy is confused.

"And he knew my name."

Trish holds Lucy's arms tight and turns her so they are face-to-face. "He what?"

"He knew my name. He called me Lucy." She bursts into tears again.

"Lucy, honey...I'm here. Everything is okay." Trish takes her in her arms and holds her until she falls asleep.

Trish dials one neighbor, then another. Neither has seen a strange man in the neighborhood. She calls yet another neighbor, no answer. Then another, but no luck.

She calls Scanlon's gas station at the end of the block. When Joe, the owner, picks up, she asks if he's seen a strange man roaming around, someone who doesn't live here, who doesn't seem to belong, someone who always wears a suit, like a business man or something.

"Nah, Trish, I don't think so. But lemme ask Donny." Joe holds the phone against his chest. Then picks up again. "Well, turns out, yeah, there's a guy, I almost forgot, but he's been here, I don't know, several times. None of us ever seen him before. Nice guy. A talker. Always in a suit and tie. Said he's from Pittsburgh, but comes to the tube mill on business pretty regular."

"Did he tell you his name?"

Joe asks Donny. "No, he didn't, but you know what? He always paid with a Diner's Club Card. Tell you what, I'll check the receipts and get back to you."

Trish hangs up. She stands in the middle of the kitchen, unsure what else to do. She brews some coffee, pours a cup, drinks it, then another. Jesus, she thinks, what's taking so long?

She goes upstairs to check on Lucy. She's sprawled sideways across her bed, one arm hanging limp over the side. She slips quietly into the room, sits on the floor beside Lucy and holds her hand. It's almost as big as hers. She moves each finger and traces the lines on Lucy's palm.

The phone rings.

Trish gently lays her daughter's hand on her pillow and pulls the blanket over her shoulders. Then she sprints into the hall, down the stairs, across the living room and into the kitchen.

"Joe?...Yeah, hi, so did you...You did?...That's great...Yeah...so who is this guy?"

Trish thinks she's hearing him wrong, so she asks again. This time, the name is clear as glass. The phone slips from her hand and hits the table, knocking over the salt and pepper shakers; her hands fly up, like a shield, to cover her face; she gasps for breath, then slips, inch by inch, to the floor.

CHAPTER 50

Everyone piles into Pop's car as he watches from the door. With heavy rain in the forecast, they decide to see a new movie, *The Longest Day*, at the Manos Theater. Willie is introducing Lucy and Pres to Becky, who leans on one crutch and shakes their hands. It's clear she's explaining how she broke her leg.

It's Pop's idea to invite Preston. Willie is surprised when he says 'yes'.

From time to time, Pop checks in with Pres's mother, Megan. "It will be a long, long haul," she says. Pres's grandmother is coming to stay with them for a while. Megan says Pres is struggling. "A day at a time," she tells him each morning when he doesn't want to get up for school.

Pop waves at the car as it backs out of the driveway. Denny toots the horn once. Pop closes the door and then leans on it. What to do with Denny and Willie's request?

"Pop, why haven't you ever told us what actually happened to Mom and Dad?" said Willie, Denny at his side, nodding. They weren't angry. They weren't accusatory. They were curious, they were trying to get what was rightfully theirs, an explanation.

"You never asked."

This was true. Well, maybe they did ask right after they got the news, but what was he to say? They were such little boys. Why burden them with something they couldn't possibly understand?

"When you never talked about it, we figured you didn't want to."

True again; he didn't want to; didn't then and doesn't now. And when they got on with the business of being kids and growing up, he assumed they'd left the question behind.

He told them, okay, you want to talk about it, we'll talk about it. "Tomorrow," said Denny, insistently. Pop agreed, but when tomorrow arrived and the weather was awful, he suggested a movie. They liked the idea so much, that he offered to treat them all, even Willie's friends. He hoped they would forget, at least for a couple of days, about having the talk. By then Denny and Becky would have to go back to school. He'd suggest talking about it at Thanksgiving. Then Christmas. Then Easter. Then never?

But before everyone piled into the car, Willie reminded him, "Tonight, Pop, we'll talk then. Thanks."

How much to say? And how to say it? Pop goes into the kitchen and picks up the phone. He flips through the directory, looking for the number. When he finds it, he clutches the receiver in his hand for a moment and then dials.

. . .

Everyone enjoys the Three Stooges short and the Baby Huey cartoon, but there is a split decision about the movie. Becky's eyes nearly bug out of her head during the opening scenes, which are jam-packed with military personnel, military weapons, military everything.

Becky stands and points at the screen. "What's this?" her voice echoing into the balcony.

"It's about D-Day," whispers Denny, trying to model a more acceptable volume for theater-talk. But, to no avail.

"Why didn't you tell me?"

"Shh, you've got to keep it down a little."

"How was I supposed to know this was a war movie, for God's sake! It's about wrapping a flag of patriotism around barbaric behavior! It's about killing and plundering and cruelty!"

A man, a vet, by the looks of him, ups the ante: "You're damn right it is! So shut up!"

Becky, shocked by his rejoinder, sucks so much air, that it's impossible for her speak.

About then, Denny suggests they make a strategic retreat to the lobby for some candy, maybe a Black Cow and some Milk Duds or popcorn. Becky pushes past him yelling, "Come to your senses, people! War is just wrong!" Denny follows at a distance, hoping no one will associate him with the splendidly crazy lady who is hobbling gallantly toward the exit.

"Hey, kid!" calls a dark shadow in the corner. "You better put a muzzle on that girlfriend of yours! I was there! If it hadn'ta been for guys like me, there'd be Nazis running this country today!"

"Thank you for your service!" calls Denny, as he picks up his pace.

In the meantime, Pres is hiding on the floor in front of his seat.

Willie kneels beside him. "What's wrong, man?"

"Nothing, I just dropped something."

"What did you drop? I'll help you look for it."

"I don't know what it was; I just can't..."

Pres's eyes are shut tight. He's shaking like a worm on the end of a fishing line. Willie raps his arms around his friend.

"Hey, man, you know what? I think this movie stinks. Whadaya say we get outta here?"

"Okay, yeah," says Pres, ducking his head as he stands.

Lucy, who dashed to the lady's room after the cartoons, returns to an empty row. Maybe she's got the wrong section, she thinks, so she goes to the other side on the theater, and has the same outcome. Confused, she calls, "Willie!" and a chorus of voices respond, "Shut up, will ya!" Then a nearby woman, crunching her popcorn, says, "They all left."

When Lucy reaches the concession stand, Becky is grumbling about war and pacifism and Gandhi, while Willie crouching in a corner beside Pres, who's trying to catch his breath.

Not knowing what else to do, Lucy says: "Hey, let's go to Mena's for some hotdogs." With that, they trundle out the door and head down the street to their favorite hole in the wall.

There are two guys at the end of the store-length counter, five empty stools beside them. Everyone takes a seat. A pot of chili is bubbling on the stove, buns are steaming in a hot box under the register, grease is splattered on the metal splash guard behind the main grill. There is a brigade of hotdogs at the ready. In a flash, dogs slathered with chili and mustard, nestled in warm buns, wrapped in wax paper and cradled in plastic baskets sit in front of them. Fries not far behind.

Stomachs bulging, they drag themselves out of the shop, moaning with satisfaction.

"My God, I've never eaten anything like that," says Becky as she rests, crutches deep in her armpits.

"Welcome to Ellwood City," says Denny.

They pile into Pop's car and head for home. When they arrive, Trish is sitting on the front steps talking to Pop while waiting to take Pres and Lucy home. Everyone rehashes the movie and says their goodbyes.

Denny and Willie are puzzled when they go in the house and find Robert Ashwood and his mother sitting comfortably in the living room.

Willie turns to his brother. "What's this?"

"Got me."

The plan was clear. They would meet with Pop to talk about their parents. No one else, not even Becky, was invited.

"Who's that girl?" says Muriel, pointing.

"Shh, Ma, don't."

"Don't 'shh Ma' me. Hello girl-I've-never-seen-before. What's wrong with that leg of yours?"

Despite Muriel's rough edges, Becky is immediately drawn to her. She introduces herself and takes a seat beside Muriel on the couch. "You've got a good eye, Mrs. Ashwood---"

"Muriel, please."

"Muriel. I fell getting off the bus when we came into town."

"My God, that's the shits, isn't it?"

Pop sidles up to the boys. Their faces are rock hard. Finally, Willie says, "I thought we were gonna..."

"We are. I wanted Mr. Ashwood to be here."

"Why?" says Denny.

"You'll see."

Mr. Ashwood leans over, leverages his arms against the back of the sofa, then pushes, grunts, and finally stands. He's out of breath when he comes across the room to greet the boys. The boys nod, still confused about Ashwood's gargantuan presence. He talks about the bomb shelter, how long it took to build, what's in it, and his confidence that he'll be using it soon. Pop interrupts, suggesting that may be a discussion for later.

They retreat to the kitchen where there's a pot of coffee simmering on the burner, milk carton and sugar bowl on the table, a plate of Oreos, as well. Pop opens the cabinet and reaches for the matching coffee mugs he and Mae bought in Niagara Falls, the Horseshoe Falls emblazoned on each one. Willie and Denny look at each other; they haven't seen these mugs since their grandmother died.

No one picks up a mug. Pop and Robert lean back as Willie and Denny lean forward.

. . .

After dropping Pres off, Trish turns the corner and heads in the opposite direction. Lucy says, "Mom, I don't feel like grocery shopping. Can you drop me off?"

Her mother shifts into third. Lucy speaks again. "I'll be okay. I will. I won't talk to anyone. I'll just stay in my room, reading."

Trish wonders if she will always be afraid for her daughter. So many things can go wrong long before adulthood, long before they're supposed to.

"Mom, can we go home?"

"Let's go for some ice cream."

Something is definitely wrong with her mother. There's a faraway-ness about her, like her body's right there in front of you, but everything else, everything that makes her her is down the road and around the bend somewhere.

"Where?"

"How about J&T?"

"Okay."

Lucy turns the radio to KQV. Up goes the volume when *He's a Rebel* comes on.

As the last "He's not a rebel, oh, no, no, no" fades away, they pull into the J&T parking lot. Lucy gets a double scoop of vanilla custard and Trisha gets a single chocolate. They go back to the car, let the seat back so they can stretch their legs, and then work on their cones.

"Lucy, you know the day when the guy came to the door?"

Here we go, thinks Lucy. "Uh huh."

"Well, when you fell asleep, I made some calls around the neighborhood. Nobody had seen him---"

"So, you think I made it up."

"No, not at all. So, then I called Joe over at the gas station. Turns out the guy's come in there several times?

"You're kidding."

"No and, well, turns out I know him. Dallas Grove, that's his name."

"What?"

"We went to high school together. We even dated for a while."

She never expected to hear that name again, let alone say it out loud. She had never loved anyone as much as she'd loved Dallas Grove. His jet-black hair all slicked back, his bashful smile, his tenderness. Too bad his promises were only bubbles in the wind.

He enlisted in the Marines without a word. The only thing he left behind is sitting beside Trish right now. She was a pregnant fifteen-year-old child with no boyfriend, no father, a bitter, scornful mother and a bad reputation. Even now, her insides curdle to think of it.

For months she waited, hoping for a letter or a call. For a year or more, she watched for a tall, thin boy who would walk up her sidewalk and carry her off to a different future. She feels foolish now, but it was real and it was true.

When Lucy was born, Trish was relieved she didn't look like her dad. There was no evidence, no proof, no reminder of the boy she'd loved and who'd loved her. It would have been too much if there were.

When Joe told her the name a second time, she stumbled and fell, as if an earthquake had erupted in her heart. First shock, then fury, then fear, then sadness. Lying on the floor, the phone dangling beside her, she felt like she'd never get up again. But she did.

After all the years and all the questions Lucy has asked about her father, the time had finally come. This is a secret she can't keep from her daughter any longer.

"You dated the man in the suit?"

"Yeah, I did. I dated him. So, there's nothing for you to worry about. He's not some creep."

"This doesn't make sense. Why would he come around here?"

"You know, he grew up here, has a job that brings him to Ellwood from time to time, wants to go down memory lane." Because he's your father and probably feels a lot of remorse for being a shit. "I don't think he was really following you. I think he wanted to see me again."

"But he knew my name."

"Small town, easy to find these things out."

Still doesn't make sense, thinks Lucy. Some old boyfriend just shows up out the blue looking for his lost love? Why doesn't he pick up the phone and call? Why wander aimlessly around the neighborhood like a creep?

Trish wipes her hands on a napkin and starts the car while Lucy finishes.

"So, Mom, this old boyfriend, where was he in the line of boyfriends?"

"I don't know what you mean."

"Was he the first, the middle, somewhere closer to the end or was he, like, your last boyfriend?"

Trish laughs. "You make it sound like I had a gazillion boyfriends. Like I gave them numbers instead of names."

"So? Where was he in the mix?"

"If you must know, he was my last high school boyfriend."

"What?"

"Well..." Shit. The words are out now and there is no way to get them back. "I mean, it was so long ago, I don't know...maybe there were others after him..."

"Huh...He was your last."

Lucy rolls her window down and tosses the rest of her ice cream cone onto the pavement. Then she turns face forward, arms folded and doesn't say another word.

. . .

When they were younger, he held things back for their own good, or at least that's what Pop told himself. 'Accident' was the word he always used, a word that didn't explain anything while appearing to cover everything. And it worked. As long as it worked, he didn't think seriously about the day it wouldn't.

"So, Pop, me and Denny, we would like to know, like, what happened to Mom and Dad. Really?"

How much to tell them? What to leave out? Pop had hoped they would make it to adulthood without crippling childhood memories or scars. Who would have thought having no memories might be worse than having too many, that a memory vacuum might leave its own scars?

"Well, I will tell you some of the story, the things I know. But I've asked Mr. Ashwood to join us tonight, because he knows more than anyone."

"What do you mean?"

"Not now, Denny. Let me start. The family planned on going for a picnic. Your mom packed a lunch of, I believe it was cold fried chicken, probably potato salad, I don't know. Your dad decided on the location, which was that little beach on the river, the one everyone calls bare you-know-what beach. But, at the last minute, you, Denny, decided you didn't want to go."

"Why didn't I want to go?"

Because your father squeezed your arm so hard it left hand prints. "Who knows? You were eight. You came upstairs to tell your grandma and me you didn't want to go on the picnic. So, I took you to the lumber yard with me, a place you loved. And your parents and Willie, went on the picnic. And that's where everything happened."

Willie leans on his elbows, chin in his hands.

Pop says, "I'm going to ask our good neighbor to tell the rest, because other than Willie, he's the only one who saw what happened."

Willie looks at his brother who gives him an I-don't-know shrug.

Robert Ashwood wipes his brow with his shirt sleeve and coughs. He makes eye contact with Pop who raises his eyebrows slightly.

"Well, you know, your Pop and I weren't neighbors back then. You all lived on the North Side, but I knew your grandfather from the dealership. He sold me a car or two and we got to know each other a little. He had all kinds of pictures of the family on his desk---Mae, of course, and you guys and your mom. Even your little dog, well, little back then. So proud he was." Robert swallows hard. He drinks a little of his cold coffee.

"It was just luck, I guess, I mean bad luck, that I saw what happened. I took a walk through the park every day back then, like it was a religious ritual, you know, something you did because it was important even though you didn't know why."

Pop clears his throat pointedly.

"So, okay, your grandfather is right in what he said. I was walking along the brim of the hill. I stopped to take a look at the river, and, sure enough, you, Willie, and your mom and dad were getting ready for a picnic. And Smoochy, she was running around and jumping on you, Willie." Robert's and Pop's eyes link. "Your mom, she laid out a blanket of some sort and I think there was a basket, or something, there. It was a sunny day, although it had rained for a few days before and the river was running high. I watched for a bit, then turned away and headed down the road again. But I heard Smoochy barking, more like yelping, I guess. So, I went back to the edge and...I saw Smoochy, and she was in the river. And, Willie, you wanted to jump in but your mom held you back and made you sit on the blanket.

Anyway, I think that's how it went. It's hard to..."

"Take your time. And Smoochy fell into the river...," says Pop.

"Yeah, okay. And your parents, they tried to reach her. I mean they reached as far as they could and then they took a few steps into the water to see if they could get closer. But your mom, she, well, she slipped, and fell in and the river, my God, the water was rushing like crazy, and it just pulled her in and wouldn't let go." He looks at Pop who's staring at the table, his arms folded.

"And I'm like yelling, 'No, no, no!', I mean I could see what was happening and I couldn't..."

Tears trickle down his fleshy cheeks. He doesn't try to dry them. "And then your dad, he jumped right in, thinking maybe he could get to her, but instead, he just disappeared, too. I mean, just like nothing." He looks at Willie. "And you, you were sitting there with your blanket around you. Just sitting. And I called out as loud as I could, but you didn't seem to hear me. By the time I got down there, I mean, by the time...well, you were lying there holding your blanket. Then Smoochy, wet to the bone showed up a little further down the river. She ran to you, wagging her tail like nothing had happened. And you hugged her. Everything was quiet. Except for the river. It's never quiet. And I tried to talk to you, but all you would tell me was your name."

Willie and Denny sob, their shoulders shake, their arms hang limp at their sides. Pop stands, then sits again. He holds his head in his hands. "I'm so sorry," he says.

Finally, they know what happened. They will discuss, time and again, how their parents slipped away and disappeared, senselessly. For the rest of their lives, they will wrestle with all the unanswered questions that were swept away by the river that day. But on this day, this day of revelation, they feel certain knowing is better than not knowing.

As Robert and his mother walk back up the street, holding onto one another so neither will fall, Muriel says, "Well, did you tell them what happened?"

"Yes, I did."

"Hm."

"What?"

"Did you tell them all of it?"

"No, both of us felt it wasn't necessary."

"Hal agreed?"

"It was his suggestion."

They walk a few more steps, both trying to catch their breath, until Muriel has to stop.

"So...you lied," she says.

"No. What I told them was truth enough."

"'Truth enough' and 'truth' aren't the same thing," says Muriel.

"Maybe, maybe not."

CHAPTER 51
1953

Smoochy lifted one paw and dipped it into the calm inlet water. Willie clomped along behind him, then stopped and placed one foot in the water, as well.

Ruthie clapped her hand loudly. "Willie, get back!"

"He's soaking wet," said Ruthie, glaring at Cliff. She grabbed Willie and wrapped him in the blanket they'd used for the picnic and returned to the warm rock above the beach. Willie laughed and struggled to break free of his mother.

"He's fine. Look at him. It's a big deal. His first time in the river." Cliff climbed back on the massive boulder.

Ruthie glared at her husband. "He's just a little boy, Cliff. A little boy who doesn't know any better than to walk right into a river. It's nothing to celebrate."

"He's all boy, Ruthie. There's no denying it. And boys like to do things, the riskier the better; that's how little boys become men, they test the limits. They color outside the lines."

"Cliff, that's a fantasy. I don't know where it ever came from, but it's a lie. Little boys are little boys. They need protection. Especially when there's danger around." Her jaw was set, her eyes narrowed.

Cliff stood, his arms at his sides. "I can't win with you, can I? Your old man has filled you with all kinds of nonsense about me and until you recognize that fact, nothing's gonna get better."

"Nonsense? You slapped my face. And that wasn't the first time."

"Jesus God, I told you a million times it'd never happen again. I just had a few; I had a few and you were all over me about God knows what."

"Getting a job, Cliff, getting a job! For the umpteenth time, I was asking you, begging you, to put the bottle aside and get a job. Unbelievable." She turned her back on Cliff.

High on the hillside a man heard loud voices, sharp and desperate. He turned and spied a family far below him. He watched as a man and woman circled each other, hands gesturing menacingly. Nearby, a little boy sat quietly, his dog beside him.

Cliff grabbed Ruthie by the arm and yanked her toward him. She slipped on the mossy rock and fell, but quickly regained her balance. "Let go of me!"

"Ruthie, you've got to listen to me. We've got to make this work. I love you! I can't live without you."

"Let go of me!" Ruthie hit his hand with her fist over and over.

"Stop it!" said Cliff. "Stop it!"

Cliff slipped and they both fell. She got up again and pushed him as hard as she could. He toppled into the water. He reached for a crack in the boulder looming above him. He tried to get a grip, but the white water surged over him again and again..

"Ruthie!" he said, a look of desperation in his eyes. "Ruthie, please!" He lifted his leg to get some leverage, but the river held fast.

Ruthie took one step forward, then stopped. She covered her face with her hands.

Cliff's fear turned to rage. He reached for her foot but she pulled away. He reached again, this time grabbing hold of one ankle. He pulled her with all his strength.

"My God, let go of me!" Ruthie struggled not to fall, like an ice skater backpedaling to stay afoot. But Cliff's weight was too much. As he disappeared, she slid across the rock, clawing at it with her fingernails until she, too, was drawn into the swirling, brown water. She bobbed once, twice, a searing look on her face before she slipped away.

The river careened onward, indifferent. The trees swayed in the breeze, uncaring. Crows cawed and a squirrel scampered and clouds raced by and a little boy laid on a blanket, eyes shut. When he opened them, everyone was gone.

He sat up, laid his head on his knees and closed his eyes again. Smoochy whimpered. Willie reached for her and pulled her close. He took the blanket from his shoulders and wrapped it around her. She licked Willie's cheek and slobbered on his shirt. Willie patted her but said not a word.

The man on the hillside, gasping, coughing, came thrashing down the hill. The man stood on the rock beside the boy and yelled at the water, over and over again---"Can you hear me? Are you there?"---until his voice gave out. "Oh, Jesus Christ, no."

"Are you okay?" he said. The boy was curled in a fetal position, sucking his thumb and clutching his dog.

CHAPTER 52

Trish dials zero and asks for the long-distance operator. "May I help you?" the voice says. She gives the woman the name and the city. After a few seconds, the operator returns with the phone number. Trish writes it down on a scrap of paper that she tucks in her jeans pocket.

She opens the fridge and reaches for the Chardonnay behind the orange juice, milk and ketchup. She puts a juice glass on the table beside the wine, then pulls the chair out and sits. She looks at the bottle, then at the stack of dirty dishes piled in the sink. No contest. She pulls the cork and fills the juice glass to the top. She drains the glass in two gulps and fills it again.

She feels loose and confident. She takes the paper from her pocket and puts it on the table, atop a smudge of grape jelly. She licks the jelly off the paper, and wonders how they decide which grapes end up in a jar and which ones end up in a corked bottle.

She flattens the scrap of paper out on the table again. There it is. With the help of the long-distance operator, she's only five digits away from talking to Dallas Grove.

"Look, Mom, you can't keep lying to me. The man in the suit is my father, isn't he?"

Lucy was standing outside her bedroom door in her Barbie pajamas and bare feet.

She asked again and again and again, each time with greater force, "He is---right? Tell me!"

Trish was stumped. How many times could she respond to this question without giving an answer? How many times could she zigzag and twist, swerve and bob and weave to avoid the constant queries Lucy hurled at her? Exhausted and unable to think of a new evasion, she answered, "Yes," just like that. Lucy gulped and her eyes bulged. She wasn't ready for the answer she'd hoped for.

"Was that a 'yes'? Did you say 'yes'?"

"Yes."

"This Dallas Grove person is my father?"

"Yes." Trish started crying, not because of Dallas and what had happened, but because she'd never seen such innocent surprise and joy on her daughter's face. It was wonderful and worrying. She knew what Lucy would say next: I want to meet him. He's my father and I have a right to meet him. And she did.

But now? Trish is just getting established at work? Her boss told her she's doing a good job. Everyone seems to like her. Doors are opening. There might be a better life out there after all.

If Dallas re-enters her life, he'd want to visit all the time, he'd want time alone with Lucy, maybe even time alone with her, he'd want to go places and do things as, like, a family. It has taken years for Trish to snuff out the flame she carried for him. Does she want to risk reigniting that flame and being disappointed again? Is she ready to hear what Dallas has to say about leaving her the first time? Does she want to?

The scrap of paper in her fist, Lucy takes another sip of wine, then tops off her glass again. Now that she knows his number, she will have to call.

She pulls the curtains back and looks out the living room window to see if Lucy is around. She stares at the black phone on the wall mount. She picks up the receiver and puts her finger in the first digit of Dallas's number. Then takes it out. Then in again. Then out again. She waits and then on impulse, picks up the phone and quickly dials the number.

It rings once, then twice, then a third time before someone answers. She's ready with her opening line, "I'll bet you can't guess who this is." She takes a deep breath, all ready to go. But the voice. It's not Dallas. It's a woman. "Hello," she says, sounding upbeat. Trish can't speak. She can't even move. She's stiff as a mannequin. "Hello, is anybody there?" Trish hears voices in the background, young voices, boys' voices. "Maybe you've called the wrong number." Little does she know. The woman's voice trails off as she speaks to someone else, a man: "Honey, there doesn't seem to be anyone there." Then he says, "That's odd, maybe---" and all Trish can hear is a dial tone. She grips the phone to her chest.

When Lucy comes home from a friend's, Trish is ready.

"Mom!"

"I'm upstairs, honey!"

She hears Lucy take off her shoes and throw them in the closet; then she hears the soft padding of bare feet on the steps.

"I'm in here."

Lucy stands in the doorway, then sits on her mother's bed.

"How's Carol Anne?"

"She's fine."

"That's good. What did you two do?"

"Mom, really. That's not what I came up here to talk about."

Trish finishes putting the ironing back in her chifforobe.

"So, did you like, did you find his number?"

"Yes, I...I did."

"You did?" Lucy didn't expect her mother to look for the number. She assumed when she came home, her mother would be all set with a litany of reasons why she couldn't contact her father. "That's great...I mean, yeah, that's great. Did you call him?"

"Yeah...yes, I did...I called him---"

"And what did he say?"

"Actually...uh...he wasn't home."

"He wasn't?"

"No, but I talked to his wife."

"He's married."

"With some kids...boys, I think."

"Okay...so...hm."

"His wife said he was in Coraopolis, near Pittsburgh. Looking at...they bought a new house, I guess...and they're getting ready to move, so she said this isn't a good time...but she'd let him know I called...and..."

"Did you tell her why you were calling?"

"Yeah, you know, I told her we were friends in high school, I heard he was coming to Ellwood from time to time---"

"No, did you tell her about me? Did you tell her who I am?"

"That's not something you do over the phone, honey, it isn't."

"So, he wasn't there, you didn't tell his wife why you were calling, I never even came up, right?"

"Well...look...I almost forgot...She said when they are settled in, I can call again. So, there's that."

"C'mon. Don't do that. Don't make things up."

"What?"

"Geez, look at you. You can hardly face me. You just can't...never mind."

"'Just can't' what? What were you going to say?"

Lucy stands and points her finger at her mother. "You can't be honest. You've never been straight with me about things that are important, like where I really came from, who my father really is...You know, it's like your whole life has been some kind of, I don't know..."

"Lie? Is that what you think?" Trish's back is up now. "You want to know the truth? Here's the truth. I knew your father for maybe five, six months. We were dumb kids, but we were in love. I mean, real love, the kind that makes a girl feel like the sun's always out, day or night, rain or snow. You can't wait to get up in the morning, just for the chance to see him. And you know good things are coming, because life is such a goddamn dream. I'm telling you, after all the others, the others who treated me like garbage, I thought this guy, this Dallas Grove hung the moon."

Trish stops for a moment so she won't cry.

"Mom, are you ok?"

"Listen to me, your mother was a lost cause at the age of fifteen and then Dallas Grove dropped into my life. And I felt like, for the first time, I was worth something, because some boy loved me. We were going to make a life together, no matter what.

"And then he went away. He went away without a word. A week later, I found out I was pregnant with you. He was gone, and I was broken. Then I had this beautiful, innocent baby, so little, who needed all the love she could get. And it was up to me to love her and make sure she grew up okay. Even without a dad. No one else to help. No one else to give a shit. And look, I haven't always been a good mother, but godammit, I loved you with everything I had. And I love you now and always will.

"That's the truth. All of it. You can do with it what you want. If you really want to meet your father then I'll find a way to make it happen. If you want to---"

"I thought I was the problem you couldn't get rid of."

Trish grabs her daughter, embraces her daughter, kisses her daughter, won't let go of her daughter.

CHAPTER 53

Becky rests her head on the back of her seat. She reaches for Denny's hand and closes her eyes as the bus pulls away. She loved meeting everyone, doing everything. She's happy Denny got the whole story about his parents.

She lifts her casted leg and wiggles her toes. She shakes her head, thinking about The Fall and her Oscar worthy performance. Perhaps someday she'll tell Denny, but not soon.

Far and away, the most intriguing person she met was Muriel. When Becky was alone with her during The Big Talk, in less than a minute she felt like she'd found a fellow traveler.

"There's gotta be more to that leg than just the cast, am I right?" Muriel was looking at Becky with one eye closed. A moment earlier, she asked Becky whether the cantaloupe sitting on the mantle was ripe. Taken aback and unsure of what to say about her leg (or the invisible cantaloupe), Becky said, "What was that?"

Muriel explained it was "obvious" that the break wasn't the only thing wrong with Becky's leg. She surmised it was a problem from birth. Without asking for confirmation, she then tsked Becky for hiding herself in a cast. "And I said hiding *yourself* not hiding your leg." She'd closed her open eye and opened her closed one.

"What do you think?" asked Muriel.

With a sheepish grin, Becky said, "I think you are a smart cookie."

Muriel then mistook Becky for her own mother and asked why she hadn't yet finished sewing her dress for the dance.

Just as quickly, she returned to Becky's leg, repeating some of what she'd already said, but adding, "It is tempting to pack yourself away in a trunk full of mothballs, hoping you'll be hidden and safe and protected from moths or silverfish. Or glaring, critical eyes full of judgment. Anything that might threaten, harm or even destroy you. This is always a mistake, even with clothes."

Muriel gestures to her own body, head to toe.

"This stuff (she pinches the skin on her arm), this stuff is our clothing; this is what we wear day in and day out from our first cry to our final yelp. Clothes are for wearing, not for hiding." There was a sparkle in her eyes as she spoke. "Take yourself out of the trunk, dear; shake off the stench of hiding; wear yourself as you are; and anyone who suggests you are out of style, or too colorful, or too loud or nothing about you matches or the styles you wear are too unconventional, or that you are a 'cripple', well, they can all be damned."

Muriel looked in every direction, gestured for Becky to come near, and whispered, "Wear yourself as proudly as you can."

Then Muriel asked again, politely, if the dress would be ready in time.

Spirits and angels, angels and spirits, thinks Becky.

.   .   .

Robert shovels more dirt onto the cement block that's poking through at one corner of his shelter. Everything's got to be covered and covered good. He walks around his creation, proud of what he's built, happy his neighbors no longer think he's crazy. He knew they'd come around.

With Denny and his girlfriend back at school, Hal and Willie are the only ones that may join them when the time comes. They still have to decide about Smoochy. One big problem is where would she do her business. On the plus side, though, Mr. Ashwood suggested if things got really dire and they were going to starve, they could eat her.

Hal crosses the backyards, cup of coffee in hand. He joins Robert in yet another tour of the shelter. They sit on the cold concrete bench.

"You know Robert, I didn't get a chance to thank you for what you did."

"No need for that."

"Yes, there is. Thank you, thank you very much," says Hal.

"Glad to help."

"I wasn't sure how much to tell them, you know?"

"Yessir."

"To be honest, I never wanted them to know any of it. Neither did Mae. What kid should know about the awful way their parents died, the awful way they treated each other at the end. If I could erase a single damn moment in time, just one...well..."

"Hm," says Robert, his tone solemn.

The men exchange their goodbyes and Hal walks back across the yards.

Earlier, just after sunrise, before anyone woke up, Denny and Willie dressed and noiselessly sneaked out of the house. They walked to the woods where Willie had seen the deer, where he and Pres and Lucy had hunted leaves, where they'd played on the tiny beach and the massive rock, not knowing then what had happened there, not knowing the angry brown river was a watery graveyard.

The brothers don't see deer, but they do see a family of red foxes, two racoons, and busy squirrels, their mouths full of nuts for winter. Willie points to the beach below. "It's been a while," says Denny. He takes the lead. They push their way through bushes and brush, fallen limbs and tree stumps. The river's churning water fills the air with mist.

Willie joins his brother atop the boulder. He carries a cluster of yellow mums in his hand. Denny takes two pictures from his pocket, Willie's most recent school photo and a picture of Denny taken by Becky. They sit on the front edge of the boulder, their feet dangling just above the water.

Willie speaks. "Denny and me, we just found out what happened. And we decided we should do something to show, well, to show you we're so sorry and we haven't forgotten you. You will always be our parents and we will always love you." He throws the flowers into the water; they watch as they're carried away.

Denny speaks. "We wanted you to know we're doing pretty good. Willie's in sixth grade; he's a good student, and has good friends. And I'm a freshman at Weston College and I've met someone kind of special. We wanted you to know this, how your children are doing, so you wouldn't worry. Here are two pictures. We thought you'd like to know what we look like now." He holds the pictures in his open palm, then drops them into the lapping water.

They bow their heads for a moment of silence. Then they go home so Denny can pack and get ready for the long bus ride ahead.

CHAPTER 54

"What do you think?" asks Pres.

He and Willie are hanging onto the chain-link fence around the football practice field. The Ellwood City Wolverines are getting ready for the biggest game of the season. On Friday night they'll host the hated New Castle Hurricanes. Ellwood takes this rivalry with the utmost seriousness. Pep rallies, bonfires, harassing drive-byes to intimidate the opponent's student body, shared recollections by past Wolverine heroes. There are pick-up games galore at school. Sixth graders force fifth graders to be the Hurricanes and then beat the snot out of them every day at recess.

"I don't know," says Willie.

"I don't know either, but don't our guys look small. I mean, look at 77, his shoulder pads are so big he's fallen over three times. And our quarterback, maybe he should try throwing with his other arm. I bet New Castle doesn't even realize this game is a big deal. For them, it's just a chance to carve another notch in their belt. What are they, seven wins no losses this year? And we're...I think we've won one game, maybe two."

"When they get out on the field, you never know what the outcome will be. That's why they play the game, my young friend," says Willie with his best sports announcer's voice.

"I guess."

"Let's go."

Willie and Pres throw a football back and forth along the way. Pres says Willie should play quarterback in high school. "You throw better than the kid we got now."

"Look at me, I'm skin and bone. I'd get killed."

"Point taken."

Before turning toward their respective homes, they check in.

"How's the thing with your dad going?" says Willie.

"Slow."

"Sorry."

"Yeah. Long haul, for sure. How's your nuclear-war-end-of-the-world-thing going?"

"Still going, I guess."

"How's the thing about Lucy's long-lost father going?"

"She doesn't say much about it, but she seems okay."

"Well, see ya."

"You, too. Hang tough."

When Willie opens the front door, the smell of macaroni and cheese fills the air. His favorite meal, hands down. Pop usually includes something green with all the starch. Tonight, it's peas, which will fit perfectly under the rim of Willie's dinner plate.

"I'm home!"

"Just in time."

Willie turns the television on and sets up the TV trays. He watches a few seconds of the Three Stooges before the show is interrupted. *Bulletin* fills the screen. Then Walter Cronkite appears, his complexion gray, his face dour.

Pop takes the macaroni and cheese out of the oven and calls Willie. "Why don't we eat in the kitchen tonight." When Willie doesn't answer, Pop tries again. He sets the table but still no Willie. He goes into the living room and finds Willie standing in front of the TV, his arms folded as he watches Cronkite.

"What's this?"

"It's happening."

The president of the United States sits behind a desk in the Oval Office and speaks to the nation, "Good evening my fellow citizens..."

Pop puts a hand on Willie's shoulder and guides him to the couch.

"...unmistakable evidence...offensive missile sites..."

"I can't believe this," says Willie in a whisper.

"It'll be fine, it will." Pop's tone of voice is unconvincing.

"...medium range ballistic missiles capable..."

Is this another day that will "live in infamy"? thinks Pop. He and Mae were sitting in their tiny house in Beaver Falls glued to the radio when another president announced the Japanese had bombed the American fleet on some island in the Pacific. They sat in silence after the president concluded his remarks. The Milton Beryl Show came on again. The audience was laughing hysterically at Uncle Miltie's antics, oblivious to what was happening on the other side of the world.

"...explicit threat to the peace and security..."

Did he say two thousand miles? The missiles can blow things up two thousand miles from Cuba? Willie pulls the *World Book* off the shelf, the one with maps of almost everything. He finds the western hemisphere and measures the distance from Cuba to western Pennsylvania, thumb to pinky, then looks at the map scale in the corner and does a rough calculation. They could annihilate us, thinks Willie. He calls Smoochy who jumps on his lap.

He holds her tight.

"...Nuclear weapons are so destructive..."

"What did I tell ya, Ma? Huh?" says Robby, bobbing his head with pride.

"What?"

"The bomb shelter. I told you. It wasn't so stupid after all, was it?"

"Where are my feet Robby?"

Robby gets up from his chair, bends over as far as he can and pretends to fish out his mother's feet from under the sofa.

"There you go, Ma." He points. "Back where they belong, right at the end of your legs."

Muriel holds her shoes in her lap. "What are these for?"

Robby feels both giddy and disappointed. Giddy that he and Ma will be saved, but disappointed Ma won't have a clue what's happening. All the work, though, is still worthy of praise, he thinks. He's a proud man today. He bets his neighbors, and maybe the whole town, wish they were Robert Ashwood now.

Ma notices her shoes are on her hands. "What the hell is this?" she says.

Robert doesn't hear a thing his mother is saying. There's too much to do; too many decisions to make. He has to recheck all the supplies, make sure the radio is working, put some blankets on the beds, shovel a little more dirt on the mound. He must reach Hal to see if they're going to accept his offer to shelter them.

"...a clear and present danger..."

Pop tries to call Denny's dorm phone, to no avail.

Willie sits on his bed staring out the window. The day has finally come. Unbelievable.

Now that it's here, why is he surprised? Did he think if he worried about it enough, it would never come? That waiting and worrying was enough to stop a nuclear war?

"...a strict quarantine on all offensive military weapons on shipment to Cuba...I call upon Chairman Khrushchev to halt... Our goal is not the victory of might but the vindication of right..."

CHAPTER 55

The next day and the day after dawn like any other. People go to work and school; they shop at grocery stores and smell fruit to see if it's ripe; they get haircuts, brush their teeth, shine their shoes, hem their dresses; church bells chime; traffic lights go from green to red and back again; pot holes get filled; restaurants serve hungry customers; people buy tickets to the movies; the Wolverines continue to prepare for a different kind of attack. And the world teeters on the brink.

New words, like "stalemate," "brinkmanship," "silos," are on the tongues of adults and children alike. Air-raid practices are stepped up and more people duck and cover. News bulletins are as common as scheduled shows. Churches are full to the rafters with the newly devout, hoping to improve their prospects for the afterlife.

Each day at recess, Willie, Lucy and Pres convene under the maple tree at the far end of the school playground. Mostly they talk about nothing and then go back to class feeling better because they have each other.

On the fourth day of worldwide craziness, the three of them go to the river after school and sit on the boulder beside the tiny beach. Pres and Lucy don't mention the obvious, and neither does Willie. He'd come once more since Denny left. The place is horrible and sacred at the same time.

"Yesterday was the first time I've ever seen Air Force jets fly right over our houses. Just a little creepy," says Willie. "How will they ever work this thing out?"

"I don't know. They will, though. Maybe they just need more time. You know Craig McDonaldson and Marky Everstone, how they've hated each other since the first grade? You think they could work out their differences in just a few days? I don't think so," says Lucy.

"See what you mean," says Willie.

"Let's hope Kennedy and the other guy have a little more brain power than Craig and Marky," says Pres.

"Does your dad know what's going on?" says Lucy.

"Not from us, that's for sure. But I think he knows; he knows without anyone telling him. Maybe it's like a sixth sense you develop when you've been in a war."

Willie picks up a piece of bark and crumbles it in his hand. "You've seen the films, I'm sure, the films that show atomic bomb tests, where the mushroom cloud billows up, like, thousands of feet. Can you imagine sitting here under a mushroom cloud?"

"I don't think anyone wants to look up and see mushroom clouds instead of the sun. I have to believe they'll work it out," says Lucy. "Things'll get better."

"You know that saying, 'If life gives you lemons, make lemonade'? Maybe if life gives you mushroom clouds, you're supposed to make, what...mushroom soup?" says Pres.

Willie and Lucy look at Pres, then at each other, and then at Pres again.

"Words to live by," says Lucy.

"That came so close to being helpful," says Willie.

"Thank you. I'm always here if you need me."

· · ·

Robert Ashwood waves to Willie just as he's getting home from school. No, thinks Willie. Not today. He waves back and smiles. Mr. Ashwood's wave changes into a cycling motion, indicating he'd like Willie to come by. Willie drops his books on the front steps and heads toward the Ashwood house.

The front door creaks and Muriel comes out onto the porch, then down the steps, where she checks on the peony bushes, their blossoms long gone.

She shades her eyes and looks at Willie. "Hello, young Mr. Blevin. So pleased you haven't been blown up yet."

"Hi, Mrs. Ashwood," says Willie. "I'm pleased you haven't either."

Robert scoffs at his mother, then turns to Willie.

"The time has come," he says. Since the Kennedy speech, Robert opens every conversation with an apocalyptic phrase.

"Uh huh."

"Yes, it has. And still people act like there's nothing to fear, no reason to be alarmed. Fools, all of them."

Sometimes it helps to talk to Mr. Ashwood. When he expounds on things Willie's worrying about, he sounds so nutty that Willie feels a kind of relief, like if Ashwood believes it, it must be crazy talk and nothing more.

"Ma and me are probably going into the shelter tomorrow night if nothing changes. And I wanted to know if you and your Pop were gonna join us."

"I don't know, actually. I'll have to ask him."

"Good, could you do that, I mean soon, like when he gets home from work?"

"Okay."

"Cause if you're planning on being our guests, we'll have to decide what to do with Smooch." He makes a sad face.

Willie tells Pop as soon as he gets home and, without saying a word, Pop heads to the Ashwood residence. Willie doesn't ask what he's going to say to Mr. Ashwood. He knows Pop's voting 'No'. Back when Ashwood first made his offer, Willie thought it would be a reasonable thing to do. Knowing they had an open invitation had a calming effect.

Lately, though, He's less certain about the value of Ashwood's hole in the ground. Willie's had plenty of experience with the junk life can drop on you. Bomb shelters wouldn't have helped with any of them. The only shelters that made a difference were skin and bone, flesh and blood.

Anyway, Smoochy would never adjust to living with the Ashwoods inside their concrete cave. And, for sure, Willie'd never let anyone eat her.

CHAPTER 56

Willie is lying on the floor behind the couch, Smoochy beside him, scratching his leg, wagging his tail. Willie's breathing is labored. He struggles to wriggle in a little further. He sees food crumbs and dust balls and two green spiders. I can't believe we've never cleaned back here, he thinks. He reaches with one arm as far as he can, but it's not far enough.

There's a knock on the front door. Geez, he thinks. He grunts hard, turns one shoulder slightly and he's got it. He backs out as quickly as he can and holds the ball in front on Smoochy's face. "If I've told you once, I've told you a million times, don't leave your ball behind the couch." Smoochy sits, cocks his head and whimpers. There is another knock on the door. He tosses the ball across the room and Smoochy's off like a flash.

Willie looks at the clock on the wall. It's 12:45pm. Lunch recess is over and he hasn't eaten a thing. There is a third knock. Willie raps on the window. Lucy and Pres glance his way, both of them tapping their wrist watches. He gives them the one-minute sign and then runs upstairs to his room, grabs one Clark Bar, then another, from the stash in his pillow case. He dashes back down the stairs, his heart thumping.

When he opens the door, Lucy is sitting on the porch, rocking in Pop's favorite chair. Preston is practicing headstands in the yard. The three of them fall in behind a group of kindergartners being led by a school safety.

They should make it back in time.

"Ready for the social studies test?" says Lucy.

"Yeah, I think." says Willie. "Glad we're ending the unit on South America."

"Goodbye Lake Titicaca," says Pres. They all laugh.

"Been to see your dad again?" says Willie.

"Tonight."

"Bet he's glad," says Lucy.

"I think everyone's glad it's over," says Willie.

. . .

It was raining hard the night Robert had planned on retreating to his bomb shelter, hoping they would be protected for either the duration of the crisis or the duration of World War III. Whichever way it went, he felt confident they'd make it through.

Robert and his mother packed a few last-minute items.

"How long will we be gone?" said Muriel.

"As long as it takes, Ma."

"This should be fun. The last time I went to Niagara Falls was before you were born."

By the time they were ready to depart, a storm had blown up with torrential rain and driving wind. Pop considered carrying Ma to the shelter, then thought better of it. This will blow over, he figured.

"Ma, we're gonna wait a bit. It's a mess out there. Why don't you relax and I'll tell you when it's time?"

"Okay, Robby." Muriel took a seat in her platform rocker and rested her head on a pillow. "Don't forget me."

Soon she was snoring softly. Robert stood by the window, taking the measure of the storm. Rather than tailing off, it seemed to be revving up. Thunder claps and jagged lightning filled the night sky.

"Well, I hope they don't launch anything while we're waiting," he said. Robby moved his overstuffed chair to the middle of the room so he could keep an eye on the storm and the shelter. Then he took a seat. And promptly fell asleep.

He is startled awake by someone knocking on the back door. He rubs his eyes and gets up as quickly as he can. Ma is still asleep. When he gets to the door, Hal is peering back at him through the window. It has stopped raining. And the sun is up.

Hal had listened to the news first thing that morning. The Russians were backing away. War had been averted.

He looks out the back door to see if there is any activity at the bomb shelter. When he doesn't see any, he worries Robert's radio system isn't working. Maybe they didn't know what had happened.

When he gets to the Ashwood's back door, he looks through the window and sees them both fast asleep in their preferred chairs. After all his hard work, Robert had missed the whole thing. The crisis had come and gone while he slumbered, his mother close by. He is left with an unused bomb shelter, suitable for any war. Hal knocks.

When Robert opens the door, Hal asks, "How'd it go last night? Did you do okay in the shelter?"

Robert stares at his neighbor through racoon eyes. He stumbles and stutters.

"I hope you were safe and sound."

Robert's mouth still hangs open.

"You were able to come out sooner than you thought. Good news this morning, huh? That president of ours stared down the bear."

"Oh," says Robert.

"Hey, your mother is lucky to have you watching out for her."

When Hal reaches his own house, Robert is still standing at his back door.

Hal is surprised to see Willie sitting at the kitchen table, hunched over his social studies book taking notes.

"What are you doing up so early?"

"Got a test."

Pop pours himself a cup of coffee, leans against the refrigerator, and watches his grandson work away. Pop blows on his coffee and sips it slowly. Willie's red hair is shaggy from sleep. He is barefooted and his toes are curled into little knots. He cradles his head in one hand; his forearm looks lean and sinewy. His cheeks are hollowing, his wrists are thickening, everything about him is in flux. He smiles at his grandson.

"Did you hear the news?" says Pop.

"Yeah," says Willie, his head still in his book.

"Pretty good, huh."

"Yeah, pretty good."

"Any updates?" says Willie.

Lucy cocks her head and pulls one corner of her mouth in tight. "Well..."

"Yeah?" says Pres.

"Sunday's the day."

"For real," says Willie. "Very cool."

"Yeah," says Lucy, as she pretends to bite her fingernails nervously.

"Pretty amazing."

"Tell me about it. I never thought Mom would call him. I guess she talked to him a few times. I asked her how it was and she said 'Fine', but I don't know. Anyway, it's gonna happen."

When Trish finally reached Dallas, she was surprised his voice sounded the same as it had in high school, only a little lower. There were silences and anxious laughter as they measured each other. Who were they now? Was there anything left of who they'd been? They steered clear of their relationship and how it had ended, releasing it to the wake of time. He asked about Lucy. She told him what a special girl she was. He said she looked like her mother. He said, "It's amazing that we have a daughter." At last, a simple acknowledgement, so long awaited. She was relieved she didn't cry until after they hung up.

Plans were made during subsequent conversations, one that included Dallas's wife, Maggie. Closing one chapter, opening another was awkward and good and frightening and hopeful.

. . .

Willie sits on the porch scratching Rocko's ears, his newspaper bag at his feet. Rocko, once his nemesis, lays his head on Willie's lap. "Don't tell Smoochy, okay? She'd be all kinds of jealous."

The days are getting shorter, the nights colder, the mornings darker. It will be Thanksgiving soon. Denny is going to Becky's for the holiday, but they will come home for Christmas.

Willie pats Rocko's head one more time. "Gotta go. Papers to deliver." Rocko barks at Willie as he walks away. He tosses papers onto the Anderson's front porch, the Linghampton's side porch and the Hazelberry's back steps.

He takes a side trip to the tired little house that once was home. He sits on the porch steps and surveys the neighborhood. A car pulls up and parks at the curb. A man in a suit emerges, opens the trunk and pulls out a sign that says, "For Sale." He grabs a hammer and pounds the stake into the ground, then notices Willie sitting on the porch.

"Hi, there."

"Hi," says Willie.

The man approaches, his hand out. Willie shakes it.

"You don't live here, do you?"

"No, I don't."

"I didn't think so. No one's lived here in a long time. It's been a very hard sell, but I'm going to give it another try. You never know what can happen. A young couple with a lot of energy and imagination might come along and see something in it that others don't see, you know. Beyond the mess of it, they might see a home with kids playing in the front yard, a swing set in the back, flowers bordering the porch, maybe even a nice white fence along the sidewalk."

"I can see that," says Willie.

"Yeah, right now it wouldn't provide much shelter for anyone, would it? But fix it up a little, put a family in there and you've got a home, don't you?"

"Yes, you do."

The man goes back to his sign. Willie stands up, puts his bag over his shoulder, begins to leave, then turns back at the end of the walkway. He looks at the house one more time. "So long," he says.

ABOUT THE AUTHOR

David B. Seaburn's first novel, *Darkness is as Light*, was published in 2005. He followed with *Pumpkin Hill* (2007), *Charlie No Face* (2011), a Finalist for the National Indie Excellence Award in General Fiction, *Chimney Bluffs* (2012), *More More Time* (2015), and *Parrot Talk* (2017), which placed second in the 2017 TAZ Awards for Fiction and was short-listed for the 2018 Somerset Award. *Gavin Goode* (2019) was an American Book Fest Finalist for "Best Book" in General Fiction and Semi-finalist in Literary, Contemporary and Satire Fiction for the Somerset Award. His latest novel is *Broken Pieces of God* (2021) which was a Finalist for the National Indie Excellence Award in General Fiction (2021).

Seaburn and his wife live in western New York. They have two married daughters and four fabulous grandchildren.

NOTE FROM THE AUTHOR

Word-of-mouth is crucial for any author to succeed. If you enjoyed *Give Me Shelter*, please leave a review online—anywhere you are able. Even if it's just a sentence or two. It would make all the difference and would be very much appreciated.

Thanks!
David B. Seaburn

We hope you enjoyed reading this title from:

Subscribe to our mailing list – *The Rosevine* – and receive **FREE** books, daily deals, and stay current with news about upcoming releases and our hottest authors.
Scan the QR code below to sign up.

Already a subscriber? Please accept a sincere thank you for being a fan of Black Rose Writing authors.

View other Black Rose Writing titles at
www.blackrosewriting.com/books and use promo code
PRINT to receive a **20% discount** when purchasing.

Made in the USA
Middletown, DE
15 February 2024